VAN

Kurtzman remembered the information from the Intel package he'd put together. Another series of commands and he had the information about the drop. "Used to be a tributary to the Irrawaddy River that cut through there. Dried up fifty or sixty years ago."

"Is it deep enough?"

"Forty feet," Kurtzman replied, reading through the text file he'd opened up. "Less than half the one we'd targeted."

"Those trucks won't survive it," Barbara Price said. "Get Gary to break off and see if he can beat that convoy back to that bridge. Let's see if we can still salvage this operation."

Kurtzman opened the communications link to McCarter, but the first thing he heard was an assault rifle blasting a full-throated roar and someone yelling in pain.

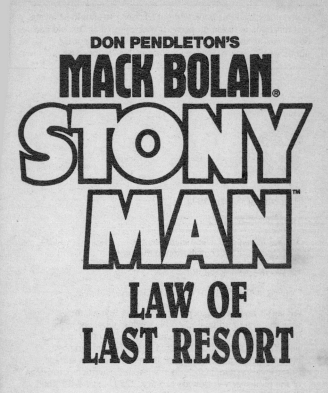

DON PENDLETON'S
MACK BOLAN®
STONY MAN™

LAW OF LAST RESORT

A GOLD EAGLE BOOK FROM

WORLDWIDE®

TORONTO • NEW YORK • LONDON
AMSTERDAM • PARIS • SYDNEY • HAMBURG
STOCKHOLM • ATHENS • TOKYO • MILAN
MADRID • WARSAW • BUDAPEST • AUCKLAND

First edition January 1998

ISBN 0-373-61916-2

Special thanks and acknowledgment to
Mel Odom for his contribution to this work.

LAW OF LAST RESORT

LAW OF
LAST RESORT

CHAPTER ONE

Tokyo, Japan
Thursday

Kesar Grishin lounged in the back seat of the stretch limousine, watching the colorful neon lights of Tokyo's *rappongi* district scale the walls of the dark concrete valley around him. The seductive colors and shapes of the lights advertised a number of products. He whistled almost imperceptibly between his teeth, conscious of the habit but doing nothing to check himself. He'd picked up the trait during his one and only stay in the Siberian prison camps of the country of his birth.

The *rappongi* district brimmed with nightlife that spilled over into the streets. Young men and women dressed in Western-style clothing mixed with corporate businessmen in traditional black suits. The young intended to imitate their American counterparts in celebration of their rebelliousness, while the older generation retreated to the nightclubs, discos and bars to extend their business day.

Both, Grishin knew, would be unloading yen, and some of the businesses he had interests in or businesses whose interests he managed would be raking in the money. He grinned in spite of the black mood that filled him. Despite the power and wealth that he now commanded, he knew he possessed the dark, cynical soul of a Russian peasant. Perhaps it was true that a man couldn't completely avoid his past. His mother had slept with several peasant men in an effort to ensure their room and board outside Moscow. Maybe even she hadn't known who his father had been.

No one dared remind him of those facts now. Not if they valued their lives, or their futures. Grishin had made himself capable of taking either—or both. At six feet tall, with craggy features and gray eyes so pale that they looked like they'd been freshly chipped from glacial ice, he presented an imposing figure and knew it. He dressed accordingly. The dark suit came from the best Italian tailors. His knee-length black leather outercoat was also Italian. His deep tan spoke of a year-long acquaintance with the sun and surf of the Caribbean. That same sun had bleached highlights into his curly light brown hair, which he left slightly long in spite of the receding hairline at his temples. His smile was perfect and white.

"I would feel more comfortable," Gerahd Dobrynin stated in a tone of practiced politeness, "if you would stay in the car while this is handled."

Grishin looked at the younger man and grinned. "You would, would you?"

Dobrynin dropped his gaze, but he answered truthfully. "Yes sir." He was slightly under six feet tall, muscular without being beefy, though the suits still came tailored to conceal the physique, as well as the tools of Dobrynin's dangerous trade. Guns were only the beginning for a man of Dobrynin's lethal talents. His thick black hair had been razored to fuzz that barely showed on the scalp beneath, a military-style cut that was in vogue everywhere these days and didn't attract much attention.

"Thank you," Grishin said, "for sharing that with me." He laughed, bright and earnest. It was an American saying that he really enjoyed, the sheer dichotomy of the announcement of thanking someone for telling a listener something the listener had no interest in.

Dobrynin retreated further within himself, not from injured feelings, but from a certain knowledge that he couldn't win the argument.

"You know," Grishin went on, "I was thinking to myself this morning how I should let you start running this business. What do you think of that?"

"I think that it would be a stupid idea." Dobrynin lifted his eyes.

"That," Grishin said with a condescending nod, "was my very *next* thought." He gathered his coat around himself as the limousine glided to a stop at the curb.

A host of curious onlookers stayed back against the building, and the ones cruising the sidewalk made room as the liveried chauffeur got out of the limousine and walked around to open Dobrynin's door.

"You've got your men in place?" Grishin asked.

"Yes," Dobrynin replied, sliding out of the car. The ear-throat microphone that connected him with the rest of his unit was carefully concealed in the lining of the ankle-long duster.

"Then what could possibly go wrong?" Grishin slid out of the car after his bodyguard.

"Jiro Ishikure won't be happy to see you. That's what could go wrong."

"Well, Ishikure-san should have thought of that before he tried to double-cross me, shouldn't he?" Grishin went into the lobby of the building, knowing the layout from the pictures and video Dobrynin's men had briefed him with.

The lobby bustled with people, mingling and waiting for the elevators that would take them to the upper floors where the nightclubs and theaters were located. The air was fouled with cigarette and cigar smoke, and with the odor of stale beer and perspiration.

Grishin scanned the map of the building in the center of the lobby as he passed by, taking in the list of names very quickly. Learning Japanese had been difficult, especially the written form of the language, but he'd made himself master it.

"Doctors' and lawyers' offices," he said to Dobrynin, taking in the four men flanking them to the left and the four men to the right. They were under Dobrynin's command, all of them hard men and killers. "Three nightclubs with excellent ratings in European reviews. A four-star Japanese restaurant, as well as a British one. A prominent television station with programs that transcend the region. Two publishers with authors who hit the bestseller charts regularly. And a first-run theater featuring American films. Amid business offices and private, very expensive apartments. It only makes sense that there would be a whorehouse, as well, doesn't it?"

"Yes, sir," Dobrynin answered automatically, his hands deep within the pockets of his duster. He moved with sinuous grace, his head rolling slightly as it moved from left to right, then back again with the timing of a metronome.

Grishin felt entirely safe. The bodyguard had been looking after him for almost nine years. He'd seen Dobrynin take three bullets for him during assassination attempts over those years. He made a mental note to make up for his behavior to Dobrynin, perhaps a salvaged icon from one of the churches that had remained in hiding during the Communist days of Mother Russia. Dobrynin had always maintained an unexplained fascination for such things.

"The security offices?" Grishin noted the security camera mounted on the wall behind a black-lensed filter that looked decorative.

"Third floor," Dobrynin answered.

"We'll stop there first."

"Yes, sir."

The group flanking them on the left took the lead, obeying Dobrynin's half-whispered orders immediately. The people in the hallways parted instantly as they became a flying wedge.

Grishin checked his watch. It was a thick silver disk, a diver's watch in the beginning, but his cybernetic-development people had also supplemented the usual bells and whistles with other programming, shown primarily in the miniature numeric keypad nestled beside the watch crystal. He'd tagged the timer as soon as they'd exited the limousine, knowing the building's security systems would have picked them up even though there was no reason for the security guards to.

Less than a minute had passed since they'd entered the building.

Halfway down the hall, the forward team spread out in a spearhead, covering a section of the wall. The corridor was lined with prints depicting the traditional cherry-blossom festivals. The people who'd been coming down the corridor gave ground at once, halting, then going back the way they'd come.

"Here?" Grishin came to a stop, bouncing on his

toes, feeling the old excitement flaring through his stomach.

"Yes." Dobrynin leaned forward, pulling on a surgical glove.

The thumb-pad of the glove carried the replicated thumbprint of one of the men who'd worked security in the building that afternoon. The man wouldn't be reporting to work the following day, and would be minus his right thumb when they found the body.

Dobrynin examined the wall briefly, then pressed against a section of it, sliding it aside and revealing the lighted ellipse beneath. He pressed the glove's thumb-pad against it.

They heard a small click, but the sound died before it reached the opposing wall. Almost instantly, a section of the wall peeled back, revealing a small, compact elevator. The doors parted and opened to the sterile stainless-steel cage beyond.

Personally Grishin would have thought to put a heat register into the system. Body heat wouldn't transmit so easily through the glove, and the heat register would have denied access. But then, not everyone was as security conscious as he was.

"They'll know we're here now if they're looking," Dobrynin said.

"They'll be looking with Ishikure here, their security will be tighter." He glanced down the hall at the black-lensed decorative panel over another security camera that had them in its field of view. He thought he spotted a flicker of light on polished metal. Then he stepped into the cage.

Without hesitation, Dobrynin stabbed a finger onto the unmarked control panel. With the intel they'd paid blackmail prices for, they'd learned the blank panel was cross-wired so buttons didn't necessarily escalate in order. Once the door closed and the cage was under way, Dobrynin gave the order for his men to take out their weapons.

The sleek Heckler & Koch MP-5s were the SD-3 models, complete with machined sound suppressors. The machine pistols were favorites of special forces across the globe. They were also costly. Grishin spared no expense when it came to his field operatives. A man didn't become worth millions by undercutting expenses.

At the third floor, Dobrynin stepped out into the hallway. His H&K MP-5 came up at waist level, and he unleashed a spray of 9 mm parabellums that lasted only a handful of seconds and cut down several men where they stood. Then Dobrynin stepped back into the cage and motioned one of his teams into the hallway. When they were clear, he punched another button on the control panel, then changed magazines in his weapon, dropping the empty one into an inner pocket of his duster.

"Messy," Dobrynin announced. "Even with the team erasing the security office's video logs, there is a possibility for a lot of exposure here."

Grishin grinned like a teacher addressing a prize pupil who'd made a rather common mistake. "Mr. Dobrynin, you're thinking like a KGB officer too much again. In your continued association with me, I'd like very much for you to pay attention to the education I'm giving you."

"Yes, sir."

"The Japanese are, as a people, unwilling to admit their mistakes," Grishin went on. "Even if our team was not at this moment destroying every video recording of our presence here, the Japanese corporation Ishi-kure-san works for would hush up all that transpires here tonight. They'll never let this out.''

"I'm sure you're right, sir.''

"Of course I'm right. The Yakuza has a regular business over here of professional blackmail. They even have a name for it—*sokaiya*. One of the Yakuza's tactics is simply to buy into a corporation's over-the-counter stock through cutout men. Just OTC stuff, not even any of the blue-chip stuff. You following me here?''

"Yes, sir,'' Dobrynin answered politely, but his attention was on the doors in front of him. He had his wrists crossed before him, the hand holding the machine pistol on top so it would be immediately accessible.

"Do you know what the Yakuza does to threaten the corporations and coerce them into paying exorbitant amounts?''

"No, sir.''

"They tell the board of directors they're going to go public with their ownership of stock unless the board buys them back for much more than those stocks are worth. And the corporations, rather than be linked to the Yakuza, pay up. I find that incredibly fascinating. Graft and corruption are almost badges of distinguished service among the Western nations, and a fuel that fed much of Russia's Communist government, as well as the dictators of the Eastern European countries before the Berlin Wall fell. Here, all that is kept from public view.''

The elevator slid to a quiet, controlled stop that left Grishin with a spinning sensation in the pit of his stomach. He followed Dobrynin into the corridor.

Dobrynin went left, splitting the four-man team that accompanied them into two-man groups. One two-man group covered the elevator, keeping it open. The other flanked Grishin. Dobrynin took the lead.

The whorehouse was at the end of the corridor. Around it were offices that did mail-order business in manga and other collectibles, including a video-game outlet Grishin had purchased after finding out the businesses were there. Other offices offered travel arrangements, temporary services and domestic help. All of them, Grishin had learned in his research of the building, routinely closed down before the whorehouse opened up for business.

At night, the elevator service to that floor was monitored, and people were allowed up only by appointment. No lists were kept, and everyone involved, including the security staff and building management, took a cut of the action. There was enough to go around. The whorehouse pandered to very special, very expensive tastes. And it offered a disposal service for those needs that were truly unique.

The door that fronted Dobrynin was simple and plain. The modest script across it announced the name in Japanese, which loosely translated to String of Pearls.

Dobrynin stepped to one side of the door, talking briefly over his headset, then he raised the machine pistol.

Usually the door had to be released from inside, but the building security had a release switch in its main office on the third floor. Grishin paused less than six paces away. No noise escaped from the hive of apartments he knew to be on the other side of the door.

A moment later Dobrynin shoved the door open, following it inward. A splash of gentle light filled the doorway, releasing the sweet, acrid scent of burning incense and oils.

Scantily clad women met Dobrynin as he stalked forward. They backed away when they saw the machine pistol in his gloved fist.

Grishin followed, taking in the ornate teak panels that covered the foyer walls, the antique vases in specially constructed niches, and the large Louis XVI desk visible in the office to the immediate right of the foyer. A petite woman who could have passed for anywhere between twenty and forty, but whose real age was fifty-three according to the information Grishin had, stared up at the intruders from behind the desk.

Grishin stepped toward her, smiling easily. "Nariko Takemori, trust me when I tell you your pictures don't do you justice."

Takemori stood up slowly behind her desk. She wore a flowing green dress that somehow managed to hide yet flaunt the lissome curves. She spoke Japanese as he did. "Do I know you?"

Grishin shook his head. Behind him, he heard Dobrynin's machine pistol snarling in its protracted whispered cough. Breakable things broke, wooden things splintered and living things died with cries of pain that were quickly cut off. Some of the women screamed.

"No, dear lady," Grishin replied, "you don't."

"What are you doing here?"

"Business." Grishin approached her cautiously. The reports he'd seen indicated the woman was dangerous.

Without warning, she lifted a small pistol and pointed it directly into his face. He could see the bullets in the cylinder less than a yard away.

CHAPTER TWO

Palm Beach, Florida
Thursday

"Shouldn't there be more guys? I mean, I don't want to sound like I'm questioning your ability or your professionalism, but these are dangerous people we're going up against."

Mack Bolan flicked a glance at the man sitting in the passenger seat of the BMW, then turned his attention back to his driving. Palm Beach maintained a laid-back way of life, and even on weekdays serious commerce didn't really start before ten o'clock, so traffic was sparse. Morning sunlight burned down bright and hot against the sandy beaches fronting the breakers rolling in from the Atlantic Ocean. Bolan had turned on the luxury sedan's air conditioner, but kept a window rolled down slightly to let in the bracing salt air.

"No," the Executioner said, "there shouldn't be more guys." He looked in the rearview mirror, making sure the other two vehicles that made up the convoy were present.

Only a few car lengths behind, a baby blue Ford Econoline van with surfing murals airbrushed on the sides and a late-model hunter green Trans Am trailed the BMW. None of the vehicles would attract much attention from the Palm Beach residents.

"I was thinking maybe five wasn't enough," Del Westin said. "Six, I guess, if you count me. But usually I do my work at a desk, after the fact. I've never been in the field before."

And that was the luck of the draw, Bolan knew. The present operation had needed a cybernetic cryptographer on short notice, and Westin had been the best the FBI could provide. "It'll work out."

The Atlantic filled the view in front of him as he made the turn south off 704 onto A1A and followed it down to Worth Street.

Palm trees lined the avenue, followed almost immediately by the scores of shops that imitated the Spanish architecture and Old World flavor of the area. Narrow alleys and spacious courtyards with high walls fronted many of the businesses.

Bolan took the second right he came to off Worth Street, breaking through a yellow light. He was running point on the operation. The four men under his direction wouldn't enter the target premises until he and Westin were inside.

He rolled on half a block, then took a left, coasting the BMW onto an incline leading to a barred gate. Stopping the vehicle, he glanced over at the security outpost and reached for the stun gun between the seats. Beside him, Westin tensed.

"Relax," Bolan said.

A uniformed security guard left the safety of the guardhouse and approached with a large clipboard at the ready. He was young and intense, eyes narrowed in an effort to add ten years to his age. He was also, intel on the operation suggested, innocent of the crimes taking place in the building he guarded.

"Kind of early, aren't you, sir?" the guard asked, stopping five feet away. He checked the list on his clipboard.

Bolan raised his arm, brandishing his Rolex watch. He was dressed in a black Armani suit, tailored for the Florida heat. "Time zones," the soldier explained. "Never have gotten used to flipping them around. Teagan said be here. I'm here."

On the other side of the barred gate, a parking lot fronted a white three-story building that looked more like a manor than a commercial interest. A small copper plaque beside the double doors in front announced Palm Beach Fiduciary Inc.

"What time have you got, sir?" the guard asked.

Behind him, Bolan spotted the second guard still in the guardhouse. The trick was going to be to put both men down before an alarm could be sounded. "About nine-thirty."

"You're an hour ahead, sir."

Bolan nodded, then glanced toward the bank. "Is Teagan in?"

"Sir," the guard said, "if Mr. Teagan told you to meet him here at a specified time, then I'm sure he'd rather meet with you at that time. You can bet that he'll be here at that time. He's very prompt concerning his appointments."

"I'm sure he is. Maybe we could wait inside."

"I'm sorry, sir, but that's not possible." The guard shrugged apologetically. "Regulations."

Bolan nodded. "I'd heard he ran a tight ship. Bet you don't get many customers coming here just to cash a check, right?"

"No, sir. Could I have your name? I'll tell Mr. Teagan you stopped by. There's a bistro not far from here that serves excellent cappuccino that I'd recommend. You could wait there. If you leave your name with the host or hostess, they can see that you're paged if Mr. Teagan càn arrange to meet you at an earlier time."

"Where's the bistro?" Bolan asked.

"Are you familiar with the city, sir?"

"Just what I saw of it when I got here last night, and what I've seen of it this morning."

"That's fine, sir. If you'll get back on Worth Street, the street you came up from—" The guard turned to point back the way Bolan had come.

The soldier lifted the stun gun over the lip of the door window and fired. The gleaming dart sped out with an explosive *chuff* of noise that didn't sound any louder than a strangled sneeze. The thin wire connecting it to the weapon spun out behind it, gleaming in the morning sunlight.

The dart struck the guard low on his left thigh, well below where any concealed body armor would be. Immediately the fifty thousand volts that accompanied the dart surged through the unit along the wire. The guard jerked spasmodically, dropping his clipboard and going slack at once.

Bolan was in motion before the unconscious man hit the ground. He popped open the BMW's door and ran toward the gatehouse. On the other side of the wire-meshed glass of the security door, the remaining guard shoved himself out of his seat, clawing for the revolver on his hip.

The Executioner tried the doorknob and found it unlocked. Since going into business almost three years earlier, Palm Beach Fiduciary hadn't had any robberies or attempted robberies. The majority of its transactions were electronic, and security was tight. Bolan opened the door and raised the stun gun.

The guard managed to get his revolver clear and was bringing it up when Bolan fired the second dart. It struck the man in the neck, and the electric current took him out of the play, sparks jumping from the metal filings inside the man's mouth.

Dropping the weapon, Bolan stepped inside the gatehouse and looked over the communications and alarm systems. His intel packet had included the probable setup of the controls, and he found the specifics were close. A brief glance assured him that no alarm had gone out. The six security monitors on the console in front of him covered the periphery of Palm Beach Fiduciary. He scanned them, marking their positions in his mind, knowing the system would be duplicated inside the bank.

He reached for the electronic storage controls, ran the footage back and pressed Play. There was a flicker, then the security-camera monitors filled with images that were only minutes old. If the security team inside the bank hadn't been on its toes, there was a chance they wouldn't have noticed the change or spot the time discrepancy on the time-date stamps. Bolan also disabled the silent alarm that fed into the Palm Beach police department, then triggered the gate release.

He returned to the BMW, unleathering the silenced Beretta 93-R. The guards inside the bank weren't going to be as guiltless as the hired security working the perimeter.

The gates whirred mechanically back into their reservoirs as Bolan dropped behind the steering wheel. He pulled into the parking lot and came to a rocking stop less than five yards from the series of stone steps leading up to the bank's double doors.

He uncoiled from behind the wheel, the Beretta hard and sure in his fist. He moved on the door at once, flanked by Westin, going up the small flight of stairs at a trot. The soldier dropped a hand into his jacket pocket and took out the ear-throat headset connected to the radio transceiver on his belt. He put it on and keyed it up. "Stony Base, this is Stony One."

"Go, One," Aaron Kurtzman replied, "you've got Base." Kurtzman was Stony Man Farm's cybernetics expert and was running the com-links for the operation.

Bolan walked toward the double doors, noting the receptionist behind the desk through the dark, polarized glass. "Have you got a vid-link?" The audio link was provided by the compact satellite system set up in the BMW.

"Got you five-by, One," Kurtzman replied. From the hidden base in Virginia's Blue Ridge Mountains, Kurtzman managed the communications and video uplink through a low-level satellite he'd appropriated. He would have Palm Beach in workable view for almost seventeen minutes—enough time to complete the operation and download the data they needed if everything went by the numbers.

And Bolan could hear those numbers whispering through his mind as he moved. He walked through the double doors, keeping the Beretta out of sight behind his leg.

"Can I help you, sir?" the brunette receptionist asked, turning to face him.

"Mr. Teagan, please," Bolan said.

"To see both of you?" The receptionist reached for

the desktop planner. "Do you have an appointment? I'm sure I would have remembered."

"Surprise visit." Bolan reached inside his jacket and produced the FBI credentials Kurtzman had readied for him.

The ID froze the receptionist in place for just a moment. "A surprise visit to Mr. Teagan generally involves a court order," she said evenly. It was the voice of experience and carried a demand with it.

"Next trip." Bolan showed her the Beretta without pointing it at her. "Move away from the desk without touching anything and leave the office."

The woman's face blanched, and the soldier felt bad about that. Innocents were in the trenches here, but moving them out of the direct line of fire was the best he could manage, even at gunpoint.

Quickly the woman vacated her seat behind the desk and ran for the door.

"Camera," Westin said, pointing.

Bolan nodded. He'd already spotted the lens fitted nearly flush against the wall to the left of the receptionist's desk. He took the lead, moving for the door to the right. The intel packet Kurtzman had sent included a detailed blueprint of the bank.

Trying the door, Bolan found it locked. He stepped back, waving off Westin, then leveled the 93-R and fired three rounds. The sound suppressor kept most of the noise out of the reports, and the brass dropped soundlessly to the thick carpet.

The 9 mm parabellum rounds chewed through the door, reducing the locking mechanism to junk.

Bolan raised a foot and rammed it into the door, shearing away the last of the latches that held it closed. He went through cautiously, following the Beretta's lead, his senses alert. Mitchell Teagan hadn't risen to the top of his particular sewer by being careless.

Gunfire sounded from outside.

Tapping the transmit button on the headset, Bolan said, "Springer Two and Springer Three, your positions?"

Another office was beyond the door, housing a long rectangular conference table with two dozen chairs. A mobile wet bar stood in one corner. Bolan kept moving forward, aware that Westin was staying only a couple steps behind him.

"In place," Springer Two advised. "Periphery is aware that we're active. We'll keep your back door open."

Movement to Bolan's left attracted his attention. He swung on point, reaching behind him for Westin's jacket and shooting a foot back to trip the man.

A tightly centered burst of double-aught buckshot punched a fist-sized hole through the wall less than two feet from Bolan. Splinters cascaded against his face, and the deep detonation boomed down the corridor.

The man standing at the second doorway of the office wore a pastel tank top and swim trunks. He racked the slide on a pump shotgun.

Bolan squeezed off two rounds, aiming slightly above the big bore of the scattergun. Both bullets smashed through the man's face and staggered him backward. The soldier reached down for the FBI computer expert. "Come on."

"I can walk," Westin protested.

The Executioner let the man go once he had him on his feet. He crossed the room to the next door and found the corridor the blueprints indicated would be there. A brief glance showed him the two men in the hall. Both had guns, moving fast to flank the conference room, which had two other doors.

"Over here!" the nearer man yelled, bringing the full-sized Uzi he held to bear. A harsh spray of rounds smacked into the wall and floor, chopping an uneven line toward Bolan.

The Executioner ducked back for an instant, unable to get off a shot before the line of fire had overtaken his position. Holding the Beretta in both hands, he waited for the Uzi to cycle dry, then turned around the corner of the doorway.

The man was trying to fall back and recharge his weapon at the same time.

Bolan put a double-tap over the man's heart, no more than a finger's width between the rounds. The second man was nowhere to be seen. "Springer Two."

"Go, you've got Springer Two."

Bolan raced halfway down the hall and reached the door located on the right side. "Close up ranks, Two. I've left at least one man up and moving behind me."

"Affirmative, Springer One. We'll bat cleanup."

Bolan didn't doubt it. The four men with him weren't standard FBI issue. They were blacksuits from Stony Man Farm, culled from the very best military special forces had to offer.

The door was locked. He fired two rounds, and pockmarks in the wood showed the metal underneath. "Move back," he told Westin.

The man stepped aside immediately, one hand holding his briefcase and the other wrapped around his 10 mm Delta Elite pistol. He had his mouth open, breathing hard.

Bolan took a preassembled block of plastic explosive from his jacket pocket, jammed it against the doors and activated the preset timer. "Five seconds," he said to the FBI agent. "Stand clear."

Westin nodded, turning away from the blast area.

CHAPTER THREE

The plastic explosive detonated with a loud bang. The shaped charge blew most of the debris into the room beyond, but tailings came rushing out into the hallway. On the heels of the explosion, Bolan moved into the small room.

The room was merely a staging area for another reception room with heavier security. Three men were inside the room, confirming Kurtzman's intel. Deep into a hell zone where anything could happen, it was reassuring to know the intel was on the mark.

One of the men was down, apparently killed or knocked unconscious by the explosion. Another was scrambling out from behind a heavy chrome-and-glass desk that had been blown to pieces. The third man was on his feet, an Ingram MAC-10 tucked into the crook of one arm. Beside him, the elevator doors to the lower level of the bank stood buckled within their housings.

Acrid smoke burned Bolan's nostrils and throat as he swung on the man with the Ingram. The MAC-10 chattered death, pockmarking the door frame beside the Executioner. Bolan squeezed off a 3-round burst from the 93-R, the 9 mm bullets tracking upward from belt level and punching the man back.

The Executioner snapped off another round that

ripped into the man's throat, slapping him back against the wall behind him. The dying man dropped his weapon and fell to his knees.

The other man threw his pistol away. Blood leaked down his chin. "Don't shoot! I'm done with it!"

Keeping the Beretta trained on the other man, the Executioner moved forward. His combat senses were alive, tracking sounds and movements. He took a pair of disposable handcuffs from the back of his pants and secured the man's hands behind him. Then he turned his attention to the buckled doors of the elevator.

"Stony Base, this is Stony One." Bolan wedged his arm between the elevator doors and shoved. They shrieked as they moved back into their housings.

"Go, Stony One," Kurtzman answered.

"The target?" Bolan peered inside, through the swirling dust that had been stirred up by the explosion. The elevator cage was at the bottom of the shaft, locked down. The blueprint specs hadn't indicated another way out of the lower levels, but he guessed that there would be one.

"The target's trying to make the electronic transfer to the off-site memory station in the Cayman Islands," Kurtzman said. "If he gets it done and destroys those computers down there, we're bust on this operation."

"Can you block the telephone lines?" Bolan reached into his jacket again and pulled out a second C-4 charge. He set the timer and dropped it down into the darkness, then stripped off his jacket.

"I'm blocking every phone line I know about, but the guy could be using a cellular phone or have a land-line I don't know about," Kurtzman said. "The only way I know the transfer is going down is because I tied in through the web page Fiduciary has set up on the

World Wide Web. The accessibility to other links on-site dropped a couple minutes ago, indicating that a major portion of the operating system just became occupied. I can't see that many potential customers suddenly deciding to check out Fiduciary's interest rates or account plans. Whatever's eating up memory is coming from an internal source.''

The second C-4 charge detonated in the elevator shaft, belching out smoke and debris.

Bolan wrapped his jacket around the cable severed from the remains of the elevator cage and swung out into the shaft. He breathed shallowly as he dropped, trying to get as little of the smoke and dust into his lungs as possible. Stopping the transfer of data to the off-site storage wasn't necessary. Getting to the data base at the bank before it was erased or corrupted was.

Light streamed into the broken skeleton of the elevator cage and shaft below. The brunt of the explosion had sought out easier passage, boiling up inside the short shaft. But it hadn't been high enough to take all of the concussion. Enough had remained to crack open the elevator cage like an eggshell and blow out one of the doors below.

Conscious of the littered area below, Bolan released his hold and dropped the remaining five feet. He landed rough and hard, sliding for a moment on the loose debris.

Bullets ripped into the elevator shaft, generating sparks momentarily before they penetrated the wall behind him. Keeping the 93-R on 3-round-burst mode, Bolan flipped down the forward handgrip and rushed into the room on the other side of the elevator doors.

The room was large, spacious, filled with electric-white light and a steady hum that droned into his body despite the spotty deafness left over from the gunfire in enclosed spaces and the two explosions. Computers lined two walls, while a third wall held a power generator cabinet. Three desks filled the center space.

Four men were inside the room, and Bolan recognized Mitchell Teagan at once. Whipcord thin, with a face carved onto his skull by the best plastic surgeons money could buy, and sporting a salon-induced tan, Teagan sat at a mainframe, his hands poised over the keyboard.

Bolan went to ground to his right, throwing himself across the tiled floor. Turning on his side, he raked two bursts that took out two of the men guarding Teagan.

The third man held a CAR-15 and unleashed the assault rifle's full firepower before the other two shooters hit the floor. Teagan went into motion behind the man, running for a door set into the wall to his left.

Bolan pushed himself to his feet, coming up behind one of the desks. The Beretta's action had blown back empty. He ejected the clip, then rammed a new one home. The desk vibrated from the assault maintained by the shooter with the CAR-15. Bullets ripped through it, spinning by the soldier and striking the front plate of the generator cabinet.

When the autofire died away, he pushed himself up, knowing he had a heartbeat that was on his side. He let the Beretta lead him around, the front sight falling over the shooter as he dropped the CAR-15 and brought up a big handgun.

The Executioner fired twice, hitting the man in the head and driving him back. Whirling quickly, he dropped the Beretta into target acquisition as Teagan reached the doorway. He fired, putting a bullet into the running man's right ankle.

His foot knocked out from under him, Teagan went down in a tangle in the doorway. He cursed, reaching for leverage to pull himself back up.

Bolan crossed the room to the man and leveled the Beretta. "You're done," he said.

Teagan hesitated, one hand reaching down to clasp his wounded ankle, then he nodded. "I want a lawyer and a doctor. In that order."

Bolan raised his voice. "Westin."

"Here." The FBI agent stepped into the room carrying his briefcase. Dust caked his suit.

"Get the computer."

Westin moved to the mainframe where Teagan had been seated.

Bolan pulled Teagan's tie from around his neck. Rolling the man over, he quickly bound his hands behind his back. He hit the Transmit button on the headset. "Springer Two and Springer Three. Give me your status."

"Springer Three is secure."

"Springer Two is secure. We're knee-deep in locals, though."

Finished with Teagan and certain the man wasn't about to bleed to death from the ankle wound, Bolan crossed the room to Westin. "Stony Base, did you copy?"

"Copy, Stony One. You'll have an interface from the Justice Department who can take care of the locals. The PD's getting a phone call now." Kurtzman and Barbara Price had arranged the umbrella over the operation. The IDs Bolan and the blacksuits had would hold up under scrutiny, and the interface would make sure there weren't any jurisdictional disputes.

Westin tapped the keys rapidly. Screen after screen

opened up on the monitor, scrolling through bank accounts, balances, transfers, legal records. He kept up a litany of curses, then finally relaxed back in the seat. Perspiration filmed his forehead as he drew a shaky breath. "Okay. We're okay. He had a worm in there, poised to delete all the data bases at this location once the transfer was complete. I nuked it."

"Good." Bolan slipped his hand under his jacket and pulled out a cellular phone. "Let's get it sent." He punched in the local number Kurtzman had set up to take the download. The call would be rerouted through several cutouts, then sent to Stony Man Farm.

Westin slotted the cellular phone into the PCM/CIA outlet and hit more keys. "The transfer's going through."

Bolan nodded. He moved around the room, identifying possible information areas. Stony Man would be sending in a forensics team in the next few hours to scrape up every lead they could glean from the site. Palm Beach Fiduciary Incorporated was the weakest link they'd been able to find in the chain they were presently tracking down.

And the chain was immense, bigger than even Stony Man Farm's resources had indicated until nine days ago when the picture had come in from a *National Geographic* shoot in the Caribbean. When Brognola had dropped the dime and contacted him, explaining the situation, Bolan had come at once. There'd been no choice. Too much was on the line.

Now, looking at the seemingly endless data scrolling across the computer monitor in front of Westin, the Executioner had to wonder how effective the Stony Man teams were going to be against the forces they were facing. Kesar Grishin's organization stretched across the planet.

And Bolan knew the stranglehold was already being applied.

KESAR GRISHIN NEVER LOST the smile as he faced the woman with the gun. He spread his hands at his sides. "If you pull that trigger, you'll be dead."

"Then we both will be," she replied calmly.

"Please," the Russian told her, "I didn't come here to harm you. If I had, trust me when I say that you'd have been dead before you saw my men coming."

"What do you want?"

"I have business with Ishikure-san."

"I don't know him."

Grishin shrugged good-naturedly. Behind the woman, he saw the ornate vases and textured paintings that were her passion. Candles burned in holders that were hundreds of years old. He'd never understood the passion to hold on to things so old, not when there were so many new things out there to be acquired.

"I knew you'd feel compelled to lie," he told her. "I expected that. So I don't fault you for it."

She watched him with predatory eyes over the gun barrel.

"There are a number of things I know about you," Grishin said. "That pistol you're holding? It's a Marley .32-caliber revolver, given to you by your father. He himself received it for services rendered during MacArthur's occupation of Japan after the Second World War. I know you're a good shot with it." He laughed generously. "I know you couldn't miss me at this distance."

"No," she stated, "I won't."

"I want to reach into my pocket and show you something." Grishin moved his left hand toward his vest pocket.

Takemori eared the hammer back on her small pistol with a quick flick of her thumb. The barrel never wavered. "No."

Grishin looked at her for a moment, never losing the smile, but letting her see it turn cold and hard. "Yes."

"And you'll be dead when you do."

"Then you'll just have to kill me, because I didn't come here to back down." Grishin was conscious of one of Dobrynin's men at his back. The woman's eyes had flicked to the side only long enough to register his presence. "If you don't kill me with your first shot, you won't get another. But you will be dead yourself. Needlessly I assure you." Grishin reached into his vest, feeling the thrill of excitement course through him as he called her bluff.

She kept the pistol trained on him.

He took out the coin he'd been given, holding it up between his thumb and forefinger so Takemori could easily see it. Three holes had been drilled through it, and strands of human hair had been threaded through the holes, secured in a knotted bead on the side he had facing her.

"You know what this is?" he asked her.

"Yes."

He flipped it at her. "I was told I'd have your complete cooperation if I showed it to you."

She caught the coin, then lowered the .32 and put it back in her desk drawer. "What do you wish?"

"Ishikure, as I stated."

"He is here."

Grishin grinned, lowering his hands at his sides. "I

knew that. I was told you have a surveillance system capable of peeking into all the rooms."

"Where did you get that knowledge?"

"I'm sorry, I can't say."

"It isn't known by many."

"I know. It is to your credit that that piece of knowledge was very expensive to acquire."

She sat behind the desk and pressed a button underneath. The dark teak paneling behind her slid away, revealing a wall of monitors. All of them were in color and peered into small, bedroom-styled compartments. In many of them, couples and sometimes more were engaged in active sex. Grishin knew the rooms were extremely soundproofed. No one in the rooms knew about the gunfire or violence that had been dealt in the outer areas. Thin bars across the bottoms of the monitors showed that all of them were being recorded.

"Nice system," Grishin said with real enthusiasm. Electronic systems, especially computers, had always interested him. "I don't suppose you ever use those tapes to blackmail anyone."

Takemori gave him a cool stare. "Of course not."

"But it's a hell of a retirement plan if you ever get out of the pussy-palace business, isn't it?"

"You're very crude."

Grishin shrugged. "Forgive me. I'm in a hurry. Perhaps I could be more charming over dinner some other time."

"I don't think so," she replied neutrally. "But I would like to know how you came by that coin."

"Yes, I'm sure you would." Grishin looked at his watch, checking the time. He returned his gaze to the Japanese madam. "But that would cost you dinner."

She paused, then a slow smile twisted her ruby lips.

"Granted, as long as I get to make the arrangements and pick the place."

Grishin laughed, delighted. It was an unexpected coup, and someone with Nariko Takemori's connections would be a treasured addition to his Japanese operations. She would have access to those already in power, and to those who would be moving into positions of power. "Placing myself in your hands is an alluring thought, dear lady, and I'll gladly take you up on your intriguing offer as long as I can bring an entourage."

She twisted her head slightly and nodded, amusement flickering in her eyes. "Of course. When may I expect you?"

"Soon. I'll call you and set it up on an evening we will both find convenient." Grishin nodded at the wall of monitors. "Ishikure-san?"

"Room 18."

Grishin ticked off in his mind the rooms, finding the monitor that showed room 18. Jiro Ishikure was indeed inside the room, lying back on a king-size bed while a young woman labored over him. He watched for a time, intrigued by the woman's performance, then he left to join Dobrynin in the foyer.

Bullet holes stitched two of the walls. At least two vases lay in scattered ruin across the Oriental rugs over the hardwood floor. Most of the working girls were hunkered down and staying quiet, in various stages of undress that would have been erotic if the circumstances were different. Some of them had tears in their eyes.

"You heard?" Grishin asked Dobrynin.

"Yes, sir. Room 18."

"Well, then, what are we waiting for?"

Dobrynin stepped over one of the dead security guards who'd tried to block their entrance. The man had never managed to get his weapon from his shoulder holster. A bullet hole was placed almost perfectly between his widely staring eyes.

Grishin followed, his nostrils pinching tight at the smell of death now lingering among the scents of the burning incense and candles.

CHAPTER FOUR

Squaring himself in front of the door to room 18, Dobrynin waved the two men accompanying Kesar Grishin into position along the corridor. They moved quickly, without a sound.

"I want him alive," Grishin said.

"Yes, sir." Dobrynin drew back a booted foot.

Screws shrieked as Dobrynin kicked the door, which banged back, sagging on its hinges. The room beyond was outfitted in red, from the bed to the mock window curtains surrounding a color monitor that projected a view of a forested summer day with a babbling brook. The water noise underscored the action in the room, broadcast by what Grishin assumed was a state-of-the-art sound system.

The woman, slim hipped and small breasted, was still atop Jiro Ishikure. The sheets swaddled around her, bright crimson against the warm butter of her skin. She uncoiled like a striking snake, with no warning whatsoever. Something glittered in her hand as it rose above her head.

Grishin instinctively moved, getting out of the flight path of the thrown object. Before it reached him, though, Dobrynin slapped it from the air with the back of his free hand, squeezing off a single round from the

H&K MP-5. The woman spun away, taken high in the shoulder by the round. The throwing knife Dobrynin had knocked from the air thudded point first into the carpet at Grishin's feet.

"No," Dobrynin said harshly to the woman. He spoke in English.

Grishin hoped the woman understood the language; otherwise she'd be dead.

The prostitute got to her knees on the floor at the foot of the bed, facing them, one hand pressed to her wounded shoulder. Blood streamed between her fingers.

"Down on your face, woman," Dobrynin commanded. "If you move any other way, you die."

Quietly the woman leaned forward and placed her forehead against the floor.

Grishin watched her, then turned his attention to the Japanese man lying on the bed. He shifted his smile into a higher wattage, feeling good, even though with the building security moving around him, he was almost as exposed as Ishikure.

"I see I've come at an inopportune moment, Ishikure-san," he said in an oiled voice.

Ishikure shook with fear and repressed rage. "How dare you!" He was in his late thirties, no more than five and a half feet tall. Raven black hair lay close against his skull, contrasting with his light hazel eyes.

Grishin clapped his hands, never once losing the smile. "How dare I?" he repeated. He stepped closer to the man, bending so his lips were only inches from his ear. "How dare I? I'll tell you how, you son of a bitch. Because I can point at anyone tonight and make them dead." He drew back and smiled at Ishikure again. "Maybe you want to keep that in mind."

"Do you think you can scare me?" Ishikure demanded.

"Quite frankly," Grishin said, "yes."

Dobrynin walked across the room to the monitor in the wall, the machine pistol covering the woman. He reached under the monitor, pressing on sections of the wall, then popped a panel loose. Inside was a VCR hookup. Taking a VHS tape from inside his pocket, he slipped it into the VCR and punched the Play button.

"What is this?" Ishikure asked. He turned his head slowly, as if afraid to take his eyes from Grishin.

"Watch." Grishin waited calmly as images filled the screen. It was good that the monitor was top-of-the-line. Ishikure would see exactly how good the work was that he'd had done.

When the image cleared, it showed Ishikure at a restaurant, which was packed with a lunch crowd, the bars dense with men and women ordering from the cooks stationed at their tables. Ishikure sat near one of the chefs. Light played and flashed along the man's knives as he prepared plates.

"Do you remember this?" Grishin asked.

"This is a restaurant that I favor. It could have been taken at any time."

The time-date stamp said that the footage had been shot only a handful of days earlier.

"Yes," Grishin said. He paused, his attention riveted to the screen, letting Ishikure know that he was watching intently, as well. "But that's not important. Watch this."

A man came to stand behind Ishikure, hesitated for a moment, then took the seat behind him. The two men spent some time ignoring each other, then started to talk briefly.

"Do you know this man?" Grishin asked.

"No."

Grishin grinned widely. "Well, it sure appears that he knows you."

On the monitor, the conversation continued for a few more seconds, then ended with Ishikure handing over a legal-size envelope. The other man took it and left, pausing only to finish the drink in front of him.

"That never happened," Ishikure said.

"I know," Grishin agreed. "However, according to this tape, it did." He shrugged, a smile still in place. "I'm sure you could convince the other members of the board of directors at Wakaba International that someone set you up, though." He paused, looking at the stilled picture monitor. "Although, that piece of footage is pretty damning."

"You did this!" Ishikure's eyes bulged, and his face darkened as blood suffused his features.

"Yes. And trust me when I say the computer-graphics utilities that were used for the blue-screen effects were the absolute state-of-the-art. When that video goes out, every specialist you can dig up is going to tell you they can't find anything in it to indicate that it's a forgery."

Ishikure swore at him in Japanese.

Grishin ignored the stream of invective. Ishikure was trapped, and they both knew it. All that remained was to show the CEO of Wakaba how bad things really were. He nodded at Dobrynin.

The video continued, closing out the sequence at the restaurant and opening up to a file on the other man, identifying him as a known member of the Yakuza who specialized in corporate crime. The man had been totally enamored of being captured for posterity on the video frame.

"No matter what you do," Grishin said as police file photographs of the Japanese gangster scrolled across the screen, "you're not going to be able to escape this." He looked hard into Ishikure's eyes. "You should have come across when you had the chance, instead of trying to use what I told you against me. I'd have kept you in business." He paused, gesturing to Dobrynin. "I'd have kept you *alive*."

"Then kill me, gaijin filth!" Ishikure shouted, pushing himself out of bed. "Kill me now!"

"And give Wakaba International a martyr?" Grishin shook his head. "Where's the percentage in that?"

Furious, fear brimming in his eyes, Ishikure threw himself toward Grishin, arms outstretched.

Dobrynin raised the machine pistol reflexively.

"No!" Grishin ordered. He moved into a defensive *kata* himself, blocking Ishikure's attack, but swung a very American right roundhouse that exploded from the point of the Wakaba executive's chin.

Ishikure sat down heavily, having trouble focusing his eyes. Blood trickled from a corner of his mouth.

Grishin waved at Dobrynin, catching the videotape the other man tossed to him. Breathing hard, more from the release of emotion than any real exertion, he dropped the tape on the floor in front of Ishikure. "If I make a phone call," he said, producing a cellular phone, "a copy of that tape goes to every member of the board of directors through an overnight courier service. And copies go out to every stockholder, as well. Do yourself a favor, Ishikure-san, and do the right thing." He reached behind his back and took out a holstered Tanto Cold Steel knife with nearly eight inches of gleaming double-edged blade. "Do it with honor."

For a frozen moment, Ishikure regarded the long knife. Then he reached back and grabbed a fistful of the bright crimson sheets. He wrapped the sheets around the handle of the knife and pointed the blade at himself. He took a fresh grip on the handle, staring off into another world as he steeled himself for the effort. Forcibly he pulled the blade into the loose flesh of his left side, miraculously allowing only a thin shrill of pain to escape his compressed lips. Muscles in his neck and arms bulging, dark red blood already discoloring the sheets, he started pulling the knife across his stomach.

Stony Man Farm
Thursday

AARON KURTZMAN SAT in his wheelchair on the raised dais behind the horseshoe-shaped desk that gave him a full view of the covert-operations nerve center. He was a big man with broad shoulders, and would have stood tall if it hadn't been for the chair.

Three computer monitors filled the desk in front of him. In the lower quadrangle of the monitor on his left, the live broadcast of arriving Palm Beach reporters flocking to the bank where Bolan and his team were on-site filled the window. A line of uniformed policemen held back the news crews.

"Aaron."

Kurtzman glanced up, tracking the voice back to Carmen Delahunt.

"The com-links and vid-links to Able Team's operation in Puerto Vallarta are on-line." Short, red-haired and feisty, Delahunt was old-line FBI, straight from Quantico. She'd mastered computers there and welcomed the chance to move into the Stony Man Farm hardsite when the offer was extended.

At the other end of the long room, three wall screens blazed with color, light and intensity. On the left, the screen in front of Delahunt showed the interior of a hotel suite, revealing two of the men working quickly to finish setting up surveillance on the room. They worked with mutual ease and a familiarity with each other. Kurtzman knew them both. Rosario Blancanales—called the Politician by his friends because of his ability with words and emotions—was dressed in a green coverall and wore a tool belt, looking like a maintenance worker as he put a light fixture back together.

Next to a wall of glass with a sliding door, Hermann Schwarz looked wiry and hard. Like Blancanales, he wore a green coverall and a tool belt. However, Schwarz worked the battery-powered drill and screwdriver like they were extensions of his own body. Those who knew him called him Gadgets, and the talents he displayed with machinery and electronics could range from innovative to pure, hellish destruction.

"Where's the Ironman?" Kurtzman asked. The operation in Puerto Vallarta was coming to a head, as well. "Ironman" was Carl Lyons, an ex-LAPD police officer who'd joined the team at Stony Man when the Farm had been put together.

"Floating," Delahunt answered. "I'm monitoring the conversation between Blancanales and Schwarz. There's been some concern about their target."

"What concern?"

"The DEA agents Lyons is coordinating the local

traffic with said the target deviated from SOP in-country.''

Kurtzman tapped the mouse, brought up the operating system and opened a new window on the third monitor in front of him. Accessing the pull-down menu he'd created, he punched up the file he wanted.

A woman's picture formed in another window to the upper left of the file. Chela Escelera had made a big career for herself in what was normally considered a man's world. The Colombian cartels where she did business didn't allow weakness, and every cartel head would have taken her territory long ago. If they'd been able.

Escelera had proved to have a vicious streak, as well. In the past, when men working under her in her organization had tried to stage a coup, she'd not only had the men killed, but their families, as well. The picture on the computer monitor showed none of that viciousness. In it, Chela Escelera looked like a beautiful woman in her forties, dark skinned and dark eyed, black hair pulled up on top of her head, tangerine lipstick covering full lips.

"What have you got on the deviation?" Kurtzman asked.

"So far, nothing. Lyons left almost eighteen minutes ago.''

"With the DEA liaison?''

Jacinto Montoya, the DEA liaison, had six years in the agency and had been a career vice cop before that.

"Yes,'' Delahunt replied.

Kurtzman felt tense. Deviations weren't a good thing, especially when the plan had been a good one. "What about communications with Lyons?''

"Limited to his cell phone only. Should I call?''

"No." If Lyons needed them, he'd be in touch. Kurtzman wished the ache in his stomach would go away, but knew it was wasted effort. The Farm's operations had for months been nipping at the toes of the organization they were up against, never really knowing it was there in the size it was. And a handful of men was being asked to go in to break it up. "Set a timer on him. Give him an hour. If we haven't heard from him by then, we'll start turning over rocks."

He worked on archiving the files arriving from Palm Beach. The phone rang, and he scooped it up in one big hand. "Yeah."

"Me," Bolan said. "Are you getting everything at that end?"

"It's coming through fine," Kurtzman replied. "Any problems there?"

"Nothing we couldn't handle. Westin did good in the crunch. You might pass that along."

"I will." Shifting behind the desk, Kurtzman noticed a blinking asterisk on the left monitor. He tagged it, then watched as it blossomed to unveil a link to a live CNN broadcast from Washington, D.C. An electronic note dropped from the top of the screen and unfurled in front of the video link: *"U.S. Attorney General Ramona Thompson's speech."*

Kurtzman started to record the broadcast, downloading it into the monster data base he'd set up for the operation.

"Have you got my flight set up for Jamaica?" Bolan asked.

"Jack's standing by there in Palm Beach," Kurtzman answered. He watched the news broadcast, tapping another series of keys that switched on the caption box.

He read the opening quotes of the CNN anchors as they got ready to unveil their story.

"As soon as we shut down this site," Bolan said, "I'm on my way."

"You've got a full intel packet waiting for you. Some of it you may already know, but you'll get it again. Remember, Dionis Santos has set himself up on the island pretty well. He'll be dug in tight, and we need to get a feel from him, then decide if he needs to be taken off the board."

"I'll let you know how tight he's dug in," Bolan replied, then broke the connection.

Kurtzman cradled the phone, staring at the images coming over the CNN link.

U.S. Attorney General Ramona Thompson was a good-looking woman in her early fifties. She kept her frosted blond hair cut short, allowing the silver strands to show. Her face held strong lines of character, and some wrinkles, as well. They'd been earned. Her second son had died of an overdose seven months into her first year of holding the attorney general's post. Instead of breaking under the adverse publicity or hiding from the media fallout, Ramona Thompson had stood her ground and faced it.

And in doing so, she'd won over the hearts of the majority of the nation.

Watching the footage roll from the congressional organized-crime meeting the previous month, Kurtzman didn't think the woman was so lucky now. The aggressive stance Thompson had taken against the growing criminal cartels linking up across the world had marked her for death.

Although Stony Man Farm hadn't been sanctioned for the maneuvers Able Team, Phoenix Force and Bolan were taking, Harold Brognola, director of the Justice Department's Sensitive Operations Group, had ordered them into action. The strategic strikes they'd planned were designed to break down the organization Thompson was taking on, hopefully collapsing it under some of its own weight as it went to ground. Maybe the assassins would be thrown off their targets for a little while.

Watching the growing list coming in from Palm Beach, though, Kurtzman really doubted it was going to go down like that. He felt a growing certainty that what they were doing now could be compared to tossing a firecracker into the path of an avalanche, hoping to break the slide.

The organization was too big, had been hidden too well. "God keep," he said quietly to the woman's image, then turned his attention to the middle wall screen in the distance. The sat-link focusing on Phoenix Force's efforts in the Myanmar Republic were up and running, and he had to give it his attention for the moment.

CHAPTER FIVE

Kesar Grishin knelt in front of Ishikure as the man kept pulling the sharp knife through his midsection. He could smell the coppery scent of the man's blood spreading out over the sheet-wrapped haft of the Tanto Cold Steel. Grishin's face only inches from Ishikure's.

"Wait."

Ishikure halted in disbelief riddled with bright pain, blood spilling over his broken lips.

"After you die," Grishin said, "I'll still release the tapes. Your name will still be dishonored. Everyone will think you took the coward's way out."

Ishikure cursed him, bloody bubbles breaking against his cheeks and chin.

Grishin turned a palm up. "But if you tell me who you talked to, who convinced you that you were smart enough to double-cross me, I'll make sure all those tapes are destroyed."

Ishikure stared at him. Blood had pooled on the floor in front of him, the sheets well past the saturation point.

"So, what do you say?" Grishin prompted. "Do we have a deal? Or do you just spill your guts on the floor here, and I still show your corporation how you betrayed their secrets to the Yakuza?" For a moment, he thought Ishikure's stubbornness would put the man past the point of compliance as death took him.

"Anthony-san," Ishikure groaned, his hands shaking on the handle of the knife embedded in his stomach. "A man named Lucas Anthony."

"Who is he?"

"American."

Grishin looked into the mortally wounded man's eyes. Ishikure wanted him to believe that was all of it; the Russian could see it in the man's desperate gaze. But he needed everything. "A businessman."

"Yes."

"And no," Grishin said immediately. He knew when he was being lied to, especially when it came to business. "What else is he?"

"American Central Intelligence Agency," Ishikure gasped.

"The CIA?" Grishin shot a look at Dobrynin. They knew of seventeen CIA operations that were investigating various parts of his global infrastructure. They also knew the names of all the men involved. Lucas Anthony wasn't among those names. "You're sure?"

"Yes." Ishikure coughed.

"Do you know anything more?"

"Yes." Ishikure smiled through the pain. "The Americans are going to get you. They know about you. And the American attorney general, Ramona Thompson, is going to be the one who puts you away."

"You think so?"

Ishikure started to answer, but before he could get a word out, Grishin grabbed the man's hands, holding them tight around the knife, and yanked the blade across Ishikure's midsection.

The Japanese man let out a long groan and collapsed on the floor, writhing in pain.

Grishin wiped his own hands clean of blood in the twisted sheets and stood. He looked at Dobrynin. "Get us out of here."

Dobrynin nodded, waving his two men out into the hallway, then following Grishin. He stepped across Ishikure's twitching corpse. Grishin leaned back into the room long enough to drop the videocassette onto the floor. He nodded a brief goodbye to Nariko Takemori.

They took the elevator down, and no one tried to stop them. Obviously the crew that had been assigned to the security offices had been successful.

"We don't know Lucas Anthony." Dobrynin shoved the H&K MP-5 into a large holster along his right hip, then pulled his jacket in place over it.

"No. Evidently Attorney General Thompson has more resources than we previously gave her credit for."

"If we didn't know about the man, he's some kind of deep-covert operative. Maybe he's not even exactly a CIA agent in some respects. A ringer, as the Americans would say."

Grishin nodded. "Thompson has managed to get an operation past us. I don't like that." He shook his head as the elevator reached the first floor and the doors slid back. "You know, she has always been such an aboveboard kind of player. I respected that about her. That's why I've let her live so long even after she started poking around in my affairs."

"I advised you against that. She's a clever woman."

"I know." Grishin sighed. "I had such a good time

playing this cat-and-mouse game with her. She's a very refined lady, and very intelligent.''

"She thought of using the DEA against you," Dobrynin reminded him, "when the others didn't want to involve that administration.''

"That's because everyone takes such a dim view of the DEA these days," Grishin said, stepping out of the elevator cage. Only a few people were in the lobby when they reached it, and none of them gave him a second look. "They all think of the DEA as intractable cowboys, and shot through with corruption.''

"And it is true.''

"Of course it is. But it was a logical and brave decision to make, knowing it could backfire and create even more information leaks within her organization. That's what I like about her.''

"I think," Dobrynin said, "that it's time for your infatuation with the attorney general to end.''

"I suppose you're right.''

They swiftly crossed the foyer and went out into the Tokyo night. The chauffer stood beside the limousine and hurriedly opened the door.

Safely esconsced in the back seat of the armored vehicle again, Grishin took out a slim-line cellular phone and punched in the programmed number.

At the other end, the phone was answered on the first ring. "Yes." The voice was very feminine, very polite and gave away nothing of heritage or geographical location.

Grishin loved women. He loved them in all sizes and shapes, all the things that they did. On the whole, they were as clever as men, he believed, and much more deceitful. "Ah, Salome, how good to hear your voice. Did I wake you?''

"No, Kesar. And how is your trip?"

Grishin glanced back over his shoulder at the building fading rapidly in the dark. The high-pitched keening of police vehicles registered through the window Dobrynin had cracked slightly as he listened. "Profitable. All that I could ask."

"I know this wasn't a social call," the woman prompted.

"No. I need you to get into those files at Langley again."

"Of course. Who am I searching for?"

"An agent," Grishin said. "His name is Lucas Anthony."

"Spelling?"

"Any way you'd wish. I believe you'll find Anthony is a covert agent, probably buried very deeply. Do be careful."

"As always. I'll call ahead to the airport and make certain your jet is ready and waiting."

"Thank you."

"Efficiency," Salome said sweetly, "that's what you hired me for."

"I'd like you to check on something else for me, as well."

"Yes?"

"Your brief from two days ago indicated that U.S. Attorney General Ramona Thompson would be involved in a charity event tomorrow night."

"The Clairborne-Hill Charity Dinner benefiting abandoned crack babies."

"Where is that being held?"

There was a brief hesitation, then the sound of a computer keyboard and a hard drive whirring filled the line. "Milwaukee, Wisconsin."

"GenCon," Grishin said.

"GenCon?"

"A gaming convention. The biggest of its kind, and a national event in the right circles. Not as big as the computer gaming festivals in Las Vegas, but huge in its own sphere. Some of our software holdings are going to be introducing games there. The convention actually opened today." Over the years, he'd been there a handful of times. He glanced at his watch. "Still going on, as a matter of fact. But tomorrow is Friday, and it will be an even bigger day. Where is the charity event going to be held?"

"The Ivanhoe Arms. A newly remodeled hotel with a real past, according to the brochure."

"That's across the street from the convention center. Can I get an invitation?"

"You won't be on the A list."

"That won't shatter me," Grishin replied. "Still, those doors will open to someone wanting to make a sizable donation. Use one of the holding companies we have in Chicago and work it so that no one knows I'll be the representative."

"Leave it to me."

"I am. And one other thing, Salome."

"Yes?"

"See to it that those videocassettes concerning Ishikure are mailed. I want Ishikure's sacrifice to have been in vain. The corporation he chaired *will* come around to my way of thinking."

"Of course."

Grishin punched the End button on the cellular phone and put it back in his pocket.

"Going to see the U.S. attorney general now?" Dobrynin asked.

"Only briefly. Long enough to pay my last respects. In fact, it might make a fitting introduction to tomorrow night's meeting aboard the *Royal Flush*." He smiled at Dobrynin. "Even though Ramona Thompson has become a thorn in the side of everyone who will be there, I think her demise would be the perfect ice-breaker. Don't you?"

Mandalay, Myanmar

"LOOK ALIVE, MATES," David McCarter stated as he walked through the guts of the de Havilland DHC7-7 air freighter. "We may be seven minutes ahead of schedule, but that doesn't mean we're going to spend the time lollygagging." He listened to the de Havilland's four prop engines whirring steadily, the vibrations running confidently throughout the cargo plane.

Tall and lanky, McCarter had been with the British SAS before signing on with Phoenix Force. He had sharp, foxlike features, but camou cosmetics masked most of the sharp angles. He carried an Ithaca Model 37 Stakeout pump shotgun on a Whip-it sling along his right side. Not all of the work this night was going to be at a distance. They'd been sent in to deliver a bloody message as violently as possible. He also carried two Browning Hi-Power pistols, one in a shoulder rig and the other in a counterterrorist drop holster low on his right thigh.

"Has Stony Base confirmed the transport?" Calvin James asked. He was on the periphery of the other three members of Phoenix Force, sorting through the medical supplies in the backpack that was his responsibility. Six foot two and slender, the black man carried an M-16/ M-203 combo over his shoulder, pointing at the cargo hold's floor. A matching pair of Beretta 92 pistols rode in twin shoulder rigs. He was dressed in a black battle-dress-uniform blouse and paratrooper pants like the rest of the team, the cuffs tucked into hiking boots that were tightly laced.

"They're there," McCarter replied. He glanced over the rest of his crew.

Gary Manning, Rafael Encizo and T. J. Hawkins continued their preparations. All of them were professionals, and no one needed to be told what to do.

"Are they on time?" Manning asked. He was the team's demolitions expert. Barrel-chested and looking deceptively easygoing, the Canadian had received military training, as well as commercial experience in his specialty field. Like James, he carried an M-16 and twin Beretta 92 pistols.

"They're behind," McCarter answered. "Four, maybe five minutes according to the intel's best guess. We're almost that much ahead."

"Never hurts to be early in a situation like this." The Cuban-born Phoenix Force commando wore body armor over his black clothing and he, too, sported two Berettas, one in a counterterrorist drop holster and the other in boot holster in his calf-high hiking boots. His combat harness held garrotes and knives for the silent killing he was so skilled at. He reached down for his M-16 and smiled thinly. "Gives us time we need to make a bigger surprise for our surprise party."

McCarter flashed his teammate a grim grin. The people they were after deserved no mercy, and none would be given. "What's the word, T.J.?" he asked the youngest and newest member of the team.

What he lacked in years of experience, though, McCarter knew Hawkins made up in sheer determination. Grit, as Hawkins himself would call it with his Southern upbringing and lineage. That lineage had also produced a number of military men over generations.

Hawkins looked up from the square case he was closing. He smiled, and a devil-may-care glint flashed in his eyes. "It gets down in one piece, it'll work like a dream. Batteries are charged and ready, and everything seems operational by remote control." Something under six feet and built broad and rangy, well muscled without acquiring a bodybuilder's physique, he moved smooth and sure. He wore black as if he were made for it, and carried twin Berettas in double shoulder holsters. A Barrett .50-caliber sniper rifle in its case lay on the floor beside him.

"As long as the cargo plane remains in range," McCarter said, "we'll be able to manage a com-link through the onboard sat-link systems. But it's going to be hustling out of the area bloody fast. You're only going to have minutes to reach that sat-link and get everything set up."

"It'll be done."

McCarter checked his watch. That old, familiar curious looseness and tension mix filled him as he got ready to go into action. At thirty-three thousand feet, they were all in for a long fall tonight before they got to the killing ground, and it was going to be a right and proper hurly-burly when they reached it.

"Mount up, lads," he growled.

The Phoenix Force members gathered their gear and went to work on the motorcycles, which had been painted matte black and equipped with a baffling system to cut down on the harsh popping sound that the engines normally gave off.

"Phoenix One." The intercom inside the cargo area connecting them to the pilot crew crackled.

"Go," McCarter responded.

"Drop area's coming up in two minutes."

"Affirmative. Drop this tailgate, mate, and let's be quick about it."

With a mechanical grate, the tail section of the de Havilland started to drop open, leaving a flat ramp with a downward inclination.

McCarter rolled his bike to the edge of the ramp. The wind whirled around him, passing in a dull roar. Thin, spidery wisps of clouds and low fog hung in the airspace above the ground. McCarter watched them with interest. If the fog remained on the ground, it stood a chance of mucking up the infrared systems they were going to be dependent on to maintain their cover. According to Price's and Kurtzman's intel reports, though, the fog wouldn't be a problem on the ground.

He took the matte black helmet from the catch on the side of the motorcycle and pulled it on. It was a full-head racing helmet, with chin protection built right in. The face mask, though, was the deepest jet, looking like an oil film. Upon close inspection, McCarter could see the microweave of computer circuitry embedded in the face shield.

He pulled the helmet over his head and switched on the power. The built-in voice-activated transmitter picked up his words at once. "Com-link check. Count off, mates."

The team members counted off in quick succession.

McCarter secured the chin strap. "Pilot, count us down when we're over the drop area, then cut and run."

"Affirmative, Phoenix One. Drop site's in forty seconds and counting."

"T.J.," McCarter called.

"Yeah."

"Your package goes first, then your bike, then you."

"Got it."

"No matter what happens down there, your assignment is that sat-link."

"Understood." Hawkins moved forward, shoving the sat-link crate with him. Mounted on casters, it moved easily.

"Give enough room in between, mates," McCarter said, "then we follow down. Machine and man. Machine and man. Maintain radio silence until you get the call from me."

"Mark," the pilot called back over the helmet com-links. "You have your go, gentlemen, and have a safe landing. You make it through, we'll be there waiting for you at the pickup point."

McCarter waved Hawkins into motion.

With a surge of strength, Hawkins sent the sat-link crate tumbling into the de Havilland's airstream. Manning shoved out Hawkins's Enduro almost immediately afterward. The commando tossed them a nonchalant salute, then went into the slipstream with an acrobatic display of twists and turns before dropping into a glide path that followed the motorcycle and the sat-link.

"Step lively, Cal," McCarter warned.

Then James hurled his Enduro through the door and followed it out. The other two Phoenix Force members quickly trailed him through the tail section.

McCarter went last, shoving the Enduro into the slipstream wrapping around the big cargo plane, then leaping into it himself. Despite the jet black outer appearance of the face mask, he could see through it easily. He went into the starfish glide position instinctively, throwing his arms and legs out to control his fall. He tracked the falling motorcycle effortlessly.

"Phoenix One." Aaron Kurtzman's voice came from inside the helmet.

McCarter shoved a finger inside the small plastic mask that covered his lower face inside the helmet. A thin hose connected the mask to the miniature air tank in the pocket of his BDU blouse, which held ten minutes of air, more than enough for the parachute jump. Once on the ground, it would be discarded. "Go, mate."

"It'll be another few minutes before we make the satellite uplink change from here. Once we do, we'll have visuals of you and your team, and the terrain below."

"Affirmative, Stony Base. We should be on the ground by then."

"Understood. You're going to lose your com-loop in another minute or so because the transport plane will be out of range."

McCarter could already hear the onslaught of white noise coasting through the sat-link forwarded through the cargo plane's onboard satellite dish.

Kurtzman's next communiqué broke up entirely. Evidently he knew it, because he repeated himself. "Stay hard down there, and we'll make the link changeover as soon as the spy satellite comes into position and the sat-link at your end is operational."

"Roger, Stony Base."

Then the sat-link severed entirely. Silence filled McCarter's helmet as he fell through the dark sky. He felt the pressure of the wind hammering against his body as he dropped, rocking him. It was a lot of work staying on track.

A high-altitude low-opening drop would have worked better, the Phoenix Force leader knew, but the risk for equipment failure would have been too great. The motorcycles would probably have taken the brunt of a HALO jump, but the sat-link Hawkins was responsible for might not have.

And without that sat-link, Phoenix Force would have been five men dropping into the night filled with an army who'd kill them as soon as they knew there were intruders among them. The tech involved was the only thing that would allow them to do the job they were there to do.

He glanced left, feeling even the small change create new and different pressure on his neck muscles as he compensated. He glanced at the altimeter on his wrist, counting down silently from ten. Hawkins should be out there with the sat-link package.

When he hit four, he saw the black mushroom of the sat-link crate's chute blossoming into view, just a slightly discolored ripple against the night. The chute packed onto the crate was set for an altitude release, as were the motorcycles. Hawkins's Enduro popped first, no more than three seconds after the sat-link's. The other motorcycle chutes popped in rapid succession, followed almost immediately by each member of the team.

Closer to the earth now, his parachute deployed, McCarter could see the broken terrain below. The target site was approximately eighty kilometers north of Mandalay. The trail the convoy would be following came down from the mountains in a lot of the same wallows the Irrawaddy River had created on its way down to the Bay of Bengal.

He swooped in pursuit of the Enduro, adjusting the chute's flight in direction and rate of descent to keep near it. Juicing the helmet's infrared capabilities, he picked up the other members of the team easily. The helmet was a prototype based on the Soldier Integrated Protection Ensemble designed for special-operations teams. General SIPE guidelines provided global positioning satellite uplinks, infrared vision and data bases that could include first-aid instructions, topographical maps or anything else that could be assembled in an electronic digital package.

With the winds in the area, McCarter knew the team was going to touch down and be more spread out than they'd counted on. He glanced down, knowing the terrain should be within the light-amplifying abilities of the helmet in short seconds.

Slightly to his right, he caught flickering purple darts that sped up from the ground. Only occasional at first, the flickerings quickly became a solid curtain that leaped skyward.

Even before the first few bullets ripped through the black folds of the parachute over his head, McCarter knew the team was descending into terrain filled with enemy guns. More of them came on track. He dumped air from the chute and sped downward, trying to keep the Enduro in the periphery of his vision as he plummeted toward the enemy waiting below.

CHAPTER SIX

Hal Brognola stood near the window overlooking the White House grounds and watched the live television broadcast on the TV-VCR combo built into the wall in front of the President's desk. He felt tired and achy from surviving on a handful of hours of sleep spread over the past two days. His stomach rolled, and the antacid tablet he'd last taken still tasted fresh.

"She won't see it your way, Hal," the President said. He sat behind the desk, fingers toying nervously with a pen. He looked haggard and worn himself, his tie hanging loosely over the back of his chair like a waiting gallow's noose.

"She's a target."

"Ramona knows that." The Man sighed, then rubbed at his face with a hand. "She's a stubborn lady."

Brognola nodded. He was acquainted firsthand with exactly how stubborn the woman could be. "You could order her to step down for the time being."

The President stood and walked to the coffee service near his desk long enough to refill his cup and to take the pot to where Brognola sat. "I thought of that."

"And?"

The Man returned the coffeepot to the service table

and shot the head Fed a rueful grin. "When I mentioned it, she told me she had some sick leave coming and could probably better promote her programs if she wasn't tied up with the day-to-day business of her job anyway."

"Damn it. Did you mention anything in there about this being a joint effort? That she isn't exactly standing out there alone?"

"Lots. Big broad suggestions. Just short of telling her about the Stony Man Farm operation and the fact that I'd asked you people to check around on things."

Brognola knew that revealing the Stony Man Farm operations was over the line. The Farm operated strictly on a need-to-know basis, and remained one of America's most covert counterterrorist measures. At the moment, Ramona Thompson didn't need to know. Truth to tell, the head Fed didn't think it would have made much difference anyway.

"I tried to warn her away from the interview with ABC news because it would help push her into a high-profile position," the Man went on. "You know how well that went over."

"Yeah. I saw the interview." In the interview, Thompson hadn't hesitated a moment about naming names and pointing fingers. One of those names she'd mentioned was Kesar Grishin, though evidence wasn't there to support her. Brognola watched the news anchor announce again that U.S. Attorney General Ramona Thompson would be joining them live in front of the U.S. Department of Justice building in a short while.

"It's politics. She's hot right now, got quite a following in the public, and she's been around the block long enough to know that she's got to move while she's full of lightning."

"I know it." And Brognola did. Thompson didn't have the opportunity to work behind the scenes like he did. She was out front, hanging in the breeze.

"I don't hold it against her," the President said softly. "She's always been a team player. But with the international crime organizations shaping up the way they are, the legislation she's helping to promote among other countries regarding the banking and financial arrangements between nations is damned important."

Brognola nodded. The reluctance of several European countries to seize assets and investigate exactly where those assets had come from was holding back the international initiative to close down organized crime's resources. Thompson had gotten the attention of several of those countries in the past three years of her post because she didn't hesitate to place the blame squarely on the people who deserved it.

The television suddenly cut away from the anchor. Evidently the delay of the U.S. attorney general's arrival had worried programming editors that their audiences would begin channel surfing.

Stock footage rolled of the hostage situation that had played out twenty-seven months earlier and had first propelled Ramona Thompson into the media eye. A militia group calling itself Freedom's Sons had held a trio of lawyers from Minneapolis for twenty-three days. The lawyers had successfully represented two men who'd raped and killed a St. Paul college student in the months before the kidnapping. The two men were also closely tied to a cocaine ring doing business in Minneapolis. The law firm had a history of handling business for the cocaine operations in Minnesota, including setting up dummy corporations and shell holdings to move money back and forth across the Canadian border.

Thompson had successfully negotiated the terms of the release of the hostages. In order to accomplish that, she'd set up a sting operation that netted the two men who'd murdered the girl. The two murderers later went down on drug charges, while the militia members were given reduced and suspended sentences for aggravated assault instead of kidnapping. The trio of lawyers involved decided not to press charges, and Thompson was known to have had a hand in their decisions, as well.

Less than eighteen weeks after that, both of the drug dealers were murdered inside federal prisons, and their killers remained unknown. During that time, Thompson's career had taken a major step forward and thrust her into the public eye.

The woman had made the most of it.

The old footage ended abruptly as the network cut back to Ramona Thompson's current passage down the steps in front of the Justice building. Reporters swarmed her instantly, held at bay by plainclothes U.S. marshals.

Brognola felt unease clench like a claw in his stomach. In the chaotic movements of the crowd, all it would take was one determined man with a rifle, and one bullet.

Brognola knew. He'd put that one man into play several times himself.

Thompson came to a stop only a few steps up, facing her audience. The U.S. attorney general looked slim and attractive in a dark olive business suit. Her short, frosted blond hair blew slightly in the breeze, somehow making her seem more vulnerable. She had a strong face with lean features, icy gray eyes that seemed to always catch the light just right to leave an impact. She smiled at the media as questions were hurled at her. She lifted her hands.

The crowd quieted immediately. Brognola had to give the woman that, too. She knew how to work a room, and had the charisma to weave a web that would draw in the listeners.

"Ladies and gentlemen of the press," she said, "I don't have much time at the moment, so we'll have to forego any long, drawn-out questioning." Her voice came across clearly for the most part, but the gusts of wind across the mikes made long, hollow sounds under her words.

"Ms. Thompson," the "CBS Evening News" reporter said as he pushed forward, "sources I've talked with indicate that you're on the verge of an agreement with Russia regarding a crackdown on banks laundering drug money."

"Can you tell me how close, Mr. Harris?" Thompson showed a cynical smile. "I'd really like to know. I've been in conference with representatives from that country for the past three days, and I can't make that assumption."

The reporter didn't let the gibe touch him. "You are after an agreement of that sort, though."

"Of course. If the government can take away the money these drug empires accumulate, we take away their reasons for being in business. *That* we do agree on. Exactly how we should go about it is still something we're debating."

"Are you still of the opinion that the international community is turning a blind eye to the money laundering that takes place within their borders?'' a woman reporter asked.

"It's not an opinion," Thompson stated. "It's a fact."

"In past months," the CNN correspondent shouted out, "you've made reference to a growing conspiracy of criminal organizations. How big is this conspiracy you're talking about?"

"In the next few days," Thompson said, "you're going to be hearing a lot more about that. Now, if you'll excuse me, I've got a meeting to attend."

The U.S. marshals assembled themselves into a flying wedge and started cutting through the ranks of the reporters. A sleek black limousine pulled to the curb, only partially caught in the view of the camera following Thompson's departure.

"Who's your target?" a reporter bellowed after her. "Can you give us a name?"

Thompson ignored the question, getting into the limousine as one of the marshals held the door open for her.

Brognola breathed a sigh of relief as he watched the limousine pull away into the Washington, D.C., traffic without incident. He took a sip of his coffee to wet the back of his throat.

"So how are we coming on your end of this operation?" the President asked.

Brognola turned to face the Man. "Striker took down the Palm Beach bank this morning."

"I'd heard a little about that. There was some gunplay involved."

"We knew going in we weren't going to get away clean with that," Brognola said. "The money laundering going on at that bank was a big part of the food chain we uncovered. They would have defended it.''

"You were after the computer records.''

"Yes.''

"Did you get them?''

Brognola nodded. "It'll take some time to figure out how damaging they're going to prove.''

"I understand.'' The President took his seat behind the desk again. "What about the assignments Phoenix Force and Able Team were given?''

"Phoenix has just made the jump into Myanmar.'' Brognola rolled over his wrist and checked his watch. A brief communiqué from Barbara Price had brought him up-to-date on both teams. "They should be within satellite range in another few minutes. Able Team has experienced a hiccup in the game plan.''

The President glanced up with raised eyebrows. "A hiccup?''

"The DEA wasn't exactly forthright in its debriefing with us,'' Brognola admitted. He was certain that declaration didn't surprise the Man. It hadn't surprised him, but there'd been no way to finesse the needed information ahead of time.

"What is it they weren't exactly forthright about?''

"Saunders had an agent in place that he didn't tell us about, a man who'd dug himself in pretty deep into Escelera's Puerto Vallarta operation.''

"Able Team is operating independently of the DEA,'' the President said, "so I don't see a problem.''

"With Able on the ground there in Puerto Vallarta,'' Brognola went on, "Saunders decided to up the ante. He had the agent in place move on some of Chela Escelera's local holdings.''

"Give me a translation.''

"The agent took a chance and burgled one of the homes of Escelera's lieutenants in the area."

"Did Saunders's agent tip off Escelera about Able?"

"No," Brognola said. "The agent got caught."

"Damn it!" The President glanced at the continued news coverage on the television briefly. "So what is the status of this agent?"

"The last we heard, he's alive," Brognola said. "Escelera wants to question him. Lyons is on his way to help pull him out of the fire. If he can."

"The last thing we need down there is a hostage situation we have to deal with. Especially if Saunders got caught with his damned hand in the cookie jar on an illegal search. What about Able's own objective there?"

"They're going to salvage it if they can."

"I tell you, Hal, the one thing that really angers me about all these different agencies getting involved in the same pie is that everybody tries to make sure they get their own piece of it. They don't care diddly about anybody else's piece. You hear what I'm saying?"

Brognola nodded. He'd been at his position long enough to learn about the infighting between the various law-enforcement divisions. The war on drugs had only escalated that infighting, especially after the search-and-seizure laws had kicked in regarding the funding of the agencies. Some of them depended on major cash and property confiscations now to stay within their budgets.

"I'll give Saunders a call," the Man said, "to make sure his people down in Puerto Vallarta give Lyons all the help he can use and to make sure they stay the hell out of the way." He picked up the phone. "In the meantime, Ramona Thompson is going to be in Milwaukee tomorrow. I'd like for you to be there.''

Brognola nodded.

''She's going to be more vulnerable there,'' the President went on. He spoke briefly to his secretary, asking for the DEA and Saunders. ''If I can't stop her, I at least want the best people there that I can manage.''

''I'll need to make arrangements.''

''Do it.''

Brognola started to go, but the President drew his attention once more.

''A final question. What about Turrin? Are you still going to be able to get him in down there in the Caribbean?''

''Katz and Kissinger are working on it now,'' Brognola said. ''I'm expecting some kind of resolution within the hour.''

''Keep me posted.''

''Yes, sir.'' Brognola left the room, drawing his scrambled cellular phone from his hip. Secret Service men flanked the door, dressed in black suits and wearing earplugs, the wires coiling back down over broad shoulders. He made the call to the Farm and was apprised of the situation going down in Myanmar.

CHAPTER SEVEN

"How many?" Aaron Kurtzman demanded.

At the other end of the room, bright blue blips showed up on the wall screen. The image was a digitized representation of the Myanmar terrain Phoenix Force was dropping into. The satellite that had drifted into range had brought up the visuals first. Communication was supposed to be a close second if everything had gone as planned. So far, it hadn't happened.

"Sixteen, seventeen separate units," Akira Tokaido replied. "At least that many, and possibly a few more." Slim and intense, he hovered over his keyboard, punching in commands. He was by far the youngest person in the room. American born and Silicon Valley bred, Tokaido was possibly the most brilliant computer hacker Kurtzman had ever met. As usual, he wore a black concert T-shirt and jeans. A compact disc player was strapped to one thigh, a wire running up his side to the plug in his ear, and his foot moved in time to the beat despite his attention riveted to the events on the wall screen. "Maybe more. I'm expanding the original parameters of the satellite scan."

Kurtzman watched in tense silence as more of the bright blue blips materialized on the wall screen. Several of them moved around with astonishing speed, letting him know the infrared capabilities of the spy satellite were only picking up the muzzle-flashes of the enemy waiting below instead of the human beings. Counting the flickering spots would give them an estimate of the group waiting for McCarter and the others.

Phoenix Force showed on the wall screen as spinning orange triangles. During the long fall from the cargo plane, the team had spread far apart. From the way they were moving, he knew they hadn't even touched ground yet. There was no way the satellite dish had been set up. Communications were out, and so were most of the technological advantages the SIPE armor would have given the team.

"What about the convoy's movement into the area?" Kurtzman asked. "We should have picked that up."

"They weren't moving when I picked them up," Tokaido replied.

They'd been waiting. The realization hit Kurtzman like a physical blow. He cursed the communications satellite he'd been forced to use to get Phoenix Force into the area. If they'd had more lead time, he could have arranged for time on a spy satellite earlier. The problem was, that particular area of the country was under no real surveillance. The trail where Phoenix Force had planned on intercepting the convoy was out of what DEA agents normally considered to be the Golden Triangle proper. Anything north, anything south, and Kurtzman could have covered it.

But he had no idea who had been waiting.

"Pull it together," the cybernetics expert growled. "Once that satellite dish completes the uplink, they're going to need everything we can give them. Let me have the raw stuff, and I'll get it ready for burst transmission.''

Tokaido nodded, and his hands flew over the keyboard.

Kurtzman accessed the files as Tokaido framed them. He archived them with practiced ease, dropping build utilities into the small but complex programming he'd written and developed for use with the SIPE armor. When new data was acquired and transmitted, it would automatically be shunted off to the five backpack computers that tied the SIPE systems together as a unit, and the build utilities would make the data available immediately. Once the armor was up and running, it would knit the Phoenix Force members more tightly than the fingers of a hand. He'd increased the SIPE's programmed abilities, as well.

He worked grimly, knowing it would take everything he could give McCarter and his team to survive the encounter.

HAWKINS WATCHED the Enduro motorcycle crash through the branches of the trees below. He worked the lines of his own parachute and managed to pull himself nearly twenty yards closer to the impact area where the crate containing the satellite dish had gone down.

However, he'd also drawn the attention of at least three hostile guns. Bullets, interspersed with occasional cherry red tracer rounds, cut through the air around him. One struck him in the left thigh, bringing an instant though temporary numbness. The lightweight ceramic plate in the built-in pocket over his thigh kept the bullet from penetrating and spread out some of the blunt trauma.

Fifteen feet from the ground, he hit the quick-release

on the chute. The harness pulled away from him, and he plummeted, one hand clawing for the Beretta snugged under his left arm while he used the other to balance.

As soon as his feet met the ground, he dropped into a combat roll.

Bullets bounced from the tops of the rocks, and stone chips peppered the Stony Man commando's armor with light taps. He went to ground at once when he heard the familiar chatter of an AK-47.

Pulling up behind a jutting rock, Hawkins scanned the area, spotting the muzzle-flashes of the Russian-made assault rifle with ease. At least three men dogged him.

He returned fire with his Beretta, zeroing in on the muzzle-flashes. During the short break he got, he pushed himself hard, sprinting forward.

The gunners chased him, closing ranks and drawing closer. The rounds got near enough that he had to seek cover behind a stand of trees. They were thick with foliage, but they also stood alone. If he made a move to break away from them, he knew he'd be skylined.

He dumped the empty clip from his Beretta and reloaded. His breathing sounded ragged in his ears. The backpack with all his equipment slowed him down, but he couldn't abandon it. There were spare parts for the sat-link that might be needed.

The enemy fire came from less than forty yards away. The bullets chipped bark from the trees, showering debris over him.

Hawkins remained hunkered down. Even over the din of the gunfire, he heard the sound of approaching engines. He wondered if it was the rest of the convoy, but that didn't make sense. The convoy was supposed

to be minutes out from their position even now. There
was no reason for them to send out an advance group.

At least, he amended, there was no reason for the
convoy to do that—unless they knew they were about
to be ambushed tonight. The thought swirled around
inside Hawkins's head. Price and Kurtzman had been
responsible for the intel on the mission. Going in,
McCarter had mentioned that the operation was taking
place on the fly. Phoenix Force had been pulled off
another operation to engage this one, so Hawkins knew
the one they were on now had gotten hot.

Hawkins traded shots with the three men creeping
up on him. Their bodies were indistinct, green appari-
tions that drifted into and out of focus between the trees
and undergrowth of the jungle. His attackers seemed
content to keep him pinned down, and he wondered
why they felt comfortable spending the manpower to
achieve that.

A glance to his rear revealed the sheer face of a
hillside. He sheathed the Beretta, walked back a few
paces and started up, finding the handholds and foot-
holds automatically. He was no stranger to rock climbing.

When he was halfway up the incline, he glanced
below to check on the three gunners. They remained
in hiding themselves nearly twenty yards out. The thick
leaves filling the branches of the trees kept his own
position up the hillside concealed.

Hawkins considered why the men would halt and
content themselves with keeping him pinned down.
The answer came to mind quickly. He looked back up
the hillside and redoubled his efforts to get to the top.

Almost at the crest of the hillside, he spotted the gray
shadow that suddenly took shape against the black sky.

He froze, pulling himself in tight against the uneven surface, the roots he was holding on to quivering in his hands. He tucked his head in close and breathed shallowly.

With the light-amplifying capabilities of the helmet, he could see the AK-47 the man carried. He studied the gunner, making out as many details as he could, knowing the man didn't belong to the group Phoenix Force had been sent to intercept.

Kurtzman's intel package had suggested the convoy would be manned by Myanmar irregulars, men who'd been conscripted through the Khmer Rouge military. They weren't soldiers, just killers in uniform. Khun Sa, the opium warlord who'd staked out his own part of the Golden Triangle including Laos and Thailand, operated independently of the nationalized heroin trade. His men were better groomed than the nationals, and reflected the military background of their leader.

The man standing before Hawkins was neither. His uniform was night black, neatly pieced together so there were no loose edges to cling to the trees and brush. He moved easily, in no hurry, a professional at stalking.

Hawkins clung to the hillside, the muscles along his arms, back and legs trembling and burning with effort. He pressed himself against the stone face with its root webbing overlay and made himself as small as possible.

The man above him leaned over and peered down. His voice was soft and measured when it reached Hawkins's ears. "I don't see him down there." And the man spoke English with a British accent.

Hawkins considered that, wondering if the guys were part of a covert British operation they didn't know about. Even Price and Kurtzman were privy to only so much. Every intelligence agency played its cards close to the vest.

"I've looked all over for the son of a bitch," the man said in his quiet voice. "He must have slipped by you bloody bastards in the dark." The man stepped back, moving to another part of the hilltop.

Hawkins reached cautiously upward, uncoiling cramped muscles and forcing them to shift his weight. He gained another yard on the hillside and found a root under his boot that would bear his weight. Sounds of the men moving below reached his ears. Even in the weak moonlight, he knew that one glance upward by any of them would give him away.

The gunner on top of the hill was turned away, scanning the terrain with a pair of binoculars. He carried the assault rifle easily in the crook of his arm.

Hawkins catfooted to the top of the hill and pulled himself over the edge. He breathed in through his nose as he gained his feet, willing his body to be limber despite the punishment he'd put it through.

Someone below had to have yelled a warning over the gunner's radio. The man came around quick, dropping the binoculars and bringing up the AK-47.

Throwing his weight forward, Hawkins raced for the other man. There wasn't time to draw one of the Berettas. Even if he'd gotten one out, the last thing he needed on top of the hill was a gunfight.

He closed with the gunner, sweeping the AK's muzzle aside with an open-handed block. Twisting, the Phoenix Force commando swept an elbow around, bringing the point of contact expertly against the gunner's chin.

The man's mouth snapped shut from the impact, and

teeth broke. His head jolted backward, eyes glazing momentarily.

Inquiring yells came from down below, demanding answers. A few bullets tore through the edge of the hillside, scattering clods and coming within inches of hitting Hawkins.

He snagged a high-explosive grenade from his combat harness with one hand, keeping hold of the dazed gunner with the other. The man's reflexes were coming back quickly, and Hawkins knew his adversary was going to be a real threat in seconds. He pulled the grenade pin with his teeth and spit it out. Slipping the spoon, he thrust the HE grenade into the man's Kevlar jacket.

The man lost interest in trying to fight Hawkins. Instead, he dropped the assault rifle and struggled to rip his jacket off. "You crazy bastard! You're going to kill us both!"

"Not both," Hawkins replied. Grabbing the other man's jacket in both hands, he bulldozed the gunner toward the edge of the hill. Nearly two yards from it, knowing the precious seconds had almost leaked away, the Phoenix Force commando moved into a perfect side throw, yanking the other man's weight clear of the ground easily.

The gunner's eyes widened, and he screamed as he went over the edge backward, his hands still working at the Kevlar jacket.

Hawkins counted down the final two seconds as he scooped up the abandoned AK-47. A flash of light arced up to the edge of the hill like a small sun dawning, then it was gone.

Making his way to the edge of the hill, Hawkins dropped the magazine from the AK-47 and checked it.

More than half the rounds remained. He slid it back into place and made sure the action was clear. Keeping a low profile, he peered over the side of the hill.

The grenade had ripped the man apart and had also killed or knocked out two of the three men below. The remaining gunner fled.

Hawkins figured the man would be radioing the position in to the other men who were with the covert team. He settled the AK-47 against his shoulder as he lay prone, then took up the trigger slack. Breathing out, Hawkins zeroed in on the back of the man's neck, then stroked the trigger.

The 7.62 mm round caught its target at the base of the skull and nearly decapitated the man.

Satisfied that he'd cut down the odds against him in the area considerably, Hawkins pushed himself to his feet. He got his bearings quickly and made his way down the hill. On more or less level ground, he aimed himself in the direction the sat-link crate had taken. He found it less than a hundred yards away, hanging from the thick boughs of an ironwood tree. The crate itself hung only six feet from the ground.

Using his combat knife, he cut the chute cords, guiding the crate gently to the ground. Slinging the AK-47, he used an all-purpose tool to cut the metal bands holding the crate together, then rammed the thickest blade between the boards of the end panel. Nails screeched as the wood pulled free.

He reached inside the crate and took out the large attaché case. The exterior was matte-finished metal, thick enough to take a lot of abuse before caving in.

Glancing around, Hawkins decided there was no better place than the hilltop he'd just left to set up the sat-link. The AK-47 once more in hand, he lugged the heavy case across his shoulders and hoofed it back to the hill.

The climb up the back side was arduous with the steep grade. At the top, he unlocked the case and flipped it open.

The newly improved and even more lightweight version of the LST-5C lay inside foam cutouts. Hawkins removed the sat-link, flipped the tripod into the locked-out position and aimed the twelve-inch dish skyward.

Satisfied all the connections were in place, he turned his attention to the keyboard tucked inside the foam. It was hooked into a computer built into the case, powered by a five-hour battery that had been constructed under it. With the flip of a switch, the computer began to power up. The small monitor built into the keyboard framework showed the systems were on-line.

Hawkins activated the seek program. At his side, the small dish immediately started shifting with mechanical precision. Less than five seconds later, the dish was in proper alignment with the necessary telemetry.

White noise filled Hawkins's hearing from the ear-throat headset, then it cleared. He tapped the Transmit button. "Stony Base, this is Phoenix Five."

There was a brief pause. Hawkins walked to the edge of the hill and took out his compact binoculars. He focused them north, the direction the opium convoy was supposed to be coming.

There, maybe only four miles away, he spotted the headlights of the approaching vehicles. The yellow glare appeared and disappeared between tree trunks. He knew it wouldn't be long before the sounds of the gun battle reached the drivers even above the grind of their engines.

Then radio static popped in his earphone. "Phoenix Five, you've got Stony Base."

Hawkins grinned and put away his binoculars. He didn't know how many men lay out there in the night, but they were all about to get an introduction to what the SIPE gear was capable of. "Nice to have you with us, Stony Base. As you can see, we've got something of a situation here."

"Standby for downloads," Kurtzman advised. "We're going to be feeding you direct."

"Affirmative, Stony Base. Everything kosher here?"

"That's affirmative, Phoenix Five. Systems at your end check out. We're in the green."

"Good enough." Hawkins retreated to the sat-link long enough to check the C-4 charge wired into the computer. "Check also on the kill switch?"

"Check," Kurtzman said. "Systems are go."

"Then let's get to it." Hawkins started down the cliff face, taking the shortest route to the area where he believed the motorcycle was.

CHAPTER EIGHT

"Who are they?"

Aaron Kurtzman pumped the wheels of his chair with his hands, bringing it about to look at the woman who'd addressed him. Intent on the wall screen in front of Akira Tokaido, he'd never heard her walk up behind him. "We're working on it."

Barbara Price crossed the room, her attention also on the wall screen. The mission controller was a beautiful woman, honey blond and tall. "The convoy?" she asked.

"No." Kurtzman turned back to the keyboard, then spoke briefly into the mouthpiece of the headset he'd put on. "Let me have it, Hunt."

"Coming." Huntington Wethers was the final member of Kurtzman's handpicked primary team of cyber-warriors. Tall, broad and black, the former computer science professor was hunched forward in his chair at the console to the right. An empty pipe was clenched between his teeth, his jaw muscles clearly defined.

Kurtzman opened windows on the trio of monitors in front of him. Footage of T. J. Hawkins's fight on the hilltop rolled on one of the monitors. The cybernetics expert stroked keys, activating the screen-capture utilities he used to take a series of pictures. The utility instantly put them up on a second monitor. It took eleven of them, shot in rapid succession, before he got one of the man's face. The definition afforded by the big spy satellite going through its suborbital route was incredible.

Choosing the full-face shot, Kurtzman keyed in more commands. The utility blew up the picture, adding more definition and washing out the night's darkness until the man's features were clearly revealed.

"He's European or American," Price stated, staring at the frozen digital reproduction.

"Could be Russian or Eastern European," Kurtzman replied. "He was using an AK-47." He'd already identified the rifle. Wethers was running the serial numbers they'd turned up, as well. If they got lucky, they'd find the number on something Interpol, MI-6 or GSG-9 had on file.

The mission controller shook her head, then leaned forward to tap the monitor screen. "No." Her finger rested on the bit of metal on a necklace around the man's throat. "That's a zodiac sign. Pisces. The Russians and Eastern Europeans haven't had that much exposure to astrology in popular culture."

Kurtzman blew up the picture more, concentrating on the necklace. Despite the strains put on the digitized image by the capture utilities, the image held its integrity. And the necklace medallion turned out to be exactly as the mission controller had called it. Two silver fish swam in opposite directions, hooked to the silver chain.

"My guess is British," Price said. "You might start checking there first."

Tapping the keyboard, Kurtzman opened a window and altered the priorities of the search utility Wethers had initiated, moving Great Britain to the top of the list. "Why?"

"A few years back," Price replied, "zodiac signs were the rage in Great Britain. This man is young enough to have gotten caught up in it."

"Get that out of *Mademoiselle?*" Kurtzman asked.

"A CIA report I skimmed through at the time," Price answered with a slight smile. "This guy wearing the medallion while on night maneuvers suggests free-lance talent rather than a military background."

"He moved pretty good against T.J." Kurtzman replayed the video footage on the first monitor.

Price watched and nodded. "You're right. Try the known mercenaries in that country first. Maybe this man has a short history with the military, picked up his initial training there and moved on to greener pastures."

"Meaning the action down in South Africa." Kurtzman tagged a brief message to Wethers defining the new search parameters.

"That's my guess." Price looked back up at the big wall screen.

Kurtzman looked, as well. The bright blue blips had settled out to a small force circling the orange triangles that were the men of Phoenix Force.

"How many?" Price asked.

"Twenty. Twenty-five." Kurtzman tapped keys, bringing the sat-link feed directly into his CPU. He opened windows across the monitors, accessing the camera feeds mounted on each of the Phoenix Force warriors' helmets. So far, all of them remained operational.

"The SIPE armor?"

"They're locked into the system."

Price nodded. She'd pushed hard for the prototype armor, determined to outfit her teams with the very best she could get. The target they were up against had unlimited assets and a brilliant mind. "Where's the convoy?"

"Two miles away." Kurtzman cleared a monitor on the right, then changed perspectives. The convoy, all seven trucks, showed up as lemon-colored rectangles against the terrain.

"Still closing?"

"So far." Kurtzman adjusted the feed, bringing up an actual picture of the convoy vehicles.

The monitor filled with a rainbow-colored haze for a moment, then cleared. The perspective was still from above, but the canvas tarp over the cargo section of the big ten-wheelers could be seen as distinct from the metal hull of the cab. The lights cut irregular swaths over the terrain, cut into by overhanging vegetation. The satellite link was sensitive enough to pick up the man smoking a cigarette as he stood on the running board of the truck. The cigarette's coal burned a bright orange for a moment.

"Have you been in communication with McCarter?" Price asked.

"He knows I'm here."

Price nodded. "There's no way that engagement is going to go unnoticed by the convoy."

Kurtzman agreed. "When they see or hear what's going on, they're going to rabbit. Turn right around and scoot back into the mountains as quick as they can."

"There was another bridge."

"Yeah." Kurtzman brought up the topographical files on the left computer monitor.

"How far back from the convoy is it?"

"Five miles," Kurtzman answered.

"How big is it?" Price asked.

Kurtzman punched a few keys, and an eyeblink later all the pertinent distances appeared in carmine letters on the screen. "Something over two hundred feet."

"And only one lane wide."

"Right."

"It's over a chasm."

The digitized map didn't show the defile clearly. Kurtzman remembered the information from the intel package he'd put together. "Yeah." Another series of commands, and he had the information about the drop. "Used to be a tributary to the Irrawaddy River that cut through there. Dried up fifty or sixty years ago."

"Is it deep enough?"

"Forty feet," Kurtzman replied, reading through the text file he'd opened up. "Less than half of the one we'd targeted."

"Those trucks won't survive it," Price said. "Get Manning to break off and see if he can beat that convoy back to that bridge. Maybe we can still salvage this operation."

Kurtzman opened up the communications link between himself and McCarter, but the first thing he heard was an assault rifle blasting a full-throated roar and someone yelling in pain.

KESAR GRISHIN SAT in one of the opulent seats in the passenger area of the private Learjet he'd used for the flight to Tokyo. The flight attendant, a young Swedish woman he'd hired less than three months earlier, handed him a glass containing vodka over the rocks, then sashayed away, twitching her hips under the short uniform skirt.

Grishin watched her go, then sipped his drink and peered through the circular window again, feeling the jet's engines shiver through the plane as it taxied forward in the line of waiting aircraft.

He hated delays. At least here at Haneda Aircraft, the delays weren't as great as those at Narita International Airport. When the Japanese had put in the big airport to service Tokyo, the Chinese had opted to continue their contracts at Haneda. His joint business interests with certain forward-looking men inside the Chinese government had allowed him a special dispensation to use the Haneda airport as he chose.

Gerahd Dobrynin walked back from the cockpit, keeping his feet easily despite the pitch and yaw of the jet. He dropped into the seat across from Grishin.

"The Japanese National Police have been alerted to Ishikure's death," Dobrynin said. He drew the first two fingers of his left hand over his brow, smoothing his temple. His face gave nothing away.

"And?" Grishin asked.

"They are keeping it quiet."

Grishin smiled, then he took a big drink of the vodka. "I told you they would."

Dobrynin spread his hands. "Still, I worry."

"I pay you well for that."

"As you say." The bodyguard relaxed back in his seat. "These chances you insist on taking near the end of this concern me."

"If I am to sell this whole operation as I have, I must remain in control of it," Grishin responded.

"You can do that through others."

"Yes." Grishin nodded in agreement. "But then I

have to ask myself how long it would be before some of those others would start wondering if I'd gotten afraid of putting my ass on the line."

"To the Japanese and the Chinese," Dobrynin argued, "removing yourself from the direct line of fire would be seen as prudent." His lips twitched slightly, signaling his attempt at humor. "The Americans and Europeans might not approve, but none of them would dare throw stones."

"But we're not just dealing with them, are we?"

Dobrynin laced his fingers together and dropped them over one knee, stoically accepting the recanting of his proposal.

"No," Grishin said, "we're dealing with the Colombians, Cubans and the Eastern Europeans, as well. None of those people really favor working through seconds, and they have very defined ideas of what a man's courage should be."

"Savages," Dobrynin pronounced.

"You might be right."

"If the military was more of a positive influence in those countries, they might have had a chance to understand the mind-set. Instead, the armies are mere collections of thugs in those countries, have never been anything more than an enforcement arm for the dictators. For those leaders, the unity you propose is only attractive because of the power you offer. Not the wealth."

Grishin tapped the side of his glass with a manicured fingernail. "Very succinct and very insightful." He held up his glass in a salute.

"We would be better off without them."

"Maybe. But they form a large part of the empire I'm proposing."

The plane taxied farther, picking up speed rapidly.

"I say this," Dobrynin said, "only so that you will think about the business you're considering in Milwaukee with the U.S. attorney general."

"I've already thought about it." Grishin drained the vodka from his glass.

"Let me handle it for you."

Grishin gazed at the other man. "You can handle it, but I'm going to be there."

Dobrynin hesitated. "Look at the risk."

"No. I'd rather remain focused on the dividend."

As the jet leaped into the sky and began a sharp climb, the air phone rang abruptly.

Grishin picked it up. "Hello." He recognized Salome's voice at once.

"The stock option you chose to exercise in Myanmar isn't going according to plan," the woman said without preamble.

"What is the problem?"

"There appears to be the threat of a hostile takeover."

"By whom?"

"I don't know yet."

Grishin rattled the ice in his glass in irritation. The operation in Myanmar was important, designed to make the independent parties in that small country aware of how vulnerable they were. The heroin trade they controlled, though considerably smaller than Khun Sa's operation, was big enough to warrant letting them buy into his organization, or crushing it entirely. Competition wasn't going to be allowed. Control was the only issue Grishin was interested in. Khun Sa's empire could be his if he assembled enough of the smaller opium-based organizations.

"Is it the DEA?" Grishin knew the American drug administration kept a covert force in the area. But given the contacts he'd cultivated within the group, Salome should have known if the DEA was going to mount an offensive against the heroin traders.

"No." The woman sounded distant, preoccupied. The noise of a computer keyboard clacking carried over the connection. "This is a small group. No more than four to seven men."

Grishin considered that. The DEA would have gone in with a much larger group just to survive an encounter. The heroin traders would have outnumbered a group that small by four or five or six times as many men. "The situation?"

"We've engaged them."

"The convoy?"

"No. The other interest group."

"And?"

"We've come up short."

"That can't be true. Our representatives are among the best of their profession." Dobrynin had made certain of that, picking through the candidates himself. Grishin trusted the man's abilities.

"It is. There are at least six men down now."

"Make sure our team stays with it," Grishin ordered. "I want those stocks." The raw opium would pay for most of the mercenary contracts that had been necessitated by the action. If they failed, Grishin would be out an enormous amount for the effort. It was a drop in the bucket, given the money he commanded, but the thought of losing was unacceptable.

"I need to get back to it," Salome said.

"Keep me informed." Grishin broke the connection and stared out the window.

"Is there a problem?" Dobrynin asked politely.

"Possibly." Grishin brought the other man up-to-date with the situation developing in Myanmar.

"Those men will never be tracked back to you," Dobrynin said.

The Russian knew it was true. They'd been paid through a bank in England, with money he'd funneled in from the accounts in the Caymans through Austria. None of those countries allowed prowling through financial records by anyone in-country, much less from another nation. But if word got out somehow about his involvement in the strike against the independent Myanmar warlords, there'd be hell to pay. "If they are," he promised Dobrynin, "I'll hold you responsible."

"Of course." Dobrynin accepted the burden without complaint.

Grishin found it aggravating to a degree, except that he knew from experience that Dobrynin would bear up under the brunt of any anger directed at him. Even to the point of death. Dobrynin prided himself on his ability to be the consummate warrior.

Grishin made himself relax in the big seat as the jet leveled off at its cruising speed. "However this turns out, it makes the operation in Milwaukee even more important. Do you understand?"

"I can see where you would think that," Dobrynin stated. "I don't agree."

"I'm not paying you to agree," Grishin snarled. "I'm paying you for results. And when we get to Milwaukee, I want to see some return on that investment."

CHAPTER NINE

Crouched behind a broad-leafed bush, Calvin James watched the two men closing on Gary Manning.

Armed with assault rifles, both gunners hurried through the tropical jungle as fast as they could, angling for a shot at the big Canadian. Manning was tracking the cargo parachute that had brought down his motorcycle and the demolitions materials he needed.

James eased a branch back into position, obscuring his view, and went after them. He drew one of the silenced Berettas and held it close at his side as he took long strides through the jungle. Without warning, the SIPE helmet came to life, letting him know Hawkins had reached the satellite relay.

The infrared circuitry in the helmet had been operational, putting him on equal footing with their adversaries, but the true abilities of the SIPE programming were far more than simple night vision. His peripheral vision picked up the incoming data on small monitors on both inner sides of the helmet. On the right of the face mask was a small digital readout that looked like a radar system with him at the eye as an orange blip. Three other orange blips were staggered around him at varying distances, shifting across the monitor as a result of his own movements. Blue blips identified the bogeys on the screen, the gunners who'd already been on the ground. A compass was below the top monitor, indicating that he was headed in a southeasterly direction.

The two men ahead of him pulled up short, mistaking Manning's sudden halt as proof that the big man had heard them, not knowing he was assimilating the sudden influx of information coming in over the relay. They raised their weapons to their shoulders, willing to risk the shots.

James hit his Transmit button, activating the helmet's built-in microphone. "Phoenix Three, drop! You're gridlocked, pal!"

Manning went to cover instantly.

Both gunners fired after the Canadian, moving forward more hesitantly.

Forty yards out, James lifted his pistol and ran flat out. It bothered him that five orange blips hadn't shown up on the screen. But he also knew the radar distance was selective and might not have been set up for enough distance to pick up all the team members. They'd been spread out on the way down, having no choice but to follow the equipment chutes. Hawkins had needed to cover a lot of ground to get to the satellite uplink.

Tracers hammered into Manning's position behind a dozen small trees, finger-thick saplings and branches falling like wheat.

Some combat sense had to have warned the two gunners of James's approach. Less than ten feet out, they turned to face him, bringing their weapons around.

James sidestepped to the left, not breaking his headlong charge. He aimed at the center of the man's face on his right and squeezed the trigger five times. The man's face shattered into bloody pieces. The Phoenix Force commando only had a brief impression of the destruction, then he was on the second man with no time at all to make another shot.

The surviving gunner was bigger, heavier than James, and was determined to take advantage of his size. He launched himself at the Phoenix Force commando, trying to bring his pistol to bear.

Barely having time to set himself, James brought his right arm across his body and caught the man's outstretched wrists, knocking the pistol to one side. He tried to sidestep the man's charge, but couldn't get clear.

From the pain of the impact, James figured the man had to weigh 250 pounds at least. All of it was hard-muscled flesh. He felt the breath explode from his lungs as he was driven back. Digging in his right foot, he managed to spin away, losing most of his opponent's driving force.

The man brought himself up short and came around quicker than James had expected. He swung a bunched left fist in a hammer blow that caught James on the side of the SIPE helmet.

Even in the impact-resistant helmet, James had his bell rung. The monitor lights on either side of the face mask seemed to splinter and streak. He stepped back to give himself some room.

The man took the room away immediately, stepping into the Phoenix Force warrior's face, and trying to come around with the pistol.

Running a hand down his combat harness, keeping his eyes on the man, James felt the haft of his Randall survival knife. He sidestepped again, keeping low and staying too close for the man to bring the pistol into play. The orange and blue blips skated around the miniature monitor as James shifted, bringing them all relevant to his own position.

The man changed his step, backing away to bring the pistol between them.

James went after him, the knife ripping free of the combat-harness sheath. When the man pointed the pistol at the center of James's body, the Phoenix Force warrior feinted to the right, then drove hard left.

The man fired at where he expected his target to be, the pistol backing in his fist. Cursing, he tried to bring the weapon back on track.

James struck without hesitation, dragging the broad blade of the Randall across the back of the man's gun hand. Blood sprayed from the wound.

The pistol dropped from the man's grip. Giving ground again, he fell back into a martial-arts stance.

James pressed his advantage, reversing the blade so that it ran along the inside of his forearm. He struck, unleashing a flurry of blows, concentrating on whipping the Randall forward at the right time. Blood streaked his hands and arms from the man's wound.

Blocking one of James's thrusts, the man spun back, pivoted on one leg and delivered a roundhouse kick. James went low under the kick and raked the knife across the man's thigh, opening the femoral artery. A dark line of blood surged along the man's leg, running to his foot.

Stunned, the man stepped back. ''You son of a bitch,'' he said in a neutral tone. ''Well, then, you've killed us both.'' He pulled a grenade from his hip and reached for the pin with his other hand.

James closed at once, his empty hand reaching for the deadly orb. He managed to clamp it over the man's two hands, feeling his opponent's strength ebbing quickly. Left with no defense, the man tried in vain to avoid the knife. Using his weight, James ripped the Randall across the man's throat.

As the man dropped backward, James claimed the grenade. A quick glance showed him the pin had gotten lost. Not knowing how much time he had left, he wheeled and took a reading from the miniature monitor inside the helmet. He lobbed the grenade at the closest pair of blue blips and away from his teammates.

The grenade detonated less than two heartbeats later. James's throw had been close to his chosen targets because when the ground erupted, it tossed one of the men into the air in a loose and slowly spinning collection of limbs.

Manning burned down the second man with a burst from his M-16.

James sucked in a deep breath, pushing his face mask away slightly. Cool drafts of air fed into his lungs.

"Thanks, buddy," Manning called out. On the other side of the thick wall of foliage, he gave James a thumbs-up, then moved out at once.

Getting his breathing under control, James gathered up his equipment and weapons. He scanned the terrain again. He also bumped up the radar sensitivity on the helmet's readout by using the buttons on the wrist pad. Some of the tension over the mission left him when he saw the fifth orange blip come into view. All of the others were moving. He was the only stationary one.

"Phoenix Four, this is Stony Base." Kurtzman's voice sounded as deep as usual, but distant.

"Go, Stony Base," James replied. "You've got Phoenix Four."

"If you can manage it, we need pictures at this end. We've managed some, but we can't divert the satellite too much without interfering with the feed we're providing the team."

"You got it." James reached into his upper BDU blouse pocket and took out a digital computer camera. Instead of recording on film, the camera captured images in binary code that could be transmitted along the satellite link.

James crossed to the man he'd killed with the knife. The moonlight and the loss of blood had leached all color from the man's features. He adjusted the camera and started taking pictures.

The gunfire had died down to a degree. Evidently the group they'd jumped in on was aware they'd bitten off more than they could chew in the short amount of time before the heroin convoy arrived. It just remained to be seen whether the other group decided to fish or cut bait.

DAVID MCCARTER FOUND his Enduro only a handful of seconds after a member of the opposition had. Moving quietly through the brush, the Ithaca Model 37 shotgun in his hard-knuckled fist, he clambered down the defile, dodging trees.

McCarter saw the man clearly through the light-amplifying properties of the SIPE helmet's face mask, watched as he came around, bringing a silenced Uzi and a blurring arc spitting fire. Both hands on his weapon, the Briton fired at the center of the man.

The gunner staggered backward, shoved by the impact of the razor-edged fléchettes that had sliced through the body armor.

Ducking under the man's line of fire, McCarter

threw himself into a paratrooper roll to the left. He pumped the shotgun as he got to his feet and blasted another round at the man.

The fléchettes nearly decapitated the gunner, dropping him backward over the Enduro as the Uzi spilled from his lifeless fingers.

McCarter ejected the spent casing and reloaded the shotgun as he ran for the bike. Fisting the dead man's uniform blouse, he yanked the corpse clear.

Righting the bike, McCarter thumbed the electronic ignition. The high-performance engine turned over and roared to life. Letting the Ithaca hang from its sling, he pulled in the clutch and dropped the gearshift into First with his foot. Besides being a crack pilot, the Briton loved race cars and motorbikes. He twisted the throttle and let out the clutch. The rear wheel broke through the loose loam and spun it out behind him in a rooster tail.

He left the light off, running on the night-vision optics provided by the SIPE system. Powering out from behind a copse of trees, he checked the radar system with his peripheral vision and located the nearest of the blue blips on the screen. Most of them were in motion, as were the other Phoenix Force members. He tapped the Transmit button on the helmet. "Stony Base."

"Go, Phoenix One," Kurtzman replied.

"Going to have to reconfigure this one, mate." McCarter stood on the pegs, keeping his knees bent to ride out the shock of traveling over an outcropping protruding from the hillside. "There's no way that convoy will make our target bridge unmolested. We've lost the surprise we were counting on there."

"We're already working it," Kurtzman replied.

"I'm getting a new intel package together now for Phoenix Three."

"Affirmative." McCarter cut around a tree, leaning the bike steeply enough into the grade that he dragged his knee for an instant. "I'm thinking we need to convince those lads heading up the convoy that they need to turn around now. There's no telling what nasty little surprises might be waiting up ahead for them."

Barbara Price came on over the communications link. "Agreed, Phoenix One. Can you get it done?"

"I'm already on it," McCarter answered.

CHAPTER TEN

David McCarter tagged the helmet buttons on his wrist, increasing the viewing field of the radar system being fed to the SIPE system via the satellite. "The trucks, Stony Base, they're showing up as yellow?"

"That's affirmative," Kurtzman said.

"Phoenix Two," McCarter said as he aimed his motorcycle down a small game trail he spotted.

"You've got Two, One." Rafael Encizo's voice was calm, controlled.

"You're bringing up the back door on this."

"I'll be there."

McCarter cut a low profile across the bike, making himself as small a target as he could for the wind and the gunners. "Phoenix Three, this is One."

"One, you've got Three," Manning answered.

"I'm going to turn them, maybe buy you a little time, but you're going to have to rush in and out of there."

"Understood."

"Four and Five."

Hawkins and James called back.

"Up to you two blokes to hold the fort down here," McCarter stated grimly. "Can do?"

"Can do," Hawkins replied.

"Affirmative," James answered.

McCarter swung wide around another stand of trees, still following the game trail. Another sixty yards, and it cut across the mountain road used by the convoy. He saw the yellow lights from the trucks splashing out against the foliage draping the trees and jutting from the earth.

Locking up the rear brake, McCarter brought the Enduro around at the side of the road, throwing dirt out across the hard-packed earth. He gazed down the road, matching what he saw with his naked eye against the information being fed to him over the sat-link.

He threw a glance behind him and saw Encizo speeding toward him. With the motorcycle's headlight off, the Cuban showed up only as a fast-moving black shadow against the nightscape. Dropping his foot on the gearshift, McCarter shoved the Enduro back into First and flitted along the side of the road toward the approaching convoy.

There were four main trucks, just as their intel packet had indicated there would be. However, there were also six military-style jeeps running blocker. Two of them were in front of the first ten-wheeler. Both had .50-caliber machine guns mounted in the back, and McCarter saw no reason to believe that the others didn't, as well.

"Two, this is One. Do you see what we're up against?"

"Affirmative, One. How do you want to work this?"

"We'll take out the first jeep or two, creating a roadblock. That'll keep those blokes from deciding to make a run for it, then trying to turn back later on and risk them getting too spaced out to take down at one time."

Encizo agreed.

McCarter rolled up on a small promontory and stopped less than seventy yards from the lead vehicle of the convoy.

He chose his attack point with a practiced eye. The convoy continued to roll, down in a defile now between rows of trees that obscured their view of the hellground that had shaped up higher in the hills. In a few more seconds, the lead drivers would have a view of the battleground.

McCarter jammed down the gearshift and popped the clutch. The knobby rear tire bit into the ground and shoved the Enduro forward. Resting easily on the motorcycle, he used his body to aid with the steering, leaning to and fro.

McCarter burst from the jungle foliage less than forty yards in front of the lead jeep. For a moment, the harsh glare of the vehicle's headlights washed over the face mask and almost blinded him. Then the circuitry kicked in and compensated for the light.

The lead jeep's driver hit his brakes. The gunner manning the .50-caliber dropped his cigarette and jumped to his weapon, trying to bring it around. The man in the passenger seat leaned forward over the dash and fired a burst over McCarter's head.

The Briton swooped toward the jeep, staying on the driver's side of the vehicle. He caught up the compact shotgun, aimed his weapon as best he could, then squeezed the trigger. The shotgun blasted and jumped in his grip.

The fléchettes cut into the jeep's hood, scratching sparks from the metal and starring glass in the fold-down windshield. Some of them also struck the driver. The jeep went out of control almost at once, veering off the road and smashing into a tree. The deck-mounted rear gunner flew from the rear of the vehicle with a long yell that McCarter picked up even through the other noise of the crash. The man in the passenger seat exploded through the windshield.

The gunner in the second jeep came to life with a vengeance, his .50-caliber rounds chewing holes in the ground beside the Phoenix Force leader.

Slowing and cutting the handlebars sharply, McCarter found passage through the thick jungle growth. He let the shotgun drop at his side to steer with both hands, angling for the road less than ten yards behind the lead jeep.

The jeep's gunner swiveled his weapon, having difficulty bringing it about on the pintles because the jeep was heaving so much. He unleashed a barrage of fire, not trying to work bursts at all. The heavy rounds slapped against the trees, shearing branches and scarring the trunks, and digging into the ground.

Staying low over the handlebars and using the small, disk-shaped Kevlar fairing for cover as much as he could, McCarter raced for the jeep. Gunfire suddenly raked sparks from the side of the vehicle ahead of him, letting him know the ten-wheeled truck behind him was taking action as well. He activated the headset. "Phoenix Two."

"Go."

"I'm going to have to lose the Enduro. I'll be depending on you to make the save."

"I'll be there," Encizo promised.

Backing off on the throttle, the Phoenix Force leader lost ground until he was almost even with the ten-wheeler rumbling along in his wake. The enemy drilled more gunfire at him, and at least one round hit him in the back, smashing against the ceramic plate of the body armor hard enough to knock the breath from his lungs.

McCarter swerved across in front of the ten-wheeler, the bumper only inches from his rear tire as the driver accelerated and tried to run him down. Ahead of him, the jeep's driver hit his brakes in an attempt to sandwich him between the two vehicles.

The Briton swerved again, coming up beside the jeep before the passenger or the rear gunner could bring their weapons around. He reached for the Ithaca, fisted the pistol grip and squeezed the shotgun's trigger. The fléchettes caught the machine gunner in the chest, ripping him away from his weapon. He disappeared over the side.

The ten-wheeler had drawn to within a dozen feet of the jeep. Lights flared suddenly behind it from another jeep that was edging up in the slightly wider run along the road.

Bringing the motorcycle over to the side of the vehicle, McCarter set his feet solidly on the pegs, then leaped for the rear deck of the vehicle. The Briton managed to pull himself across the rear deck as the ten-wheeler closed from behind and smacked into the jeep hard enough to jar it off track but not enough to knock it from the road.

The gunner in the jeep's passenger seat struggled to keep his balance and bring up his assault rifle. McCarter pulled one of the Browning Hi-Powers and fired across the assault rifle's barrel, punching both rounds into the man's forehead. The AK-47 dropped away without being fired.

The driver tried to point a pistol at McCarter and keep the jeep on the road as the Briton scrambled forward and slammed the Browning's muzzle against the man's temple. The driver went slack, then he fell from the jeep.

"Phoenix One, this is Two."

"Go, Two." McCarter dropped into the driver's seat and took hold of the steering wheel in time to keep the jeep from going headfirst into densely packed trees.

"One, you've got another jeep coming up fast from behind."

The Phoenix Force leader controlled the vehicle with difficulty, then managed to secure the seat harness.

Bullets from the gunners in the jeep behind him hammered across the back of McCarter's vehicle, jarring his seat. One of the rounds penetrated the back and hit the Briton's body armor. Another ricocheted from the helmet and bounced his head off the steering wheel.

"Two, standby," McCarter said grimly. "I'm going to lose the jeep and see if I can choke down this bleeding freeway." He thought he saw Encizo's Enduro racing across the hillside above and in front of him to the left, but he wasn't sure. There were too many other things occupying his attention.

Getting the speed up where he wanted it, feeling the jeep float off its springs as it came out of a depression, McCarter cut the wheels sharply to the left. Off center and racing along, the vehicle turned turtle at once. The wheels on the left cleared the ground and kept rising as McCarter forced the jeep into a tight semicircle.

The seat harness held McCarter in. He felt the jeep tremble as the vehicle behind it rammed into the side. The headlights speared into his eyes from only a couple feet away as the jeep continued to flip, coming over on the roll bar. The impact knocked the breath out of him.

Rocks and clods of dirt plowed up by the overturned jeep flew against the helmet's face mask.

Gradually the vehicle slowed, plowing deeply into the dirt. Then it stopped entirely, slammed up against trees or boulders, McCarter wasn't sure. He reached into his boot for the Gerber knife and ripped the sharp blade across the seat's restraint straps.

Off balance, gravity working against him, McCarter spilled to the ground. He pushed himself to his feet on the other side of the overturned jeep. A quick glance over his shoulder showed him that the jeep that had been tailgating him hadn't given up the chase.

Even worse, the overturned jeep didn't totally block the roadway. The other vehicle swung around it, caroming off tree trunks briefly. McCarter swept his gaze back to the jungle around him, trying to find a spot to make his getaway. He dug in and ran hard, but it didn't take a rocket scientist to know that the jeep was going to run him down before he got clear.

CHAPTER ELEVEN

"Show me the bridge." Aaron Kurtzman shifted his attention to the monitor in front of Akira Tokaido.

"Coming up." Tokaido played the keyboard in front of him like a virtuoso. The huge wall screen shifted away from the global view of the combat area and focused on the terrain, zooming closer and closer in seconds.

Kurtzman glanced over at Barbara Price. The mission controller stood beside him, her face neutral. Kurtzman knew from experience that her thoughts were nowhere near as relaxed as the exterior she presented.

"We could back Phoenix off at this point," the cybernetics expert stated. "Give it up and get them clear of the situation."

Price nodded. "I've already thought about that. The statement we were going to make with the strike tonight has had the ante upped by whoever the other players are. The thing is, with the third party involved, we need information now more than ever. We need to know who's zooming who."

Kurtzman watched as Tokaido sharpened the view of the secondary bridge that had become Phoenix Force's objective. In the darkness gathered above and below it, the bridge glistened slightly, wet from the dew point. The bridge looked vaguely like a gossamer construction stretching between the two sides of the chasm, almost ephemeral.

"Someone out there in that killing field has information we need," Price went on. "We're just going to have to hope Phoenix can get it for us."

"Then they're going to need us to do our part," Kurtzman growled. He reached for the headset's mike and levered it back up in front of his face. "Akira."

"Yeah."

"Where's Gary?"

"I've got a lock on him, too." Deftly Tokaido opened another window in the upper left of the wall screen. The satellite peeled away the night, revealing a man hunched over one of the motorcycles.

Kurtzman watched the new video footage briefly. "How far out is he?"

"Two minutes," Tokaido said. "Three."

Another window opened on the wall screen, this one only inches below the first but slightly larger. It started out the same as the first open window, panning in directly on Manning. Then it pulled away, shifting over to an orange-blip representation of the Phoenix Force demolitions master. The terrain around Manning changed, as well, becoming a computer-generated representation as the computer tracking utility shifted over to animation interpretation rather than a direct feed. The view continued to pan back on the second window, blinking and redrawing itself in quick syncopation. In seconds, the picture related the proximity of Manning to the target bridge.

"Any signs of pursuit?" Kurtzman asked.

"No."

Another window opened then, this one showing the

entire battlefield that had erupted on-site. The other four Phoenix Force members were quickly identified. So were a number of the blue enemy blips. Some of those blue blips, however, were crossed over in scarlet, indicating confirmed kills.

Kurtzman felt a short-lived glow of confidence and pride. The Stony Man Farm support team was the best he'd ever worked with. But the bottom line was McCarter and his team were still in dire straits. "Have you got the workup on the bridge?"

"Here."

In the next second, three purple asterisks dropped onto the video link of the bridge. Once they touched the actual surface of the structure, they slid around and locked into place with mechanical precision. Yellow arrows suddenly branched out from the purple asterisks, spanning the distance of the bridge in two dimensions, marking the exact placement.

"I recalibrated the demolition site using the new specs," Tokaido said, "and factored in three explosions. The first one will set up internal vibrations. The other two will follow almost immediately and slam the bridge to pieces. It'll work. I used the software Gary designed to set the limits."

"Have you uploaded the new intel to him?" Kurtzman asked.

"It's on its way. He'll have it by the time he reaches the bridge."

"Good enough."

"Aaron," Carmen Delahunt called.

"Yeah."

"I've identified one of the men facing Phoenix Force. It's coming over to you now."

Kurtzman checked the monitor on the left side of his

desk. A window opened in the new screen showing part of a face that belonged to a middle-aged man with a strong jawline and a burn scar under his right eye. The mouth was missing, though, and the cheeks and jawline were almost two-dimensional in their rendering. The top of the head was missing, as well.

"What you're looking at," Delahunt stated, "is the best Hunt could capture from the target in the battlefield."

"He had a tight-fitting hood on," Huntington Wethers explained. "It covered his head and lower face."

Kurtzman watched another picture take shape on the screen, bumping the face with the missing features one space to the right. The original picture of the man filled the new window. The hood he wore was tight-fitting, almost blending in with the night around him.

"I lifted the features I could get," Delahunt went on, "then cross-referenced them, using the correlation points I was able to work with. I scored a hit at Interpol."

A third window opened on the screen, to the right of the first two. This one showed a man in military dress.

"Barbara called it right when she said British military," Delahunt said. "This was Sergeant-Major Jason Wallaby of the SAS."

The picture flickered twice, then suddenly swelled up and filled the monitor screen. The man in the picture seemed only a little younger. Lines of computer-perfect script lay in the wake of a speeding cursor that darted in the lower-right quadrant of the picture. Height, weight, hair and eye color and distinguishing marks marched in orchestrated abandon.

Kurtzman took in the information instantly, as well

as the biographical information that scrolled upward. "Is Wallaby still with British military?"

"No. He mustered out eight years ago with honorable mention."

"Then why does Interpol have him on file?" Price asked.

"He's become a known mercenary in recent years," Delahunt answered. "Some involvement with the Middle East and South Africa. Lately he's been handling arms-running work in Bosnia and other Eastern European hot spots."

"Arms?" Kurtzman asked. "What about involvement with drug shipments?" It wasn't unusual for ex-military types to hire on to ride shotgun over important shipments. Or the men who made them.

"Nothing in his dossier," Delahunt assured him.

The big cybernetics expert tapped a forefinger against the side of his keyboard, pushing the pieces around mentally. "Dig as deep as you can into his background. Let's see if he ties up anywhere else."

Price lifted the cellular phone from her hip and punched in a series of numbers. "I'll give Langley a call. The CIA's got personnel who watch over men like Wallaby. I've got some markers owed to me."

Kurtzman nodded and turned his attention back to the wall screen at the other end of the room. He watched the blip that was Gary Manning no more than a hundred yards away from the bridge. The purple asterisks on the structure remained unwavering. The only thing left to be seen was whether Manning had enough time to plant the charges before the convoy raced back down on top of his position.

"Damn!" The muffled curse came from Hunt Wethers.

Unaccustomed to hearing the man sound ruffled, Kurtzman snapped his head around. He took in the wall screen in front of Wethers at once, saw the satellite uplink's close-up of David McCarter trying to scramble from the overturned wreckage.

The Phoenix Force leader barely managed to clear the flipped vehicle as the second jeep bore down on him.

RAFAEL ENCIZO LOCKED the rear brake of his Enduro and brought the machine to a yowling stop. The motorcycle's back tire dug into the black loam and clawed through roots and dead leaves. He killed the engine with the flick of a switch, hoping the carburetor didn't flood before he could get back to it as he laid the Enduro on its side.

He kept his eyes focused on the action taking place down the trail, shaking the M-16/M-203 combo off his shoulder and stepping away from the motorcycle. He'd raced ahead of the jeep McCarter had overtaken by seventy yards or more. Encizo was almost still ahead of them at that distance now. The 40 mm warhead the M-203 had locked down in its thick, stubby barrel would easily make the range, but the trees between them made the shot uncertain.

McCarter ran, skirting the jungle line as he drew .50-caliber fire from the pursuing jeep's rear gunner. The vehicle swerved around the wreckage of the jeep the Briton had usurped, but the convoy of trucks slowed.

Encizo hit the Transmit button inside his helmet as he sprinted. "Phoenix Five, this is Two."

"Go, Two, you have Five," Hawkins replied. The

transmission carried the deep-throated roar of the Barrett .50-caliber sniper rifle Hawkins had deployed.

"Can you pick up One from your position?" Encizo raked the surrounding foliage with his gaze. He needed an opening soon. If he had to travel much farther, he wouldn't have a chance at doubling back for the Enduro and getting to McCarter before the convoy's ground forces or the unidentified team arrived.

Scanning the screen inside his helmet, Encizo saw that three blue blips had closed on McCarter's position. He spotted tracer fire next, blazing through the jungle undergrowth. Having no choice, McCarter had gone to ground. His pistol was up in his hand, firing. The jeep raced at him, the driver low behind the steering wheel.

"I can get to him, Two," Hawkins replied. "It won't be easy."

"When?" Encizo knew time had all but run out on the play. He threw himself to the ground and prayed the undergrowth would leave him a clear shot. He marked the range to his target automatically.

"I'm tracking now," Hawkins said.

Encizo brought the rifle to his shoulder, staring through the scope and locking on to his target. He squared it up against the padded area of his shoulder and reached forward until he had his finger in the M-203's trigger guard. He tightened up slack, settling the crosshairs slightly elevated over the jeep streaking for McCarter.

From the periphery of his vision, Encizo knew McCarter was firing at the rampaging jeep with both pistols as it closed to within thirty yards of his position. The Cuban let out a half-breath as he judged the jeep's speed, then squeezed the trigger.

"Stay down, One," Encizo said.

The grenade launcher shoved the M-16's stock against Encizo's shoulder, and flame spit from the tail of the 40 mm warhead as it rushed under the low-hanging limbs of the trees separating the Cuban from his target. The smoky white vapor trail left an uneven zigzag suspended in the air.

At slightly more than twenty yards from McCarter, the grenade took the jeep in the right side just slightly behind the front bumper. The resulting explosion ripped the wheel from the well and flipped the vehicle onto its side in a slow roll as gravity gave over to raw force.

Encizo reached for another 40 mm round as he watched the crippled jeep slide forward, missing McCarter by yards now, and slam into the dense tree wall fronting the jungle on the other side of the trail. The advancing line of mystery ground troops had pinned McCarter down, and gunfire stabbed at his position.

"Come on, T.J.," Encizo growled to himself as he drew a bead on the next jeep trying to make the gap around the vehicle McCarter had demolished. The jeep drew abreast of the gap, then Encizo's second 40 mm grenade slammed into the front end.

The phosphorous round Encizo had selected for the second target belled up in a massive gout of white-hot flame, fire engulfing the jeep. Burning men leaped from the vehicle, tumbling onto the ground.

Encizo didn't spare any pity for his victims. They dealt in death, and they made the payoffs with the lives of others. If he'd been closer, he might have used mercy rounds to put the flaming men out of their suffering. But McCarter was still in the thick of it.

The Cuban slammed another HE round into the

M-203. He snapped up the barrel, jacking the round into the receiver, then swiveled and aimed in the general direction of the line of assassins advancing toward McCarter. He pulled the trigger and watched the 40 mm grenade spin toward the tree line.

The grenade exploded against a thick tree bole, setting the surrounding branches on fire. The proximity of the detonation sent the men scrambling for the ground. Wreathed in flames from the explosion, the branches made a blazing pyre that lit up the area.

Three men garbed for the night sprinted away from the epicenter of the grenade's impact. Encizo loosed a stream of 5.56 mm tumblers after them, but doubted he hit anyone. He tagged the helmet's Transmit button. "One, this is Two. I'm on my way."

"If it looks like it can't be done," McCarter gritted, "don't do it."

Encizo didn't say anything. He ran, dodging trees, and recovered the Enduro. Throwing a leg over the seat, he grinned in satisfaction as the engine turned over effortlessly when he flicked the ignition. He jammed the gearshift into First, then let out the clutch.

He took the shortest route down the side of the hill, picking his spots with care, depending on the infrared systems. A boulder jutted out almost ten feet up from the road.

Sparing a glance at the convoy, Encizo saw that the trucks had halted. Two of the jeeps running blocker milled at the wreckage. A man shouted orders over a large military walkie-talkie, waving wildly.

Then Encizo's attention returned to the large boulder. He aimed the Enduro's front wheel toward it and geared down, his stomach lurching threateningly as he goosed the throttle and went airborne. A heartbeat later, he was sailing out over the road, descending rapidly.

He landed squarely, both wheels soaking up the impact at more or less the same time. He kicked out a foot to recover his balance as he accelerated again. McCarter was less than twenty feet away, already rising up from a crouch.

Encizo gunned the motorcycle and aimed it toward the Phoenix Force leader. Bullets pocked the ground around them, and one round spanged from the handlebars in an arc of sparks. Encizo felt the vibration shiver through his arms.

McCarter slid onto the seat behind Encizo. The Briton had a Hi-Power pistol in each fist, and muzzle-flashes leaped from both barrels. "Go, Rafe! Stay here and they're going to turn us into bloody hamburger!"

Encizo accelerated, the rear tire spinning for a moment before finding traction. Small-arms fire from the convoy chased them, and they had no option but to brave the broken teeth of the assassins' guns waiting ahead.

"What about it, Five?" Encizo asked over the headset. "Can you assist?"

CHAPTER TWELVE

"I'm there," Hawkins replied. He had the Barrett's stock snugged against his shoulder. A fiber-optic jumper wire connected the sniper rifle's scope to his helmet, allowing the computer to download the extra information coming via Stony Man Farm.

Hawkins swept the hell zone where McCarter and Encizo had halted the opium convoy. The crosshairs rested briefly on the two commandos on the motorbike. They flickered, limned in orange.

Shifting the scope ahead of them, Hawkins found the mystery aggressors falling in position to intercept the fleeing Phoenix Force team. He dropped the sights over the man closest to him. If he could get the shots off fast enough, he knew he could have two or maybe even three of them down before they knew he'd targeted them. It would take seconds for the heavy boom of the sniper rifle to roll over their position.

Hawkins took up trigger slack, then hit the Transmit button on his helmet. "Stony Base."

"We're here, Phoenix Five," Kurtzman replied.

"Give me a range." Hawkins couldn't judge accurately in the night, but the satellite's systems would be able to triangulate the two points to within inches. Maybe less.

"Five hundred and eighteen yards," Kurtzman replied.

Hawkins reached up and adjusted the scope to five hundred yards. The distance was easily within the specs of the big Barrett. "Windage."

"Twenty-three miles out of the east," Kurtzman replied.

He made that adjustment, as well, and saw Encizo racing toward the waiting assassins. Set on infrared, the scope picked up the muzzle-flashes from their weapons. Hawkins squeezed the trigger and felt the big Barrett slam against his shoulder. Even built in a bullpup design with the receiver in the stock, the .50-caliber rifle had a heavy recoil.

He shifted to the left, recentering the crosshairs, and chose his next target. He didn't try anything fancy, merely shooting for the greatest mass of his targets. No matter where he hit the assassins, the .50-caliber bullets would put them down, punching through most conventional body armor even at five hundred yards.

He'd squeezed the trigger through on the third target before the first bullet hit. The .50-caliber bullet evidently hit squarely, because the man suddenly lunged forward. The second man went unscathed, and Hawkins thought the bullet probably was deflected by a branch that hadn't shown up on the scope. The third man caught a round through his left shoulder and went sprawling.

The fourth man abandoned his position, diving for deeper cover. The infrared systems fed into the scope through the SIPE from the satellite scan took that cover away. Hawkins led the man, aiming high because the terrain went up. He squeezed the trigger through, then adjusted the scope to pick up a larger view again. With the distance against him, he needed the scope to see clearly.

He got the scope into focus again a moment later, just in time to see the fourth man's head explode. The headless corpse stumbled and dropped to its knees, then fell forward.

Scanning the battlefield again through the Barrett's scope, Hawkins said, "I see three down, Stony Base. Can you confirm?"

"Stony Base confirms," Kurtzman said. "Three down. Two remain viable."

"Ping them for me." Hawkins found one of the men scrambling through the underbrush. He gave the man a lead, then fired.

The assassin spun away and dropped.

"Stony Base confirms only one target."

Hawkins swung the scope wide, seeking the remaining man out of the small group he'd locked in on. "I've lost him, Stony Base. Can you assist?"

"Your target's at two o'clock."

Hawkins brought the scope farther to the right, taking in the broken terrain and the tree burning in the background. Blurred movement, slightly grayer against the true night, alerted him. He let out a breath and bracketed the man in the crosshairs. The rifle slammed against his shoulder when he fired. The gunner collapsed when the heavy bullet hit him in the sternum and shoved him backward.

Encizo and McCarter had cleared the zone. Hawkins turned his attention to the convoy.

With the overturned jeeps blocking the road, the trucks had reached an impassable snarl. Uniformed men ran between the vehicles, already drawing fire from the approaching troops that had braced Phoenix

Force. From the way the attacking team had set up on the convoy, Hawkins was certain they were there to take possession of the trucks.

Settling in behind the Barrett's stock, Hawkins used the information relayed through the sat-link from Stony Man to take out more of the attackers. He finished off the sniper rifle's clip, and punched through half of another before the convoy trucks got turned and headed back along the trail the way they'd come.

"Five, this is One," McCarter transmitted.

"Go, One." Hawkins scanned the terrain around him, finding none of their attackers interested in trying to overtake his position.

"Wrap it up, T.J.," the Briton said, "and let's get out of here. We've done about all the damage we could. The rest is up to Three."

"Acknowledged." Hawkins grabbed the Barrett by its handle and jogged toward his Enduro. In the distance, the lights of the convoy trucks slashed through the darkness, jerking and bobbing over the rough jungle road as they raced away.

Even with the lead that Manning had, Hawkins knew it was going to be a close shave for the Canadian to plant the charges, take down the bridge and get out of the situation alive.

"Phoenix One, this is Four," Calvin James said.

"Go, Four."

"I'm picking up vehicles other than those with the convoy."

Standing astride his motorcycle, Hawkins stared hard into the shadows draping the broken jungle below him where the hillside sheared away. He saw the first two Range Rovers pull into view, running without headlights. Gunmen stood on the running boards, assault rifles canted at the ready.

"Five confirms," Hawkins said. As he watched, a third vehicle roared from the jungle.

"Stony Base is picking them up now, too," Kurtzman called over the communications loop. "You have five unidentified vehicles on-site."

"Bloody hell," McCarter said. "Where are the other two?"

"North of your position, Phoenix One. On the opposite side of that road."

"I see them. Do you have a fix on these people yet?"

"The ones we've identified," Kurtzman said, "are known mercenaries. Their background comes out of England."

"Definitely not local boys, then." The Briton's tone carried the bite of sarcasm, but Hawkins knew it wasn't directed at anyone.

"No."

Hawkins squared up behind the sniper rifle again, judging the speed of the Range Rovers. He laid the crosshairs over one of the men clinging to the vehicle's side. With both eyes open, he could see the other two Range Rovers running in tandem with the three on his side of the jungle road.

"They're going to try to cut off the convoy," McCarter said. "Three, do you copy?"

"Three copies," Manning replied, sounding breathless. "I'm coming up to the bridge now. If you can keep them coming, I'll be ready for the convoy when it gets here."

"I'm going to hold you to that, Three," McCarter

promised. "We'll see how much time we can buy you."

Hawkins's finger tightened on the trigger. The bullet sped from the Barrett's muzzle and plucked the gunner from the side of the Range Rover. Immediately, following the course Hawkins had figured on, the Range Rover's driver hauled on the wheel hard, instinctively dodging from the spray of blood that glistened across the windshield in the moonlight.

Sighting again, aided by the computer input coming through the Stony Man Farm systems, he targeted the driver, then fired. The bullet caught the driver in the head, killing him instantly.

Pandemonium erupted aboard the Range Rover. The man clinging to the driver's side dived off as the big truck roared for a steep drop in front of it. The passenger-side door banged open just as the Range Rover started over the drop. The soft side of the drop-off gave way under the truck's weight, sending it over the edge. The truck hit nose first, then turned over.

Hawkins was already seeking his next target.

GARY MANNING DIDN'T SEE the edge of the ridge in front of him until he was on top of it. Then he felt the Enduro jerk under him, the shocks bottoming out for a moment. The sick, twisted feeling in the pit of his stomach told him he was airborne before he saw it for himself. The high-pitched keen of the motorcycle's engine screamed into his helmet as the rpm shot up.

Branches whipped across the face mask of the helmet as he fought to keep the Enduro under control. He was a big man and athletic, used to controlling his weight and using it to his advantage. He managed to stay on top of the motorcycle and ease off on the throttle. The rear tire bit into the black loam when it hit.

In control again, he raced down the slope of the hill to the bridge. The wood construction was decades old, a simple-span timber stringer that had seen a lot of wear and tear.

Manning shot out of the jungle and landed with a thump on the dirt road snaking from the bridge. His backpack pinched at his arms, the weight slamming solidly between his shoulders. He hit the Transmit button on the helmet radio. "I'm here, Phoenix One."

"Get on it, mate," McCarter answered. "We've managed to put a hiccup in their operation here, but that's about the size of it. And the competition's burning up the backtrail."

Manning gunned the engine and streaked out onto the bridge. He felt the structure quiver and quake beneath him. Occasional moonlight sparked off the dark ribbon of shallow water that remained in the basin.

"Stony Base," Manning called.

"Here," Kurtzman replied.

"Get ready to mark off the demolition points." Manning brought the Enduro to a shuddering halt at the center of the bridge. Blowing a simple-span bridge was easy work. If he set the charges at the ends and timed them to blow together, he could effectively drop the whole structure into the chasm below. Even with the fall, there was a good chance that it would survive the impact well enough to be easily replaced.

But that would have meant perhaps some of the trucks in the convoy might survive intact, as well. That would also mean the cargo aboard could be salvageable. And Manning didn't intend to see that happen.

He shoved out the motorcycle's kickstand and

moved away from the bike. He unslung his M-16, then shrugged out of the backpack. Stepping to the edge of the bridge, he peered over the side. The trickle of dark water below was barely visible.

"Stony Base is standing by," Kurtzman said.

"Give me the first one," Manning said. He reached into the backpack for the plastic explosive. His hands moved with skill, shoving the grayish white C-4 into the desired shape.

"Another eighteen inches forward," Kurtzman directed.

Perspiration fogged the inside of the face mask. Manning touched the release studs on either side of the helmet and shoved up the face mask. Cool air, wafted from the chasm below, blew into his face. The wind carried the scent of dead vegetation and stale water.

He moved forward, stopping when the cybernetics expert cued him. Peering over the edge again, he made certain where the support pylon was. He knelt and pushed the ball of C-4 into the gap between the bridge floor and the support pylon. With some effort, he was able to scoot the explosive under a cross timber that helped shore up the bridge floor. When the deadly packet went off, most of the force would be directed downward, especially since the weight of the convoy would help push the concussion in that direction. He stuck a remote detonator into the center of the explosive and flicked it into operation.

"Come on, Three," McCarter called over the headset. "They're almost on top of you now!"

"Understood, One, but this is as fast as it gets." Manning peered back at the convoy. In the distance, he could see the headlights paling the horizon.

He placed another charge in the middle of the bridge

along the same side, this one shoved up under the infrastructure so the blast would be directed upward. At the other end, over the support pylon, he fixed the remaining charge so it would again direct most of the destruction downward, shearing the support pylon.

Finished with the backpack, its contents now packed around the bridge, Manning threw it over the side, then tapped the headset Transmit button. "It's done, One."

"Then get the hell out of there."

Manning sprinted for the Enduro.

"And make sure your arse is on the right side of the bridge when it goes tumbling down!" McCarter added.

Reaching the motorcycle, the big Canadian threw a leg over and thumbed the electronic ignition. The engine rumbled to life. He booted the kickstand up into place, then walked the motorcycle around in a tight circle, trying to get it headed back in the direction he'd come.

Just as he reached the end of the bridge, Manning saw the lights of the convoy. He made it to a copse of trees that provided enough cover for him to wait, unseen, while the convoy approached.

As the last of the trucks raced onto the bridge, Manning flicked the first remote detonator. Immediately the C-4 package in the middle of the structure blew, throwing a gust of gray smoke into the air. A huge hole suddenly appeared near the middle of the structure. One of the trucks skidded into the hole, then tilted at a crazy angle, not quite falling through. The rear tire on the opposite side of the hole lifted and cleared contact with the bridge. A handful of men abandoned it, jumping onto the structure.

Thumbing the secondary detonator to the two charges at either end of the bridge, Manning watched as the structure suddenly listed to the right. The initial explosion had served to weaken the structure and to set up the internal vibration that would cause the bridge to shake itself to pieces when the ends sheared.

The explosions went together, cutting the support posts. The bridge dropped to the right, turning on the remaining support pylons as if they were hinged. The trucks fell into the chasm, and the men fell with them.

In seconds it was over, and the convoy plus most of the jeeps that had been guarding it were at the bottom of the chasm. A lone vehicle struggled at the edge where the bridge had been, all four tires digging furiously at the ground. The passenger and the gunner on the rear deck abandoned the vehicle, tilting the odds in favor of gravity. The driver seemed determined to save the jeep or hadn't thought of leaving it himself. As soon as the weight shifted, the jeep slid over the chasm's edge and disappeared. The man's scream, all the way to the end, seemed to hang in the air.

Another veil of headlights showed across the crest of the ridge leading to the bridge area. Manning peered up the incline and saw two Range Rovers pull to a stop overlooking the defile. Inside his helmet, the miniature radar screen flickered into renewed life, taking in the new information being pumped in from Stony Man Farm.

"All right, gents," McCarter said as the Range Rovers started to roll cautiously forward, "let's leave them to pick over the bones. We're done here. Rendezvous at the pickup site. Do you copy, Stony Base?"

"Stony Base copies," Kurtzman replied. "Your transport will be in place."

Manning let out the clutch and guided the Enduro up the incline. He drew brief fire from the gunners aboard the Range Rover, but it seemed only a half-hearted effort at best. The prize had been snatched away. But he was curious about the men the team had confronted so unexpectedly. Engaging the convoy was supposed to put pressure on the organization the Stony Man teams were stalking and bring more of the players of the international network into view. Evidently someone else had planned along the same lines.

And judging from the manpower and information the other team had put into the play, Manning knew that whoever they were ultimately up against had resources that might even rival those of Stony Man Farm.

CHAPTER THIRTEEN

Barbara Price stared at the wall screen at the other end of the room. With the sophisticated systems available through the low-level spy satellite Kurtzman had accessed, the broken bodies of the men who'd been aboard the trucks when they dropped were visible against the hard, unforgiving surface of the rocks at the bottom of the chasm.

"What about the cargo?" she asked.

Kurtzman hammered in commands on his keyboard. The wall screen split into four separate screens, defined by a thin purple border. All of the screens maintained the same view-from-above perspective, but the magnification indexes and the target areas were different.

One of the new screens focused exclusively on the wreckage left at the bottom of the chasm. The view panned from north to south, according to the digital legend that flared to life on the screen.

"We don't know how much opium they were shipping for sure," the cybernetics expert said, "but it's probably a safe bet that Phoenix got it all."

Price nodded. During the past few days of putting all the missions together and piecing together the spotty intelligence reports from dozens of national and international agencies, she hadn't gotten much sleep. She felt the fatigue now. "What about the team Phoenix intercepted?"

"All of them trace back to England."

"All of them mercenaries?"

Kurtzman nodded.

Price took the cellular phone from the pouch at her hip and started punching in numbers. "Put a package together containing the pictures of the men we've identified so far." She glanced at the wall screen at the end of the room, noticing the way the satellite's relay systems moved around the chasm area. Akira Tokaido had taken over the satellite's video feed.

As Tokaido locked on to one of the men in the area, he saved the image to a screen-capture file. The video feed froze momentarily in each quadrant where a target was imaged, and a turquoise field flared to brief life around the merc. Carmen Delahunt took the stored images from Tokaido via the Cray mainframes their computers could access, then assembled them in order.

The phone rang at the other end, setting off sonorous bongs that echoed over the line. Then the receiver lifted and an answering machine kicked in. "Fletcher's Seed. I'm sorry, all our lines are tied up at the moment, but if you will be patient, someone will be with you shortly to take your order."

Price entered a four-digit number. If she stayed on the line, she would have been directed to a seed-catalog representative. The extension number sent her to a place that had nothing at all to do with agriculture.

"Hello." The voice was male and deep, quietly reassuring in a stuffy kind of way that Price had always felt seemed grandfatherly.

"Sir Blakely," Price said.

"Ah, dear child, so good to hear from you again.

How good of you to call. And how are you doing these days?"

"I'm fine," Price said. "But I'm afraid I called for business reasons rather than social ones." She watched as Kurtzman used a zip utility to compress the pictures they'd gathered from the business in Myanmar. Open screens flipped across Kurtzman's central monitor as he readied the zipped files for transmission, then opened his access to the Internet. As with all the phone lines that came out of Stony Man Farm, the Internet connections bounced off a half-dozen different points, changing origins as they went until they were untraceable. Replies were dumped into any of fifty or more electronic mailboxes operating at any given time. When the messages were received by an independent operator, they were shunted on to Stony Man Farm, clear of any tracing utilities.

"I'm afraid these days," Blakely said, "business is social with types like ourselves. I can be of assistance, then?"

"I think so," Price replied.

Sir Winston Blakely was a curmudgeon of a man. In his salad days, he'd fought in World War II, often behind the lines and without support teams. His field then had been assassinations.

Now the man was in his early eighties, firmly entrenched in the intelligence-gathering part of his chosen vocation in the service of his country. Over the years, Price had found the man to be erudite and cunning, his mind still his most effective weapon.

"Then may I be of assistance?"

"I'd like to send you a batch of computer files containing pictures," Price said.

"I trust these pictures are not for public consumption."

"No."

"Very good. Allow me to give you an address where you may send them."

Price waited, knowing the Internet address would be secure and invisible to any prying eyes. She relayed the address to Kurtzman when it came. The cybernetics expert entered the address, then sent the files.

"They're on their way now."

"Do you want to wait while I review them?"

"No. This is probably something that will take a little time at your end." Price glanced at the wall screen, wondering if Phoenix Force had made its ex-filtration. "It'll take a few minutes to upload."

"Very good. How may I reach you?"

Price checked her personal digital assistant, queuing the phone-numbers section. The PDA pulled up the list in seconds. All the phone numbers on the list were available only for a few hours each, the time frames marked beside them. Some of them were also earmarked for Bolan, Phoenix Force, Able Team and Brognola. She chose a free one in Depoe Bay, Oregon, that was good now and could be used for the next three hours.

She read off the number. Kurtzman instantly picked up on her use of it and made the necessary field changes in the phone program that routed the mission controller's calls to and from the Farm.

"Perhaps it would be helpful to know something of what I am looking for in these photographs," Blakely said.

"We've tagged some of them as mercenaries," Price replied.

"And you believe I would know of them?"

"Most of the ones we've identified had spent some time in the British military."

"*Had?* That aspect certainly intrigues me. Will you elucidate more on how you came by these photographs? I was not aware of any infractions within my sphere of influence that would involve such people."

"The trouble I'm looking into isn't in-country there," Price said.

"Then you're searching for the debarkation point of this operation."

"Yes. If you can turn up a contact, someone who put that team together with a buyer, I'd be interested."

"Of course, dear lady. A dozen names are already in mind. I shall endeavor to winnow out the one most likely, then get back to you."

"I'll owe you one."

Blakely chuckled. "No, dear girl. Over the years of our association, I believe it is I who still owe you. I should, at some point, like very much to meet you."

"I'm afraid that's not possible." Price had kept her identity secret from Sir Blakely, as she did with all contacts when using the full clout of the Stony Man operation. Only a handful of people knew she was connected with the counterterrorist hardsite.

"If by chance it should ever become possible—"

"I would love to meet you myself," Price said.

"Then we'll chat again soon." Blakely broke the connection.

"He's got all the pictures," Kurtzman said.

"Good. What about Phoenix?"

"They're en route to the pickup point." Kurtzman tapped the keyboard. The monitor on his left cleared and refocused. The image was dark at first, then he entered more commands. The picture lightened immediately, letting Price know the light-gathering feature of the satellite had kicked in again.

Five orange blips showed up on the monitor, quickly magnifying enough that they became bubbles around the men of Phoenix Force. The field of view also showed pursuit by the Range Rovers, which were having a harder time getting through the jungle, but keeping the distance close just the same.

"The plane?" Price asked.

"It'll be on the ground when they get closer," Kurtzman said. "We've got an added problem."

"What?"

Kurtzman keyed in new commands. A moment later, the middle screen displayed military vehicles bucking and charging through jungle growth, headlights flaring into the darkness. "Their mission has gotten the attention of the locals."

Price looked at the gathering of military men and hardware. There were too many for this to be a routine patrol. "They were riding backup on the delivery."

"I'd say that was true," Kurtzman growled. "But then, we didn't expect any less, did we?"

"How far away are they from Phoenix?"

"Maybe an hour." Kurtzman changed the view from the spy satellite. "And they've got enough firepower to knock the de Havilland from the air if they get close enough." The monitor zoomed in on an oversize vehicle trailing a jeep. The neon red skeleton of the vehicle suddenly exploded onto the screen. Sharpening its image, the vehicle's skeleton shunted the main video feed down to the lower-right corner, then occupied the upper-right corner itself. Technical writing quickly filled in the upper left corner of the monitor. "The satellite data base confirms that this is a Soviet ZSU-23-4 self-propelled air-defense gun.''

It took Price only a moment to run the specs through her memory. The ZSU-23-4 had four 23 mm machine guns linked to a valve-technology radar. It was quite capable of taking the de Havilland down, or damaging the plane too much for Phoenix Force to exfiltrate.

''Advise Phoenix One and the pilots,'' the mission controller said.

''I did.'' Kurtzman shifted in his chair. ''There's a window of opportunity, and McCarter knows we can't do much once that window closes.

In silence, Kurtzman and Price watched the Phoenix Force leader head for the makeshift landing strip the de Havilland pilots had targeted.

CHAPTER FOURTEEN

Puerto Vallarta, Mexico

The mobile phone inside the Dakota King Cab pickup rang stridently.

Carl Lyons shifted his gaze from the street and glanced quickly at the caller ID printed across the back of the handset. No name appeared, but the number was familiar. "Saunders," he said.

Seated behind the pickup's steering wheel, eyes watching the early-morning traffic closely, DEA Agent Jacinto Montoya nodded. "He's getting antsy."

"He called a busted play," Lyons said. "He knows his ass is in a sling." Max Saunders was the senior DEA agent in the Puerto Vallarta district. Saunders was also Montoya's boss.

"If Rudy's neck wasn't on the line here," Montoya said, "I'd sympathize with him. We'd been working this beat for months, hoping for a shot at Escelera, before you people just showed up and took over."

The phone stopped ringing.

Lyons swiveled his gaze back to the street, ignoring the cynicism and accusation in Montoya's voice. Lyons didn't blame the guy. He'd been an LAPD cop himself and had suffered through Feds landing on a case and snatching it away from the PD people originally assigned to it.

He scanned the street. They were in a part of Puerto Vallarta that was well away from the touristy section of the city. Buildings rose and fell around them, some of them three stories tall, and most of them in various stages of disrepair. Clotheslines hung in alleys, well above the rusting hulks of cars and trucks where scantily clad children played hide-and-seek and other games.

There was enough traffic on the road to provide cover for Montoya as he followed Escelera's late-model black Lexus. Dawn was blossoming hard against the eastern sky, ripping through the night and leaving dark purple and deep rose tatters in its wake. But the heat was already filling the streets and the city.

Lyons sat in the passenger seat, saturated by the humidity. It was cooler down by the beach where the big ocean liners and cruise ships were. That was where the action was supposed to have gone down; not in the inner city, and not with the DEA involved.

He wore jeans and a sleeveless chambray shirt left outside his pants. A loose black leather vest covered the .357 Magnum Colt Python in a shoulder rig under his left arm and the Colt Government Model .45 tucked inside his waistband at the back. He wore a baseball cap to cover the blond hair that would mark him instantly as a foreigner in the community.

Montoya looked at home on the streets. He wore faded jeans with homemade bell-bottoms, the inserted cloth panels containing a festive print depicting amber Aztec designs against a field of blue that had lost some of the color with time. His red T-shirt stretched tight across his broad chest. A matching bandanna covered his head, keeping the wild black hair beneath mostly under control. Wraparound sunglasses hid his eyes. His caramel-colored skin showed darker markings of scars along his arms and on the right side of his face. He wore a Fu Manchu mustache, and his two front teeth were capped in silver. Gold-hoop earrings hung from both ears. The last thing he looked like was a DEA agent.

Two other DEA agents sat tensely in the back, both of them outfitted like Montoya. Lyons had picked up their names from brief snatches of conversation, and from the perfunctory introductions that had been made earlier.

Dominic Arrias was the oldest of the three agents, well into his thirties. With his rough-hewn peasant's features, hard looks and the gray threading through his hair and his full beard, he looked like an old *bandido* gone to seed. He didn't talk much, but he was the kind of guy Lyons knew to listen to when the action went down. Arrias had been stationed in the Puerto Vallarta area for more than twelve years, working the streets and working the local graft along the docks. He dressed the part of a dock worker, wearing stained and ripped dungarees. A gray-and-black kerchief hung around his neck.

Raul Orosco was the youngest of the group, scarcely in his twenties. From the prelim Price and Kurtzman had offered via computer link, Lyons knew Orosco was once part of the Puerto Vallarta police department. Orosco's older brother had been with the local PD, as well, but had been ambushed and killed three years before, sold out by dirty police officers within his department. Rumor had it that the killers had belonged to Escelera's organization. Raul Orosco had cut a deal with the DEA, getting his mother and two sisters out of the country so they wouldn't be targets, as well. He'd stayed on in Puerto Vallarta, changing his looks and his street identity and working deep undercover. He wore leather despite the humidity. Sitting in the back seat beside Arrias, he absently stroked the French tickler growing down from his lower lip.

The Lexus took a sudden left at the next intersection, skating through and cutting a red light.

"Son of a bitch!" Montoya growled in frustration, slapping the steering wheel as he braked to a stop.

Lyons watched the luxury sedan pull away. Following now wasn't an option. They'd have stood out like a sore thumb.

"I don't think they made us," Arrias said from the back. "Probably just being careful."

"If they did spot us, Rudy's a dead man," Montoya said.

"He's a dead man anyway," Arrias warned, "unless we get up on them before they can do the job."

"We'll do our best," Lyons promised as he reached into the duffel at his feet, shoving the H&K MP-5 SD-3 machine pistol to one side, along with the spare clips that went with it, and fisted the IBM ThinkPad notebook computer. The computer had been retooled in a more durable casing, and upgraded under Kurtzman's own specs.

The Able Team commando flipped the top open and tapped the space bar. The small screen filled with color, then shifted immediately to the tracking utility that he'd used. He flicked the red mouse button in the center of the keyboard and dropped the menu window into view. Only three file entries were available for selection.

The first was for the *Pearl Serpent*, Escelera's private yacht, anchored just out of Puerto Vallarta. The second was for the small jet the woman kept at the local airport, and the third was for the Lexus. All of them had tracing devices on them, courtesy of specialized teams Price had put on the ground in Puerto Vallarta before Able Team had arrived.

Escelera had her vehicles swept regularly for bugs, so Lyons knew the tracers wouldn't stay in place long. But for now, they worked.

Lyons double-clicked the menu bar for the Lexus. Neon blue letters floated to the top of the screen. "Trace in progress." He reached into his duffel and took out the cell phone tucked into one of the pockets. After punching in the two-digit speed-dial code for the access number that would tie him in with the global positioning satellite Kurtzman had set up for the operation, he slotted the lead into the computer's PCM/CIA outlet.

An overlay in fluorescent green shadowed the "Trace in progress" announcement. Icons of a phone, satellite and car showed up on the overlay. A dotted line connected the phone to the satellite, then the satellite to the car.

"GPS connection complete—stand by."

"I've got them," Lyons said as the message dropped away and returned to the trace utility. The screen shimmered briefly, then a street map formed in the restless wake. Lyons clicked on the mouse button, increasing the magnification. The programming didn't give actual video footage, creating instead a digitized representation of the area and the trace subject.

Street names painted themselves on the streets. A compass rose formed in the lower-right corner of the screen. The blocky car looked nothing like the Lexus, but glowed against the representations of the other vehicles on the street with it.

Lyons read off the directions and the street names.

Montoya waited for the light, then cut across oncoming traffic. Horns blared in frustration, and angry shouts sailed in through the open windows. "How sure are you this thing works properly?" he demanded.

"The guy who put this package together," Lyons replied, "is the best in the business. I'd trust my life to him."

Montoya shot Lyons a hard look as he pulled around a slow-moving flatbed truck. "We're trusting Rudy's life."

Lyons nodded at the man but didn't say anything. There was nothing he could say. He'd been in operations during his LAPD days that had left an undercover cop dangling in the breeze. Over the years, he'd helped save a lot of them, but they'd lost three good men, never able to recover the body of one of them for his family to bury.

"Rudy wouldn't have been in no damned hurry to get his ass in a sling," Orosco said, "if Saunders hadn't made the call."

"Saunders wouldn't have made that call if we hadn't suddenly had so much competition here," Montoya replied.

"If Rudy hadn't been so anxious to get out from under in Escelera's organization," Orosco argued, "maybe he'd have told Saunders to go screw himself. He was too damned ready to get home."

"Shut up," Arrias said irritably. He poked a forefinger at the computer screen. "Looks like they're taking Rudy out to Cuale Island."

Lyons racked his brain for memory of the area as he

glanced out the window. He'd been through much of
Mexico at different times, on vacation and on business.
They'd passed Guadalupe Church a few blocks back,
putting them deep into Gringo Gulch along the north
bank of the Cuale River. Looking to the south, Lyons
could see the houses still maintained by the movie people, as well as by other rich, transitory dwellers.

"If they get farther south," Orosco said, "there's
plenty of places to lose a body and never have it turn
up again."

Lyons was aware of that. He read off the streets in
a flat voice, knowing the closer they got to their des-
tination, the less chance Rudolpho Guarano had of surviving the encounter. Escelera's people, like the
woman herself, were ruthless.

At the Cuale River, two bridges extended across the
water. The Lexus aimed itself at the one upstream,
slowing slightly in the thronging pack of people at the
northern edge of the bridge. Cuale Island lay beyond.

"Take the downstream bridge," Arrias directed.
"We can gain on them even though it's farther around.
That damned marketplace will only hold us up."

Montoya turned at the next intersection, then raced
down the street beside the river.

Lyons glanced up from the computer to scan the upstream bridge. The Lexus had bogged down in the traffic and the market-goers. To avoid the heat of the noonday sun, the market hawkers had already filled the
bridge area. Bright green stuffed toy iguanas and olive
armadillos jutted out from poles, along with flags and
festive banners.

Montoya shrilled around his turn, bluffing a station
wagon full of musicians out of their turn through the

intersection. He roared onto and across the downstream bridge.

As they passed under an arch, Lyons watched the monitor screen fragment.

"Shit," Orosco said. He heaved himself up from his seat and tried to peer through the buildings and houses up the river.

"It's okay," Lyons told him as the monitor reformed the picture. The tracer aboard the Lexus pulsed like a heartbeat, strong and true.

The link remained clear as the Lexus wound through the streets. Lyons watched the restaurants, low-rental bungalows and motels parade by. They approached the sea in a direct route, leaving no questions as to what was in store for the undercover DEA agent.

"Escelera's not with them," Arrias announced.

Lyons stared at the back of the Lexus. The passengers were still too far away to see with the unaided eye. Arrias had a pair of binoculars.

"She was there," Orosco said.

Lyons took out a compact set of binoculars and peered through them. Escelera wasn't with the hard crew inside the Lexus. The Able Team warrior counted two men in the front and two in the back. When they'd first began the trip, Escelera had been sitting in the right rear passenger seat.

"She's not now," Arrias said.

"She's trying to keep her hands clean," Lyons said, putting the binoculars away. There were almost out of town and out of island. A patch of jungle remained just beyond the strip of beach the locals called Playa de los Muertos. Loosely translated, Lyons knew it meant "Beach of the Dead."

"Pissed her off that Rudy got so deep in her organization," Montoya speculated. "She probably faced him off, let him know she knew and took time to tell him what her men were going to do to him. Then she split."

And the woman could also have killed the agent herself and left his corpse for the men to dispose of. Lyons brought his thinking back from that possibility. He concentrated on making the save.

The brake lights of the Lexus flared bright ruby.

"They're stopping," Orosco stated.

"Park there." Arrias pointed into a space between an old GMC three-quarter-ton truck whose cab had mostly rusted away and a battered yellow Cadillac.

Montoya brought the pickup to a stop. The tires crunched in the sand. His hand slid under the seat and pulled out the rolling gun rack. He took out the scoped Marlin lever-action rifle lying there and checked the action. Brass gleamed as the cartridge slid into place.

The men inside the Lexus sat and watched the fishermen cresting the waves on the ocean. Cigarettes glowed softly.

Lyons closed the notebook computer and took out the H&K MP-5 SD-3. "They're taking their time."

"No hurry," Arrias said bitterly. "Who's going to stop them, right?" He snorted in disgust. "Escelera's probably breaking some of the treaties she's got with the locals by choosing to execute a federal officer of the United States here, but I don't think that's going to stop her."

"We will," Lyons said. He gazed back behind the pickup. "The tree line starts back there just a few yards away. If we can make it over there without getting spotted, maybe we can put them down without endangering Guarano."

"Man's already in danger," Orosco said. "We take time to talk, he's going to be dead."

Montoya shook his head. "If we walk up on them, Rudy's going to get just as dead. This isn't Tombstone. If we get lucky, we can come up on them, maybe shave the odds." He fixed Lyons with a hard stare. "You any good with that chattergun, or are you just going to hose the area and hope to God?"

"I hit what I aim at," Lyons replied.

"So do I." Montoya craned his neck and glanced at his two companions. "We'll circle around if we can." He held up a compact walkie-talkie. "I'll let you know when we get there."

"Do it," Arrias said.

Orosco gave a short, quick nod. "I'm not going to wait on you forever."

Lyons attached a sling to the machine pistol and tucked the weapon inside the reusable plastic shopping bag Arrias passed up from the rear. He threaded his fingers through the bag's straps and through the H&K MP-5's trigger guard. Extra magazines for the machine pistol and his .45 went into his vest and pants pockets. He clipped a pair of speed loaders on his belt under his shirt. The position was unwieldy, but he'd proved over the years that he could get to them fast enough.

Montoya moved from the pickup, the rifle in a loose duffel.

Lyons caught up easily, his longer stride eating up the distance. Sand crunched under his feet. Perspiration trickled down under his shirt and caused the material to stick to him. A pair of mirror shades covered his eyes. The salt of the sea hung in the air around him, and the humidity was like a warm, wet slap.

The cellular phone was clipped to Lyons's hip. As soon as he reached the relative shelter of the jungle growth without drawing the attention of the hardmen in the Lexus, the Able Team commando flipped the phone open and punched in the two-digit number that linked him with Blancanales and Schwarz.

"Amigo," the Politician answered in his smooth voice. "What's happening?"

"Saunders," Lyons answered in a low voice. He navigated his way through the rough brush nearly ten feet off Montoya's lead. "He called a busted play. Sent in a deep to bust up the shakedown and grab a few personal party favors early."

"The deep-cover guy?"

"In deeper," Lyons replied curtly. "I'm with a handful of DEA irregulars. We're going to try to bust the deep out. The reason I called is to find out how much longer you and Gadgets would be there."

Talking echoed in the background over the phone connection.

"Five, maybe ten more minutes at the outside," Blancanales reported a few seconds later. "The Farm had trouble picking up a few of the microwave broadcasting transmitters. Something to do with the structural integrity of the building. The blueprints Base got were good, but evidently not exact. We had to work around a few things."

"Get it zipped up and cleaned up as quick as you can," Lyons said. "We lost Escelera in the confusion. For a time she was riding shotgun with the deep."

"And now she's not."

"That's about the size of it."

"Anything else?"

"Wish me luck."

"Done." Blancanales broke the connection.

Lyons put the phone away, locking it down with the Velcro restraining strap. He and Montoya had followed the curve of the hillside, staying well within the underbrush. The heat seemed even more intense there, though the shadows weren't entirely cut by the rising sun.

Out along the sea, the fishing boats rocked on the water, resting at anchor as the crews worked the nets. Hot salsa music and American rock and roll drifted up from portable boom boxes and radios in the vehicles below.

"They're moving," Montoya called.

"I see." Lyons hunkered lower and kept moving, watching as the hardmen got out of the Lexus.

The four men walked as a unit to the rear of the Lexus, all of them wearing dark suits in spite of the heat. Escelera liked to present a professional image, and enforced it with her men, as well.

Three of them stood near the trunk while the fourth strode toward the approaching decades-old Ford LTD. Lyons couldn't tell what the car's original color had been, but it held a green patina now.

The LTD stopped only a few yards from the Lexus, throwing up a small cloud of sand and dust. The man in the suit facing the car turned to greet the five men who clambered out of the LTD. All of them wore casual clothing, layered somewhat to cover the weapons they carried.

The man in the suit talked to the five men from the LTD, then reached into his jacket to take out an envelope. The Able Team leader's eyesight was good enough to spot the quick flash of currency inside the envelope.

One of the men from the LTD took the envelope and made it disappear, then he led his group to the rear of the Lexus.

The trunk popped open, revealing the body of Rudolpho Guarano inside. Electrical or phone wire bound the DEA agent's hands and feet, and tape covered his mouth.

A member of the Lexus crew reached into the trunk of the luxury car and hauled out the DEA undercover agent. Guarano stood uncertainly on his bound feet. Like the others in Escelera's inner circle, he wore an expensive suit. Blood stained it in fat splotches, turning the gray material dark, and crusted his hair near his right temple.

Guarano was a little man with narrow shoulders, a guy nobody would really look at twice. Escelera had seen the value in such a man, and her taste had coincided with the DEA section chief's.

"They're going to take him deeper in," Montoya mouthed in a loud whisper. "Leave him in the jungle."

Lyons moved out, anticipating the direction the kill squad took. Two of them took Guarano between them and hustled him back to the LTD. A narrow dirt road led between the trees, beaten into submission by infrequent traffic. With a lurch, the LTD pulled into the jungle.

Without warning, a group of people hurried away from the row of parked vehicles where Arrias and Orosco had been. Lyons caught a brief glimpse of the younger man cutting behind a Volkswagen microbus.

Escelera's men spotted Orosco, too. They opened fire immediately. Bullets punched massive dents and punctures in the side of the microbus and shattered the windshield and windows. The DEA man returned fire at once, using short bursts from the CAR-15 he'd taken from Montoya's pickup.

A burst caught one of the men from the Lexus in the chest and knocked him down, but he was moving again in seconds, letting Lyons know they were equipped with bulletproof vests, as well.

The LTD vanished into the jungle as the men in the rear and passenger seats added their gunfire.

Slipping the H&K MP-5 from the shopping bag, Lyons charged after the fleeing LTD.

CHAPTER FIFTEEN

Barbara Price glanced at the caller ID listed on the phone she used at Kurtzman's desk. Despite the fact that the name was listed as unknown, she recognized the number at once as Brognola's. "Hello."

"Tell me it's something good," the head Fed told her.

"A little of both," Price replied. "Aaron managed to penetrate the shell companies listed on the files Mack lifted from the Palm Beach arena."

"And they lead back to Kesar Grishin?"

"Without a doubt, confirming what we know about the man. However, we still don't have the key we need to bring down his operation. We're closer."

"What about his little gathering scheduled for tomorrow night?"

"I don't know." Price opened a manila folder that contained the pictures and information they'd acquired from dozens of different intelligence agencies over the past few months. She knew every one of the faces inside the file by memory. Flipping through them casually, she stopped at Alexander DeCapra's photograph.

DeCapra stood tall and roughly elegant in the photo. It had been taken at a senatorial committee meeting in Philadelphia the previous year. In his early forties, De-

Capra cut a roguish look in his black tuxedo. Clean-shaved, dark good looks still turned the ladies' heads.

"We're going to have to move Leo into the play," Brognola said.

"I know." Price didn't like the way her voice came out so neutral. Brognola knew her well enough to read it.

"I can make the call," Brognola offered.

"It's not your place," Price replied.

"It's the right thing to do, Barb."

"I know." Price placed the photograph back on the stack and flipped it over. On the back was a yellow sticker with a location and time, and that day's date.

"So give me the bad news."

In a terse description that left nothing out, Price outlined Phoenix Force's compromised operation in Myanmar, as well as Carl Lyons's own foray off the plan down in Puerto Vallarta.

"McCarter will pull his team out," the head Fed said. "What about Lyons?"

"He had a brief communication with Blancanales. He's with a covert DEA team attempting to recover the lost deep-cover agent."

Brognola nodded grimly. "As long as Able is in the field there, the DEA won't make another move. You still don't have a clue as to what information Escelera's carrying to the Caribbean meet?"

"No." It had been the lure of that information that led to Able Team's presence in Puerto Vallarta. The intel had come by way of the PD liaison that Price had developed through her contacts in the country. Even the DEA didn't have what she had. But then, the DEA had been looking for contraband, not information.

"What about the team that intercepted Phoenix in Myanmar?" Brognola asked.

"I'm checking the angles." Price checked her watch. "I'm expecting a call back within the next few minutes."

"Let me know."

"As soon as I do." Price closed the folder on DeCapra's pictures. The information scrawled across the sticker was marked indelibly in her mind. "Where will you be?"

"On a plane."

"To Milwaukee?"

"Yeah."

"The Man couldn't talk Thompson out of going?"

"No."

Price stepped away from Kurtzman's desk, holding the cellular phone to the side of her face. Her stomach tightened at the prospect of the attorney general of the United States marching into Milwaukee. "Maybe if we told her we're working on Grishin…"

"The things we're doing," Brognola said in an easy voice, "are across the lines Ramona Thompson is comfortable with drawing."

And Price knew that.

"You and I have made our peace with them," the big Fed went on.

Price silently agreed and knew she could offer no further argument for telling Thompson about the antiterrorist hardsite. In the present world of political and economic unrest, Stony Man Farm was necessary. Congressional decisions were based on reactions, rather than proaction. Stony Man Farm had been set up and put into service for the purpose of successful retaliations and preemptive strikes that would save lives.

"If there's anything you need while you're there," Price said, "let me know."

Brognola said he would, then broke the connection.

Price punched in a number from memory and talked briefly with one of the Farm's blacksuit commanders. The blacksuits managed Farm security and worked in the orchards and fields. All of them were culled from the cream of the crop in special forces and bound by military-intelligence strictures not to speak about anything they saw at the Farm while on assignment. All of them were capable soldiers.

In just minutes, the mission controller arranged to have a small unit put into the air and gave the intel officer the password to retrieve the Milwaukee blueprints and specs from Kurtzman's computer files. Brognola might be walking into the eye of the storm with the attorney general, but the mission controller wasn't going to let the head Fed walk in alone.

Finished with the brief conversation, Price punched the cellular phone off and glanced back at the wall screen, which was split into quadrants. Clockwise, starting with the upper-left screen, the views depicted the overall battle zone with infrared that showed the de Havilland, Phoenix Force and the mercenary team rolling in pursuit. The distances separating all three didn't appear to be much.

The second screen showed a closer view of the cargo plane as it touched down in the jungle. Remote-controlled flares set into the ground by an in-country team earlier spit harsh, bright color into the sky, helping to reveal the rugged terrain.

On the third screen, Price watched the four Enduro motorcycles bobbing across the countryside through the intense tangle of underbrush and trees. The fourth screen showed close-ups of the mercs. A blue rectangle floated over the faces, occasionally locking in on one of them as Tokaido continued recording images.

"Going to be close," Kurtzman said.

Price couldn't add anything to the announcement. She waited and watched.

KESAR GRISHIN LAY on the bed in the rear of the jet and watched the flight attendant get dressed. Her muscles moved smoothly beneath the supple, tanned skin. She smiled at him as if she knew exactly what he was thinking.

Grishin smiled back because it fulfilled the rules of sexual attraction in the game she thought she was playing, and because he knew she didn't have a clue as to what he was thinking. His mind was already locked in on the events unfolding in New York. Despite her own convictions, the woman had only been a few moments' amusement.

"Will there be anything else?" She posed the question coyly, one hand on her hip.

Grishin grinned at her anew. There was nothing like power. Only few men were born to handle power, though, who would truly dare to take it to the limit.

"No," he replied. "Thank you."

"Thank you." The woman walked through the door, but she seemed uncertain about passing through it.

Grishin waved to her with one hand, flexing his fingers.

She opened the door and let herself out.

When she was gone, Grishin levered himself out of the bed. The bedroom was outfitted with everything he needed to travel in rapid and comfortable style. He went to the wet bar built into the wall and made himself a vodka with cracked ice, then retreated to the desk built into the wall at the back of the room.

Taking out a remote control, he aimed it at the twenty-seven-inch color television depending from the ceiling near the door. When the picture came into focus, he flicked to "Headline News" and scanned the stock quotes parading across the bottom of the screen. The Wall Street quotes were delayed by minutes, long enough for financial fortunes to ebb and flow in some cases.

Grishin laced his hands together behind his head and continued watching as he relaxed in the chair. There was a knock at the door.

"Come in, Gerahd."

Dobrynin opened the door and followed it into the room. He closed the door behind him and stood at parade rest, his wrists crossed before him.

"You wanted something?" Grishin asked.

"There has been a problem."

Grishin muted the sound on the television and gave his full attention to his security chief. "What problem?"

"The bank in Palm Beach," Dobrynin said. "American federal agencies raided it a couple hours ago. The person I had stationed there was only now able to call."

"What federal agencies?" Grishin glanced at the clock beside the bed. It was set on Tokyo time. He did the mental calculations to figure out what time it was in Palm Beach.

"It isn't clear at the moment."

"The Justice Department?"

Dobrynin gave a small shrug, his expression remaining neutral. "Perhaps."

"What happened to the information pipeline we have to Thompson's office?"

"It's still operative. Those people assure me they didn't know anything about the raid. In fact, they're only now finding out about the details themselves."

Grishin considered that. Despite the finesse with which he'd moved money into and out of several countries—including the U.S.—one step ahead of several international and domestic police agencies, he was aware that Thompson would assume her own office was leaking information. Details had been drying up over the past weeks, though he'd kept himself aware of the investigations into several of the holding companies and shell corporations he'd erected in dozens of countries. Still, he hadn't thought Thompson's office capable of arranging such a coup without his knowing of it beforehand.

"How bad is it?" Grishin asked.

"I don't know. I was told that the computer files were accessed and transmitted out of the offices there."

Grishin lifted the phone handset from the desk and punched a speed-dial number. Anytime he boarded one of his planes, the onboard computer databases were automatically filled with his preferences from a modem link. When he left, they were all wiped out of the master motherboard.

The phone rang in the Caribbean, but if anyone had been able to trace the call, it would have been logged in as somewhere in Europe.

"Good morning, Kesar," Salome said in a cheerful voice.

"It appears we have a problem in Palm Beach," Grishin said without preamble.

"Yes."

"That bank was one of the areas you were supposed to be watching over."

"I was. I saw every detail of the raid over the closed-circuit security system. Until the people behind the raid inserted a closed-loop interface that blinded the system and later took it off-line."

"Do you want to tell me why I have to find this out from Dobrynin instead of receiving a call from you?"

"You do know what they say about the messenger." Salome's voice remained bright and cheerful.

Over the phone connection, Grishin heard the shrill whistle and prolonged beep of her computer accessing the modem. There were a number of web sites she'd set up in cyberspace that she could use to access any number of agencies without being accessed herself.

"Is Dobrynin still living?" Salome asked playfully.

"Only until he hits the ground." Grishin looked up at the security chief, who deigned not to respond.

Salome laughed.

At times, the woman's confident attitude got on Grishin's nerves. But she was very good at what she did. "You could have called," he said.

"I knew Dobrynin's cohorts would call you soon enough. In the meantime, I've been busy trying to work damage control. I think you'd agree that was much more important."

"How bad is it?"

"The transfers from Eastern Europe were coming in. I've managed to rescue most of them through the trap-door in the Palm Beach system. Now I have to make sure they have new hiding places where they won't be bothered. Millions of dollars, as you well know, are not easily hidden quickly. If at all."

Grishin knew. "The Cayman accounts will soak up a lot of those accounts for a short time."

"True," Salome said. "I'd already thought of those. The downside is that these federal agencies may have a deep throat in the Cayman transfer offices. I would. Bringing the money to our part of the world might inadvertently point the finger at us. So far, they have some of the holding companies we've been using. But they don't have us. I want it to stay that way."

"Then where are you putting that money?"

"A quick trip through Germany, I think. It's after four there. By the time anyone gets around to checking on—and logging in—the transfers in the morning, it'll be gone again. By noon tomorrow, it'll be as if that money never went through their offices."

Grishin took another sip of his drink. He trusted Salome, trusted her skill and trusted her fear of him. If she attempted to abscond with any of the money he controlled, she knew she was already dead. But he hated having to trust her. On the jet, he didn't have access to all the software he'd designed and the systems within dozens of banks that he'd created, so he couldn't manage the money himself.

"Are you having any problems?" he asked.

"None. But the roll-over in some of the countries we're going to have to use to launder this money is going to be more steeper than we'd anticipated."

Roll-over was a banking term Grishin had become well acquainted with. With all the electronic accounts in the world, there was more electronic currency than existed in the physical world. So when a bank needed paper money to give to a patron, if enough wasn't on hand to operate, they had to buy it from another bank. Roll-over described the percentage the second bank took from the sale of the paper money. And that percentage changed with nearly every hour of a business day. The same money a bank bought in the morning could go higher—or lower—by that afternoon, when it was sold back to the bank the first bank had gotten it from.

"Using those sources is also going to leave us looking for new outlets for the other cash coming in sooner than we'd expected."

"Yes," the woman replied. "I've been working on that, as well. I've got some ideas I want to toss at you. When will you be back?"

"We're gaining on Thursday now." Since the jet had passed the international date line, Grishin was, in effect, going back in time. "Did you get the layover scheduled in Milwaukee?"

"Yes."

"I'll be back as soon as I finish up there. Probably no earlier than Saturday morning."

"You're going to miss your party at the yacht."

"So they'll have it without me. It won't be the first time."

"No, but you've got some important clientele who wanted to meet you in person. Alex DeCapra, to name one."

"DeCapra is the man representing the East Coast Families."

"Right."

"After the party at the yacht, make sure he's invited up to the estate. I'll make it up to him." DeCapra was important to the economic engine Grishin was building. The East Coast trafficked in a lot of money, and the Mafia Families there already had access to a number of legitimate businesses in the northern states and Canada. "What does Mr. DeCapra favor in vices?"

"Ladies. Lots of them."

"What are his preferences?"

"The more married, the better. He has a penchant for forbidden fruit."

"Can we arrange that?"

"I've already seen to it. While at the party, DeCapra will be introduced to Lady Beverly Wainwright of Monaco, who is a close friend of the royal family."

"Married and royalty," Grishin said. "Our Mr. DeCapra will be enchanted. Who is Lady Beverly actually?"

"A European hooker I've used before. And I've even hired a male from the service to act as her husband," Salome said. "That way, DeCapra will have someone to cheat on."

"Cunning," Grishin said.

"One of the most underappreciated traits in a woman."

"Let's return to the Palm Beach situation."

"The money's no problem."

"How much did we lose?"

"Enough to make a dent in our fee, but these are people we regularly do business with. If we jack up our charges over the next three or four months, tell them that the banks are gouging us, we can recoup our losses."

Grishin checked his watch, gazing at the date. Leaning forward, he tapped keys to bring up his personal calendar on the computer. Instantly lines of information appeared in the squares. He shifted the mouse over to the current date in Caribbean time and exploded the box until it filled the monitor screen.

The influx of accounts from the Eastern European sector had been heavy: guns, drugs, political graft and the laundering he routinely did. Potentially, in the right hands, the information was dynamite.

"Have you talked to the attorneys on the scene there in Palm Beach?" Grishin asked.

"Yes."

"And their opinion?"

"That the information the federal agencies retrieve from the Palm Beach bank will be inadmissible as evidence in a court of law."

Grishin looked at Dobrynin. "How bad was it on-site?"

"Men were killed," the security chief answered.

"Federal agents?"

"No, sir."

"Teagan's people?"

"Yes."

Grishin absorbed the information. "Gerahd says men were killed during the raid."

"Yes," Salome said.

"But no federal agents?"

"That's correct."

"The Justice Department and Thompson won't go away from this easily."

"No. You'll have to give them something. Or someone."

"Teagan," Grishin said.

"That would help," Salome allowed. "Teagan can't touch you. All you've been is a remodulated voice on the phone. What he knows about your business, I've already taken care of. Records have been changed, and accounts wiped out like they never existed."

"You had encrypted those files in Palm Beach."

"True," Salome said. "However, remember that for everything you're able to do in computer programming, there's at least twenty people waiting to undo it. There is no such thing as a completely uncrackable encryption. Still, whoever does crack it will have to be very, *very* good."

"But if someone is able?"

"There's not a judge in Florida or in Washington who would touch the case or attempt to take you into custody. Maybe they'll be able to penetrate some of the holding companies we've fostered, but we can replace those. Besides that, once you return home, there's no chance at extradition."

"No, but that island could become a prison for me if the Americans could build a case. I've had enough of prisons." And travel was one of Grishin's passions.

Salome's voice became more gentle. "Trust me, Kesar. No one is going to be able to get to you because of anything they might get out of those computer files. You hired me because I was the best. I still am."

"Of course you are." Grishin leaned back in the seat again. "I suppose I'm more tired than I thought I was. But what we've built together, it's larger than I ever thought it might be. I guess I'm feeling protective of it."

"In another forty-eight hours," Salome said, "they're going to be as vulnerable as you are. Or you're going to be as valuable to the Western world as the Americans are. Keep that in mind."

"I do." Grishin glanced at the following day on the calendar, pulling up the lists there. "Has there been any word from Escelera?"

"She's in Puerto Vallarta. I'm expecting a call from her at any moment."

"As soon as you have the information—"

"I'll let you know."

Grishin hung up the phone.

Dobrynin stood in the doorway, waiting patiently.

"You've got something more you want to say," Grishin prompted, "say it."

"Rethink the business in Milwaukee," the security chief stated. "Don't make it personal. Let me have some of my people handle it."

"Your people are handling it, Gerahd."

"You don't have to be there. Your presence is only inviting trouble."

Grishin waved away the comment. "Tomorrow night, I'm going to tell dozens of people that they can trust me with millions of dollars of their money. I've got to have something more to offer them than this winning smile."

"In forty-eight hours, you're going to be able to shake the major economies of the world. Show them that."

"Let's hope I can do that." Grishin brought up a program. A box popped into being on the screen and demanded a password. He tapped the code word in and pressed Enter, launching the program.

The screen immediately filled with programming architecture. Numeric and alphabetic strings ran in twelve-digit columns. Heavy encryption protected the programs uploading and downloading.

Grishin watched the numbers and letters spin and cycle. Getting all the information, all the ultimate destinations, ferreting out the various servers and accounts had cost him millions of dollars and taken almost six years to get accomplished.

He tapped another key. A digital readout appeared

in the upper-right corner. It counted backward: 47:51:12, 47:51:11...

"You've come this far," Dobrynin said, "and no one's detected your programming."

"No." Grishin watched the programming continue to run. It was some of the best work he'd ever done, and he knew it. "The next twelve hours are crucial." He sipped his vodka, finding it had gone tepid and watery. "If they don't find me in their systems at that point, they won't. Not until it's too late for them to do anything about it."

"You don't need this face-to-face with Thompson."

"You're wrong," Grishin said. He looked at his security chief, his hand slapping out automatically to blank the screen of running programming. "I have to sell myself to every person on that yacht tomorrow night. If I don't control the money they have to launder through me, if I can't convince them that I'm the guy who has everything in place to handle their profits, I'm not going to be in the position I need to be in forty-seven-plus hours from now."

Dobrynin remained blank faced.

"If they see me take care of Ramona Thompson at that dinner Friday night, that'll leave them with an impression that will make them mine." Grishin fixed his security chief with a harsh stare. "Make no mistake. We're going to Milwaukee. Not for personal reasons. This is business."

CHAPTER SIXTEEN

Carl Lyons charged through the dense jungle under-growth. He swiped branches and lianas from his way as he fought to keep the fleeing LTD in sight. As the sedan followed the curve of the narrow road through the trees, the big Able Team commando cursed the fact that he wasn't tied into the Stony Man Farm systems at present. If Kurtzman or one of the others had been there with him, he'd have known where the road went.

During the past few days, the area had received brief storm fronts that had dumped inches of rain across the coastline. The trail had turned to mud, and trucks had evidently still used it. Dark and deep ruts cut through the trail, making footing risky.

Gunfire still echoed behind Lyons, a more subdued thunder than the rapid heartbeat filling his ears. He kept the H&K MP-5 close to his chest as he left the trail. He couldn't outrun the car. He guessed that the trail curved out again, toward the coast, and figured that the crew in the LTD would go toward the coastline.

If he was wrong, Guarano was dead.

Lyons ran up the slope. Brush covered treacherous rocks and holes eaten into the ground by erosion, as well as covering tangles of exposed roots. He fell once, but caught himself and shoved back to his feet with his free hand. He wished he and the DEA men had been linked by radio. He'd lost Montoya.

He crested the hill, caroming from a gnarled oak tree that listed badly to the east, away from him, and spotted the LTD circling around the foothills. With the brush and tree growth, Lyons caught only brief glimpses of the vehicle. But it was enough to let him know he had gained on it.

He sprinted down the hill, heading for the clearing he'd seen near the coastline. The beach hadn't been worked in this area, and the waves didn't come in on sandy expanses. The jungle butted up against the ocean. From his position, he hadn't been able to tell how deep the drop-off was on the other side of that clearing, but it looked deep enough to conceal a weighted body. If there was any undertow in the area, and Lyons was betting the killers knew there was, Guarano's body would be washed out to sea. There'd be no evidence of Escelera's involvement aside from the DEA agents' testimony. A good defense lawyer would point out the vested interest the American DEA agents had in getting a judgment against Escelera, and Escelera was able to afford much better than a good defense attorney.

The LTD pulled to a stop, dust swirling over it from behind. The five hardmen got out, pulling Guarano with them from the back seat. The DEA agent stumbled and would have fallen, but one of his captors jerked him roughly to his feet by the wire binding his wrists.

The dull throb of the LTD's engine muted Lyons's approach. The Able Team leader ran, keeping low as he could while maintaining speed.

The man holding Guarano jerked him back toward the rear of the car, while another man opened the trunk.

Guarano tried to fight as the men pulled him toward the back of the car. Without warning, one of the men standing behind the small DEA agent stepped up and slammed a shotgun stock into Guarano's skull. The DEA undercover agent went rubber legged, but still managed to fight weakly as he was thrown into the trunk of the sedan.

Lyons fired a short burst from forty yards out. The 9 mm parabellum rounds caught one of the perimeter men across the chest, driving him backward. Blood covered his beige shirt, letting Lyons know they weren't wearing bulletproof armor.

The man went down, yelling shrilly in pain.

Lyons managed another burst, aiming now at the hardman ducking into the car.

The bullets chopped across the LTD's top, leaving jagged tears in their wake and pounding out the door glass. Some of them caught the man and hammered him against the door and down.

The car started forward, the gasoline-starved engine snarling fitfully as it managed to lumber the vehicle forward. A few trees and warped undergrowth stood as a flimsy blockade in front of the drop-off little more than twenty yards away.

Lyons dived and went to cover as return fire ripped through leaves and branches over his head. He rolled as the gunners vectored in on him. Lyons ran to a thick-boled oak tree and took cover. He glanced back down the trail and spotted Montoya. Bullets chewed bark from the tree where the DEA agent took cover.

Whirling around his own tree, Lyons unleashed the rest of the machine pistol's magazine at the three remaining gunmen. They ducked into hiding.

The LTD closed on the drop-off, mowing down the

small trees and underbrush easily. The front wheels went over, dropping the undercarriage onto the ground. For a moment, it looked like the additional friction would overcome the sputtering engine's capabilities and choke it down. Then enough of the car's weight went over the balance point for gravity to pull it over the rest of the way.

Lyons changed magazines. "Cover me!"

Bullets whacked into the tree and tore large holes in the ground around him. Montoya returned fire quickly.

Gathering himself, Lyons ran toward the drop-off. One of the men evidently felt he had Lyons dead to rights, standing up and shouldering an M-14 to get a clear shot. The Able Team commando fired on the run, never breaking stride. The swarm of bullets caught the gunner and knocked him back. The round from the M-14 cut through Lyons's short-cropped blond hair.

He reached the drop-off's edge and didn't hesitate. The LTD bobbed in the water fifteen feet below, taking on water quickly. Releasing the H&K MP-5 to hang from the sling, Lyons dived in.

He hit the surface of the ocean and was immediately engulfed by the undertow grasping greedily at him. He fought against it, squinting against the murk. Lyons spotted the LTD going down rapidly, beneath the surface now. Lungs already desperate for oxygen because of the run to the clearing and the sprint to the drop-off, Lyons stroked for the sinking car. It was possible the plunge into the ocean had killed the DEA agent. If it hadn't, the man couldn't last long trapped in the car's trunk.

Lyons overtook the car, grabbing the rear bumper as it settled on the slanted ocean floor. Bubbles continued streaming from the trunk, slowing and growing smaller.

The car's impact against the ocean bed stirred up a cloud of silt. The salt water burned Lyons's eyes, and the grit was almost blinding.

He clung to the bumper and ran his fingers across the trunk. Finding the groove where the trunk hatch closed, he reached for the third button down on the leather vest he wore.

The button was one of Hermann Schwarz's deadly little tricks. Almost an inch across and a deceptive half inch in thickness, the button contained a plastic explosive charge. It wasn't much, but Lyons hoped it was enough.

Lyons pulled the button free of his vest, found the miniature switches located on the underside and nudged them into position. The charge had a ten-second delay, enough to create a distraction and powerful enough to take a door from its hinges. Lyons hoped the water wouldn't blunt the effects too much.

He shoved the button into the gap near the trunk lock and swam back. His lungs burned, and not all of the black spots flashing in his vision had to do with the cloud of silt.

The plastic-explosive charge detonated. Water roiled, stirring up even more of the ocean bed. The concussion peeled Lyons's lips back, forcing the salty brine past his clenched teeth. Pain from not breathing mushroomed inside his head as he returned to the car.

The trunk lock had disintegrated in the blast, leaving the trunk lid warped. Lyons locked his fingers under the edge of the heated metal, ignored the burn and yanked. The trunk lid gave grudgingly.

Eyes stinging, he peered through the murk and spotted Guarano up against the back seat. He reached in and pulled the man out.

Blood streamed from a cut over Guarano's left cheek. Bubbles burst from his mouth, and he flailed weakly.

Lyons gathered the man in easily and headed them both for the surface. He clapped a hand over Guarano's mouth and nose to keep him from breathing in the brine and kept kicking them toward the surface.

Guarano fought briefly to get free, then went limp.

Breaking the surface, Lyons kept the man above water and swam toward the base of the drop-off. There was no beach, but large rocks jutted up from the shallows where Montoya was waiting.

"How is he?" Montoya asked.

Lyons shoved Guarano onto one of the rocks. The DEA agent breathed raggedly, but he was alive. "He'll live," Lyons answered. "What about the guys back there?"

"Four down. One got away."

Lyons hauled more of his weight onto the rock, trying to find a comfortable position and maintain the hold on the unconscious man. Four down wasn't bad. "What about Escelera's people?"

"They faded," Montoya yelled over the sound of the breaking surf. "What do you want to bet Escelera's called the car in as stolen?"

Lyons waved the offer of a hand away, feeling the rising sun bake into him, steaming away part of the chill. Escelera covered her bases. Thinking of her reminded him of the situation Blancanales and Schwarz might be in if the woman had walked back into the hotel room too soon. He pulled the phone from his hip but found the salt water had destroyed it. All he could do was wait.

"YOU'RE QUICK," Barbara Price stated.

"Ah, dear girl," Sir Winston Blakely said over the phone, "normally I shudder to hear those words from the fairer sex."

In spite of the tension of the moment, in spite of the satellite footage of Phoenix Force's run from Myanmar, Price smiled. "I meant it in only the best way."

"Of course." Papers shuffled at the other end of the connection. "I believe I have a candidate for the files you sent me. Have you an e-mail address to which I can download a file to you?"

Price looked at Kurtzman and lifted an eyebrow.

Kurtzman nodded. He reached for a cup of sharpened pencils he kept on the desk and scrawled a quick series of letters and numbers across a memo sheet: "Kingfisher@well.com."

Price read the address back.

Computer keys clacked at the other end. "There you go," Blakely said. "You should have the package in mere seconds, if those Internet interchanges are working properly."

Price walked back to Kurtzman's desk and peered over a big shoulder. Her attention was divided between the monitor the cybernetics expert cleared and the wall screen at the end of the room showing McCarter and his people closing in on the de Havilland as it landed. Their pursuit was only seconds behind.

"Got it," Kurtzman said. "They've got it zipped. I'll have it on-screen in two shakes."

"We've got it," Price told the British Intelligence man.

"Very good. Your people must be connected well to retrieve an electronic document so quickly."

"We try."

"Let me know when you're ready for a debriefing," Blakely said, "and I'll run your quarry down for you."

The monitor exploded into a handful of screens in a dossier utility that Price was familiar with. It came with an index, breaking the file down further into text, pictures and related files under names and organizations.

The picture of a thin, narrow-eyed man with slicked-back silver hair filled the screen. He sat at a table, in the shade of an umbrella, puffing on a cigarette in a long holder, his back to an iron-barred fence. The setting reminded Price of a French-styled outdoor bistro. Another table was also in the frame, showing a man and woman engaged in quiet conversation.

"Okay," Price said. "I'm ready."

More pictures flashed onto the screen as Kurtzman rummaged through the file. The man maintained the same relaxed appearance, dressing in casual elegance. One of the shots showed him at a racetrack, standing near a jockey and a horse. In that picture, a satisfied smile twisted his thin lips. With his beret in place and the plaid sports coat he wore, he looked like an aging landed gentry.

"Your quarry's name," Sir Blakely said, "is Percival Dickey. He's got quite an interesting little history."

"I'm listening," Price said, but her attention was riveted on the desperate escape Phoenix Force was pulling off in Myanmar.

"Tighten up the bloody line, lads," David McCarter growled over the headset built into the SIPE helmet. "Those blokes aren't going to wait up the taxi forever." He shifted on the rear of Encizo's Enduro.

The Cuban reacted, keeping the motorcycle under

control despite the redistribution of weight. The de Havilland sat on the level plain ahead of them, the exterior lights doused. The landing had been by instrument, and the takeoff would be by the same.

McCarter peered over his shoulder through the darkness. Calvin James was behind him, followed closely by Gary Manning. There was no sign of Hawkins.

The Briton keyed the Transmit button. "Five, this is One."

Only silence hung on the radio band for a moment, then it crackled as Hawkins came on. "I'm here, One. Just took a moment to leave a little surprise for the raiding party following us in."

"We don't exactly have time here," McCarter grated.

Hawkins's motorcycle came blasting around the last copse of trees that masked the clearing they were using for the pickup.

"It would have been even less time if they'd caught up with us," Hawkins replied.

Sudden lightning flared to life in the trees behind Hawkins. Only a half breath later, the sonic boom of the explosions followed.

"Should hold them up long enough," Hawkins commented. "I had a pressure detonator I thought would come in handy, and returning to base with C-4 left over kind of goes against the grain. Back in basic, I learned that the conservative guy was the one who got his ammo and rations cut the next day."

McCarter grinned. Hawkins had a lot of grit. It made a commanding officer handle him with a firm and steady hand, but it was the stuff outstanding soldiers were made of. McCarter had been on both sides of the equation.

Turning his gaze forward, the Phoenix Force leader checked the pursuit relayed on the helmet monitor via the satellite. The blips representing the mercenary force had reached a bottleneck in the pursuit. They were unjamming it now, getting vehicles rolling again, but they'd lost time and distance.

Encizo roared straight for the rear of the de Havilland. The crew aboard the cargo plane had been stripped. The mission had been strictly black ops, with risk to equipment and men cut down to the bare minimum. No lights were on inside the plane. The ramp in the tail section was open, dropped to the ground.

With less than seventy yards separating the Enduro from the de Havilland, McCarter could make out the two men standing in the open cargo hold. Both of them held 7.62 mm machine guns mounted on pintles and wore black uniforms.

Encizo cut the motorcycle's speed during the final approach, then twisted the throttle again to shove them up into the cargo area. McCarter lowered his feet from the pegs and took his own weight onto his legs, rocking for a moment to get rid of the momentum.

"Pilot," the Briton called over the headset.

"Yes, sir."

The Briton walked back to the mouth of the de Havilland's ramp. James roared by him, followed by Manning. Both joined Encizo in securing the bikes. "Get us moving."

"You've got one man outbound, sir," the pilot replied.

"I know that," McCarter said. "Get this crate moving. He'll make it."

"Yes, sir."

McCarter felt the engine vibration shudder powerfully through the big plane, which started rolling forward at once as the propellers bit into the wind. He grabbed a nearby support strut and steadied himself, watching Hawkins roar across the intervening distance.

Almost a hundred yards out, midway between the moving de Havilland and the line of trees beyond, the headlights of the Range Rovers suddenly whipped into view. Almost at once, explosions detonated on Hawkins's right, whipping up a funnel of dirt and force.

"Grenade launchers," Encizo said as he came to stand by McCarter.

The Briton nodded. "If we'd have stood still we'd have been a sitting duck."

"I know," Encizo said, "but it's going to make it tough for T.J. to make the relay."

"He'll do it. The kid can be insufferably cocky, but he's good."

The motorcycle bobbed and weaved across the terrain, losing ground speed as Hawkins took evasive action. The Range Rovers drew closer to Hawkins, their four-wheel-drives and greater weight having less trouble with the rough ground. The men handling the grenade launchers were getting the range now, too.

A big hole suddenly opened up in front of Hawkins, and for a second McCarter lost sight of the younger man as he was enveloped in a cloud of debris. Then Hawkins shot through the whirling maelstrom, jumping over the hole.

He pulled the Enduro back on track, roaring for the bouncing tail section of the de Havilland.

With the uneven terrain, the dropped tail section banged up and down as much as three feet.

Abruptly the cargo plane achieved lift, the forward

progress smoothing out entirely. McCarter hit the Transmit button. "Pilot."

"Sir?"

"Hold steady, mate. Not too far from the ground."

"We're running out of room," the pilot radioed back. "I've got a tree line that'll tear the undercarriage out from under this baby if I cut things too closely."

"Well, cut it as closely as you can," McCarter growled. Under his breath, he urged Hawkins on.

Staying low over the handlebars, Hawkins accelerated again, drawing closer. The tail section of the de Havilland slammed into the Enduro's front tire as Hawkins tried to negotiate the ramp.

The Enduro wobbled, and Hawkins fought for control as the Range Rovers closed.

"Damn," Manning swore beside McCarter.

The Briton unlimbered both the Browning Hi-Powers he carried. Bending slightly at the knees to steady himself against the plane's motion, he let out half a breath, then started squeezing the triggers. His bullets chopped into the lead pursuit vehicle. The machine gunner fell from the rear deck, and the man handling the grenade launcher from the passenger seat dropped back. The Range Rover's driver immediately took evasive action, nearly ramming into the vehicle on his left.

Hawkins's second attempt got him up onto the ramp, rocking like a child's toy. As he put out a leg to steady himself, Manning shot out a big hand and grabbed the front of Hawkins's BDUs. Powerfully built and set for the effort, the Canadian hauled Hawkins in.

"Button it up!" McCarter called. "And get us clear!"

"Yes, sir."

NO COST! NO OBLIGATION TO BUY! NO PURCHASE NECESSARY!

PLAY "LUCKY 7"
AND GET FIVE FREE GIFTS...

HOW TO PLAY:

1. With a coin, carefully scratch off the silver area at the right. Then check the claim chart to see what we have for you—FREE BOOKS and a gift—ALL YOURS! ALL FREE!

2. Send back this card and you'll get hot-off-the-press Gold Eagle books, never before published. These books have a total cover price of $18.50. But THEY ARE TOTALLY FREE, even the shipping will be at our expense!

3. There's no catch. You're under no obligation to buy anything. We charge nothing—ZERO—for your first shipment. And you don't have to make any minimum number of purchases—not even one!

4. The fact is thousands of readers enjoy receiving books by mail from the Gold Eagle Reader Service™. They like the convenience of home delivery... they like getting the best new novels before they're available in stores... and they love our discount prices!

5. We hope that after receiving your free books you'll want to remain a subscriber. But the choice is yours—to continue or cancel, anytime at all! So why not take us up on our invitation, with no risk of any kind. You'll be glad you did!

THE GOLD EAGLE READER SERVICE: HERE'S HOW IT WORKS

Accepting free books places you under no obligation to buy anything. You may keep the books and gift and return the shipping statement marked "cancel". If you do not cancel, about a month later we will send you four additional novels, and bill you just $15.80—that's a saving of 15% off the cover price of all four books! And there's no extra charge for shipping! You may cancel at any time, but if you choose to continue, every other month we'll send you four more books, which you may either purchase at the discount price…or return to us and cancel your subscription.

*Terms and prices subject to change without notice. Sales tax applicable in N.Y.

If offer card is missing, write to: Gold Eagle Reader Service, 3010 Walden Ave., P.O. Box 1867, Buffalo, NY 14240-1867

BUSINESS REPLY MAIL
FIRST-CLASS MAIL   PERMIT NO. 717   BUFFALO, NY

POSTAGE WILL BE PAID BY ADDRESSEE

GOLD EAGLE READER SERVICE
3010 WALDEN AVE
PO BOX 1867
BUFFALO NY 14240-9952

NO POSTAGE
NECESSARY
IF MAILED
IN THE
UNITED STATES

"Lock in and strap down," McCarter ordered his teammates.

The de Havilland's engines screamed as they powered to push the big plane into the air at a steeper incline than was safe. For a moment, listening to the engines lugging down, feeling the plane trying to go perpendicular, McCarter thought it was going to stall.

Then the big aircraft leveled off, and the noise of the straining engines went away.

CHAPTER SEVENTEEN

"Phoenix One, this is Stony Base," Price called over the headset.

"Go, Base. You have Phoenix One." McCarter released the cargo straps they'd rigged to hold them during takeoff. He crossed the cargo space, leaning into the slight incline the aircraft maintained as it sought the altitude it needed. They'd stay low, avoiding the Myanmar military radar as much as they could while they streaked for the Bay of Bengal.

"That was closer than we'd planned," Price said.

"No kidding." McCarter doffed the SIPE helmet but disengaged the headset and kept it on. By the time he'd reached the pilot's cabin, Hawkins joined him. The other three members of the team busied themselves with stripping down the weapons and gear, cleaning the equipment and oiling it. "Did you get a line on those blokes?"

The cabin area was generous. The de Havilland had been specially redesigned for use by black-ops crews, from military personnel, special forces, CIA and other clandestine missions. Nearly double the space needed for the normal plane crew existed within the cabin now.

Back of the control area was a computer-communications area. The de Havilland's satellite receivers kept it in constant contact with HQ, whatever HQ was overseeing it at the time.

Hawkins slid into the chair bolted to the floor in front of the computer station. McCarter stood over him, resting his arms against the low bulkhead. He ached from the abrasions and contusions he'd managed to get while heading off the convoy.

"We've got more than a line on them," Price said. "Do you feel like making a stop back on your way to the Farm?"

"Thinking of throwing another monkey wrench into the works?"

"Yes."

"I've got to hand it to you. When you start twisting the tail of the cat, you don't like to let go until you get every kink."

Hawkins tapped the keyboard, bringing up the computer. The screen popped on, bringing up the special template Kurtzman had designed for cybernetic operations in the field. The safeguards the cybernetics expert had installed in the software and the hardware were intensive, and new updates were constantly coming through. The computers were a liability, as well as a bonus. If one could be taken during a mission, and subsequently accessed, the intel could be damaging on a number of fronts. He pulled on a headset and glanced up at McCarter.

"We're ready here," the Phoenix Force leader said. He glanced ahead, seeing nothing but dark sky through the cockpit. If there'd been any kind of pursuit, the crew would have notified him.

"We turned up a probable contact for the mercenary team you encountered on the ground."

McCarter glanced back at the computer monitor. A

picture formed in the upper-right quadrant of the screen. The man was thin, with narrow, close-set eyes and silver hair that he brushed back.

"His name is Percival Dickey," Price said. "I'm going to give you an abbreviated version. The file you're getting now has quite a lot of information you'll find useful. You'll have time to look before you get to him."

The left side of the screen quickly scrolled down, listing text that was linked to embedded pictures. McCarter's quick scan showed him that the intel was of a business, financial and personal nature. From the way the package was put together, he guessed that the intel Price had gathered had come by way of British Intelligence. The format was similar.

"We just got our hands on this," the Stony Man mission controller said, "so we're still actively breaking it down and assimilating it ourselves. As we get information that you'll find pertinent, we'll give you updates. Likewise any information we collect that we haven't acquired as yet."

"Good enough, Base." McCarter nodded at Hawkins, who turned the program over to Kurtzman's or Price's control at the other end of the sat-link. "How was Dickey connected with tonight's exercise?"

"We're guessing that the mercenary team was fielded by him," Price replied.

"Someone else picked up the tab?"

"Yes. We're starting a prelim investigation of Dickey's financial dealings with help in London. Once we get in there deep enough, we're expecting a link with our main target. Dickey's very creative with his cash flow, but he's been under investigation for a long time."

"Affirmative, Base. What are you looking for from us?"

"A black-bag operation," the mission controller replied. "Once we find out where Dickey is, we want him to answer some questions."

Hawkins hooked up the digital camera that Calvin James had given to him. "We're ready to download the pictures that were taken."

A window opened on the screen. McCarter wasn't familiar with the utility that logged on, but he knew it was downloading the stored pictures from the digital camera. Just as quickly as it formed on the screen, the utility dropped to the menu bar across the bottom of the screen and continued to run in the background.

"Do you know where to start looking for our target?" McCarter asked.

"From what we've learned, Dickey has three vacation homes besides his residence in London. However, it's our feeling that the contract was taken out in Great Britain, since most of the mercenaries appear to be from there. The men you went up against in Myanmar weren't amateurs."

"No," McCarter agreed, "they weren't."

"I think we'll find Dickey still in London," Price said. "Those men would expect payment transferred at the completion of their mission. Dickey's base of operations is in London."

The computer kept cycling through pictures. McCarter tagged some of them mentally. All of the team would have a chance to look at them in the next few hours. "Any extrapolation on the object of the mission here in Myanmar?"

"The cargo you were after was running heavier than

we'd been told to expect,'' Price reported. ''Maybe two or three times as much heroin as we'd believed.''

''That would be my guess, as well.'' McCarter remembered the wrecked trucks strewed at the bottom of the chasm, all the deadly cargo spilled over the site.

''Kesar Grishin approached the Golden Triangle warlords several months ago about handling money for them, and possibly arranging shipping for a percentage. We received that information from CIA covert sources within those organizations.''

''I take it Grishin was turned down.''

''In a flat second.''

''No honor among thieves,'' Hawkins commented.

McCarter smiled. ''No trust, at any rate.''

''Grishin's trust quotient has gotten considerably higher since that time, though,'' Price stated. ''With the information turned up through Striker's mission earlier, we've been able to tie more pieces of his business together than we'd previously even thought about. From the appearance of things there, he's got some of the Golden Triangle warlords letting him handle their finances behind the backs of the others.''

''Industrious chap,'' McCarter quipped.

''Yes. Your attack on the convoy was designed to stir up trouble, to make the opium warlords think Grishin or one of his compatriots had moved against them.''

''And maybe they'd respond in kind, disrupting whatever tenuous hold Grishin has managed in the area.'' It was a plan that McCarter completely agreed with, given the present political state of the opium industry. The warlords had access to a growing market, and any of them could produce enough raw stock to make millions of dollars—if they weren't in direct competition with each other.

"Yes."

"The attack tonight by the mercs would have achieved the same end," McCarter said. "So Grishin wasn't afraid of forcing the issue."

"No," Price admitted, "but here's where Grishin's machinations tonight get cute. Take a look at the computer monitor."

McCarter directed his attention to the screen. In the midst of the pictures and text files downloading on Dickey, a window surfaced and expanded. He squinted, but still couldn't see it clearly. "It's too dark to make out."

"Wait just a moment," Price said.

The picture began to change, lightening by degrees.

"They're adjusting the gamma correction," Hawkins explained.

In only seconds, the picture was clear enough to see what had been hidden. Black material draped the jungle floor, the letters DEA stamped in white across it. Another few seconds, and it took on the aspects of a flak jacket lying on the ground.

"Those men weren't DEA," Hawkins said.

"No," Price agreed.

"Grishin's mercs salted the mine," Hawkins stated.

McCarter watched as the screen cleared. More pictures formed, showing three other DEA-type jackets and vests. Two of them were attached to dead men.

"These corpses?" the Briton asked.

"DEA agents," Price confirmed. "We've infiltrated the DEA branch working the Golden Triangle area. Three men are listed as MIA in Thailand."

"When did they go missing?" McCarter asked.

"Days ago."

The Phoenix Force leader studied the dead men. "We missed them."

"There was no chance at rescue," Price told him. "The satellite shots we've taken of them lead us to believe they were already dead. There wasn't enough blood on the ground, and they had weak infrared signatures, indicating their body temperatures were already low. They were killed somewhere else and brought in."

"The in-country team killed the DEA agents while en route with the convoy," Hawkins said.

"That's what I'm guessing," Price replied.

"Grishin planned to use the presence of the dead DEA agents as leverage against the warlords who wouldn't go along with his organization," McCarter said. "With them discovered there, they'd think the DEA was ready to start direct strikes against their operations. Grishin could have stepped in, offered to up their intelligence network and take care of transportation and cash flow."

"That's what we believe."

McCarter looked at the dead men and put himself past wondering who they'd been and how much their families would miss them. "You say these men were taken from Thailand."

"That's correct."

"Did they have any prior contact with Myanmar? If these men can't be connected with the effort in Myanmar, maybe some doubt could be spread through the warlords. Some of Grishin's influence could be taken away in that manner."

"All three of these men have prior histories with Myanmar operations. We have to assume the third man is on the ground there somewhere and we've missed him.''

"Unless he was the one who sold the other two out," Hawkins said quietly.

"Possibly."

"It wouldn't matter," McCarter argued. "Two bodies or three. The surface damage is the same. Khun Sa and the others are going to believe their convoy was attacked by the American DEA on a covert mission." It wasn't that far removed from their own initiative. Except that their efforts could never have been traced back to the United States. "What about damage control? Those blokes lost quite a few men themselves."

Choppy video footage scrolled across the screen. Black-clad forms raced through the jungle. As McCarter watched, one of the men picked up a similarly dressed man. The extremities drifted loosely, akimbo, letting the Phoenix Force leader know they belonged to a corpse.

"They're recovering their dead," Price said. "There's a chance they'll have the area clean. All that the Myanmar military will be able to confirm is that a large contingent of men were in the area."

McCarter knew Phoenix's own five-man band wouldn't have left the swath of destruction in their wake that the mercs had. A small, experienced team operated with surgical precision. "How soon before the Myanmar military arrives?"

"An hour at least," the mission controller said. "They're going in more slowly. When your plane took off, they tracked it for a time. Now they're scouring the brush, closing in the parameters."

"What are the chances of the mercenaries having the area scrubbed before the military arrives?"

"Good."

The de Havilland's engines cut back, and McCarter felt the plane sink into its final leveling-off groove. "So all the Myanmar military will be able to report is that a band of covert DEA agents took down the convoy."

"Right," Price said. "And that's when we believe Grishin's inside people will start working on the Myanmar warlords who haven't capitulated."

"What do you want to bet that some of the bureaucrats inside the Myanmar government who're fronting for the Golden Triangle interests don't pony up and put pressure on those same warlords?" Hawkins asked.

"No bet," the mission controller said. "Grishin's played this one close to the vest. And our own involvement there has only added fuel to the fire."

"Maybe," McCarter replied. "But Grishin couldn't have counted on us making some of his boys. We do have that card to play."

"We're going to have to make the most of it," Price said.

"When we get to merry old England, we'll see about rocking his world again."

"The package I'm putting together for your team in England is only going to be transitory," Price stated. "There'll be no protection, no backing from any law-enforcement body there."

"It's okay," McCarter said. "Slipping in through the cracks keeps us moving lively."

"You've got some downtime with the trip back to Great Britain. Make the most of it. I'll try to make arrangements so you can get some sleep. You'll have to equip yourselves once you're in-country."

"No problem," McCarter said. "I still know a number of chaps who do business under the table and owe me.''

Price broke the connection, but the computer continued cycling, storing data.

McCarter clapped Hawkins on the shoulder. "I'll leave you with it while I go fill in the blokes in the rear.''

Hawkins nodded.

Stepping back into the main cargo area, McCarter shifted his attention to Gary Manning. The big Canadian tossed him a can of Coke from one of the military ice chests that had been stocked with supplies for the mission. McCarter caught the drink, felt it ice-cold and wet against his skin.

He cracked the seal, taking time to breathe in the released fumes. "Ah, now that's an ambrosia that'll put the lead back in a man's pencil.'' He drank deeply, then fired up a Player's cigarette.

"So what's the score?'' James asked, wiping his hands on a red grease rag. "Are we making the jump to the Caribbean?''

"After a short side trip," McCarter said. In a few terse sentences, he brought them up to speed concerning Percival Dickey in London.

When he finished, Rafael Encizo said, "You have to think about the repercussions of what has gone on tonight.''

McCarter looked at his teammate. Encizo usually was a man of few words, but the ones he said carried a lot of weight.

"You need to consider that Grishin knows someone's knocking on his door," Encizo said. "He probably knows about Striker's action against the bank in Palm Beach, and he probably knows about the action here in Myanmar—or will know about it soon. With everything we know about Grishin, he's not the kind of guy to go on the defensive."

"Right," Manning said. "A man like Grishin is going to want to knock the wheels off somewhere else, get a little buyback for his pound of flesh."

"At this point," Encizo said, "all Grishin knows is that he's been invaded by the FBI. He's going to want to seek redress for that. And his chief opportunity for revenge is going to be the DEA agents in the Caribbean theater."

"That's why Striker's down there," McCarter stated. The plan was for Phoenix Force to join Bolan on the islands and begin to put pressure on Grishin's home front. "If anyone knows how to keep those people off balance, he's the bloke who can pull it off."

"If that's all of it," Encizo said, "I wouldn't be too concerned. Striker can keep them busy until we get there, but what I'm wondering is what else Grishin may have up his sleeve. He has that party on the yacht tomorrow night, and Escelera's escorting a package of his herself. And from her dossier, we know she *never* leaves her turf. I don't think we can count him out yet."

"We're not, Rafe. This trip we're taking to England, we're just going to turn up the heat some more. Every move Grishin makes now, we're going to feel it. And I think you're right, but we're going to have to wait and see what we can leverage."

Encizo nodded.

"T.J. is getting the files from the Farm," McCarter said. "As soon as we have it, we'll take a look, see what we have on our plates."

"Did anyone ever figure out where Grishin was?" James asked.

McCarter shook his head. And that was a sixty-four-dollar question. The man had put together the following night's meeting, yet he wasn't around any of his usual haunts. The Briton was seasoned enough in his craft to know that didn't bode well.

CHAPTER EIGHTEEN

"They're in the hallway," Rosario Blancanales said. He stared at the high-resolution screen of the notebook computer sitting on the small breakfast table on the patio balcony of the hotel room.

"Almost done," Hermann Schwarz called back from inside the room.

Blancanales remained calm and cool despite the tension filling him. Together, he and Schwarz had been in a number of dangerous situations over the years. If they were caught inside Chela Escelera's hotel room, there was a very good chance he and Schwarz would be dead men in very short order.

He toggled the notebook computer's controls, accessing the pull-down menus in the observation templates Kurtzman had rigged for the surveillance mission. His cellular phone created substantial weight in his coverall pockets. There'd been no contact with Lyons since the brief call from Playa de los Muertos, although Kurtzman had checked in to assure them everything had gone well at that end.

The morning sun baked down onto the city now, banishing the cool breezes sweeping in from the coastline. The marinas and shipping anchorages were only a few hundred feet away. The sounds of the big freighters and cargo ships cut through the noise the morning traffic generated.

The computer screen cleared, dividing automatically into quadrants. The microcamera viewpoints were numbered in the upper-left-hand corner of each quadrant, followed by a time-date stamp that counted off the recorded footage in tenths of seconds.

Blancanales tripped the sysops utility, setting the program into motion on a subsystems and analysis routine. The primary cameras quickly flipped through the rooms in the hotel suite on a two-second delay. Blancanales knew the rooms by heart, from the blueprints Price and Kurtzman had forwarded from the Farm, and from the experience Able Team had had that morning.

All the rooms were furnished lavishly and remained pristine despite the bugging devices they'd installed. The actual trick had been to leave the bugs already in place from the local law enforcement and the DEA without alerting those agencies that they were on the premises.

The problem they currently faced, and the one Schwarz was endeavoring to solve now, was in the living-room area, where the reception from two of the five minicams had been fouled by the electrical lines running through the suite.

They'd managed to finesse one minicam by relying on the reflection of the room from the desired angle through a large, decorative mirror covering one of the walls. Kurtzman had layered in another utility to the programming to reverse the effects of the mirror, making it possible for them to observe the room directly without seeing everything in the reverse.

The second problem had required rewiring the electrical delivery to the suite. In the end, Schwarz had decided there'd been no other choice. Escelera's impromptu departure from the schedule to dispose of the DEA deep-cover operative had provided enough time.

Blancanales hoped. He tapped the keyboard and flicked the mouse, selecting the control number that locked in the hallway minicams. "Gadgets, we've got to move, or we're going to blow all the time we've got in here."

Schwarz didn't reply.

Blancanales blew out a short breath. Schwarz could get locked into a project, ignoring everything else that went on around him. It was a good trait to have, but it was a dangerous one in the right circumstances. Or rather, Blancanales amended, the *wrong* circumstances.

And these were definitely the wrong circumstances; Escelera was returning. Her escort included three personal bodyguards, plus four more men. Blancanales knew them from the Stony Man Farm files. Two of the men were local talent that Escelera kept in Puerto Vallarta. The other two were deeply involved in the political scene inside the city, giving her information on police operations. All of them were killers.

One of the bodyguards took the lead as they neared the door. As he pulled a key-card from a wallet inside his suit jacket, his shoulder holster was briefly visible.

Blancanales closed the notebook computer, disconnected the second cellular phone from the modem and stashed everything in the duffel sitting on the patio table. He shouldered the duffel and drew the silenced Beretta 92-S from the shoulder rig under his coverall. Stepping back into the room, he watched Schwarz put a light fixture back into place on the wall.

"I had to work with this one," Schwarz said. "Every time I attached this fixture to the backup wire

I ran, it threw the breaker. I never did figure out why." He tugged on the pull chain. The light came on, holding steady. "So I put it on a direct-current power supply instead of the alternating one." He turned the light off, then reached for the lamp shade. "As long as they don't use the light so much they drain the battery, we're in the clear."

Blancanales crossed the room and took up the large cloth bag Schwarz had used to hold debris from his work. Wiring and alligator clips littered the small coffee table near the light fixture, mixed in with cutters, screwdrivers and pliers. Blancanales held the bag open and swept it all inside. Then he tagged the headset's Transmit button, opening the frequency to Stony Man Farm.

"Stony Base, this is Able Two."

"Go, Able Two," Kurtzman replied. "You have Stony Base."

"I need a delay," Blancanales said, pulling the drawstring on the cloth bag tight." Maybe jam the electronic reader to the room, block the swipe card." Blancanales spotted tailings from the wire cuttings, hard black plastic chips against the sculpted blue carpet. He picked them up.

"I can do it once," Kurtzman said. "Any more than that, it may not be regarded as a fluke."

Blancanales focused on the door, hearing the voices out in the hall. "If they catch us here, there's no chance Escelera will think it's a fluke. Do it."

The door shuddered as someone leaned against it and jerked the door handle. "Damned key didn't work," a man said in Spanish.

Blancanales headed for the patio doors, Schwarz at his heels. He closed the heavy draperies behind them, hoping Escelera wouldn't notice or would blame the inattention to the hotel maid service.

"Try it again," Escelera ordered.

Once outside, Blancanales shut the patio doors. Schwarz clambered over the balcony railing.

"Not a problem," Schwarz said. "Only have a ten-foot drop to the balcony below."

"Go." Blancanales used lock picks to secure the patio-door latch. It clicked into place.

"I'm gone," Schwarz replied. A moment later, a thump sounded below.

Blancanales didn't think it was loud enough to be heard inside the hotel suite, especially over the dull roar of the air-conditioning. He crossed the patio, making certain the patio furniture was back in place. Then he paused at the railing, looking down. What he saw didn't make him happy.

Schwarz had been right about the ten-foot drop to the balcony below. What Gadgets hadn't mentioned was the four-story drop that awaited if he missed. Cars moved along rapidly in the four-lane street below.

"Damn," Blancanales said, levering himself over the side of the patio.

The headset came to life in his ear. "Escelera and her people are inside the suite," Kurtzman said.

Slithering down the outside of the balcony, Blancanales tossed the cloth bag to Schwarz. The room below was empty. They'd already checked on it, even though this was to be the last possible escape route. He swung his body when he was at the bottom of the balcony, supporting his weight with his arms.

The patio door above him opened.

Trying not to think about the street four stories below, Blancanales swung his body forward and released his hold. He kept his feet under him, making less noise when he landed than Schwarz had. The duffel across his shoulder thudded against his body.

Schwarz put away his lock picks and shoved the patio doors open.

Blancanales hustled inside after his teammate. He didn't want to think about the possibility that one of the DEA surveillance teams had spotted them leaving Escelera's suite. Word would get back to the drug czarina in short order.

Less than three minutes later, they were in the outside hall headed for their room on one of the lower floors. Blancanales tapped the Transmit button on the headset. "Stony Base, this is Able Two."

"Go, Able Two."

"How's the situation on the open house?"

"Open," Kurtzman replied. "We're operational."

"Good to know. Call us if anything develops?"

"You'll be the next to know."

Montego Bay, Jamaica

"SO, WHO'S THE GUY we're going to see?"

Mack Bolan flagged a waiting cab at the curbside in front of Donald Sangster International Airport. The cabbie flicked off his light and moved forward, green and white paint gleaming with droplets of the remnants of the tropical storm still passing through the islands. Away from the covered area, rain still fell. Jack Grimaldi, Stony Man's ace pilot, moved easily at Bolan's side.

"A guy named Edgar Joule," the soldier answered as he moved to put his luggage in the trunk.

"He supplies hardware."

Grimaldi's nod assured Bolan that he understood exactly what kind of hardware Joule would be distributing. They'd come to the island without weapons. Price had offered Joule's name in the package she'd forwarded to them after the raid in Palm Beach. The Executioner had studied Joule's career on the flight over, scanning the lines of type and the assorted pictures that had been included, then moving onto his main target. Over the years, Joule had been used by the CIA and was a snitch for the local law enforcement. Truly a rogue in the seamy side of Montego Bay, Joule wouldn't have anyone to run interference for him.

Bolan dropped into the rear seat of the cab. He wore gray pleated trousers and a loose vermilion sports shirt over a light gray tank top. His loose shirttails covered both his money belt and the folding combat knife he'd taken from his luggage inside the airport building after clearing the security areas. Wraparound sunglasses protected his eyes from the tropical sun.

The cabbie was a heavyset white guy with a peeling sunburn and a faded football jersey that had the sleeves ripped off. His red hair clung to his bowling-ball head in sweaty bunches. "Damned heat and humidity," he complained as he adjusted his rearview mirror so he could look over his passengers. "It'll get you every time. Where can I take you?"

Bolan gave him the address.

The cabbie eased into the traffic, threading his way through the maze of arriving and departing cabs. He cut one man off and drew a salvo of indignant honking in his wake. He shoved a thick, meaty arm through the window and flipped the bird at the driver behind him.

Bolan's gaze swept the traffic area out of habit. No one knew about the mission he was on, but it wouldn't have been too hard to imagine someone stationed at the airport to pick up information about private arrivals. There were guys who probably picked up front money from burglars looking for marks.

Grimaldi also surveyed the field. He was dressed like a tourist, sporting a loud shirt, sandals and wraparound sunglasses.

"This your first time here?" The cabbie's voice had a curious lilt to it, like he'd been down in the islands long enough to pick up some of the West Indies speech patterns.

"No," Bolan replied.

The man nodded. "Reason I asked, that address you gave me is in a pretty rough part of town. I figured maybe you guys were buying into some hand-me-down information about Mo' Bay." He flicked a quick glance at them in the rearview mirror. "If you're looking for girls, I thought I could fix you up at a safer place."

"No," Bolan said.

"A lot of first-timers to the area," the cabbie went on, switching lanes, "they end up getting in over their heads before they know it."

"If we do that," Grimaldi replied, "you'll be the first guy we call."

The driver checked the rearview mirror. "No need to be a smart-ass about it."

Grimaldi pushed his face closer to the driver. "I don't like people who pry. If you want to drive, drive. Otherwise, put us out and we'll take another cab."

The driver got the message.

Bolan ignored the exchange, concentrating on the feel of the city. It would be dusk before long, and the nightlife would start. If Dionis Santos didn't check in at his usual spots and if Joule didn't have an idea where the man was, the soldier would have no choice but to attempt to get the information he needed from another source. He wasn't sure that was possible.

According to the files, Jamaica wasn't Kesar Grishin's base of operations. Grishin's mansion and estate were down in Nevis. But the Russian had definitely sown some seeds in Jamaica. Santos was one of the last and the biggest local crime lords who hadn't knuckled under to Grishin or pressure from the Colombians.

Bolan settled back in the cab and tried to enjoy the air-conditioning. Thoughts of the organization that Grishin commanded, of how big it could be, kept intruding, making him feel even more restless.

The situation in the Caribbean was shaping up to be a powder keg.

CHAPTER NINETEEN

Philadelphia, Pennsylvania

"There he is."

Without being obvious, Yakov Katzenelenbogen altered his stance, leaning heavily on the cane he didn't need. Anyone watching him would have thought he shifted only to find a position that offered greater comfort. "I see him."

"Guy's something else, isn't he?" John Kissinger asked. Tall and broad across the shoulders with narrow hips, he looked good in the dark suit he wore, but without his usual casual clothing, he didn't look at all like himself to anyone who knew him.

"The man has no conscience." Katz surveyed their quarry dispassionately. The Israeli wore a light gray suit and a matching beret, a blue carnation in his lapel that matched the color of his shirt. Age had turned his hair silver-gray, but his eyes were deep blue and clear. He held on to the wooden cane with his left hand. His right arm was prosthetic from the elbow down, a result of one of the wars that had ravaged his adopted homeland.

Alexander DeCapra stood inside a small knot of elegantly clad women. A handful of men stood just back of the women, wearing suits. DeCapra was in entertainment mode, his white smile flashing, his long-fingered hands accompanying his words, emphasizing the punch lines.

DeCapra was at a party for the socially advantaged, deep in the old-money section of the City of Brotherly Love. The estate was huge, including a main house and three guest houses. The party had gathered around the pool area, sandwiched in a generous allotment of space between the riding stables and tennis courts.

The house belonged to Michael Charteris, a financier who skated legalities across nations. He was a developer, a builder and an investor. He could walk into either house of Congress and call senators and representatives by their first names and get a glad handshake in return.

With the business and connections the man had, it was no surprise to Katz that Charteris should be involved with the East Coast Families. Charteris was also very good at keeping a low profile in his business. If it hadn't been for Leo Turrin's inside scoop on the Mafia, even Stony Man wouldn't have had as much dirt on Charteris as it had.

Charteris stood near DeCapra, soaking up the overflow of attention the younger man was receiving from the female audience. Charteris, in his early sixties, stood ramrod straight. He kept in shape from arduous exercise on the handball and tennis courts. One of the reasons he was so fond of DeCapra was that DeCapra knew how to lose well to him without seeming to give the game away. That had been in the file, as well, by way of Turrin's resources.

Katz shifted again, aware of the four bodyguards that accompanied DeCapra. The men were Mafia, as was

DeCapra, but they were good at their jobs. Dressed in tailored suits that hid the guns they wore, with micro-earphones and pencil-thin mikes strapped to their off thumbs, they looked like Secret Service men.

"DeCapra's going to be hard to catch alone," Kissinger commented. "We'd have been better off busting a cap on this guy from a distance."

"No," Katz said quietly. "I want him alive when we leave."

"I know."

The parameters for the operation were that DeCapra be prevented from attending the party Kesar Grishin was hosting off the coast of Jamaica. If necessary, the man could be terminated. Katz didn't intend to see it come to that. Both he and Kissinger had killed in cold blood. It was something a soldier did when the occasion warranted, and when it would keep an operation or teammate from harm.

DeCapra had no defense. The man had killed, in hot blood and in cold. And Katz had no doubt that De-Capra would kill again. If left to his own devices, prob-ably the Israeli would have killed the man and been done with it. That would have ensured the mafioso wouldn't have made the trip to the Caribbean. But the order had come from Barbara Price, who—Katz had sensed—wasn't entirely comfortable with the possibil-ity of terminating DeCapra. The man wasn't the kind of target Stony Man Farm usually pursued. DeCapra was strictly small-time, and not a national threat, not someone who had the power to harm dozens or hun-dreds of people if left unchecked. He was someone the legal system should take care of.

As such, Katz knew the man's death would weigh heavily on Price's mind. He'd seen it happen before.

And the thing that made the mission controller so good at her job was that she remained able to see the different degrees necessary in her job. The Israeli intended that she should keep as much of that view intact as was possible.

Katz took a dry martini from a passing waiter. For an ice-cream social, as the engraved invitations had promised, the event was spectacularly catered. Long tables laden with food and desserts were manned by wait staff, girls with California tans and men who could have worked as exotic dancers.

He glanced at DeCapra again, watching the man work his crowd. The women laughed readily, and Charteris clapped him on the back like a favorite son.

"I doubt," Kissinger said in a low voice, "if Charteris would feel the same way toward DeCapra if he knew the guy was occasionally sleeping with his wife."

"I agree." Katz sipped the martini, watching De-Capra.

Edi Charteris slowly, quietly and finally got DeCapra all to herself, ushering her husband off to attend to the party-goers. From his position, Katz was able to put together enough of the conversation to know what was going on. Twining her arm within DeCapra's, Edi Charteris started her escort down the stone-lined path that led to the riding stables.

"Showtime," Kissinger said, placing his empty beer stein on one of the small round tables that had been set out for guests. "I'll meet you around back. I spotted another trail that comes out around the south end."

Katz nodded. He finished his drink, giving the Stony Man weapons specialist time to work through the crowd and disappear. From the way Edi Charteris had been hanging on to DeCapra's arm, they weren't expecting to return to the party soon. Even DeCapra's bodyguards had lagged behind.

Katz left his empty glass with a waitress and drifted along in DeCapra's wake. The trail to the riding stables was beautifully landscaped, and the noonday sun kept the shadows from the trees at bay, allowing the ground cover its full glory. A scent of pine lingered in the air, but was quickly eradicated by the smell of the horses.

The stables were located at the bottom of a short hill. Katz leaned on his cane for the benefit of any watchers as he made his way down the short, steep flight of steps to the stables. The trees had been thinned out to the right, in front of the paddocks, revealing a corral.

DeCapra wasn't in sight, but his bodyguards were. Two of them lounged in front of the main entrance into the paddocks. The other two leaned against the railing and watched the half-dozen horses trotting around inside the corral.

Katz made his way laboriously to the corral. He looked out over the horses and nodded and smiled to himself, like a man who was satisfied with what he was seeing. Reaching under his jacket, he took out a pack of unfiltered Camel cigarettes and shook one out. He put the pack away and reached for his lighter, listening to the approaching footsteps of one of the bodyguards.

"Let me get that for you, Pop."

Katz looked up at the taller man, who held out a flaming lighter. "Thank you." He cupped his hand over the lighter and inhaled through his cigarette. Once the tobacco was burning properly, he pulled his head back and breathed out a satisfied stream of smoke.

The bodyguard's eyes roved over the area, then returned to Katz. "You got some business down here, Pop?"

"Merely taking in the air," Katz replied. He gestured toward the horses. "Fine animals. I was told about them by Mr. Charteris, so I thought I'd come see them for myself."

The bodyguard nodded. "I was thinking you might find a better time later."

"I was thinking of leaving the party," Katz replied. "There'll be no time later."

"Yeah." The bodyguard pinned him with his gaze. "Then maybe there'll be a next time."

Katz ignored the hard look in the man's eyes, smiling easily. "Maybe you're right." He hooked his cane over his prosthesis, rebuttoning his jacket and smoothing it out. He also removed the forefinger of the glove from his prosthesis. Tucked up inside the aluminum and plastic limb was a CO_2-powered tranquilizer pistol. The darts were scarcely three inches in length, but they packed enough anesthetic to put a man down in seconds.

The bodyguard looked away for a moment, his attention drawn elsewhere. His left hand drew up to touch the microreceiver in his ear. "Get that asshole out of there. Now."

Casually Katz turned his attention toward the paddock area. Kissinger walked through the paddock from the other end of the breezeway. The two bodyguards stepped into the breezeway after him, their hands going beneath their coats.

With an economy of motion, Kissinger swung a short pole at the lead man. The pole looked like the handle of a shovel or pitchfork. When it connected with the bodyguard's temple, the man folded up like an accordion. Before the second man could react, Kissinger knocked the gun from his hand and was on him.

"Shit," the bodyguard in front of Katz snarled. "Paulie, get over here!" He started forward.

Katz trapped the man's hand against his side, leaning in against him unexpectedly. He brought up the prosthesis and fired a dart into the man's throat.

The bodyguard's eyes bulged, and he clawed at the dart with his free hand. He stared at Katz as if he couldn't believe it. The feathered dart twitched, lodged deep into flesh. He tried to talk, but couldn't force the words out. Katz kept his gun hand blocked as the man drifted into unconsciousness.

Stepping around the man, Katz took aim at the remaining bodyguard and fired three more darts. Two of them sunk into the man's face, and one of them caught him in the throat. He went down coughing, then passed out.

When Katz turned back to the breezeway, he spotted Kissinger standing above the two unconscious bodyguards. The Israeli hurried over. He unfastened the cuff of his shirt, then pushed up his jacket and sleeve to bare the prosthesis to midforearm. Unblemished vinyl was revealed. He pried at the arm just two inches back from the wrist and pulled the cunningly concealed plug from the surface. Sticking his fingers inside the prosthesis, he pulled the depleted wheel-shaped cartridge cylinder from the CO_2 gun. He took a second cylinder from a reservoir inside the arm and reloaded, flexing the muscles inside his stump to engage it again.

Kissinger had the lead, walking back toward the center of the paddocks. He hooked a thumb at a door beside a line of saddles. He kept his voice quiet. "They went in here."

"Locked?"

Kissinger tried the door, slowly. "Yeah."

"There can't be much holding it."

"No." Kissinger braced himself against the door. "Whenever you're ready."

Katz braced the prosthesis in his good hand. He stepped toward the door, staying two yards back. "I'm ready."

Kissinger hit the door with his shoulder, driving it off its hinges and ripping the lock free. He went low, giving Katz room to fire over him.

Inside the room, DeCapra stood against the opposite wall of the small room. Edi Charteris faced the wall, her back to DeCapra. The mafioso whipped his head around.

"What the hell is this?" DeCapra demanded. He dropped the hemline of Edi Charteris's dress and reached for his pants.

"John," Katz said in a monotone.

Kissinger moved, intercepting DeCapra easily. He dropped a big hand over the man's shoulder, pulling him around. Levering an arm under DeCapra's chin and against his throat, the Stony Man armorer drove his captive against the wall.

"Oh, my God!" Edi Charteris said breathlessly. She wiped at her hair, trying to push it back into shape, and tried to smooth her dress over her hips at the same time. "Alex?"

Katz stepped forward. Part of him felt sorry for the woman, for the position they were going to leave her in after they were finished with DeCapra. But she'd been unfaithful to her husband long before they'd arrived. Without saying a word to her, the Israeli shot her in her exposed legs. The twisted pantyhose proved no defense against the darts.

"You son of a bitch!" the woman shrilled, stumbling in disbelief as she stared at the feathered darts in her thighs. "You shot me!" Before she could take another step, she toppled forward and remained still.

Katz turned his attention to DeCapra. It wouldn't be long before someone spotted the bodyguards lying against the corral.

DeCapra tried to break away. Kissinger leaned into his hold a little more enthusiastically, lifting the mafioso from his feet and keeping him pinned against the wall.

"What the hell do you guys want?" DeCapra demanded.

"Someone doesn't like you very much," Katz said, moving closer and unlimbering the cane.

"Somebody hire you to do this?" DeCapra squirmed and reached a hand toward Kissinger's forearm.

He slapped the hand away. "Yeah."

DeCapra swallowed hard. "I can pay you more."

Kissinger kept his gaze flat and hard, focusing on the man. "Don't know. Got paid pretty good for this."

Katz swapped ends with the cane, gripping it by the bottom. Letting DeCapra think the attack was vengeance motivated would help keep the heat off Leo Turrin. "How much?"

Kissinger turned his attention to Katz, giving the impression that he might disagree with the question even being asked.

"Plenty," DeCapra said.

"What do you have on you?" Katz asked.

"Eight, nine thousand," DeCapra said. "Maybe ten, if you don't mind some small bills."

Katz shook his head. Kissinger slammed DeCapra back against the wall.

"Wait, wait!" DeCapra bellowed. Fear turned his face white.

"Speak more quietly," Katz commanded.

DeCapra nodded. When he spoke again, his voice was even softer, trying not to offend. "I said ten grand, right? We can push it more toward twenty if I throw in my Rolex watch and these rings I'm wearing." He pulled his sleeve back to reveal the watch.

Katz looked at Kissinger. "What about the watch?"

Kissinger made a show of inspecting it. "Jewels. Doesn't look like a knockoff."

"Knockoff?" DeCapra sounded incredulous. "Do I look like the kind of guy who would wear a knock-off?"

Katz glanced meaningfully at the unconscious woman. "You're not a guy I would want to trust."

DeCapra forced a laugh. "So don't trust me. Take my money, okay?" He shrugged. "I mean, no matter who you're working for—and I don't want to know, okay—but whoever you're working for, I don't figure they paid twenty grand to get me banged up. Am I right?"

Katz let the question hang in the air just long enough to give his decision weight. He nodded at Kissinger. "Let him go."

Kissinger stepped back, letting DeCapra drop to his feet.

Released, the man tried to retain some of his dignity, but it was wasted effort. Though the legs were health-club perfect and the shoes were from the best

Italian leather, he was still half-naked. Still, DeCapra handled himself well. He smiled and reached inside his jacket for his wallet, taking it out and opening it. "Guess you guys must be pretty good to take out my boys. They're not pushovers, but I'm definitely going to dock their pay for this."

Kissinger continued stepping back.

DeCapra watched him, obviously more afraid of what the bigger man would do. Bills flashed between his fingers. "You boys, though, you're going to come out ahead today. And me, I'm going to be a lot happier about this."

Katz swung the cane without warning, too quickly for DeCapra to react. The cane connected with the man's hand, and one-hundred-dollar bills went flying, flipping and fluttering to the wooden floor. DeCapra yowled with surprise. Stepping in, Katz swung the cane again, connecting with the man's jaw, listening with a practiced ear to the fracture.

Unconscious, DeCapra dropped to the ground.

Cool and under control, Katz used the cane methodically. He broke the man's fingers on his right hand, then broke the right ankle. He added a few contusions to his face. If the East Coast Families thought DeCapra could tough out a couple broken bones for the meeting with Grishin, they certainly wouldn't want to send him looking like a poster child announcing they couldn't take care of their own. When Katz was finished, he wiped the cane clean and took it with him.

Kissinger had paled slightly.

"Are you okay?" Katz asked.

"Not my usual style," the weapons expert stated without apology.

"Nor mine. Still," Katz said, looking at the unconscious man, "it's better than killing him."

"Yeah."

Katz led the way out of the riding stables. No one approached them as they took their leave. Kissinger presented the claim check for their car. A few minutes later, the valet drove it up.

Kissinger slid behind the wheel.

Katz took the passenger seat, then he reached inside his jacket for the cellular phone. He dialed the number he'd been assigned for the Farm.

Price answered on the second ring.

"It's done," Katz announced. "We left him alive, Barbara."

There was a hesitation. "Thank you, Yakov."

"Of course. If there is anything else…"

"Not yet."

"Keep us apprised." Katz punched End and folded the cellular phone in two as Kissinger pulled back onto the highway that would take them into Philadelphia. The Israeli turned to his companion. "The pilot will let us set the time to fly back to the Farm. I was thinking, perhaps, a good meal. Some wine."

"Sure."

Katz took out his handkerchief and cleaned the cane again, removing all his fingerprints. He let five miles pass, then tossed the cane to the roadside where it would doubtless go unfound.

"Even doing it right," Kissinger said, "and keeping Price's conscience clear, it wasn't easy."

"No," Katz admitted. "God forbid that something like that should ever become easy to me. The man I would be then is someone I wouldn't want to be."

"There's a lot of distance between them and us, buddy."

"I know." Katz turned his thoughts from the beating he'd given DeCapra and the embarrassing way he and Edi Charteris would be found. It was all part of the cover they needed to get Leo Turrin into play in the Caribbean. And considering the danger Kesar Grishin posed, Katz couldn't allow himself to second-guess the need to act as he had.

Now, though, things were left to the three Stony Man teams and Turrin once he was in place. Katz kept them all in his prayers.

CHAPTER TWENTY

Barbara Price sat at the desk in her office off to the side of Aaron Kurtzman's theater of operations. She checked the clock and found that enough time had elapsed that she could take another couple analgesics from the bottle she kept in her top desk drawer. She shook out the last two, then downed them with a couple swallows from the tepid orange juice she'd brought in earlier.

The office represented the mission controller's thoughts to a large degree. Everything was neat and in its place, organized. Life wasn't like that, so Price had learned to make do with her environment.

On the wall opposite her was a TV-VCR combination. She kept the channel on CNN and the sound off, relying on her visual acuity to let her know if any of the hot spots the teams were involved in showed up on the screen. The computer monitor on her desktop linked her with what Kurtzman's team had on tap outside, as well as allowing her access to the Farm's Cray mainframes.

The monitor held her attention for the moment. Six squares projected video footage on the screen, all of them views of the suite Chela Escelera had in Puerto Vallarta.

Escelera sat in the living-room area with three body-guards. They talked in Spanish, and Price wasn't fluent enough to keep up with the conversation. There were idioms she wasn't familiar with, and Escelera and her people talked in vague references that were empty of real information. Price trusted Blancanales to let her know if there was anything that was said that she needed to be aware of. The rooms were tapped, as well, though none of the tapes would be admissible as court evidence.

Escelera sat in a plush easy chair. She wore a magenta dress high enough across the thighs that whenever she made a move to cross her legs, every man in the room took notice. Escelera ignored them as she leafed through a stack of magazines. Price had already ascertained that they were all merchandise catalogs. Escelera made money, and she liked to spend it.

"We have action," Blancanales said softly.

Price had opened a cellular phone link with Able Team. She leaned forward and tried to ignore the burning in her eyes. One of the video windows flickered and changed. The bedroom that had been the focus of the camera suddenly gave way to the hallway just outside Escelera's suite.

Two of Escelera's bodyguards had left earlier, but now they were back with a third man. Out of habit, Price made a notation on the yellow legal pad in front of her. She knew it was a duplication of effort, because Blancanales or Schwarz would do the same thing. But it was hard to ignore what had become ingrained.

"Can you identify him?" Price asked.

"We're searching through the database now," Blancanales replied. "He didn't pop very quick."

The database Able Team had in Puerto Vallarta contained images of most of the known felons in the area. Kurtzman had assembled the database by hacking through local police records and the computer files the DEA kept on the area.

Price studied the man as the bodyguards halted him at the door leading to Escelera's suite. The man had short-cropped hair and an erect bearing, and there were no signs of nervousness in his dark features. He kept his gaze sweeping the hallway, moving slightly on his feet to stay loose.

"I'm guessing he's a cop," Schwarz said. "Guy's definitely taking stock of the situation, kind of cocky. And take a look at his left leg."

The video window suddenly expanded, focusing on the man's lowerleg. Price saw the bulge near the ankle and knew what it was before Schwarz told her.

"Doesn't cover up his pistol very well," Schwarz said.

Price picked up her headset and opened a link to Carmen Delahunt's ops center. "Carmen."

"Yes."

"Can you get access to Puerto Vallarta police department files?"

"Aaron put in a back-door system through the link they have with American immigration."

On the monitor screen, one of the bodyguards inside the suite opened the door and let the trio in. The two who'd brought the man to the room stayed with him, within easy distance.

"I've got a picture I want you to run," Price said. She used the mouse and the screen-capture utility. In seconds she had downloaded a picture of the man and imported the picture into the e-mail utility. Once she had it there, she sent it on to Delahunt. "Let me know what you find out."

"Of course."

Price continued to watch the screen. The man entered the suite. The camera view changed, then continued to change as Blancanales or Schwarz flipped through the available minicams to get the picture he wanted.

The man sat on the sofa across from Escelera, near the light Schwarz had rigged with the backup battery pack. So far, no one had used the light. The man rested his forearms on his knees, relaxed and intent on Escelera. They spoke in Spanish, too rapid for Price to follow. But she recognized Guarano, the name of the DEA agent Lyons had helped rescue.

The sound coming from the computer speakers muted. "They're talking about Guarano," Blancanales said. "They know the man is still alive, but so far he hasn't recovered consciousness."

Price was aware of that. She'd been in contact with Lyons less than twenty minutes earlier. Guarano had been moved to the hospital bay of an American freighter so there'd be less chance of any of Escelera's people getting to him. A doctor and his handpicked team had been brought in to take care of the agent. So far, there'd been no word other than that Guarano's condition was stable but critical.

"Who are they?" Price asked.

"He hasn't said. Escelera is asking how much money it'll take to get the job finished."

On the computer screen, the man spread his hands and leaned back in the sofa. Obviously he felt he was holding all the cards. The man answered, shaking his head doubtfully.

"He says he doesn't know. The American DEA is protecting the freighter, and they know steps are being taken to move the ship out to sea."

Price was aware of that, as well. All that the freighter was waiting for was enough of the crew to return to move it out of the harbor safely.

Blancanales continued to translate. "Escelera wants to know how much for the whole ship."

On-screen, the man looked surprised for just a moment, then got control of himself again. He shook his head. Price didn't need a translation.

Escelera nodded at one of her bodyguards. The man disappeared into one of the suite's rooms. The minicam system picked him up, following him into a bedroom where he took a large suitcase from the closet. He returned to the living-room area. Escelera gestured toward the floor. The bodyguard put the suitcase down, then worked the latches. When he lifted the lid, he showed that the suitcase was filled with money.

Escelera said something.

"Five million dollars," Blancanales translated. "American. Cash up front just for trying."

Price didn't wait for the man to answer. She picked up her cellular phone and punched in the speed-dial code for Carl Lyons's cellular phone. On-screen, the man leaned forward and riffled through the stacks of American currency. The one-hundred-dollar bills were crisp and tight, fluttering together like a new deck of cards.

Lyons answered the call in one ring. "Yeah."

"Has Guarano come around?" Price asked.

"Not yet. He's showing signs, though. The doc says it should be at any time now. Guarano's respiration and heart rate are up."

"How soon before they're able to move the freighter?"

Lyons's voice became muffled, like he'd covered the mouthpiece with a hand. A brief, garbled conversation followed, then Lyons came back on the line. "Twenty minutes, thirty minutes tops. What's up?"

Price explained, watching the computer monitor as the man in Escelera's suite nodded hesitantly. It was too much money to turn down, and too much responsibility to take lightly.

Escelera calmly leaned back and lit a cigarette. Price didn't need Blancanales's translation to figure out the woman was threatening the man with what would happen if he simply ran off with the money. Then the man started to talk, and there was a desperate edge to his words.

"He's telling her he can get it done," Blancanales said. "There are dockworkers he can buy, men who know explosives and have scuba gear."

Price knew the plan was possible. Her desktop phone rang, lighting up the extension that connected her to Carmen Delahunt's desk. She asked Blancanales to hold, then answered the other call.

"I've found the man you're looking for," Delahunt said.

"Who is he?" Price watched as the image she'd sent Delahunt took precedence over the video feed coming from Puerto Vallarta. The imported image slid over to the left side of the screen, making room for a new window to pop into place.

"Miguel Francisca," Delahunt answered. "He's a detective with the Puerto Vallarta PD."

The second picture showed Francisca looking younger, in an obviously posed shot. His smile was clean and neat, engaging. Stats scrolled out below the two pictures, including Francisca's birth date, address and the high points of his career. He worked the drug scene in Puerto Vallarta, which meant there were any number of dockworkers he'd become familiar with over the years.

"Has he got any priors?" Price put down the cellular phone and cradled the desktop phone on her shoulder. She tapped the keyboard, sending the information to Blancanales.

On the computer screen, barely visible under the two windows containing Francisca's pictures, Escelera's bodyguard zipped the suitcase closed again. Sitting it on end, he shoved it toward the detective. Almost drawn hypnotically, Francisca stroked the leather suitcase like a pet.

"No priors," Delahunt relayed. "According to everything I've got, he's been a clean cop. I took a peek into the jacket they've got logged in for him at Puerto Vallarta PD's version of internal affairs. Apparently there have been some concerns about him. He's been investigated three times in the past two years concerning missing evidence."

"He made it disappear?"

"Evidently someone thought so."

"What cases?"

"All ones that would have made things somewhat sticky for Escelera."

"Thanks, Carmen." Price hung up the desktop phone and resumed the conversation with Blancanales, quickly bringing him up to speed on Delahunt's findings.

"So he's a guy who can get it done," Blancanales said when she finished.

"Not for long. It won't take much to cut through channels and get a military plane in there to airlift Guarano out of the area." The only reason she'd left the DEA agent in place as long as she had was to put pressure on Escelera, and to wait for the medical team to stabilize his condition.

"Gadgets is updating the Ironman."

Price saved the pictures of Francisca to the Puerto Vallarta files she'd archived, clearing the screen. She watched as the detective picked up the suitcase and headed for the suite's main door. Escelera stopped the cop with a few words.

"Should we take him down?" Blancanales asked.

"No." Price didn't hesitate about her decision. Part of the information on Francisca included the number of his car phone. "I'll take care of it."

"If this guy gets loose, he could maybe do what he says," Blancanales said gently.

"He won't," Price promised.

On the screen, Escelera motioned to one of her bodyguards to switch on the large-screen projection television that had been hidden from view in a cabinet against the wall. The remote control for the television rested on the small table beside her, but she ignored it. The bodyguard changed channels at her request, then adjusted the volume.

Price spotted the CNN logo on the television screen when Blancanales shifted the minicam view to take in what was being broadcast. The television scene shifted from an anchor to a reporter standing at a dock area in front of a line of ships. When the signature line flashed onto the screen, Price saw the dateline was Puerto Vallarta.

Glancing up at her own television, Price saw the

story about DEA Agent Guarano was breaking. The reporter gave a lively, spirited discourse on Guarano's kidnapping by a prominent Colombian-based drug czar, and on his rescue by the DEA team that wouldn't give up on their partner. The only photos available were old academy shots and photographs from Guarano's police work before going into the DEA.

There was no mention of Lyons, and no mention of Escelera. Price recorded the broadcast automatically, archiving it into the video files on one of the secondary hard drives delegated for her use only.

"Guess she likes to stay informed," Blancanales said.

"Stay with her, and let me know the instant anything suspicious turns up. Paying Francisca five million dollars for an attempt to sink that freighter tells me Guarano's probably got something she can't afford to lose."

"It would be better," Blancanales commented, "if we knew what we were looking for."

"Maybe we will. Lyons said Guarano was on the verge of recovering consciousness." Price broke the connection, then brought Francisca's file back onto the screen. After she memorized his mobile-phone number, she cleared the video feed from Escelera's room and booted up the video archives she had recorded of Francisca's conversation with the woman. Then she dialed the detective's number.

The phone rang six times. For a moment, Price wondered if the man was going to answer.

"*Hola,*" Francisca said.

"Detective Francisca," Price said, "five million dollars is a lot of money, isn't it?"

Silence filled the phone line with white noise.

Price knew Francisca was squirming, trying to decide what to do. She let the silence echo for a bit, pushing the man into an active mode rather than a defensive one. She wasn't looking for an argument.

"Who is this?" Francisca demanded in English.

"Someone who knows you. Someone who knows what you've just done."

"Listen, I don't know what you think you know, but—"

Price tapped in the keyboard commands to play the computer recording back. The conversation between Francisca and Escelera broadcast, and the reproduction was good. "I also have video footage."

"Who are you?" Francisca demanded.

Car horns blared over the phone connection, and Price guessed that the detective was rattled enough to have forgotten what he was doing. "Someone who wants to see that you do the right thing."

Francisca was cautious. "And what do you see as the right thing?"

"As I said, Detective Francisca, five million dollars is a lot of money. Take it. Run as far and as fast as you can."

"Screw that," Francisca snarled. "You know who I'm dealing with. I take a walk with her money, I'm a dead man."

"I have the tape," Price reminded him.

"If you'd had a court order for it, I'd have known about it. So everything you have is illegal. You can't use it in a court. As far as my career goes, I was considering retiring. Even if you know about the attempt on that freighter, that won't stop the guys that I send. And if you stop them, big deal. I still go down in Escelera's books as a man who can be trusted."

"That's where you're wrong," Price said. "By the

time I get through with my story and the tape, it'll look like you wore a wire into the meeting with her today. If you call her, I'll know and I'll turn a copy of the tape over to your commanding officer. If you do anything now but leave the city, I'll do exactly as I said.''

Francisca didn't say anything.

"Any attempt at double-crossing me on this deal,'' Price promised, "and you won't be able to run far enough fast enough.''

"Are you American?''

"It doesn't matter.''

"Are you with the DEA?''

Price smiled, feeling that she had the man exactly in the frame of mind that she wanted him in. Paranoia in a man as duplicitous as Francisca had been forced to be was a condition that fed on itself. "I'm in a position to make you an offer.''

"Evidently you had to make an offer.''

"Detective Francisca,'' Price said, "I did what I wanted to. If you turned up dead, or Escelera heard about your disappearance, things would still go as I wanted them to. If you vanish on your own, you'll leave a trail of sorts. Escelera will be more worried about you taking her money than she will be about anyone watching her as closely as we are. Do you understand?''

Francisca answered reluctantly. "Yes.''

"Good. Then I'll trust you to know what to do.'' Price broke the connection and hung up the phone. Dealing with the man in such a manner was a gamble, but it was a better risk than taking the detective off the streets, when the chances were too great that they'd be spotted. Francisca's first instinct was going to be for survival.

She pushed the man to the back of her mind. Checking the television, she saw that CNN had moved on to another story. Evidently the one breaking in Puerto Vallarta wasn't going to be big enough to maintain national or international interest.

She lifted the phone again and arranged for a military jet to pick up Guarano. Lyons could stay with the man until that lead either proved out or turned cold.

Pushing herself up from the desk, she walked into the main computer room. Leo Turrin was standing by at the home he maintained in Washington, D.C. The Mafia Families Turrin remained connected with assumed that Turrin kept a house there to work the lobbying interests representing legitimate Mob interests. There were more and more these days. They didn't know about the office Turrin also filled in the Department of Justice.

Price had determined a long time ago that she wouldn't have wanted to live the stocky little Fed's life. There were too many lies involved, too much to get right at any given time.

And she was responsible for putting his life on the line again, under the watchful eyes of the Mafia and Kesar Grishin, hoping all the time that Turrin would be able to betray them all again.

Price walked to the back of the computer room behind Kurtzman and took a cold bottle of orange juice from the iced bins against the wall. The headache had abated somewhat, but the throbbing had only been muted, not silenced.

The cybernetics expert hit the wheels of his chair and flipped it around to face her. He stripped off the headset and laid it aside as he caught Price's eye. "We've got a problem."

CHAPTER TWENTY-ONE

Leo Turrin's life was made up of lies. As he stood by the big charcoal grill with a meat fork in one hand, a beer in the other, the sharp edge of those lies bit into him. If he'd been alone, he could have taken the lies better. As it was, he knew the war zone was approaching his home and he couldn't even take time off from the lying to set himself up for it.

"How are the steaks coming, honey?"

Turrin turned slightly, taking in the svelte form of his wife, Angelina. He smiled at her. "You've got a little more time."

Dark haired and dark eyed, wearing a one-piece bathing suit that showed off her mature curves, Angelina Turrin climbed up the steps leading from the big oval pool. Worry lines etched the hollows around her eyes, but only he would have seen them. She let no one else close enough to know her like that.

"I think I'm done with the pool."

Turrin nodded and checked on the steaks. They were coming along nicely.

"Would you like another beer?"

Turrin glanced at the bottle in his hand, then finished the dregs. "Sure."

Angelina took the empty from him, then walked

back to the house, draping a towel across her shoulders. Turrin admired her walk, the sway of her hips.

After all these years, there'd never been anyone like Angelina. It was strange thinking back on how she'd almost killed Mack Bolan in the early days, trying to save him from the Executioner's misplaced vengeance. Of course, that had been before the hellfire warrior had learned Turrin was an undercover agent. And that had been just after Angelina had found out Turrin was in the Mafia.

Turrin gazed out over the spacious backyard. Over the years, they'd lived in a lot of places, following his business around. At first, it had been because of his ties to the Mafia, to the East Coast Families, and the things they'd needed from him. Then, as he eased into a partial retirement, he'd moved to get closer to the cop work he was doing, keeping various agencies apprised of the organized-crime moves.

Now he was pretty much out of that business, handling only the special assignments required by the connection to Stony Man Farm. He was in a peaceful place.

Something cold touched the back of his neck. He recoiled, thinking for just a flash that it might be a gun barrel. Then he felt the droplet of water skate down between his sun-browned shoulders beneath the knit shirt.

"Sorry," Angelina said, extending the cold beer toward him. "You just looked so serious standing there."

Turrin pushed the tension away and took his wife in his arms. "I was serious. I was seriously contemplating taking you to bed after we finish these steaks."

Angelina laughed at him. "You've got big plans."

"Yeah, well."

She sat at the table and munched a soda cracker. "Leo, a big meal or sex. One or the other and you'll be ready for a nap. Both would prove overtaxing, if not dangerous."

Turrin clapped a hand to his chest and collapsed into a chair next to the picnic table. "Ouch! Man, you know how to hurt a guy."

Without warning, the gate next to the house opened with a squeak. The privacy fence was tall, but the man peering over it was taller.

Turrin's hand slid automatically for the Airweight Bodyguard .38 under the towel in the chair next to him. He fisted the short, curved butt, cocked the hammer and brought it into his lap. Dropping a nearby napkin over the pistol, he stood and moved toward the man. "Something I can help you with?"

"Leo Turrin?" the man asked.

"Yeah. I don't know you."

"No, sir."

The tone of respect allayed Turrin's suspicions a little, unclenching the white-hot fist that had twisted his stomach. Turrin stopped in his tracks. "What can I help you with?"

"I need you to get ready to go."

Without warning, two more men appeared. Turrin recognized both of the new arrivals.

"What's up, Jimmy?" Turrin asked.

Jimmy Venturo was old-line Mafia, one of the few soldiers who'd actually worked with Sergio Frenchi years ago when the Executioner had whipped through organized crime. He was a short, dapper man carrying a headful of gray hair these days and a pugnacious face that hadn't recovered from a life filled with violence.

He wore a suit that fit him well, testimony to the fact that he'd come up in the world.

"Sorry about this, Mr. Turrin," Venturo said. "I would have called first, but you know how it is with the phone lines." He was referring to the phone taps that were part of Turrin's daily existence.

"It's okay, Jimmy." Turrin relaxed to a degree. No one was going to try to hurt him here, and Angelina would be safe. But evidently the Old Men of the Families were reaching for the second-string to cover Kesar Grishin's action down in the Caribbean.

"The Old Men, they told me get down here quick, see if you were still willing to take that trip."

Turrin shook his head. "I thought Alexander De-Capra made it plain that he wasn't interested in working with me. He's got the ears of the Old Men these days."

"If you ask me, Mr. Turrin, I think it's only the hand of God setting the table straight on that." Venturo crossed himself, then kissed his fingertips. "DeCapra's jealous of you, jealous of where you been, who you been with, guys you know."

"He also knows more about money than I do," Turrin said. "And that's what this meeting's all about. That's why they went with him in the first place. The Old Men need someone down there like DeCapra to make their deals for them."

"They got something else worked out, Mr. Turrin. The don himself told me to ask you if you could do this small favor." Venturo spread a hand across his chest. "Me, I don't want to have to go back to the don, tell him you can't do it."

"What have they got worked out?" Turrin asked.

"They got a guy who's going to go with you. Let

you know if you're being played square with. A guy who understands money, economics, investing, that kind of thing. But it's going to be your handshake that seals the deal for every one of the Old Men. They got a lot of respect for you, you know?''

Turrin looked past Venturo, watching Balls Carlina moving the big man back out of the area of the conversation. "How soon do we have to leave, Jimmy?''

Venturo spread his hands. "Soon as you want, Mr. Turrin. Long as you got time to make the plane down to the Caribe.''

"I got time to finish my meal?''

"Sure, Mr. Turrin.''

"Call the don,'' Turrin suggested. "Tell him I'll take the deal, go represent the Families' interests and let him know what's what.''

Venturo smiled with relief. "I'm sure he's going to be glad to know.''

"Let him know it's my pleasure,'' Turrin said.

"I'll be sure and let him know.''

"Is he going to want to see me?''

"No. But he expects you to call before you go.''

Turrin eared the pistol's hammer back down and held it loosely under the napkin. "Soon's I finish my meal, go pack a bag and grab a toothbrush I'm all his.''

Venturo nodded.

"Jimmy,'' Turrin called.

"Yes, sir.''

"You ever been to the Caribe?''

Venturo shook his head. "Not in a lot of years.''

"Ask the don is it okay if you go with me,'' Turrin said. "Tell him I ask a favor, someone to watch over me that I know and trust, okay?''

Pride lit Venturo's eyes, straightened the posture

bowed by time. "Sure, Mr. Turrin. But there's a lot of guys would cover your back. Younger guys who still got all the quick and all the technology know-how."

"I want you, Jimmy. You see about putting a team together that you feel good about. Tell the don that I asked that."

"Yes, sir." Venturo disappeared around the house.

Turrin turned back to Angelina. "Sorry about the interruption."

She gave him a short, quick nod. He hadn't told her what was going down with the Stony Man operation. They hadn't been away from the house because he wanted everything to look normal to the people who were watching him, and talking about sensitive matters inside the house wasn't done. It was life in a fishbowl. When DeCapra got sidelined, it wouldn't have paid for anyone to be wondering if Leo Turrin had anything to do with it.

"How long will you be gone?" Angelina asked.

"A few days." Turrin sat at the table, then put the revolver away and draped the napkin across his lap.

"Can you tell me about it?"

"An investment opportunity."

"For the Families?"

"Yes." Turrin sawed at his steak.

"How much trouble can there be?"

"I've got a friend down there," Turrin said. There were usually at least a half-dozen bugs around the house, and agents were known to watch the home with shotgun microphones. To the people that might be listening, he knew they would think he was referring to Jimmy Venturo. But Angelina knew he was talking about Mack Bolan.

"It's good to have friends."

"Yes."

"I want you back safe, Leo," Angelina said, "as soon as you can get back."

He winked at her, feeling some of that old devil-may-care feeling filling his veins. It was the same feeling that had kept him alive in his tangle of lies, the same feeling that had made him push the envelope in those old days by including the Executioner as another front he dealt with. Either side had been willing to take Bolan off the board in those days. And come to think of it, those days hadn't changed all that much.

"I'll be back before you know it, Angel. And I'll tell you something else."

Angelina raised arched brows, sensing the fire in him, playing to his mood and knowing his real heart no matter what words he said.

"I think we're going to take some time packing my bag."

She laughed at him, and it almost took away the worry in her eyes.

Turrin lifted his wineglass and toasted her, feeling more alive than he had in weeks. God help him, there were days when he missed the way things had been: the challenge of keeping the lies straight and the nearness of death.

Kesar Grishin, according to the files Turrin had seen on the man, wasn't going to be an easy sell. Turrin looked forward to the challenge.

CHAPTER TWENTY-TWO

"It's now or never."

Seated across the street from Edgar Joule's law office in Montego Bay, Mack Bolan silently agreed with Jack Grimaldi's assessment. They'd watched the law office for the past hour, monitoring the people going in and out.

The office was a second-story walk-up, located over a busy bike shop and a sandwich shop that was almost empty now that lunch had passed. A few months earlier, someone had painted the sign that advertised the law office. Bolan could tell that from the way some of the white areas still gleamed under the sheen of the falling rain. Jamaica remained in the clutches of the passing tropical storm. Winds and rain whipped through the streets.

"Let's go," the soldier said, pushing up from the table they'd lunched at. He dropped money on the table to cover their tab and a generous tip.

"You gentlemen have yourselves a good day," the old black woman behind the counter called to them.

"You, too," Grimaldi called back.

"And you stay away from them bad girls," the woman added in her singsong voice. "Boys like you should find better things to do than be hanging around them clubs and bars all along this street. Next thing you know, you be out there with them hoodoo people doing snake dances and drinking chicken's blood. You be sick for sure come morning." She cackled at her own wit.

Bolan walked to the corner, his combat senses alert. From an earlier recon on the building, he and Grimaldi had determined there were no other ways into the building other than the entry between the bike shop and the sandwich shop.

He crossed the street, watching the group of youths lounging at the curb in front of the bike shop. Most of them wore American sports jerseys and dreadlocks. Their ages spanned eight to eighteen. During his observations, Bolan had also figured Joule used the bike shop as a front for a delivery service. He'd watched three different men come down the walk-up breezeway with packages that were given to different bikers.

The soldier didn't know what was in any of the packages, but the intel he had on Joule indicated the man moved drugs, as well as hardware. He walked by the group of boys, drawing harsh stares and sullen remarks that were barely audible.

The stairs were narrow and dark, and a chill from the warm rain gathered in the recesses. Single-light-bulb fixtures were mounted on the sloped roof above, but none of the lights was working.

Bolan reached behind his back and slipped the fighting knife from his belt, flicking the blade open with his thumb. He had no doubts that someone in the bike shop had called to alert Joule he was about to receive company.

"Hey, man," a deep voice called from above.

Bolan turned on the landing, facing the second flight

of stairs that led up to Joule's office. He kept moving, taking in the two black men on the landing above. The knife remained out of sight behind his thigh.

Both of the men were broad, dressed in slacks and casual shirts. One had mirror sunglasses, and the other sported a goatee on his round face.

"I think you best turn around now if you know what's good for you," the man with the sunglasses said.

Bolan didn't hesitate going up the stairs, taking away the distance in long strides. Both of the men were used to having people consider their chances before bracing them.

The Executioner was less than three feet away when they made their play for their guns. By the time they got them clear of the hip holsters, he was among them. He took the man with the sunglasses first, lashing out with the combat blade. The razor-sharp knife sank deep into the inside of the man's thigh, slicing up toward the man's groin. Bolan attacked without mercy. The men Edgar Joule had working for him were all killers.

The man he'd stabbed yelled and tried to step back away from the knife. The landing didn't have much room to work with, and the Executioner didn't break his advance. The second guard was jockeying for position to use his weapon, having a hard time getting around the man Bolan had stabbed.

The Executioner stepped to the inside of the landing, putting himself between the door and the men. He yanked on the stabbed man's gun arm, keeping him off balance, ramming him into his partner. The man with the goatee finally succeeded in getting his gun arm over his partner's shoulder, shoving the barrel toward Bolan.

The Executioner dropped, feeling the bullets cut the

air over his head and smash through the glass pane of the door behind him. Maintaining his hold on the wounded man's arm, he pushed himself back up, leading with the combat knife. He brought the blade in from the side, burying its length in the second gunman's throat.

The man started to choke on his own blood, his jugular severed and pouring fluid down into his lungs. The first man lunged at Bolan desperately, shoving the soldier back up against the wall and trying to overcome him with his greater weight and bulk.

Bolan went with the flow, yanking his knife free of the other man's throat. The dying man fell to his knees, his limbs going limp.

The remaining guard tried to bring his pistol to bear. Bolan kept an inflexible grip on the guy's arm, keeping the weapon pointed toward the ceiling. The sound of the shots the second man had fired still rang in the enclosed space of the stairwell.

"You going to die, you bastard!" the guard snarled. "You going to die!" He pushed his free hand into Bolan's face, clawing for his eyes.

The Executioner let the man's greater weight smother him for a moment, choosing his time. His knife was too short to attempt a stab through the rib cage. Whipping his arm up behind the man, he slammed the knife home into the back of the man's neck, severing the spinal cord. He twisted hard.

A shiver passed through the man as his motor control went away. He was dead by the time he sank to his knees.

Bolan plucked the pistol from the man's lax grip. Looking across the corpse, he saw Jack Grimaldi raiding the other dead body, turning up an extra magazine for the Smith & Wesson .40 the other man had held.

"You okay?" the pilot asked.

"Yeah." Bolan inspected the military .45 he'd claimed from his adversary. The gun was clean and neat, well cared for, heavy and solid in his hand. He dropped the clip into his palm for quick inspection and found six rounds still in the magazine. He knew the man had fired at least one round into the ceiling. He slammed the magazine home again, then ran his hands through the dead man's clothing.

"Joule knows he's got company," Grimaldi said, taking up a position on the other side of the stairwell. He directed his voice downstairs.

"You people want to stay back down there." He pointed the pistol down and squeezed off a round.

Cursing voices filled the stairwell.

"Getting back down the same way could be tough," Grimaldi commented.

Bolan nodded. He turned up three extra magazines for the .45 and shoved them into his hip pockets, butts up so he could get to them quickly. He faded into position beside the door.

The smashed glass pane that had once held neatly spaced lettering announcing the law office allowed a view of the outer office. No secretary was in sight.

The Executioner went forward, letting the .45 lead him. Reggae music filled the room from overhead speakers. He stepped into the office and moved for the door at the back of the small room that had been almost overfilled with a desk, chair and sofa. Plants filled desk space and the gray metal filing cabinets on either side of the room's only window.

"Stay with the door," Bolan said. "We don't want to get hemmed up in here."

Grimaldi nodded. He took up a position inside the doorway that gave him a field of fire covering the stairwell. "We're not exactly winning a popularity contest here. Couple of guys I've seen below have taken up arms."

"We won't be here long." Bolan strode toward the door at the back of the room. When he tried the door, he found it locked. Aiming the .45 at the lock, he triggered two rounds.

The bullets blasted through the cheap metal locking mechanism, then Bolan drove a foot into the door to break it free of the jamb. He used the door frame as cover as he leaned in with the pistol. A bullet thudded into the wall beside him, passing through the thin plasterboard and leaving a white, powdery vapor trail after it. Other bullets followed, hammering the wall and ripping splinters from the door frame.

The Executioner dropped the .45's open sights over the shooter. The man wasn't Joule, so he was expendable. The shooter had taken up cover behind one of the free-standing shelves of law books. He was a thin man with a hatchet face, a purple weal of an old scar beneath his left eye, a bone-and-cloth talisman at his neck. Dark blue tattoos covered his arms. He wielded the Uzi machine pistol with grim authority, yelling.

A two-inch gap between the top of a row of books and the shelf above it revealed the shooter's face when he moved back into deeper hiding. Through the din of the rolling thunder of shots, Bolan heard an empty magazine thump into the floor. He aimed the .45, then took up trigger slack. When he squeezed off the round, it whipped through the two-inch gap and smacked into the man's temple. The head crumpled under the savage impact.

Bolan moved into the room as the corpse stretched out across the floor. He kept the pistol up, covering the only other man in the room. The air stank of cordite.

"Edgar Joule," the soldier said.

The man crouched behind the big desk that was easily more expensive than anything else in the office. It was neatly organized, polished, looking completely out of place. The piece of furniture dominated the room. Two straight-backed chairs lay overturned in front of the desk.

The window behind the desk was open and led out onto the alley below. It would have been a long drop for a man Joule's age.

"Don't shoot me. Please, don't shoot me." Real terror hung thick in Joule's voice. He pushed himself up behind the desk. Almost six feet tall, the lawyer was broad without being fat, revealing an athlete's build gone past his prime. His head was shaved smooth, and a short-cropped gray beard covered his lower face, deeply cut to hollow out the cheeks. He wore an expensive suit in pale gray.

Bolan approached, keeping the .45 centered on the man's chest.

Joule blinked rapidly, turning his head away, but not so completely that the soldier was out of view.

"I came to talk," Bolan said, "and I don't have much time."

Joule kept his hands up, partially covering his face. "What do you want?"

"I want to know where I can find Dionis Santos."

"You could have called."

Bolan gave the man a cold grin. "That's not all I want."

Joule turned to face the Executioner, relaxing only a little. At least death seemed further away. "I'll tell you where to find him. But he's an easy man to find."

"Not so easy these days," Bolan disagreed. "He and Kesar Grishin are at odds. I know Santos has gone into hiding here on the island. He tried to fight the expansion of Grishin's partners into the drug trade here on the island. They put a contract out on him."

Joule nodded. "You're American? DEA?"

Bolan raised the .45 and pointed it between Joule's eyes. "I'm a trigger pull away from looking for Santos somewhere else."

"Don't! Please! I can give you an address where you'll find Santos."

"Write it down." Bolan indicated the writing pad on the desk.

Cautiously Joule leaned forward and hastily scribbled out an address on the top sheet with a pen from his jacket. "That's the last address I knew for him."

Bolan ripped the top sheet from the pad and pocketed it. "You've got a car nearby?"

Joule nodded. "In the alley below."

The soldier walked over to the window. An older white El Dorado Cadillac was parked all by itself in the alley. He turned back to Joule. "The keys?"

"In the desk drawer."

"Get them."

Joule did, handing them over reluctantly.

The Executioner glanced around the office, taking in the free-standing book shelves, the chairs, the desk and the filing cabinets. A computer system occupied one corner. The numbers on the operation were running thin, whispering through his mind. Even though the bike-shop employees and hangers-on who worked for Joule wouldn't call the Montego Bay police, other people would. They had only minutes before the first car arrived.

"Where are the guns?" Bolan asked.

Joule hesitated, obviously taking the time trying to think of a lie that would be believed. In the end, he didn't have the courage for it. "I can show you."

"Do it."

The lawyer crossed to the wall behind the free-standing bookshelves, stepping over the dead man. He pressed on the wall, tripping a hidden release that caused a portion of the paneling to pop out.

"I'll take it from here," Bolan said, motioning the lawyer back with the .45.

Joule backed off.

Bolan slipped his fingers inside the open space and tugged. The wall section rolled back on well-oiled casters. Behind the wall was a vault. The steel door looked imposing and too thick for anything less than antitank weaponry. A keypad was mounted to one side. "What's the combination?"

Joule gave it.

After Bolan entered the key sequence, a green light flashed beside the keypad. The vault door opened with a series of snicks. Pulling it open, he spotted the racks of weaponry and explosives in the area inside the vault when the interior lights came on automatically.

"Down on the floor," Bolan commanded.

The lawyer dropped to the floor and covered his head with his hands, shaking visibly.

"Jack," Bolan called, scanning the weapons that were in front of him. Besides the munitions, the vault also held stacks of paper currency from various countries, as well as bags of milk white powder. Evidently Joule ran a large, successful business.

"Yeah." Grimaldi stepped into the room. "The guys in the cheap seats seem content to stay there. But we're not going to get past them very easily."

"We've got a different way out." Bolan emptied a duffel bag containing kilo-sized packets of cocaine, spilling them across the floor. The duffel bag was regulation military size, capable of holding the M-21 Beretta sniper rifle he tucked inside.

He worked quickly, staying with the mental list he'd prepared for the foray. He found an Ingram MAC-10 that was bulkier than the H&K MP-5 he passed up, but took it because it was chambered in the same .45ACP as the long-slide Colt he'd taken. He added two Mossberg 500 shotguns with pistol grips, and another .45 to replace the S&W .40 Grimaldi had picked up. He didn't see any .40 ammo. Two blocks of C-4 plastique, a fistful of remote and timed detonators, boxes of shotgun shells, 7.62 mm for the sniper rifle and .45ACP rounds joined the weapons in the duffel bag.

Finished, he zipped the duffel and stepped back into the room. Joule remained on the ground. Footsteps sounded out in the stairwell breezeway, proof that at least some of the bike-shop messengers weren't taking the safe way out.

"If the address you gave me for Santos doesn't check out," the soldier told the man, "you're the only guy I have left to check back on."

"It's good. I swear. I do some business with him from time to time. He trusts me."

"It might be a good thing to keep in mind that after today he probably won't."

Bolan opened the window at the back of the office, then draped the duffel strap over his head and shoulders and dropped to the ground. He landed on his feet, folding down into a squatting position so he wouldn't try to take all the extra weight of the munitions and sprain an ankle or tear up his knees.

Shuffling feet sounded to his right as he pushed himself into a standing position. He brought up the .45 instantly, targeting the man drawing down on him from the edge of the alley. A shot whipped by Bolan, smashing into the large garbage bin in the back of the alley.

The Executioner squeezed off two rounds from the .45, putting them through the man's head. The corpse stumbled back as Grimaldi hit the ground beside Bolan. Tossing the pilot the keys, Bolan said, "You're driving."

The soldier followed Grimaldi to the El Dorado, switching magazines in the .45. Other bullets smashed into the dead-end alley, but the gunners were keeping a low profile.

Grimaldi slid behind the wheel and keyed the ignition. The engine caught smoothly. Bolan dropped the duffel into the back seat and got into the passenger seat. The pilot slid the gear selector into Reverse and burned rubber.

Gunfire drilled holes into the Caddie's bodywork, metal shrilling in agonized protest.

Taking a two-handed grip on the .45, Bolan provided covering fire that kept the gunners at bay while Grimaldi slewed the car into the street. A garbage truck came to a rocking stop on the passenger side only inches away. Other traffic skidded to a halt around them as the Caddie blocked both lanes.

Bolan put the .45 away, watching the people in front

of the bike shop scatter. Grimaldi put the Caddie in Drive and floored the accelerator. They quit the scene just as the first wails of arriving cop sirens cut through the air.

"Gee," Grimaldi said as he worked through the traffic, "that went well."

Bolan took his war book from behind his back and opened it. Inside were a number of maps of the area he and Grimaldi had gone over while in the restaurant across from Joule's law office. Mentally he was already preparing for the next hell zone.

CARL LYONS HAD JUST decided to take his chances with the ship's galley when Rudolpho Guarano woke with a loud groan and tried to sit up in the small hospital bed aboard the *Parker's Tramp*. The DEA undercover agent had been unconscious since he'd been hauled out of the water.

Dr. Albert Constantine, a skinny little man with cottony hair and skin bronzed by years of soaking up the sun on the beaches of Puerto Vallarta, stepped back inside the room. "Keep him from getting up," the doctor told Lyons.

"Where the hell am I?" Guarano demanded, taking in the IV tube connected to his right arm. Bandages swathed the right side of the man's face, and purple swelling was evident around the edges of the bandages.

Lyons grabbed Guarano by the shoulders and forced him back down onto the bed. It wasn't hard even though the man fought at first. Guarano was still under the influence of painkillers, and his body hadn't recovered from the beating it had taken at the hands of his captors.

"Take it easy, amigo," Constantine said, glancing

at the heart-rate monitor hooked up to his patient. The equipment had been brought in with the doctor. "You're in good hands here."

Personally Lyons figured if the doctor had been in dress whites instead of swim trunks and a tank top, the man might have been more credible. Still, he felt Guarano relax somewhat.

"There's a good lad," Constantine said with an Irish lilt in his words. "I'm Dr. Constantine. You've had a rough go of it, but you're going to be fine."

Price and Kurtzman had recommended the doctor. They'd also downloaded a file on the man to Lyons. The Irish accent was warranted, and Constantine was a capable surgeon. He also had warrants out for his arrest for consorting with the IRA back in Belfast.

"Where am I?" Guarano demanded.

"Among friends, it appears," Constantine said. He took a stethoscope from a bag on the floor and fitted it into place. He slid the diaphragm onto Guarano's bare chest. "How are you feeling?"

"Like I got hit by a truck." Guarano put his free hand to his head to feel the bandaged area. He winced in pain. "What kind of shape am I in?"

Constantine put his stethoscope away, obviously comfortable with the results. He unfolded a beach chair from the side of the bed and sat. "You have multiple contusions and lacerations. A host of bruises. I expect you should probably feel worse."

"Feels like the room is moving," Guarano complained.

"That's because we're on a ship out in the anchorage off Puerto Vallarta," Lyons said.

Guarano looked at him distrustfully. "Who are you?"

Lyons gave his Justice Department ID a workout. In it, he was identified as Charles Lightner, a special agent for Justice. "I know about Saunders, and I know you got caught up trying to do a little breaking and entering that Saunders wanted you to do."

"I told him it was a bad idea," Guarano said.

"He should have listened to you."

"Saunders doesn't like listening to anybody."

Lyons nodded. "Yeah, well, he's listening now."

"You rescued me from Escelera's people."

"I had help."

"Who?"

Lyons gave him the names of the DEA agents who'd been involved in the rescue while Constantine continued with his examination. The doctor peeled back one of Guarano's eyelids and shone a light inside.

"Where are they?" Guarano asked as Constantine started on the other eye.

"Ashore."

"Why aren't they here?"

"They weren't invited."

Constantine moved away from the bed. "I'd advise against tiring him out too much," he said to Lyons. "He's still pretty much under the weather."

"I'll only stay as long as I have to," Lyons said agreeably.

The doctor left the room and went back into the passageway.

"You're part of the special Justice team that was brought in," Guarano said.

Lyons nodded.

"Saunders got nervous that you guys knew more than he did." Guarano closed his eyes and swallowed hard. He laid a hand across his stomach. "They tell you how long I was deep on this project?"

"Yeah. Rudy, you did good. You did more than a lot of guys could have done." Lyons said the words with sincerity. It took a special kind of guy—or woman—to go deep and stay there for any length of time without cracking up or giving in to temptation.

"So where do I go?"

"There's a military jet coming into Puerto Vallarta within the hour," Lyons said. "They're going to take you out of the country."

"The military?"

"Yeah."

Guarano swallowed hard again. "If you can get the military in, you must have a lot of pull."

"I know the people who do," Lyons replied.

"So why are you here with me? I know you didn't come just to hold my hand."

Lyons took a seat in the chair near the bulkhead beside Guarano's hospital bed. "No. You're going to pull through. The people I know, they're arranging it so you've got some time down when you get back to the States. Go see your family, work on forgetting what went down here."

"My cover?"

"Blown to hell," Lyons answered.

"I didn't give them anything," Guarano said. "I knew if I did, I was dead. Even up to the end when they locked me in the trunk of that car, I didn't think Escelera would do it. Man, I was clean in her eyes."

"You stepped over the line when you did that forced-entry gig."

"I didn't know it was going to be that big of a deal," Guarano commented. "Saunders got wind through one of his little snitches that Escelera had some information squirreled away in that house I hit.''

"Who was living in the house?"

Guarano shrugged. "A nobody. A small cog in Escelera's wheel. That's why I didn't think anyone would be around when I burgled the place. Man, you'd have thought it was Fort Knox the way they came down on me outside. For a while, I thought they were going to do me right there in the house.''

"But Escelera stopped them.''

"Yeah.''

Lyons waited a moment, giving the agent time to clear his mind of the past fears and get his present situation back in perspective. "What did Saunders send you there looking for?"

"Nothing specific. He thought maybe there'd be some information regarding new shipments.'' Guarano made a wry face. "You probably know Escelera's been letting us take down shipments to keep us busy while she put others through.''

"Yeah.''

"She's been working our snitches better than we have.''

Lyons could sympathize. A snitch was only as good as whatever allegiance was felt. They were a necessary evil in law enforcement, but they worked against a cop as much as they worked for them. "There was something at the house, though?"

Guarano nodded. "In the safe. I knew it was there from earlier trips to the home. I was doing business with the guy, working with him when Escelera said.''

"Who was he?"

"Like I said, a nobody. A cipher. Lorenzo Fitch. The paper we had on him at the DEA said he was ex-CIA.

Shelled out over in Germany somewhere, caught dealing on both sides of the line before the wall fell. He got busted down through the ranks and heaved out of the CIA, spent a little fed time while the Agency tried to make up their minds what to do with him. In the end, they figured trying the guy would be more embarrassing than just letting him go.''

"And they cut him loose?"

"Yeah." Guarano struggled to find a more comfortable spot on the bed but obviously failed. "The word we got was that Fitch is some kind of industrial spy these days. Worked Silicon Valley when it was hot, then moved up to Seattle when all the computer companies went north."

"What was his connection to Escelera?"

"That's tough to skull out. Maybe she used him just for contact in the computer crowd. Plenty of blow for the white-collar guys, and Fitch was a guy who could hook her up with the people who could work distribution."

"You think it was more than that?"

"Maybe." Guarano pulled at the bandaging on his face again. "It could be Escelera was using the guy to launder some of the money she was taking down."

"She doesn't use him anymore?"

"Not as much. I've been in place for months. You know that. A guy hangs around that much, you pick up a feel for things. A few months back, Escelera shifted some of her money to a new launderer."

"You get a name for this guy?"

Guarano shook his head slowly. "No. A few names of some companies, but they didn't lead anywhere when Saunders checked them out."

"Tell me what you found in the safe," Lyons suggested.

Guarano hesitated, licking his lips. "I give this up to you, you know there's nothing I got left to make sure you don't waste me right here if you're lying to me."

Lyons nodded, accepting the man's statement. "Your call." A guy got paranoid working deep, used to living in a world where everyone was out to get him.

"But if it wasn't important," Guarano said, "you wouldn't be here."

"Yeah."

Guarano looked around. "Can I get something to drink?"

"The doc says water."

"That's probably the last thing I want after nearly drowning," Guarano said with irony, "but I'll take it."

Lyons got up from the chair and crossed the room to the small refrigeration unit that had been installed with the hospital bed. He took out a plastic bottle of spring water, then helped Guarano sip from it.

"Thanks," the undercover agent said.

Lyons nodded and put the bottle on the table beside the hospital bed. He sat in the chair again, waiting.

"There were blueprints in the safe," Guarano said.

"Blueprints to what?"

"I don't know." The undercover agent tried to shrug, but the effort came away weak, listless. "They looked like they belonged to an office building. Concentrated on phone lines, wiring, that kind of shit."

"There was nothing written on them that would tell you what they were of?"

"No. I had a camera. A little piece of work about

as big as your forefinger, shot rolls of film about the size of a pea.''

"You took pictures?'' Lyons asked.

"Yeah. Two rolls. Escelera's people got one of them when they grabbed me.''

"What about the other one?''

Guarano glanced around the room. "I'm naked as a jaybird under these sheets. You got my stuff anywhere?''

Lyons reached beside the bed and took up the suitcase he'd used to keep all of Guarano's personal effects together. He opened it, revealing the wet, torn and bloody clothing.

"I have a lighter in there somewhere.''

Lyons found the disposable lighter, noticing there were no cigarettes. When he tipped it up and held it against the track lighting overhead, drops of salt water splashed from the surface. But he could see the dark, pea-sized dot inside the plastic shell of the lighter. "The film?''

"Yeah,'' Guarano said. "I don't smoke.''

Lyons pried open the lighter, and the small roll of undeveloped film spilled out into his palm.

"If that comes to anything, will you let me know?''

Lyons nodded as he replaced the film roll in the lighter. "If I can. Is there anything else you can tell me about the blueprints or Fitch?''

"No, man. I had that safe just closed back up when they jumped me. You know the rest of it.''

"Get some rest,'' Lyons said. "You've earned it. We'll take it from here.''

"Good hunting, buddy.''

Lyons walked toward the door, reaching for the cellular phone holstered on his hip.

CHAPTER TWENTY-THREE

"What am I looking at?" Barbara Price asked. She stared hard at the numbers, letters and symbols that covered all three monitors at Kurtzman's desk.

"Programming code," Akira Tokaido replied. He leaned over Kurtzman's shoulder, eyes roving from screen to screen.

"What does it do?" Price asked.

"We're not certain," Kurtzman said. "Yet." He scribbled some cramped notations on the yellow legal pad on the desktop in front of him.

"And you found this in the data we got from the Palm Beach bank this morning?"

"Yeah."

"These strings were hidden really well," Tokaido said. He was so intent on what was happening on the screens that his earphone lay on his shoulder, totally neglected.

"Where?" Price asked.

"Where?" Kurtzman repeated.

Price nodded.

He glanced at Tokaido. "Where?"

"Man, I didn't even think about where at the time." Tokaido turned a hand toward the keyboard. "May I?"

"Be my guest," Kurtzman said, bumping the chair's

wheels with his palms and scooting it back out of the desk. Tokaido slid in at once, dropping into a crouch as he pulled the keyboard toward him.

The mission controller knew they were both in their element now. Tokaido appeared consumed by the challenge. But then, the younger man had more of an ingrained hacker's curiosity about programming and how it worked than Kurtzman did. It was one of the chief reasons Kurtzman had recruited someone like Tokaido. The younger man viewed intruder countermeasures in the cybernetic field as fences preventing exploration. What was on the other side wasn't all that important. Circumventing the programming and learning about it were the important things.

Tokaido's fingers flew across the keys. The cursor jumped from left to right, top to bottom, throwing out whole new lines of commands that cut up the confusion of programming on the screens. He shook his head and grinned. "Man, this is going to be a tough one to crack." He blew a pink bubble of chewing gum, then popped it and snapped it back into his mouth.

"Grishin put the programming into the banking files," Price said.

"Had to be," Kurtzman responded, watching his young protégé at work. "What Akira has found so far is a fraction of what the overall programming is. We may not be able to tell what it does until we have it all."

"What makes you assume this programming is bad?" Price asked. "It might be a systems-check override Grishin put in to verify all financial transactions that went through the bank at Palm Beach."

"No," Kurtzman answered, "we'd already found that. It was really cleverly designed, as well. The peo-

ple working at the Palm Beach site might have guessed
that it existed, but I doubt they found it. And if they
found it, I doubt they would have been able to tamper
with it much.''

"Careful as I was," Tokaido said, "I triggered a
virus in those subsystems that would have lunched everything we managed to download from that site. And
if it had gotten out of the environment I'd written for
it, that virus would have lunched everything in our
computers, as well.''

"The problem that I see," Kurtzman went on, "is
that this programming is incomplete.''

"Maybe we simply didn't get it all when we did the
data upload," Price said. Like the others, her eyes
stayed with the flow of data covering the three monitors. "There were areas we missed.''

Kurtzman shook his head. "From the looks of
things, it wasn't all in there.''

"The program?''

"Right." Kurtzman leaned forward, studying the
scrolling lines of data more closely. "This program
was linked to the account transfers?''

"You'd think so," Tokaido replied. "Oh, man, this
guy was slick. See how it all blends in?''

Price couldn't ferret out any information in the twisting strings of numbers, letters and symbols. "I don't.''

"Just a sec." Tokaido opened a window on the
screen, typed in a half-dozen command strings that
Price was only slightly familiar with and pressed Enter.
The window closed. A heartbeat later, a handful of the
data strings across the screens lit up in lambent green.
They were vastly outnumbered by the other data cours-
ing across the monitors.

"That doesn't look like a lot of programming," Price said.

"Good virus programming never does," Tokaido commented. He rubbed his chin as he watched the data strings organize themselves into columns. "If it's done correctly, it accesses and takes advantage from existing programming, further minimizing the amount needed."

"But it remains able to take over the host programming," Kurtzman said.

The eight-figure columns kept cycling. Gradually they coalesced. "The programming wasn't generated at the Palm Beach bank," Tokaido said. "It came in with the electronic money transfers and went out the same way. Somewhere else." He tapped on the keyboard again.

Price watched, a sense of unease growing within her. Grishin was clever, and he was ambitious. The streak of ruthlessness that ran rampant through the man completed the dangerous ensemble. "We've already verified that the Palm Beach bank was responsible for laundering money."

"Yeah," Kurtzman said.

"Assuming none of the programming was done there," Price went on, "that means the programming was generated elsewhere, then fed into the Palm Beach bank."

"I'll go along with that," Kurtzman said.

"But the programming didn't stay at the Palm Beach bank."

"No."

"Then why break it up? Why not just shove it through in a chunk, wherever it was going?"

"Grishin didn't want it to be found," Tokaido said.

"Not until it had done whatever it was supposed to do."

"For it to work," Price said; "all those random pieces of programming you've found are going to have to end up in the same spot eventually. Right?"

"Sure," Kurtzman agreed. "Otherwise, you've got a collection of useless data floating around out there in cyberspace."

"So wherever Grishin sent the data, he was counting on it getting together."

"Look at this," Tokaido said excitedly. On the computer screens, the data streams slowed. Windows opened, revealing phone numbers.

Price looked at the numbers, seeing area codes that were scattered across the nation. "There are a dozen states represented there. Fourteen, maybe fifteen."

"And the list is growing," Tokaido said needlessly. He tapped the computer keyboard, opening a memo window that instantly inscribed each new phone number as it appeared. There were already dozens, most of them listed as savings-and-loan associations.

"Investment houses," Kurtzman said. "These entries represent investments Grishin was making over the past three years."

"Investments in what?" Price asked.

"I don't know." The cybernetics expert lifted his headset and called for Hunt Wethers's attention, assigning the man to the task of tracing the numbers Tokaido's program was forcing the Palm Beach bank data to give up. "We knew he was heavily engaged in legitimizing as much money for the people he was laundering for as he could. Stocks, bonds, futurities, mutual funds, T-bills. Hell, he could have been jobbing them government savings bonds, as well. Six months after purchase, they could have cashed them anywhere in the United States and it would have been clean money as far as anyone from the Justice Department was concerned.''

Price knew it was true. Even when they knew the shell companies and fake corporations Grishin had started, the straw banks he was using in Russia, there was no way to stop the man or his business without international help. Grishin's financial empire had been growing in staggering leaps and bounds, a festering cancer that Stony Man Farm had been called on to excise.

Wethers called for Kurtzman's attention, talked briefly over the headset.

When Kurtzman put the headset on the desk, Price could tell the big man was upset. "Those numbers," he said, leveling a finger as the screens, "all belong to savings-and-loan institutions that failed in the late eighties and early nineties.''

"They're not being used now?'' Price asked. And the cold chill enveloping her stomach became an icy shield.

"No," Kurtzman agreed. "Except by Grishin.''

"The man's phreaking the phones," Tokaido said.

Price was familiar with the term. The first computer hackers had been phone phreaks, people who could hack into AT&T's long distance and access long-distance service without paying for it. Some of them had even been able to hack the service by screeching into the phones using their voices alone once they'd learned the codes. But eventually most of them got caught by the phone companies. "Saving on long-distance charges isn't something I'd see Grishin being interested in," the mission controller said.

"Not saving on long-distance charges," Kurtzman said with cold certainty. "Usually the telephone company puts a number out of commission for a while when a service has been canceled."

"I can understand that Grishin would be able to access those numbers," Price said. "I've stayed up with the news. I've read reports about hackers who used abandoned 900-numbers to run their own phone-sex-for-hire scams for months, never paying a dime for the service while pulling down thousands of dollars."

Kurtzman took the keyboard from Tokaido, entering keystrokes rapidly. "I'm going to pull up the telephone records for these accounts, see who Grishin was doing business with."

In rapid succession, over dozens of long-distance carriers that Kurtzman had access to through the programming he had in place, the bills of the savings-and-loan numbers began to appear. All of them showed a history of being paid in full, with differing dates, but all of them on time. They all also showed only one long-distance area dialed.

Price immediately recognized the 212 area code as belonging to New York City's Manhattan region. "Who do those numbers belong to?"

As Kurtzman tapped the keyboard, the numbers realigned themselves down his central screen, listing whom the numbers belonged to and what address they belonged to. "Brokers," the cybernetics expert said. "All of these people are Wall Street brokers."

"That's where he's building his program," Tokaido stated. "Those pieces are going in cloaked as part of investment packages—probably are, in fact, investment packages—and are assembling themselves. Maybe they're already in place, already functioning." The younger man's voice rose in excitement and disbelief. "Grishin's planning on hacking Wall Street."

"Can we lock out those numbers?" Price asked Kurtzman.

"I can get started," the cybernetics expert said. "It's going to take a lot of time to get them all. And there's no guarantee that we'll have them all. Grishin's probably got access to dozens of other numbers, some of them more legitimate than these."

Price looked at the phone numbers. Appearing there in white on a field of gray, they looked innocuous, nothing at all like the threat that they represented.

"If you start changing his system," Tokaido announced, "you're going to alert Grishin that we're onto him."

"Akira's right, Barb," Kurtzman said. "If we're going to go head-to-head with this guy, we need to get a look at the hand we're left with."

Price knew that it was true. "Leave it intact," she said. "For now. Keep it monitored. Let me know the instant things change."

"Sure."

Price retreated to her office, already punching in the number she had for Harold Brognola.

"SALOME," KESAR GRISHIN said as he pulled on the phone headset, "are you ready?"

"I hear a grin in your voice," the woman replied.

Showered and feeling refreshed after breakfast, Grishin sat at the computer station in his cabin in the jet. The satellite system he owned managed the triangulated phone connections from his position over the Pacific Ocean, Salome's base of operations in the Caribbean and the office in downtown Manhattan without problems. "Of course I'm smiling. And why shouldn't I be? We're about to take Wall Street by storm."

"I feel I should offer a caveat about overconfidence."

"And you would," Grishin said, "had you any reason to. How are things at the Japanese office?"

"Wakaba International logged on to the Wall Street investment broker as you suggested, and they are prepared to upload the investment package that I will send them in a few minutes."

"Excellent." Grishin looked at his watch, realized they'd probably already entered another time zone by now, and adjusted the time accordingly. The *investment* package Wakaba was going to upload contained more of the programming that he had been salting the Wall Street brokerage computers with for the past two years.

"I do have some bad news."

Grishin entered commands on the computer, accessing the mainframe he had back at his estate. The modem, though it was more sophisticated than anything coming out on the market at present, still required time to boot up the programming template. "What news?"

"Mr. DeCapra is not going to be able to make the meeting aboard the liner for the party tomorrow night."

Irritation flooded Grishin. He tried to push it away, realizing that part of the feeling stemmed from the fact that he still hadn't slept in more than twenty-eight hours. He got up from his seat and fixed another vodka. "And why won't Mr. DeCapra be there?" He was counting on bringing the East Coast Mafia Families into the fold. They represented a large block of investment potential, which would even further entrench his machinations in the Wall Street operation.

"Mr. DeCapra suffered an accident."

"An accident?" Grishin didn't like the sound of the announcement. He didn't like coincidences, either.

"Apparently Mr. DeCapra was beaten by a pair of professional thugs at a party given by Michael Charteris. You know who he is?"

"Of course." Charteris had proved instrumental in setting up some of the shell companies Grishin had used in America. "Who hired the thugs?"

"The list of possibilities is a long one."

"Forget it." Grishin watched as the program booted up, reaching sixty percent, then seventy, and continuing to climb. "Did they catch the men who beat De-Capra?"

"Unfortunately, no. Though I got the impression that a number of husbands and boyfriends would stand in line to offer a commission for a job well done."

"DeCapra is out?"

"Definitely."

"Have the East Coast Families decided to forego the meeting?"

"They want to send someone else."

An uncomfortable itch spread across the back of Grishin's neck. The software had completely booted up. He triggered the modem connection, springboarding through another line into the investment office he'd selected in the Wall Street sector. With the last series of investments coming in from Russia and the Middle East, each of them handled through brokerage firms he had interests in, enough of the program should have been intact to run. "Do you know who they want to send?"

"His name is Leopold Turrin."

"I think I remember his name from the files you assembled on those people."

"You should. Mr. DeCapra barely edged out Mr. Turrin to represent the East Coast Families' interest with you."

"Why didn't they just send them together?"

"Mr. DeCapra didn't want it that way."

"Why?"

"Apparently Mr. DeCapra feared his own light would be eclipsed by Mr. Turrin's."

"Would that happen?"

"Mr. Turrin garners a lot of respect in the right circles. Mr. DeCapra is trying to gain his own validation."

"Then why did they offer DeCapra?"

"Mr. DeCapra understands more about the computer aspects of what you're offering."

Grishin reviewed the stock quotes that scrolled across his screen. The prices fluctuated as shares were bought and sold, fortunes made and lost that day as the market flip-flopped. He utilized the software, reaching out and accessing stock quotes being pumped through on a major credit card company, a large oil corporation and an electronics firm that had been showing a steady decline as younger, more-vigorous companies came out with more-aggressive merchandise. "Turrin isn't inept when it comes to financial matters, is he? I don't want to be fucking around with a goddamned invalid."

"No."

"Another thing I don't like is how conveniently Turrin got moved up into DeCapra's spot," Grishin stated. "How sure are we that he had nothing to do with De-Capra's accident?"

"There are no ties. And Mr. DeCapra was found in a somewhat compromising situation with Mrs. Charteris."

From what he'd heard about DeCapra, that didn't surprise Grishin. "How much do we know about Turrin?"

"I downloaded everything the Organized Crime Task Force has on him. If I printed it out, I'd have enough reports, court interviews and news stories to fill a library."

"The man is what he seems to be?"

"Mr. Turrin comes from old-line power in the East Coast Families. After a stint in the U.S. Army, Mr. Turrin has been a career Family man. He's been in semiretirement through his own choice for the last handful of years."

"Why?"

"From what I interpret in the files, he took himself out of the play. A number of the East Coast Families, and some of the West Coast ones, as well, have used him in the past to mediate problem issues. He's good at what he does."

"How can we sell him?"

"You're referring to special treatment?"

"Yes." Accessing the stock quotes, Grishin cut the selling price of the credit-card company and the oil company by thirty percent, then doubled the electronics firm's stock. The software accepted the changes, then blinked "Change?" He tapped the Enter key.

The computer blinked again: "Change in progress. Updating incoming files. Global Search-and-replace."

"Leo Turrin is a man above reproach," Salome said, "maybe even approach, as well. In some ways, he could be a harder sell than Mr. DeCapra ever would have been."

Switching on the television behind him, Grishin changed channels to a financial network, watching the coverage suddenly shift to Wall Street. A camera panned in on the trading floor, showing knotted groups of men glued to monitor screens. Grishin smiled. "Are you monitoring things from your end?"

"Yes."

"Wonderful, isn't it? All the prognosticators of economic indexing are probably shitting their pants right now, wondering what the hell went wrong." The software design was something he'd worked on diligently for three years, learning everything he could about the investment communications links Wall Street had with the rest of the world. He let the stock quotes run for a minute and a half.

Then the computer monitor blinked again. "Parameters Blurring. System overload. Failure inevitable."

A minute and a half wasn't long, but it was enough time to cause a numbers of shares to change hands. Today's investor was used to a certain volatility in the market, and was quick to react. He double-tapped the Enter button.

"Change in progress. Reestablishing prior stock quotes."

Grishin picked up his glass. "I'm toasting myself, Salome. Join me."

"I believe I will. I hadn't thought the program would work so well."

Grishin sipped his drink. "You haven't seen anything yet. Wait until the rest of the programming goes in from Wakaba International. There'll be no stopping me then. Bring on Mr. Leopold Turrin. There's no way I can fail to sell his people this system." He shut down the computer with a few keystrokes.

The confusion on Wall Street's trading floor continued as the master quote board registered the return to the initial selling prices. Several investors went into another frenzied mode, struggling to recoup losses or overspending.

Grishin laughed at the antics. "You realize what the joke is, don't you, Salome?"

"Perhaps you'd care to enlighten me."

"Those people are struggling to save and recover dollars that existed only for a minute and a half. Cyberdollars. Someone's score on a tote board. Appearances can be so deceiving, but they are so necessary to doing business."

"Speaking of appearances," Salome said, "I still believe the best investment of your time tomorrow night would be to attend the party aboard the ocean liner instead of taking the trip to Milwaukee."

Grishin used the remote control and shut off the television. He leaned back in his chair, feeling exuberant. "I just pulled off one of the biggest coups of my entire career by manipulation of Wall Street quotes, something that's only been able to be influenced by major marketing pushes by corporations as big as some Third World nations. Don't presume to second-guess me at this point. You or Dobrynin. I have my own agenda. And so far, that agenda is working out."

"I'm sorry, Kesar. I spoke out of turn."

"Yes," Grishin said emphatically, "you did."

"I apologize."

"And I accept." Grishin sipped his drink and stared into the ebony depths of the computer screen. So much potential remained to be tapped within the program's reach—as soon as he had it completely up and running. "Break down the information on this man Turrin for me. I'll want to meet with him Saturday morning at my estate. If he's willing."

"I've got a package ready. I'll send it along."

"Very good." Grishin broke the connection and finished his drink. Then he turned the television back on, watching it with the volume turned down. There would be speculations, of course. The change in the selling price of the stocks he'd manipulated had been too large, and the targets had been chosen carefully. But no one would know the truth.

Not until he told them. And that, he was holding until the proper time.

CHAPTER TWENTY-FOUR

Carl Lyons peered over Hermann Schwarz's shoulder into the photo-developing liquids in the metal pans spread across the hotel suite's main bathroom. The smell of the chemicals ran rampant through the room despite the overhead duct laboring to suck the noxious odors away.

Schwarz poked at the developing pictures with a pair of plastic tongs, as if coaxing the images to put in an appearance. He worked methodically, moving from pan to pan.

The timer went off. Working quickly, Schwarz plucked the contact sheets from the pans and hung them up to dry on the fishing line he'd run from one wall to the opposite.

"What do you have?" Lyons asked.

"Blueprints," Schwarz answered. "The film was black-and-white, so we can enlarge the images and jockey around a little bit with them if we need to without losing definition."

Lyons studied each of the twenty-four pictures, using one of the magnifying glasses on the table. Guarano had done a good job with the photos, making sure to take overlapping shots so close-ups could be pieced together. The blueprints had no identifying marks, headers or legends.

"Hell," Schwarz said in disgust, "these could be from an office space anywhere."

Lyons silently agreed.

Blancanales called to them from the living room. Closing down the photo-development equipment, Lyons and Schwarz walked into the outer room.

Blancanales sat in front of the computer system they'd installed in the suite. The monitor showed the different views available over the minicam system they'd installed in Escelera's suite.

"What's up?" Lyons asked. On the screens, Escelera and her group were seated at the dining table while white-jacketed waiters catered their lunch.

Blancanales tapped the computer keyboard. One of the minicam views exploded in size, filling the screen. The view tightened, then started to magnify.

"What are we looking at?" Schwarz asked.

"A file Escelera was checking before lunch arrived," Blancanales replied. "She got word earlier that Guarano had been air-lifted from the freighter out in anchorage, and her calls to Francisca, the Puerto Vallarta police detective, have gone unanswered."

"Getting a little tense in there," Lyons commented.

"Yeah," Blancanales agreed. "I think so." The view on the monitor continued to tighten, until details were discernible. The file folder held no markings, but an eight-by-ten print had slid halfway out of the sheaf of papers. The minicam view continued to get closer, more slowly now as it started to max out its capabilities.

The picture from the file showed a tight cluster of buildings in a metropolitan downtown area. Lyons had the impression that he'd seen the area before, but couldn't summon up where or when or what the circumstances had been.

"Can you get a picture of this?" Lyons asked.

"Already done," Blancanales said. He tapped the modem-connection icon in the lower-right corner of the monitor screen. "I'm sending it back to the Farm right now. Maybe Aaron can tag it in one of the databases he has access to. But I'm going to tell you right now, matching it up anywhere is going to be a long shot."

"That's okay," Schwarz said. "Long shots are where Kurtzman and his team shine."

London, England
Friday

DRESSED IN BLACK and draped in shadow, David McCarter led the way to the expensive town house that Barbara Price had discovered belonged to Percival Dickey. T. J. Hawkins was dressed like McCarter, wearing a black turtleneck and slacks, with a casual black jacket to block the chill wind and to cover the pistol in its shoulder rig.

The town house was more than one hundred years old, McCarter judged upon seeing it. Rising three stories high, it fit in with the other structures in the area. All of the homes belonged to moneyed families, though some of them were now used only when conducting business in London proper.

A wrought-iron privacy fence stood eight feet tall, topped with cruel, edged points. A double gate fronted the entrance from the street, fish and other sea creatures in bas-relief scribed into the metal. The dark stone of the house reflected the wet gleam of headlights from a cab passing through the street.

McCarter turned up his jacket collar and tapped the Transmit button on the headset. "Phoenix Four."

"Four here, One," Calvin James responded. "You guys are clean and green."

Without breaking stride, McCarter and Hawkins stepped into the canopied area. The Phoenix Force leader slid his Browning Hi-Power from shoulder leather and tapped its customized sound suppressor, making sure it was still attached properly. It felt sure and solid. He crossed his hands in front of him as Hawkins went to work on the electronic lock securing the doors. Hawkins held a battery-powered screwdriver and quickly removed the screws from the plate containing the security connection that linked the door to the computer system inside.

McCarter studied the house, fitting everything in his mind. Kurtzman and Price had come up with house plans, including the remodeling Dickey had contracted since buying and moving into the place. No lights were on inside.

But plenty of them would come on if the security system wasn't negated.

"Here we go," Hawkins breathed quietly.

McCarter glanced down, watching.

Hawkins removed the facing plate. According to the security specs Kurtzman had forwarded, the security system would broadcast an alarm in thirty seconds if the proper code wasn't entered. Moving deftly, Hawkins attached the leads from the small microchip device he took from his jacket pocket.

They had thirty seconds. McCarter counted them down, adrenaline pumping through his system. Dickey kept at least four men on-site with him. Price had also provided information that the mercenary broker was entertaining that evening with a stay-over guest, a young woman who sold her time and was easily half Dickey's age.

The yellow numbers on the electronic device in Hawkins's hand spun rapidly.

McCarter was down to five seconds, counting them off, when the five numbers, some of them in double digits, locked in on Hawkins's miracle box.

"We're in," Hawkins said. He tapped other buttons on the device. "I'm shutting down the connection to the police station, the pressure-sensitive windows and flooring and the infrared systems inside the house."

McCarter placed his hand on the wrought-iron gate. "Tell me when."

"When." Hawkins gathered his tools and shoved them in the deep pockets of the jacket.

"Four," McCarter said over the headset.

"I'm with you." Calvin James was on the rooftop of a building across the street with a silenced Vaime sniper rifle.

McCarter tugged on the gate. It opened somewhat stiffly, grating across the stone walk beneath it. The Briton walked forward rapidly and went up the steps leading to the building. He managed the door lock with picks in under a minute while Hawkins covered his back.

They split up inside the foyer. Hawkins went to the drawing room while McCarter took the kitchen. The plan was to secure the place floor by floor until they found Dickey.

The town house was furnished with care. Period pieces filled the rooms, and paintings adorned the walls, not overly priced, but originals all the same. Sounds of a struggle came from the drawing room, then ended quickly.

"One down," Hawkins confirmed over the headset.

McCarter was coming back from the breakfast nook when the second guard walked from the kitchen.

The man dabbed at his lips with a napkin. He held an automatic pistol in his fist as he advanced cautiously. Dropping the napkin to the floor, he searched the wall for the light switch. "Bryan?"

McCarter fired without mercy, putting two rounds through the man's heart and one through his head. All of the men Dickey had in his employ were killers.

The dead man dropped to his knees and fell forward.

Stepping over the body, the Phoenix Force leader checked the kitchen area. No one else was inside. He tapped the headset's Transmit button. "Two down."

"I'm going up," Hawkins said.

"On my way." McCarter walked back toward the front of the building, aiming for the stairs that led to the upper floors. Hawkins would take the second stairway. There was also an elevator, which was in the hallway outside the drawing room.

McCarter took the steps rapidly, the Hi-Power leveled before him.

Four bedrooms were on the second floor, two of which were occupied. Only dead men remained behind as Hawkins and McCarter took the only set of stairs leading to the third floor.

Hawkins paused at the doorway to the master bedroom. The lock picks he wielded with a surgeon's precision caused the lock to sheathe back into itself. He dropped a gloved hand on the door, twisted and pushed it open.

Dim light streamed in through the French windows, cutting soft lines across the man and woman lying in the large four-poster. The woman lay curled up along the edge of the bed, her back to Dickey.

McCarter took a plastic protector about the size and shape of a cigar from his pocket. Inside was a hypodermic. He approached the woman and nodded at Hawkins.

The younger man grabbed the woman's face, clapping a hand over her lips. She came awake almost at once and reached up to grab Hawkins's arm.

McCarter held her left forearm and plunged the needle home inside her elbow. Her struggles awakened Dickey, who gaped in astonishment, then began to reach for a drawer at the side of the bed.

The Phoenix Force leader dropped the empty hypodermic and fired two rounds from the Hi-Power into the nightstand. The drawer splintered.

Dickey yanked his hand back, cowering against his bed. "Who are you?"

The woman passed out as the drugs spread through her system.

McCarter took a penlight from his shirt pocket. He switched it on and shone it in Dickey's face. "I'm the guy," the Briton said in a quiet, firm voice, "that you're about to have a long heart-to-heart talk with concerning a certain mercenary action that went down in Myanmar almost eighteen hours ago."

Dickey glanced at the woman lying unconscious beside him, then up at Hawkins standing by the bed with his pistol in hand. He looked back at McCarter. "Sure, mate, anything you want to talk about."

MACK BOLAN PULLED the rental car from the curb, his eyes centered on the luxury vehicle ahead of him. He waited for a moment, then flicked on the lights.

"Dionis Santos doesn't exactly lead the quiet life-style of a successful gangster, does he?" Jack Grimaldi asked from the passenger seat.

"No." Bolan checked his backtrail in the rearview mirror and spotted the sedan that followed Santos from the nightclub's parking area. The soldier stayed in the right lane, allowing the other car to speed past him.

Santos's chosen mode of transportation was a tricked-out Winnebago. Running lights framed the big recreational vehicle as it glided down the highway back to Montego Bay proper.

Bolan and Grimaldi had picked up Santos's trail easily after the information Edgar Joule had provided. Although he was supposedly keeping a low profile to stay out of the gun sights of the Colombian cartels seeking to protect Grishin's territory, Santos had gone clubbing. It was a rebellious action, and Santos had done business, as well.

Santos never dealt out of the Winnebago, though, according to the dossiers Kurtzman had ransacked from the Montego Bay police department and DEA files. But the RV was equipped with cellular telephones and computers, literally an office on wheels. The RV had also been reworked with bulletproof armor and bullet-proof glass, and had weapons ports added. The luxury vehicle had become a rolling dreadnought.

Bolan followed the entourage. Gradually the four lanes became a two-lane highway that would run straight back into the heart of Montego Bay. The road hugged the coastline rather than attempting to break through the jungle areas. In some places, the rolling ocean breakers were less than a hundred yards from the road, kissed by the moonlight that blazed through the remaining storm clouds.

Topping a slight rise that gave him an unobstructed view of the road for a quarter mile, Bolan made the decision to move. He pushed his foot on the sedan's accelerator and steered for the left, acting as if he were going to pass.

The car running protection from the rear moved over slightly, speeding up enough to squeeze out any perceptible space between the two vehicles. Besides the driver, there were two other men in the car. The greenish glow from the instrument panel lit their faces.

When the rental drew even with the blocker car, Bolan whipped the wheel hard to the right, slamming the vehicles together. The impact shivered through the steering column as the soldier kept the pressure on, forcing the car over.

The driver tried to recover, slamming Bolan's car back. Metal screeched in agony. The driver's-side mirror tore free of the door. The men in the passenger and rear seats struggled to free their guns.

Jack Grimaldi brought up the 12-gauge Mossberg shotgun and shoved the muzzle toward the driver's window. During the hours since the raid on Joule's law office, they'd dumped the lawyer's Caddie and worked on their weapons. After breaking into a machine shop earlier, the Executioner had cut down the shotguns, removing much of the barrels, making them pure death at close range.

The pilot pulled the trigger. The double-aught buckshot pattern chopped into the driver's-side glass. Fractures ran through the bulletproof glass, but it held its position in the door. The impact and the flare of the muzzle-flash threw the driver off. Instinctively he steered away from Bolan.

The Executioner remained in aggressive mode, gaining speed, then ramming into the car again. The rental sedan smacked up against the side of the blocker car like a breaker rolling in, going up high on two wheels for just a moment.

Grimaldi fired another 12-gauge charge into the driver's window. The pellets bounced off the bulletproof glass and spanged off the rental sedan.

Out of control, the blocker car left the road in a cloud of dust. It looked like a comet sluicing through the sand-covered shoulder before it smashed into a tree.

Turning his attention to the Winnebago, Bolan saw that the big RV had pulled ahead a considerable distance. There was no question of it getting away. The RV pushed too much air, carried too much weight. Bolan pinned the accelerator to the floor, and they gained on the Winnebago quickly.

Grimaldi reached into the back seat as autofire raked the nose of the rental sedan.

Bolan fought the steering wheel, feeling the power steering starting to slip, making driving more difficult. One of the rounds had to have clipped the power-steering unit. The guess was confirmed when a spray of hydraulic fluid splashed against the windshield. He switched on the windshield wipers but succeeded only in smearing the dark fluid and further reducing visibility.

The soldier pulled the car hard left, coming up on the left side of the RV. The Winnebago's driver took evasive action, weaving as he sped up. However, the action was restricted by the RV's bulk and lack of balance; the vehicle wasn't designed for such tactics.

"Get ready," Bolan told Grimaldi.

The ace pilot gave him a nod, holding the satchel charges they'd made out of the C-4 they'd taken during their ordnance raid. The plastic explosive was inside an ordinary backpack, but the bag had ordnance tape covering the back. Sticky on both sides, and with the C-4 as lightweight as it was, the backpack stuck easily to the side of the Winnebago when Bolan swerved the rental sedan close enough.

"Done!" Grimaldi called.

Bolan eased off the accelerator at once. Bullets chewed up the nose of the sedan, then chipped sparks from the highway as the gunners lost the range. He spotted the backpack clinging to the side of the Winnebago, the straps fluttering in the slipstream. "Take it out."

Grimaldi took a remote-control detonator from the glove compartment, flipped up the cover and pressed the button.

The explosion went off moments later, ripping out the side of the Winnebago. It also tore out the rear axle, throwing the RV totally off balance. The driver fought for control, but it was a losing battle. The rear axle swung loose from its moorings and got tangled up underneath the RV, flipping it over onto its side.

Grimaldi took up the shotgun as Bolan pulled off the road after the Winnebago.

Halting the sedan behind the vehicle, leaving enough room for the headlights to take away the night on either side of it, Bolan threw the transmission into Park. He scooped up the Ingram MAC-10 and flipped off the safety, he and Grimaldi leaving the sedan at the same time and charging for the wrecked RV.

A man clambered from the passenger side of the

Winnebago, which was now the top side of the vehicle. He had a pistol in his fist and fired it rapidly in their direction.

The Executioner loosed a blistering figure eight of .45-caliber death that punched the shooter to the ground.

"I've got the front," Grimaldi called, racing around the RV.

The Executioner scrambled on top of the Winnebago and maintained a low profile. A fire had started underneath the vehicle, and the stench of gasoline was in the air.

He reached the side door of the RV. The damage had jammed the door, but he managed to open it after a second tug. Smoke trapped inside billowed out.

Pistol shots rang out, then Grimaldi's shotgun boomed and the gunfire stopped.

Taking a flashlight from his pocket, Bolan shone it into the Winnebago.

The inside of the RV was total carnage. Though they'd been bolted down, desks and computer equipment were scattered all over. The section just behind the driver's cab had been a kitchen. Cabinet doors lay askew, and pots and pans littered the area, along with dry goods and the contents of the refrigerator.

Bolan dropped inside. Movement ahead of him in the small, short hallway that led to the rear of the RV drew his attention. His flashlight beam pinned a man who wasn't Dionis Santos, then the MAC-10 thundered in the soldier's fist. The man spun away, dropping the pistol in his hand.

With the Winnebago turned over on its side, the Executioner couldn't walk through the hallway. He crawled through, staying low. Santos's office area was in the center of the RV, with a bedroom in the back.

A dead man blocked the way ahead of Bolan, his neck twisted in a position totally unnatural. The Executioner verified it wasn't Santos, then pushed the corpse to one side and kept going.

He found Santos in the office area under a pile of furniture. The man waved a pistol in Bolan's direction, one hand over an eye as blood streamed down his arm.

Bolan dropped into the room from the hallway and took a step forward. A man surged forward from farther back in the room, roaring with rage and brandishing a pistol. The Executioner whipped the MAC-10 around and fired a short burst that danced across the man's chest. The heavy rounds bounced the man backward, sending him crashing against the back wall.

Pulling the submachine gun back onto Santos, Bolan said, "Dead or alive. However you want it."

Santos hesitated only a moment, then threw his pistol away.

Bolan worked carefully, hauling his prisoner up from the debris, then securing his hands behind his back with a roll of ordnance tape.

"Who the hell are you, man?" Santos demanded.

Bolan didn't answer, pushing the man toward the hallway.

"Who? DEA? Or are you for hire?" Santos stumbled, having trouble getting up into the hallway.

Bolan shoved the man up and through the opening, conscious of the thickening gasoline smell.

"I can pay you," Santos called back. "I can pay you more than you're getting now."

"Crawl," Bolan ordered.

"I can't," Santos protested, flopping weakly. "You

tied my fucking hands behind my fucking back. And I'm bleeding all over the goddamned place."

Bolan grabbed the man's foot and shoved him through the hallway. Santos dropped over the edge on the other side, yelping in pain and surprise. The Executioner followed.

Santos was trying to push himself up on his chin and his knees when Bolan got to the other side.

"Sarge."

Bolan glanced up at the doorway and saw Grimaldi there.

"We're clear out here. Hand him up." The pilot reached a hand down inside the Winnebago.

Bolan grabbed Santos by the shoulder and pulled him into a standing position. Taking the belt from the nearby dead man's pants, Bolan secured it under Santos's arms. Grimaldi was just able to reach the belt. He caught it and started to pull the man up. Bolan grabbed the man's legs and helped. Once Santos was clear, he clambered through the doorway himself.

"Man," Santos said, "how much money can we be talking about here? Come on."

Bolan dropped to the ground beside Grimaldi and Santos. The fire underneath the RV had gotten larger and pools of gasoline had collected in the sand.

"I got thousands of dollars in that RV, man," Santos said.

Grimaldi pushed the man from behind, starting him toward the rental sedan.

"What?" Santos said. "You just going to let that money burn up? I'm telling you the truth! Got enough in there to keep you set up and living fine for months. Maybe a year or two, you know?"

Grimaldi took a strip of ordnance tape and strapped

it across the man's mouth. "Sounds better already," the pilot commented. He stored their prisoner in the rear seat of the sedan.

Bolan lifted the hood to look at the engine. The radiator was intact. Luckily only the power-steering hose had been damaged, not the unit itself. He used ordnance tape to patch the small hole in the hose. The fluid leaked out only when he was using the power steering. He figured there was enough at least to get them to the outskirts of Montego Bay, where they could acquire another car. The name and the credit card Bolan had used to secure the rental would disappear, and the insurance would cover the rental agency's loss. He had other credit cards, and by morning, Price would have arranged a diplomatic pouch that would further equip him for a longer stay in the islands.

He slipped behind the wheel while Grimaldi joined Santos in the rear seat. He put the car in gear and pulled back onto the road, driving around the overturned Winnebago. Adjusting the rearview mirror, he caught Santos's gaze. "You want to make a deal, right?"

Santos nodded, trying to talk around the strip of tape over his mouth.

"There's only one deal on the table," the Executioner said coldly. "If you can't handle it, you don't see the sunrise in the morning."

Santos nodded again.

"I want to hear what you know about Kesar Grishin's operations. The guy's been forcing you out of your home territory, so I know you've been checking him out. You've probably got more on him than any law-enforcement agency on the island."

Santos's head bobbed up and down vigorously.

"Take the tape off."

As Grimaldi stripped the tape, the Winnebago exploded behind them. The glare from the explosion washed over the inside of the sedan, giving the appearance of sudden daylight. Yellow-and-orange flames shot up from the wreckage, casting out roiling clouds of dark gray smoke.

"Man," Santos said, "if you want Grishin, I'll give you the bastard on a plate. Been trying to give him up to the DEA, the locals, you know, but they got all these rules and shit they've got to go by."

"I'm making up my own rules," the Executioner said.

"Man," Santos said earnestly, "I got that impression."

CHAPTER TWENTY-FIVE

Hal Brognola paced his hotel room as he talked over a scrambled cellular telephone that connected him with the White House. He'd managed a couple hours' sleep on the flight from Washington, D.C., when he'd come to Milwaukee with U.S. Attorney General Ramona Thompson and her staff. He felt washed out, used up, and his stomach churned like a washing machine despite the antacid tablets he'd been chewing.

"Sir," the big Fed said, "I think—"

"Hal," the President interrupted, "don't go getting sanctimonious on me. Can you guarantee you can take out Kesar Grishin and this damned virus that he's shoved into the Wall Street computer without anything going wrong?"

Brognola glanced at the television in the hotel room. It was tuned to CNN and had been on since his arrival. The story about the confusion in the Wall Street quotes was still part of the overall thread of the stories the network was choosing to continue to cover. Market analysts had been consulted during the day, along with representatives from the three corporations involved, as well as Wall Street brokers and major players in the realm of investing. Brognola had become familiar with all of the stories.

"No, sir."

"Then we need to wait until we know we can nullify this man."

Brognola let out his pent-up breath quietly. No matter how much he breathed out, it just seemed like he couldn't empty his lungs entirely. "I know I don't need to point out that every hour we leave Grishin in place is another hour he's able to solidify his position."

"No," the President agreed, "you don't."

The Justice man forced himself to turn away from the television. It was frustrating to watch, reminding him of everything that needed doing and the fact that he wasn't getting it done. He crossed the room to the balcony windows, which overlooked the heart of Milwaukee. The city wasn't truly at rest. It was an industrial community that ran on a twenty-four-hour clock. The streets weren't congested yet, but they would be in a few short hours. In the meantime, the night shifts kept the assembly lines moving.

"Hal," the President said in a softer tone, "I understand your frustration. Hell, how do you think it makes me feel to have to tell you this?"

Brognola took another antacid from the nearly depleted roll in his pocket. He hadn't yet changed out of the clothes he wore the previous day. After his arrival at the hotel, he'd managed another hour of sleep. He hadn't even bothered to turn down the bed. And he wasn't really able to call it sleep, either. There had been nothing restful about it, just a lessening of resistance to the fatigue that threatened to claim him. He ran a hand across his face, feeling the stubble growth.

"Do we even know where Grishin is?" the President asked.

"No."

"But Grishin's supposed to be at the cruise ship in Jamaica this evening?"

"Yes, sir."

"Leo Turrin's in place down there?"

"He'll be arriving at ten o'clock this morning," Brognola answered. "Tonight he'll be at the yacht."

"There are no problems there?"

"No." And that made the head Fed uneasy, as well. The President had ordered the Stony Man teams to stand down for the time being, and no one was going to be close to Turrin if the wheels came off down there.

"The debacle at Charteris's estate couldn't have been avoided?"

"It was the only sure time to take DeCapra out of the play."

"Striker is in Jamaica?"

"Yes."

"He's talked with Dionis Santos?"

"Yes, sir. Someone should have talked with Santos long before now. He had a lot of information on Grishin's operations that wasn't in any of the intel packets we had access to."

The President's reply was dry. "Striker's methods aren't something this office would publicly condone."

"No, sir." But they were effective, and Brognola knew both of them knew it. "We're checking out the leads Santos has given us, getting a better picture of the overall laundering scheme."

"I trust Striker isn't exactly happy about being put on hold?"

"He's not happy about it," Brognola said, "but he'll stick with the call." Bolan's relationship with Stony Man Farm was a good one, but the big hellfire warrior also called his own shots in spite of public or political approval. If Bolan had seen a way clear to take out Grishin and leave the situation intact, Brognola had no doubts the Executioner would do just that.

"Phoenix Force is on its way to Jamaica?"

"Yes, sir. They'll link up with Striker this afternoon."

"And Able Team is in New York?"

Brognola glanced at his watch. "They will be by the end of the hour. Escelera left Puerto Vallarta late last night."

"Barbara tells me you found the building in Escelera's documents."

"Yes."

"Do you know what the importance of it is?"

Brognola walked back to his notebook computer and opened it on the desk. "The building is located in the Wall Street sector of Manhattan. The man who worked there was a clinical psychologist who worked with the state in a number of rehab programs."

"Could that be a tie?"

"That might be how Escelera ferreted him out," Brognola replied, "but that isn't the tie." He tapped the computer's keyboard, bringing up the file on the screen. A picture of the building formed on the right, while a picture of the psychologist took shape at the top. Lines of biographical data followed, tying in all the particulars Kurtzman and his team could find out about the man. "You've got the file in your computer." He gave the President the access number, then sipped his coffee while the Man brought up the file at his end.

"There it is. The guy's name was Peter Lawrence."

"Yeah. As you read through it, you're not going to find anything outstanding. He was a guy with bills, which he pretty much paid on time, no extravagant lifestyle, and lived from contract to contract with the state. The only significant thing you're going to find is that he had a six-month lease on the office space, and that isn't up for another two months.''

''Why is that significant?''

''Lawrence never paid ahead before.''

''That doesn't seem very significant to me. Maybe he came into a windfall and paid ahead just to get it out of the way.''

''What is significant about it is that the check for the last four months of the contract arrived in Manhattan two days before his body got back there.''

''His body?''

''Yes. Lawrence was killed in a boating accident down in Puerto Vallarta almost two months ago. Once Kurtzman found out where the building was and who the office belonged to—and I'm not even mentioning all the databases he had to go through, first identifying the state the building was in, then the area, then the actual building itself—he turned up the story on Lawrence himself. The report on the accident down in Puerto Vallarta was filed by Detective Miguel Francisca of the Puerto Vallarta Police Department.''

''How did Lawrence die?''

''The official story is that he was out scuba diving and got clipped by a passing boat. Swimmers found his body early in the morning. He'd been there all night. Lyons dropped a coin down there after we turned up the name. He talked shop with a uniformed police officer who'd helped investigate the accident. The officer said the case was closed, sure, but there was one loose end.''

''What?''

"No one knew where Lawrence got the scuba gear he was wearing."

"He didn't take any with him?"

"No. And the gear wasn't marked as belonging to a rental shop."

"Okay, given that Escelera was responsible for the man's death, how does the office tie in?"

"It's a bottom-floor office. And one of the main fiber-optic cable trunk lines leading to the Wall Street Exchange runs beneath it. Kurtzman thinks Grishin wanted the office space to run a direct-connect to the Wall Street trunk line as a backup fail-safe."

"If Grishin can already get into the Wall Street computers, why would he need this?"

"Yesterday he was testing the system. He screwed up the stock-market quotes for ninety-two seconds. Kurtzman thinks maybe Grishin's system isn't ready to go on-line for any longer than that. With the direct-connect to the trunk line, even over a cell phone, he can get a stronger access to the exchange systems."

"My, God," the President said, "do you realize what this means?"

"Yes, sir," Brognola replied. He, Price and Kurtzman had already discussed the situation. "It means that if the computer program that Akira found works the way Grishin designed it to, he can change anything he wants to with the stock figures."

"Son of a bitch!" the President said. "Do you know the panic that has already set in because of the changes that went on yesterday?"

"Yes." Brognola glanced at CNN on the television and watched it all happening again.

"If Grishin manages to invade the computer system there and wreak havoc with them, Black Monday in the stock-market crash of '29 will pale by comparison.''

Brognola judged that to be a fair assessment. "That's why you need to let the Stony Man teams pursue this, sir.''

"What do you have in mind?''

"Turrin will be at the party on the ocean liner tonight. Grishin is supposed to talk one-on-one with him regarding investments the East Coast Mafia Families are supposed to commit to. Aaron and Akira spent last night creating a virus they believe will paralyze the programming Grishin has in the Wall Street cybernetic systems. If Leo can get to the computers Grishin is using, he's going to load up the virus and bring Kurtzman's computers on-line with Grishin's. Striker and Phoenix will target the site, shut down Grishin and exfiltrate Turrin.''

"That leaves the computer system you're hypothesizing exists in Manhattan.''

"Able Team will take that down.''

"And if we make a mistake,'' the President said, "we're going to lose this country's strongest selling point. Do you know how much business goes through Wall Street every day?''

"Yes, sir, I do.'' That information had all been encapsulated in the files Price and Kurtzman had sent up from the Farm.

"People all over the world depend on the trade that goes on there,'' the Man said. "In 1987, when we were floating in a sea of debt, the Japanese came through with a series of loans that kept this country strong and viable.''

That had also been the year when the Japanese yen

became part of international currency, Brognola remembered. Nothing was done out of pure generosity.

"Everyone comes here to trade," the President went on. "When the European Commonwealth Market started up, there was some speculation that it would take away from the United States' thunder. It didn't. But this, Hal, this will kill it."

"That won't happen," Brognola assured him. "The teams are in place. We can turn this one."

"Grishin's going to use this to blackmail us, isn't he?" the President asked.

"At some point, I'm certain he will."

"If we leave him alone, let him run his business, he'll let us run ours."

"That's a slow death," Brognola said. "You've seen yourself from the reports we've put together how Grishin is turning nearly fifty percent of organized crime's cash flow into legitimate business enterprises. Countries won't be run by governments in the future he's building—they'll be run by cartels and organizations. You've seen how the Mafia, the Yakuza, the Triads and the Colombian crime syndicates work." He paused. "You can't allow that to happen."

There was a long silence. "For now, Hal, the order stands. This is Friday, one of the most vigorous trading days on Wall Street. Find Grishin if you can, and leave him alone. Let me know when you do. We'll take a look at things then, make a better decision about what we should do."

Brognola stood quietly for a moment, then he lifted the phone to place the call to the Farm.

"HELL OF A PARTY, ain't it, Mr. Turrin?" Jimmy Venturo asked.

Leo Turrin glanced at the hardman standing beside

him and smiled. "Sure as hell is, Jimmy." He turned his gaze back to the ballroom floor on the *Royal Flush*'s main entertainment deck, feeling slightly intoxicated by all the pomp and splendor. "Feels like I'm standing in the middle of the United Nations."

Venturo nodded, then hooked a finger inside his tuxedo collar, trying to make it more comfortable. "This mook putting this on ain't no slacker when it comes to a bank book, hey? He's laying out a lot of bread for this shindig."

"Glitter money," Turrin announced. "Kesar Grishin's pockets go a lot deeper than this."

"I heard that," Venturo said. "Guys I was talking to were telling me this guy does business all over the world. Handles money the way Fat Eddie the Tuba does back in the old neighborhood. You know Fat Eddie?"

"Yeah." Fat Eddie was a money launderer for the Mob, primarily working the East Coast. Turrin had gotten to know Fat Eddie during his days with Sergio Frenchi.

"Nobody does business like the Tuba," Venturo said. "Makes money appear, disappear, just like that." He snapped his fingers. "Fat Eddie has told a couple guys that this Grishin mook was good, but he's kind of shy about trusting him."

Turrin nodded. The Families were reluctant about letting anybody but Family handle Family business. "That's what we're here to decide, Jimmy, just how far we can trust this mook."

Venturo clapped Turrin on the shoulder. "Anybody can spot a guy trying to shine on about something, Mr. Turrin, that's you. Nobody can lie to you, and you've always been a stand-up guy. I'm proud to be here with you. Thanks for squaring it with the don.''

"No problem, Jimmy.'' Turrin snagged a beer from a white-jacketed waiter passing by. The alcohol was all imported and served in German glass.

Long tables surrounded the dance floor. A band occupied one corner of the huge room, and belted out dance music that ranged from island reggae to seventies disco to salsa to big-band sounds. Spinning globes overhead reflected sparkles of light over the party-goers.

The European and American criminals were the most gregarious, actively seeking out the young women who'd been hired as part of the entertainment. The Japanese, Chinese and Vietnamese factions stayed primarily in their own groups, declining to mix.

Beyond the representatives of the various crime organizations, though, were the bodyguards who protected them. The atmosphere of inherent violence was too thick to ignore, and Turrin knew he contributed to it by having Venturo and his people staying close to him.

The rest of the ocean liner was open to Grishin's guests, but it had been his request that they be in the main party area between nine-fifteen and nine forty-five. Turrin's stomach had been tightening as he watched the minutes tick down.

"Mr. Turrin.''

Turning, Turrin found a beautiful woman standing behind him. She was petite, only a little over five feet tall, and had a figure that made the white spandex dress she wore cling in all the right places. Her hair was almost bone white and straight, cut so that the ends curled in and followed her jawline, framing her face. Topaz eyes caught Turrin's hypnotically.

She offered a white-gloved hand. "Pardon me for startling you, and permit me to introduce myself. I'm Salome."

Turrin took her hand. He'd noticed her earlier in the crowd, circulating through the guests, getting her hand kissed by the various European representatives. He held her hand only long enough to feel the smooth strength of it, then released it. "Leo Turrin."

"I know who you are. Mr. Grishin asked that I check on you, make sure you were having a good time."

"Thank you. I am." Turrin peered over her shoulder. "Is Mr. Grishin around?"

"He'll be joining us in only a few moments. Is there anything I can do for you?"

Turrin raised his stein of beer. "I'm all set. Just waiting to talk to Mr. Grishin."

"Are you always all business, Mr. Turrin?"

"No."

"Perhaps you'd like to dance?" She took the beer stein from his hand and gave it to Venturo, who made a silent whistle of appreciation behind the woman's back.

Having no choice and choosing to avoid a confrontation, Turrin gracefully surrendered. "Sure." He let Salome lead him onto the dance floor while Venturo smiled and shook his head.

"You make it hard for my guys to do their job," Turrin commented.

"Oh, you're safe here, Mr. Turrin. Mr. Grishin left strict orders that you were to be well taken care of." Salome slipped her arms around his neck and placed her body at a discreet distance from his.

Turrin could still feel the heat. He put his hands on the woman's hips cautiously. His attention was divided between the woman and the people around them. He couldn't imagine why she would want to guide him out on the dance floor and have someone slip a shiv between his ribs, but the thought was there.

The number was a big-band favorite. Turrin kept the steps easily.

"You're a marvelous dancer, Mr. Turrin," Salome said.

"Thank you. So are you."

"Lessons," she replied. "It took lots of work on my part to get this good. I have a feeling that you're a natural."

"My wife," Turrin explained. "She made me learn."

"You have a very wise wife."

"And a very beautiful one."

Salome raised her eyebrows and smiled slightly. "Are you telling me, or are you reminding yourself?"

Turrin grinned, and the expression was filled with honest amusement. "Maybe a little of both."

"You don't have to worry about me, Mr. Turrin. I'm merely attempting to get to know you, not seduce you. You represent a rather large consumer bloc that Kesar Grishin is interested in entering into a business relationship with. He'll be more than willing to talk with you about it."

"I'm ready." Turrin had scoured the ship as much as he was able under the careful watch of the guards and crew that floated freely through the guests. He hadn't found Grishin, nor had he found the computer command post that might control the virus that threatened the Wall Street Exchange.

"Soon." Salome drew back one of her arms and touched one of the dangling earrings she wore. "Henri, bring the number to a close, please."

In seconds, the band music drifted away, leaving only silence in its wake.

"Fallon, give me the media center, please," Salome said, "and patch me through to the ship's PA system."

Turrin had already picked up the fact that the earrings were microtransceivers. He stepped back from the woman, giving her space to work.

Overhead, a huge octagonal assembly of television screens descended from the ceiling. The ceiling tiles slid back smoothly, allowing entrance.

Salome turned toward the crowd as a baby spotlight ignited the dress and turned her into a bright phantasm of ivory. The lights around the ballroom dimmed, presenting a curtain of indigo behind her.

"Ladies and gentlemen," Salome said, and the PA system broadcast her words throughout the area, "Kesar Grishin asked me to convey his regret at not being able to be here in person."

A rumble of conversations started up at once. Evidently most of the congregation wasn't happy to learn that at all.

"However," Salome continued, "Kesar would like to have a few words with you."

The baby spotlight winked out, and Salome disappeared into the darkness. Turrin watched her cross back to him as the octagon of television screens flared to life overhead.

Kesar Grishin appeared on the screen. He wore a black sports coat over a red turtleneck, smiling and confident. He sat in a recliner, one leg crossed over the other, black slacks tailored well enough that only a small portion of the black socks showed.

"Friends and business partners," Grishin said, "I hope you're having a good time at the party. I threw it for you, so damn it, you should enjoy it. I extend my apologies that I couldn't be there. However, maybe next year." He smiled, and Turrin saw that the expression was devoid of any warmth. "I have the feeling that we're going to be together for a very long time." He reached to his side and hoisted a champagne glass. "Toast with me."

Salome took two glasses of champagne from a passing waiter. Other waiters were hurrying through the crowd, passing out the fresh drinks. The woman gave one to Turrin.

Grishin gazed at the bubbly liquid trapped in the clear crystal. "To your health, and to our continued successes. May we leave our enemies broken behind us. And may we never know a time with lean profits." He drank.

Turrin drank, as well, noticing all of the people around him doing the same. He didn't think the recording was live, but he couldn't figure out why it would be taped.

Grishin put his empty glass aside. "On this, the eve of the greatest partnership ever known, I come to you—at least in a sense—bearing gifts. The party. The food. The entertainment." He laughed. "The booze, and whatever other recreational needs you have. I think we've covered nearly every vice known to man. If you happen to have thought of a new one we don't know about, let me know."

A ripple of laughter went through the crowd.

"He's a good showman," Turrin said to Salome.

"That's merely a by-product of being a good businessman," she replied.

The camera view tightened on Grishin, filling the screens with his features. His glacial eyes blazed with power and confidence. And Turrin had to admit there was enough about the man to make people believe in him.

"I also come to you to speak of an enemy," Grishin said. "You all know U.S. Attorney General Ramona Thompson in one capacity or another. She's been trying—unsuccessfully, I might add—to get other countries to take the hard-line approach regarding property-seizure laws. Since she has been unsuccessful, I've held no real feelings about the woman. But I recognize the threat she might offer, should feelings shift in enough of those countries. And she has made business difficult for some of your U.S.-based businesses. Tonight I give you my gift. And we're going to send a message to the United States government."

A sick sensation twisted Turrin's stomach. He wished he could reach a phone and send a message to Stony Man Farm. But the cellular phones had been confiscated as the parties boarded the ocean liner. Bodyguards had been allowed to keep their weapons, but no communications devices.

"Tonight," Grishin went on, "the illustrious U.S. attorney general is speaking in Milwaukee, Wisconsin. We're going to join her there."

The camera view shifted from the static environment to one that was constantly shifting. Turrin knew from experience that they were watching a broadcast from a minicam, probably hidden as a lapel button or another piece of jewelry.

People milled in front of the camera. But slowly the

focus returned to Grishin. The Russian still wore the red-and-black outfit, smiling and shaking hands with people, and moving confidently through the crowd.

Turrin's breath locked in his throat as he watched Grishin, followed by his cameraman, work his way through the crowd. In seconds, he was standing only a few people back from the U.S. attorney general.

Onscreen, Ramona Thompson, dressed in a simple gray business suit, stood at the front of the room. She smiled pleasantly and greeted her supporters at the anti-crime convention in Milwaukee.

Turrin spotted Brognola in the background, the Justice man appearing watchful. The little Fed could tell the exact moment Brognola spotted Grishin, because the man started straight for the Russian.

CHAPTER TWENTY-SIX

Hal Brognola couldn't believe his eyes when he spotted Kesar Grishin stepping into the line to shake Ramona Thompson's hand.

The big Fed moved forward, raising the fingertip microphone to his lips. "Close in around her," he said. "Now, damn it!" He shouldered his way through to the U.S. attorney general, excusing himself as he drew angry and perplexed stares.

Ramona Thompson saw Grishin, as well. She hesitated just a moment, but realized she was on television in several American cities and perhaps international channels, as well. She stood her ground.

Brognola couldn't help but admire the woman, but silently swore because she didn't back away from the man.

"Quite a party you're having here," Grishin said enthusiastically. He gestured to the gathering of people in the room.

Brognola reached Thompson's side. The attorney general checked him with a palm. Having no choice and not wanting to make a scene, Brognola halted. He kept his eyes on the Russian, aware of the 9 mm Glock pistol snugged in shoulder leather.

"But you should see the party I'm having at my place," Grishin said.

"What are you doing here, Mr. Grishin?" Thompson kept her voice low enough that it didn't carry far. The television microphones were kept at a distance so her conversations with people giving donations could be kept discreet. Her speech had been broadcast earlier, promising a long, hard fight against organized crime.

"Why, dear lady," Grishin said in mock affrontery, "I came here to show my support." He extended an envelope.

Thompson didn't take it.

"Oh, come now," Grishin said. "Don't be a spoilsport. Surely you don't want to be seen turning down donations. What kind of message will that send to all your supporters?"

Brognola stepped up. "Maybe I should take it."

"No," Thompson said without turning to him. She reached out and took the envelope.

A million thoughts slammed around inside Brognola's head. Grishin had never used poisons or biological agents to kill someone before, but he could choose any moment to start.

Grishin remained standing there, a wide grin on his face. Other people stood behind him, waiting their turn. The security staff moved in around him, flanking the attorney general.

"I must say," Thompson said, "you're probably the last person I expected to see here."

Grishin shrugged. "I always try to do the unexpected. It keeps me ahead in the game."

"Was there anything else?"

Grishin shook his head. "No. I just wanted to see you, tell you goodbye. So, goodbye!"

At the change in Grishin's voice inflection, Brognola's cop's radar went off. He reached for Thompson and started to pull her back.

Then the windows to their right exploded as bullets crashed through. Pandemonium erupted in the room.

Brognola felt Thompson's body shiver from the impacts of bullets. Her head snapped back, her face a sudden mask of rushing blood. Fear and surprise gleamed in her eyes. Brognola tried to cover her body with his, counting on the body armor he wore under his jacket to shield them. Instead, it felt like a burning brand thudded into his left shoulder, throwing him off balance. He retained his hold on the attorney general even though all feeling in his left arm went away.

On the floor now, Brognola covered the woman, suddenly joined by other security men. Shrill screams tore through the room, punctuated by the continued drumroll of rifle shots. Reporters and convention attendees went down.

Brognola checked Thompson and found her unconscious, but found a pulse, as well. She was bleeding heavily from the abdomen. "Get off her!" he ordered. They were below the level of the windows.

The security guards pulled back.

Brognola reached to a nearby table and pulled off the tablecloth. "Get a doctor up here," he yelled at one of the blacksuits Price had sent to Milwaukee with him.

The man nodded, produced a walkie-talkie and spoke rapidly.

Tearing off a section of the tablecloth, Brognola folded it, then pulled open Thompson's blouse. The wound was nasty and deep, but it hadn't cored through her heart as the shooter had probably intended. With any luck, it hadn't touched a lung. But it was ugly, ripped and bleeding profusely. He pressed the folded section of tablecloth over the wound.

"Where's Grishin?" Brognola demanded of the blacksuit.

"We lost him in the confusion, sir." The blacksuit nodded toward the broken windows along the side of the building. "The shooting came from outside."

"Grishin ordered it."

"Yes, sir, but our first priority was to shut down the shooters and minimize casualties."

Brognola knew that. "Get the building shut down."

"Security's already been notified."

Brognola turned to the blacksuit next to him. "Are you familiar enough with field med to manage this compress?"

"Sir, I am."

Brognola left him to it. He turned Thompson's head gingerly, looking for the wound, hoping that he wouldn't see something that would offer him no hope at all. "Son of a bitch, we got lucky," he breathed, as much to the woman as to himself.

The bullet had skated along her head, leaving an open furrow that would require plastic surgery to repair. But she'd live, provided she didn't lose too much blood and there hadn't been any internal damage from the impact. He made another compress out of the tablecloth and covered the wound, finding it hard to work with his arm still partially numbed from being wounded himself.

"I took a hit," he told the blacksuit.

"Yes, sir." The man came over and looked at Brognola's shoulder as the head Fed surrendered the second compress to another blacksuit.

"Through and through, sir. Lot of blood and some tissue damage, but you're going to be okay."

Brognola said a silent prayer for Thompson, then pushed himself to his feet. He drew the Glock and headed for the door. The blacksuit trailed him, his own weapon out.

A number of people were down. One of them was a definite casualty, a female reporter with most of her head blown away.

Taking his cellular phone from his pocket, Brognola punched in one of the numbers he had for Stony Man Farm. Kurtzman answered it on the first ring. "Are you monitoring the situation?" the big Fed asked.

"As much as we can," Kurtzman said. "We have the satellite overhead, but our visibility is limited. And the gaming convention has spilled over into the street. There's a lot of people in town."

"Get back to me if you get anything."

"The very minute."

Brognola broke the connection. Guests who were staying in the building had come out in the hallway to see what was going on, and many of the convention-goers had retreated to what was perceived as safer territory, as well.

Several of the people moved back from Brognola at once, some of them crying out when they saw the gun in his hand.

The head Fed kept moving, trying to make himself believe they had a shot at catching Kesar Grishin.

TURRIN'S STOMACH flipped over as the crowd aboard the ocean liner began to clap. A few of the more boisterous party-goers let out cheers.

"Ding dong," Salome said, "the witch is dead."

Kesar Grishin's image filled the screens again. Turrin knew the man had staged the whole presentation at that point, predicting the outcome. The camera view pulled back, revealing Grishin sitting in the chair again. He had a fresh glass of champagne.

"Want to see it again?" the Russian asked, grinning. He made a pistol out of his forefinger and acted like he shot the audience.

A small dot formed on the screen, then exploded to fill it. Turrin wanted to turn away but knew Salome was watching, judging his reaction. He watched as one moment Thompson was standing there so straight and tall, confronting Grishin. In the next, Brognola grabbed the woman and they both went down in a hail of gunfire.

This time the digital footage slowed. The image expanded, showing Thompson's head jerk back as the bullet hit her. From the angle and the confusion going on, Turrin didn't know if the wound had been fatal.

"You don't look happy," Salome commented, looking at him.

"Killing federal politicians isn't exactly good for business," Turrin replied.

"On the contrary, Kesar knows what he's doing. A message has been sent tonight. And another will be sent later."

"More killing?"

She looked at him. "Would that trouble you?"

"It would trouble the people I'm with," Turrin told her honestly. "A lot of them have gotten their images clean over the past few years. People stand between them and any serious falls. If someone got a copy of this film out to the American government system, Grishin's going to be in a world of hurt."

"Trust me when I say that the American government is going to be in no position to stop him."

The television screens refocused on Grishin sitting in the chair. "And there it is, people. My gift to you." He cupped his hands together in front of him. A digital gift box appeared between his hands, put in through computer-animation techniques. The gift box was roughly a square white paper with a big red bow securing it. He moved his hands forward, as if offering the gift box.

The gift box exploded onto the screen, blocking out everything else. The red ribbon pulled through itself, and the box fell open, revealing a tombstone with Ramona Thompson's name on it. The current date was below, with RIP under that.

The tombstone fragmented, flying off the screen. Grishin returned, hoisting his champagne glass. "Enjoy the party." The television screens blanked, and the lights came back on. The rush of conversations filled the dance floor.

"What do you think?" Salome asked.

Turrin turned to her. "I think Grishin is going to be lucky to get out of town."

She smiled. "You're an amusing man, Mr. Turrin. Kesar is going to do more than get out of Milwaukee. He would like to have breakfast with you tomorrow at his estate on Nevis."

"Breakfast?"

"Yes. I'm going to be leaving within the hour. Certain of the attendees tonight will be there, as well, but Kesar has talked to all of them before. Breakfast tomorrow morning he has put aside to talk to you."

"Does he want me to meet him there?"

"I'll be leaving by helicopter. If you wish, you can

join me." Salome looked pointedly at Jimmy Venturo and the other hardman. "Your friends will have to stay on the ship. They'll be well taken care of."

"They were told to stay with me."

"Mr. Turrin, I'm sure they'll do exactly as you wish. If you want to do breakfast, meet me aft in an hour. Ta." The woman turned and walked away.

Turrin watched her go, knowing he didn't have a lot of choice if he wanted to pull the mission together. And after seeing what had happened, he had no doubts about the need to stop Grishin.

"How are you doing, Hal?"

Brognola paced the hospital waiting room with the cellular phone clutched in his good hand. His other arm was in a sling. The wound had been treated in the ER, and he'd been given pain pills that had eased the throbbing that filled his shoulder but failed to slow the frantic wheels turning inside his head. "I've been better."

"What about Ramona Thompson?" Price asked. "The television news has been filled with a lot of speculation but nothing concrete."

"She's still in surgery. The surgeon I talked to doesn't expect to be out for a couple more hours. The bullet nicked a lung enough to collapse it before the EMTs were able to take her out of the building. There was a lot of internal damage. What the surgeon is primarily concerned about is getting all the bleeding stopped inside. If they don't, she could hemorrhage to death by morning."

"At least she's got a chance."

"Yeah. Did Leo get in?"

"We were monitoring the ocean liner by satellite," the mission controller said. "He left by helicopter."

"Where to?" The thought of Turrin out there wandering around loose didn't sit well with Brognola. He was too far away to keep safe.

"We're tracking him now. They're islandhopping. We'll know something soon. We've got good coverage down there."

"I thought we had it on the hotel," Brognola said irritably. "We lost Grishin."

"He'll turn up. Any word from the President?"

"Not yet."

"He needs to turn the teams loose. Able is ready to go in Manhattan, and Phoenix has joined Grimaldi and Striker in Jamaica. I've got a transport plane standing by for them that has enough ordnance to mount a full-scale assault."

Brognola sighed tiredly. "Get a plane for me, Barb. I want to get back to the Farm. Things always seem better there. I've done all I can here."

"It's already done," Price responded. "I'll have McDonald take you to the airport." McDonald was the young blacksuit who'd been in charge of the unit attached to Brognola at the hotel. "I've assigned the rest of them to remain on security detail there at the hospital in case Grishin finds out Thompson's still alive and wants to make another attempt."

"Thanks. I'll see you soon." Brognola punched the End button and took out another antacid pill. It was going to be a long time until dawn broke.

"THEY'VE LANDED."

Barbara Price lifted her head from her arms and blinked blearily at Aaron Kurtzman. It took a second for all the thoughts to sort themselves out. "Where?" she asked. She knew the big cybernetics expert was referring to Turrin and the helicopter that had taken off from the *Royal Flush*.

"Nevis."

"I know where it is." Price pushed her hair back out of her face, stood and followed Kurtzman out into the computer room. She checked her watch. "I've been asleep for the last hour and a half. You should have woken me." She suddenly felt guilty. Kurtzman and his staff had worked straight through.

"You've had less sleep than anybody here," Kurtzman said. "If something had happened, I'd have let you know."

Price came to a stop at Kurtzman's desk, her arms crossed over her breasts. She was so tired she felt almost frozen.

The wall screen at the other end of the room showed an infrared view of a large house and an estate. A pool was in back of the house next to a breakfast patio nook. A large garage was on the other side of the building and looked capable of holding perhaps as many as a dozen cars. A tennis court was between two guesthouse bungalows. Farther out was an airstrip that would accommodate small jets. A trail led along the west side of the estate to the ocean below. A helipad was on the shore, currently occupied by the same helicopter that had airlifted Turrin from the ocean liner. A dock stretched from the landscaped shore, leading to a marina. Two speed boats, a yacht and a large sailboat were moored there.

"What am I looking at?" Price asked.

"Kesar Grishin's little hideaway," Kurtzman answered. "If you look close enough, you'll see the satellite dishes on top of the house. Sure, maybe some of them are to improve television reception, but I don't think they all are. Do you?''

Price didn't. She stared at the house, at the imposing hugeness of it. ''How the hell did we miss something like this?'' They hadn't ever found a residence for Grishin in all the information they'd turned up.

''The house isn't listed with any of the holding companies that we turned up for Grishin,'' Kurtzman answered. ''I found it while I was looking through the information McCarter and Striker gave me. The house is owned by a corporation that does business in England, supposedly managed by a parent company in Germany. The parent company doesn't exist in Germany except on paper. Took me a while to figure out that much. That corporation is the one Grishin used to make the payment to Percival Dickey in London. Nothing else popped up on any of the business he's done there. That corporation was relatively clean.''

''Then why did he use it?''

Kurtzman shrugged. ''The money he paid Dickey for the merc action was big. Maybe he didn't have any other companies that could come up with the money in the amount of time. No one thought about it in England when he transferred the money. If we hadn't made Dickey, we wouldn't have made the corporation, either. Then he does some fancy footwork when he moves the paperwork on the corporation down to the Caribbean. Slick stuff, Barb. If Striker hadn't turned the name from Santos, we'd never have made it. The guy really knows his trade. In Nevis, the corporation becomes a legitimate business under another name. Actually handles real estate on the island. High-value property stuff. Grishin doesn't own the house under his name.''

"Where are Striker and Phoenix?"

"En route to Nevis. I used one of the contacts the CIA has in Jamaica to get them into a Bell LongRanger helicopter."

"When will they get there?"

"Within the hour." Kurtzman tapped the computer keyboard and brought a map of the Caribbean up on his central monitor screen. He tapped it again, and a bright blue blip showed up not far from Nevis. A moment later, distance and air speed were calibrated. "Make that thirty-seven minutes."

Price consulted her watch. "They can be ready to roll by five-thirty. Can we link up the LST-5C?"

"When they juice it up, we'll be in touch."

"Is Grishin there?"

"I haven't seen him. He had farther to travel than Leo. When he gets there, though, he's ours."

GRIMALDI LANDED the LongRanger at a point one and a half miles north of Grishin's estate. When Barbara Price checked the time, she found it was 4:53 a.m., exactly thirty-seven minutes after Kurtzman had told her the time the chopper would be landing.

Hooked into the scene through the space-based satellite, the darkness stripped away by the on-board infrared systems, the mission controller watched Bolan and Phoenix Force debark. The Stony Man warriors covered the distance to a vantage point near Grishin's estate in little more than thirty-three minutes even with the gear they were packing.

Hal Brognola entered the computer room five minutes later, at the same time as Bolan and Phoenix Force came onto the communications grid through the portable satellite dish they'd packed in.

"Stony One to Stony Base," Bolan called.

"Stony One, you have Stony Base," Price answered.

"What about the mission?"

"We're on hold," Price answered, "pending."

"Affirmative. What about our target?"

"His position is unresolved."

"Sticker is here?"

Sticker was a code name for Leo Turrin that went back to his active undercover days for the Organized Crime Bureau. "Confirm that, Stony One. Sticker is on the scene."

Brognola pulled out a fresh cigar and stripped the wrapping. He shoved it into his mouth without lighting it and started to chew.

"There's a plane in-bound," Akira Tokaido called from the front of the room. "I've picked it up on radar."

Price glanced at the wall screen, watching as the radar tracked the plane, increasing in focus as the craft neared the estate. Less than four minutes later, it touched down.

Tokaido swapped over from the radar screen to infrared. There was no mistaking Kesar Grishin as he stepped from the aircraft and walked to the golf cart waiting to take him to the house.

"Stony Base," Bolan called over the headset, "we confirm the presence of our target."

"Affirmative, Stony One," Price replied. "Target confirmed at this end, as well."

"Well, then," Brognola said, "it's time to put this to a vote." He moved to one of the phones on Kurtzman's desk. Price recognized the number the head Fed punched in. Brognola straightened his tie as he waited for the phone to be answered.

"Sir?" He punched the phone over to intercom mode. "We've confirmed the target. How do you want us to handle it?"

"Turrin is there?"

"Yes."

"And he has the virus program your people have developed?"

"Yes."

There was silence for a time. "You know, old friend, we've made a lot of tough calls over the years of our association."

"Yes, sir."

Price breathed shallowly. They'd been ordered to back off operations before, sometimes never finishing them as the Man tried to keep the overall world picture in view. Power behind the scenes like Stony Man Farm represented had to be used wisely; otherwise, other checks and balances could be lost.

"It occurs to me," the President went on, "that Ramona Thompson went to Milwaukee to meet her fate, whatever that might be, with her head held high, willing to take whatever she was dealt. I can't see that we can do anything less without disgracing ourselves."

"I agree, sir, for what it's worth."

"It's worth a lot, Hal. Tell your teams that they've got a green light. And God keep them safe."

CHAPTER TWENTY-SEVEN

Mosquito Bay, Nevis
Saturday

Cold gray dawn slashed through the eastern horizon, driving away the remainders of the night. Mack Bolan watched it spin out over the island as it broke through the cloud layer. The soldier hunkered down next to a tree, dressed in combat black, his face smeared with camou paint. His position was slightly elevated from the outer walls of Grishin's estate to the south.

"You know what this place reminds me of?" David McCarter asked. He dropped slowly into position beside Bolan. Like the Executioner, he was dressed in combat black, wearing bulletproof armor with ordnance strapped about his body on a combat harness.

"No." Bolan raised his binoculars to his eyes and peered at Kesar Grishin's home. So far, there'd been no sign of the Russian. He kept close watch over the front doors and the patio area, thinking Grishin would probably spend his time there—if he left the building at all.

"Scotland," McCarter said. "The way the water comes up into the cliffs and everything."

Bolan silently agreed. The land did have that familiar feel of Scotland.

"Could be Grishin's all done in and is going to sleep for a while, mate," McCarter commented.

"I don't think so." Bolan lowered the binoculars. "He's got people there waiting on him." Already that morning, they'd logged in a half-dozen people who comprised a small, deadly who's who of international crime syndicates. "And he's got the smell of blood on him. He's tried his programming on the Wall Street quotes. He knows the damage he's capable of doing, and he hasn't even had the chance to play that card. He'll want to do that."

"Yeah, well, unlucky for him, the stock market's closed today."

Movement on the patio drew Bolan's attention. He peered through the binoculars again. Service staff in brilliant whites began to set up a buffet around the patio. A moment later, he saw Leo Turrin walk onto the patio with a blond-haired woman clinging to his arm.

Turrin was dressed in a polo shirt and slacks, managing an elegantly casual look that still set him apart from the other guests. He appeared confident and calm, not at all like a guy who'd shoved his head into the lion's mouth.

"That bloke's one cool customer," McCarter said. "I've gone undercover before, sometimes for a few weeks. But not my whole life."

"Leo's a special guy," Bolan said.

"He has to be, because nobody without ice water in his veins could do what he does."

Bolan tapped the Transmit button on his headset, accessing the communication link Stony Man Farm was providing through the LST-5C portable satellite dish they'd deployed. "Stony One to Phoenix team."

Phoenix Force quickly and quietly checked in with him. Calvin James, Gary Manning and Rafael Encizo were farther up the hill, spread out with different vantage points to spy on the estate. T. J. Hawkins was with Jack Grimaldi in the LongRanger, which had been fitted with pontoons.

"G-Force," Bolan called.

"Reading you five-by, Stony One," Grimaldi replied.

"Stony Base is standing by," Kurtzman said over the headset.

Bolan continued to watch Turrin through the binoculars. Until they received a signal, there was nothing they could do but wait. The next move was Turrin's.

"If you don't have any swim trunks, Mr. Turrin, there are plenty in the house. One of the servants can get them for you."

Turrin looked down at Salome. He guessed that she had gotten less sleep than he had—if she'd gotten any sleep at all—but she acted as fresh as if she'd gotten a full eight hours. The way she looked in the bikini was nothing short of incredible. Her complexion was flawless.

"Give me a rain check," Turrin said.

"Honestly I'm beginning to think that there's nothing daring about you," Salome complained. "I read this dossier on Leopold Turrin, a guy who's been in the Mafia all his life. I saw *The Godfather.* I have to admit, it kind of romanticized the whole Mafia thing for me."

"Yeah, I can see how you'd confuse me with Pacino.'' Turrin knew the woman was playing up to him, working on his ego and getting him ready for Grishin. But he was also aware that she was intelligent enough to know that he was playing back, not really buying anything she was selling. That got confusing because he had to wonder if she was continuing her efforts because she didn't know what else to do, or if she wanted him to think she didn't know what else to do. Either way, he'd decided she was dangerous.

''If you get to feeling adventurous later,'' she said, moving toward the sky blue pool at the end of the patio, ''you just whistle. You *do* know how to whistle, don't you?''

Turrin grinned and gave his best Bogart imitation, which Angelina had always assured him was atrocious.

''Bogie always made the best gangster, didn't he?''

''Yeah.'' And that comment made Turrin wonder about his cover.

Salome walked to the edge of the pool. She poised, picture perfect, her tan dark and rich against her white bikini, aware of all the male attention she was getting, then dived into the water.

''Leo.''

Turrin turned toward the man's voice and found himself suddenly face-to-face with Kesar Grishin. The Russian proffered his hand, and the stocky Fed took it.

Grishin looked out at the swimming pool, grinning widely. ''That's an invitation you don't turn down very often. I have to wonder about a man who shows no libido.''

Turrin smiled, looking up at the taller man. ''What you call a lack of libido, I call self-respect.''

''How so?'' Grishin seemed honestly intrigued.

''Have you ever seen a dog chase after a car?'' Turrin spread his hands. "I mean, what the hell's he going to do with it even if he brings it down? That lady is rack-and-pinion steering, a full-blown engine, and I'm not vain enough to think she's really interested in me. And if she was, I'd think it would be because of you. Thinking like that would screw up my business dealing with you. Should I be grateful? Should I be angry?" He turned to look at Salome swimming gracefully through the water. "Me, I think maybe I should just love from afar."

Grishin laughed. "A wise man with a philosophical bent. Always the hardest sell."

"Yeah, but once sold, probably sold for life," Turrin said.

The Russian turned to the taciturn man behind him. "Gerahd, this is a man to take stock of. See, he can be business, but still wield a rapier wit."

Turrin recognized Dobrynin from the files Stony Man had sent.

Grishin returned his attention to Turrin, clapping him on the shoulder. He gestured toward the breakfast bar with his free hand. "Have you eaten?"

"No."

"Then let's eat." As Grishin walked across the patio, members of various crime organizations, including Chela Escelera, called out to him.

None of them approached, though, and Turrin got the feeling that Grishin had scheduled them in for other times.

"Do you recognize these people?" Grishin asked.

"Most of them." Turrin picked up a plate.

"The ones you don't know, you'll meet before the weekend is up." Grishin picked up a silver cup containing an egg. "Three-minute egg. Would you like one?"

"No, thank you."

"Is everything here all right? I have a fully comple-mented kitchen and staff inside if there's something else you'd care to have."

"No, this is fine." Turrin filled his plate with gen-erous helpings of French toast, bacon and chilled fruit, guessing that if he didn't eat well, Grishin would talk about that instead of anything else.

"Coffee?" Grishin asked when they reached the end of the line.

"Please." Turrin noticed Dobrynin didn't take any-thing, standing a polite but accessible distance away. The stocky Fed took the cup he was handed.

"Have you ever been to Nevis before?"

"No."

Grishin guided them to an unoccupied table. "I'll have to arrange a tour for you before you go." He sat across from Turrin. "The island isn't much, maybe fifty square miles altogether, but there's some really nice stuff here to look at. Alexander Hamilton was born here."

"I'd heard."

"There are other attractions."

"Kesar, let's cut the crap. I'm here representing the East Coast Families, and maybe the West Coast Fam-ilies, as well, because they may follow our lead in whether or not we should do business with you."

"Okay." Grishin maintained his winning smile. "I want your business, the business of the people you rep-resent. What do I have to do to get it?"

"Personally," Turrin said, "I don't think you can."

Grishin waggled a finger. "That's where you underestimate me, because I believe I can interest you. And those people.''

''This is going to have to be a hell of a sales pitch,'' Turrin said. ''The way the Families look at it, they don't need anyone.''

''The American Families have done very well for themselves these past years,'' Grishin admitted. ''They have legitimized a number of their businesses, hidden away the graft and corruption they depend on for profit. If you let me handle your money laundering, I can help you get away from any competition you're presently experiencing.''

''What competition?''

''I could offer you part of the drug trade,'' Grishin said.

Turrin held up a hand. ''Hold it right there. That was one thing,'' he said truthfully, ''that the Old Men told me explicitly to stay away from. If someone gets busted on a drug beef, the U.S. government has the tendency to take away anything else they think might have stemmed from the profits on those sales. The Old Men don't want to lose what they've worked hard to acquire.''

''I understand.''

''Also, the Rastafarians and Colombians are crazy. You try muscling in on what they consider to be their territory, they'll kill you and anyone else they have to in order to get you to stop.''

''The lesser gangs can be dealt with,'' Grishin replied. ''It might take some time, but they can be eradicated if we all work together. We can take away their markets, take away their product, and—if it comes to it—take away their lives.''

''Money for nothing? That never happens.''

"I take a percentage," Grishin said. "That's all."

"Even if you could finesse the gangs and take them out of the play, there's still the government to consider. They don't screw around with those property-seizure laws."

"Let me show you something," Grishin said. "Finish your breakfast."

Turrin had to work at eating the meal and keep the excitement out of his posture.

TURRIN SAT in a chair in the large computer lab inside the main house. It was in the basement, protected by reinforced walls.

Grishin sat in the center of the huge machines, his eyes intent on the screen. Dobrynin lounged in a corner, his eyes roaming the room. "You know about the stock-market quotes that fluctuated two days ago?"

"Sure. I've got some investments there myself."

"What would you say if I told you I was the one who caused it?"

Turrin let the disbelief show on his face.

Tapping the keyboard, Grishin brought up a demo file he'd programmed, relaying how he'd infected the Wall Street Exchange with the override virus, allowing him to change figures as he wished.

Excitement flared in Grishin's eyes as he turned away from the computer screen. "This is the hammer I have, Mr. Turrin. If the United States government wants to pick a fight with me, with us, they risk losing everything. I may jumble up a few stock quotes at first, or I may wipe out the Wall Street Exchange altogether."

"That wouldn't be a good idea," Turrin said. "A lot of the Families have invested there these days."

Grishin shook his head. "It won't come to that. The President, Congress, they'll all fold before they try to stay in a game like that. No, Mr. Turrin, in the long run, they'll have no choice but to deal with me. If they want their economy, they'll have to give us ours. Hell, I can see a time when they might want investments from us. Look at how many foreign investments and loans the American government takes every year in spite of the public outcry against deficit spending. Your people are hooked on spending, and when they run out of money of their own, they want to spend someone else's. No matter how much it costs."

And Turrin knew that was the true evil of what Grishin was suggesting. Crime turned a profit every time, no matter what the economic index was like or whether it was a bull or a bear market. American business and government didn't always. It was that need for a steady influx of cash that kept loan sharks and deficit spending operational.

"What is the saying in your country, Mr. Turrin? 'Money talks, bullshit walks'? In a few years, working together, we can build an empire that's even more global than anything that's out there. So what do you say?"

"I say that you're probably going to get a favorable response from the Families," Turrin answered.

AARON KURTZMAN WATCHED the wall screen closely. Now that daylight had arrived in the Caribbean, all of the spy satellite's visual abilities could be accessed. He studied the breakfast area. Hunt Wethers was assembling pictures of the motley crew while Delahunt matched them up with law-enforcement dossiers scattered around the world.

Brognola and Price stood behind him. No one spoke, and the only sounds in the computer room were the noises from the machines.

"There," Brognola said. "Grishin and Turrin are back."

"I've got them," Kurtzman said. He and Tokaido were linked, ready to jam through Grishin's systems the virus they'd concocted. The view tightened on Turrin as the stocky Fed and the Russian took their earlier places at the table.

Turrin was laughing, animated, his gaze roving around the crowd as Grishin continued speaking and pointing out different individuals. Then Turrin reached into his pocket and pulled out a lighter, which had one white side and one black side, a gift from a gambling casino that was a legitimate Mob operation in Atlantic City. Turrin had ties there, so having the lighter on him wasn't a big deal.

The big deal came when Turrin held the lighter in his right hand and placed it white side up on the table while he continued talking.

"He's been to the computer room," Price said. She reached for the microphone connecting the computer room to the teams. "Stony One, do you read the signal?"

MACK BOLAN PICKED UP the white side of the lighter through the lenses of the high-powered binoculars as Turrin placed it on the table. He tapped the headset's Transmit button. "Affirmative, Stony Base. We confirm reading. G-Force."

"G-Force reads you, Stony One."

"Showtime."

"Affirmative, G-Force is on the way." The solid

throb of the helicopter rotors growled to new levels as the communications died away.

"Phoenix Force, this is Stony One," Bolan said as he put the binoculars in his chestpack. "Let's do this one by the numbers." He picked up the M-16/M-203 combo from where it lay in the tall grass beside him. McCarter was at his side as he broke into a distance-eating jog. The estate was less than an eighth of a mile away. They could do the distance even with the heavy gear they were carrying in under a minute.

He glanced to his right and saw the other Phoenix Force members break their cover. Before they made half the distance, staying within shelter of the trees as much as possible, Grimaldi streaked by overhead. The helicopter hugged the ground, the pontoons less than a dozen feet above the treetops.

Bolan carried the assault rifle in his arms and sprinted for all he was worth. McCarter kept pace with him. The sudden appearance of the helicopter would buy Turrin some time inside the estate, but there would still be no one to stand alongside him when he was found out.

JACK GRIMALDI FLEW the helicopter with a practiced hand. Hawkins was in the cargo area, the door pushed back so the wind whipped inside. The Phoenix Force commando manned a .50-caliber door gun mounted on a support system.

Grimaldi gazed downward and saw Bolan and the rest of Phoenix Force charging at the estate. "Give 'em hell, Sarge," he said quietly, then they were gone from view, the wall of the estate coming up quickly.

Men working the estate security had taken notice of

the LongRanger, but no action had been taken to prevent it from flying over.

Grimaldi grinned. ''Time to wake them up, T.J.,'' he called over the headset.

''Ready,'' Hawkins called back. The .50-caliber machine gun chattered to life, ripping bullets across the manicured lawn.

Guests and security men began to scatter at once. Several of them unlimbered weapons and returned fire.

''We're going to be losing speed,'' Grimaldi said. ''We'll make a bigger target that way. I'm going to be depending on you.'' Bullets were already ricocheting from the chopper's body, and a sudden crack ripped across the Plexiglas nose. He jockeyed the aircraft around, bringing Hawkins to bear on the pocket of resistance that had formed along the front lawn of the estate.

The .50-caliber weapon cut loose, running wide open and chewing through ammo belts. Brass spilled across the cargo floor, glinting in the morning light. Several of the security people went spinning away as the bullets caught them.

Grimaldi kept his head moving, surveying the field. The .50-caliber door gun hadn't been the only thing added to the helicopter since the Stony Man teams had gotten it. He and Hawkins had also mounted nineteen-tube rocket pods on both sides of the aircraft. The pods were armed, keyed into the chopper's yoke.

Bringing the aircraft around, Grimaldi lost more altitude and raced for the guest-house bungalows. ''Stony Base, this is G-Force.''

''Go, G-Force,'' Kurtzman replied.

''Can you confirm bungalow number one as a fair target?''

"Affirmative." That's where Escelera is staying."

Locked on to his target, Grimaldi tripped the rocket launcher and sent three rockets into the bungalow. The explosions ripped the building into shreds. Smoke curled up from the ruins, and flames followed in short order. Whether Escelera was inside or not, at least she'd know she'd been targeted.

Grimaldi gained altitude and turned the helicopter around, taking another pass. He took aim and fired five rockets into the empty pool, ripping it from one end to the other. Water spumed up, and the explosions drenched several nearby people who had gone to ground. The torrents and concussions also wiped out the breakfast bar, sending patio furniture skittering across the patio, smashing some of it through the floor-to-ceiling glass walls that fronted the patio area.

The pilot knew Bolan and Phoenix Force would have a hard time separating Grishin's handpicked hard crew from the innocents below in all the confusion. Hawkins kept the .50-caliber gun chattering. Grimaldi unleashed more rockets, wreaking total carnage on the estate grounds.

CHAPTER TWENTY-EIGHT

New York, New York

"Hey, who the hell are you?"

Carl Lyons turned around while giving the appearance of being relaxed. He hadn't even heard the men come up behind him. He kept his body between them and the door. The lock picks he'd been using were still in the lock. Blancanales and Schwarz were elsewhere, setting taps into the security system in the central office so the legitimate security personnel in the building would have less chance of discovering them.

"Didn't you read the back of the coverall?" he asked. Then he tapped the red-and-white patch over his left breast that identified him as a member of Kelley Cleaners, the business that took care of the office building's cleaning needs.

Two men stood in front of him, dressed in suits. The taller one said, "It's kind of early for building maintenance to be here."

Lyons's gaze took in the special tailoring in the suit jackets that took away evidence of the shoulder holsters both men wore. "Shift boss had a special come open later today. If we get done here early, maybe we can catch a little over-time." The usual maintenance crew would be in by ten o'clock. By then, Lyons knew it was going to be all over, though there would be a bigger mess to clean up than the cleaners usually dealt with.

"You had this job long?" the other man asked.

"The job, sure," Lyons said. "Seven years. First time on this site."

"That explains it," the tall man replied. "You don't know about this office."

Lyons glanced back at the doorway he stood in front of as if he were trying to read something there. The door was plain, only a room number in black letters—112—painted across the metal surface.

"That room doesn't get cleaned by the regular service. We have our own people. They'll be along later."

Lyons shrugged. "One less office puts me one office closer to the next job." He straightened his ball cap and gave them a smile. He knew it was all going to break loose when he stepped away from the door. They would see the lock picks then, and he had no chance of removing them without being discovered.

He moved away to the other side of the hallway. He wore bulletproof armor under the coverall, but the men moved like professionals, staying out of each other's field of fire while they'd talked to him.

There was no warning. If Lyons hadn't been listening hard, he wouldn't have heard the sharp inhalation of breath behind him, wouldn't have heard the scrape of leather on the carpet.

Lyons spun and went to ground, pulling the Colt Government Model .45 from the shoulder harness under the loose coverall. He'd left it unzipped to allow access to the weapon. The .45 came up slightly slower than normal, weighted by its customed-made sound suppressor.

The men got off three shots. Luckily all of them were silenced, as well. One of the rounds thudded into the carpeted floor beside Lyons's face, gouging carpet and exposing the concrete beneath. The other two went over him, lost somewhere along the wall behind him.

Lyons squeezed off a double-tap at each man. The bullets caught them in the face, throwing them back. Neither moved again as motor control immediately left them.

Pushing himself up, Lyons approached the gunners. Both were dead. Then he noticed the concealed earphone that had popped out onto the floor. A brief check of the other man showed that he was similarly equipped.

He took out his own headset and pulled it on, then tapped the Transmit button. "Pol. Gadgets." He turned his attention to the locked door.

"We're here, Ironman," Blancanales called back.

"We're blown," Lyons said as he worked the picks, the .45 tucked up under his arm. "I had to off a couple of the guards watching over this room. They had radios."

"We'll be there," Blancanales said. "We've finished here."

The door lock gave, and Lyons pushed his way inside.

The office was a simple affair. A large secondhand desk occupied the space against the opposite wall. Sports prints of basketball and baseball players decorated the wall, easing some of the Spartan look of the room, their bright colors adding some life to the gray wall. A computer was on the desk, as well as a telephone and a small color television.

Lyons closed the door behind him and peered at the floor, searching for any signs of the trapdoor that Kurtzman and Price had figured would be cut through the floor to allow access to the main telephone trunk line a dozen feet below. Spotting a rectangular area that stood out from the rest of the room under the desk, Lyons shoved the furniture aside, scattering the computer, telephone and television. He knew from the reports over the headset that the mission was under way in Nevis.

As a precaution, he fisted the telephone line and ripped it from the wall. He knew it probably wasn't the only connection Grishin would have to the hookup below, but it did cut down on the possibilities.

He pulled a fold-out hunting knife from his pocket and rammed it through the crack surrounding the rectangle. He levered up the section with greater ease than he expected, realizing the section had been hollowed out.

Shoving the piece of flooring aside, Lyons peered into the tunnel it revealed. A ladder had been added to the side of an uneven tunnel. Below, it was so dark that he couldn't see the bottom of the trunk-line shaft.

He started down the shaft, using the ladder. The air turned muggy and hot as he descended, which surprised him as he thought it would be cooler. After all, the trunk line ran under the city.

At the bottom of the shaft, he found another hatch, this one set carefully in place. In complete darkness now, he reached into his pocket and took out a penlight. It took only a moment to find the handle built into the hatch below. He fisted it and yanked it up, discovering a hook on the side of the shaft opposite the ladder that he could hang it on.

The trunk line yawned below him, the bottom a good eight feet down. From the schematic Kurtzman had sent, Lyons knew the trunk line was basically the same distance across.

His peripheral vision alerted him when the light above him suddenly dimmed. He looked up, already knowing what he was going to find.

A man leaned into the shaft, shoving a pistol in front of him.

Lyons released his hold inside the shaft and dropped through the hatch into the trunk line. He lost the penlight when his hand struck the side of the shaft, and he watched it spin away.

Then gunfire from below blasted the penlight out of existence. Lyons fell into the darkness, knowing part of Grishin's on-site team was in the trunk line with him.

LEO TURRIN RAN, staggering through the debris left by the exploding pool when Grimaldi had struck out with the rockets from the helicopter. He spotted Grishin in the barbecue area, tucked behind the L-shaped corner of the grill, safe from the onslaught of bullets.

Turrin sprinted through the smashed patio doors, glass crunching underfoot as he raced across the room. He followed the maze of rooms and hallways from memory, reaching the pantry area behind the kitchen where Grishin had hidden the door leading down to the basement computer lab.

A man stood guard over the door, an Uzi machine pistol in his fist. He looked at Turrin and started to say something.

Turrin beat him to it. "Where's Grishin? He said he'd meet me here."

The guard hesitated, and Turrin gained another step. The stocky Fed had noticed earlier that all of the staff knew him. Grishin briefed his people well.

He took another step, then reached into his pants pocket and took out a credit card, palming it so the man couldn't see what it was. "Grishin told me to get down here as fast as I could. Jesus Christ, all hell is breaking loose up there. I hope he didn't get hit." Another step and he was close enough to the guard, who was still undecided about what to do.

Turrin flicked the small release on the edge of the credit card, flipping out the razored blade from hiding. He moved toward the guard with all the speed he could muster, raking the blade across the man's throat. Blood erupted, and the guard tried to bring around the Uzi.

Grabbing the machine pistol, Turrin managed to hold on to it, keeping the barrel pointed away from him until the man died. The subsonic rounds chopped into canned stuffs and jars, then the machine pistol cycled dry.

The little Fed grabbed the Uzi and helped himself to a fresh magazine in an ordnance pouch at the man's waist. The metal door behind the false wall was featureless except for the electronic lock. Turrin stripped his belt from his waist, finding it slim enough to slide between the door and the jamb. When everything fit but the buckle, he turned the buckle harshly, tearing it free of its housing and setting off the four-second timer built within the belt.

He took shelter, ramming the fresh magazine into the Uzi. The belt was lined with C-4 plastique, undetectable for the most part to conventional X rays.

The explosive blew, ripping out the door and filling the pantry with smoke.

Moving quickly, Turrin went into the computer room. He crossed to the unit that Grishin had used to demonstrate the Wall Street virus. The computer was password protected, and he hadn't seen the sequence of keys that the Russian had used to gain access to the programming.

He pushed the desk chair out of the way, his heart hammering in his chest.

Pulling up his shirt, he slipped the CD-ROM disk from his back, the surgical tape holding it in place giving reluctantly. He reached for the phone beside the keyboard and dialed the Stony Man number.

Kurtzman answered.

"We're burning daylight here, Aaron," Turrin said as he inserted the CD disk he'd brought.

"Let me have it," Kurtzman said. "Akira and I can take it from here."

Turrin cradled the phone, then reached down and swapped the phone line with the one in the computer that was hooked to the modem.

Glancing at the screen, he watched as the computer booted up the modem. A template formed on the screen, letting him know the Stony Man Farm cybernetics teams had succeeded in gaining the necessary connection. A heartbeat later, the CD-ROM light winked on and the drive started to whir softly.

"Kill him!"

Turrin turned, scrambling for cover and grabbing the Uzi. He spotted Kesar Grishin in the doorway, making way for Gerahd Dobrynin.

Lifting a hand, Dobrynin unleashed a spray of full-autofire at Turrin. The bullets caught the desk chair and sent it spinning.

Turrin went to ground, knowing there was no place to hide.

AARON KURTZMAN STUDIED the lines of programming scrolling rapidly across his screen. He tried to access the virus he and Akira Tokaido had assembled, feeling his eyes burn as he focused on the screen. Tokaido was accessing the modem drive, as well, playing in the artificial environment Grishin's computers had established, trying to launch the virus code.

The antivirus programming Grishin maintained in his systems kicked in automatically, stopping the virus. Kurtzman and Tokaido reshaped it, reformed it and returned it each time, like a tennis game with an increasing tempo.

Less than a minute later, Grishin's programming assimilated the virus, drinking it down in one long gulp.

"It's done," Kurtzman announced, pushing back from the keyboard. "Now it's survival of the fittest. And I'm telling you now, Grishin's never seen anything like this."

MACK BOLAN GAINED the main house without much struggle. Grimaldi's rockets had turned the sculptured landscape into a battlefield of gaping craters. The soldier hugged the house, using it for cover. He kept the M-16 at the ready.

"Stony One," Grimaldi called over the headset, "you're coming up on two men stationed at the corner of the house. They'll be at ten o'clock as you make the corner. You've got three, maybe four others trying to hold the line at the patio."

"Affirmative, G-Force." Bolan slowed his approach, spotting the helicopter hovering less than eighty yards away, in direct line of sight of the patio area. "What about civilians?"

"Can't confirm either way. They're packed in there too tight. Otherwise, we'd be able to assist."

Bolan spun around the corner, bringing the assault rifle to his shoulder, becoming a human gun sight. The two men at the corner spotted him at the same time, bringing their weapons around as they tried to fade into position behind the stone wall lining the barbecue pit.

The Executioner burned them both down with 3-round bursts. Return fire drove him back to cover. He'd gotten a glimpse of the men holding the patio, but still couldn't confirm if any of the waiters or waitresses was in the area.

He ripped a smoke grenade from his combat harness. Pulling the pin, he lobbed the bomb around the wall into direct view of the gunmen. Startled yelps filled the air, followed by the sound of running feet.

The Executioner came around the corner, staying low. He swept the area with his eyes, picking up his targets, automatically marking them in his mind as he dropped to one knee and took aim. He squeezed the M-16's trigger deliberately. The first round went through a man's open mouth. The second round cored another man's temple. A third face flashed into the assault rifle's sights, and Bolan held his finger and moved on, recognizing the features as those of a woman. He spared her, tracking his next target, finding himself looking down the sights of an AK-47.

Bolan felt the burst brush by his head, held his ground and squeezed through the trigger. The round took the gunman squarely between the eyes.

The grenade popped then, releasing a heavy cloud of dark blue smoke that swirled over the area.

The Executioner rushed forward, staying to the left. He located the waitress by her screams and yanked her off her feet. "Stay down," he told her, "or you're going to get shot."

Then the soldier was on the other side of the smoke cloud, inside the house. He spotted the fourth man just as he felt bullets smash against his body armor. He fired a burst that cut the gunman down.

Changing magazines in the assault rifle, Bolan ran through the house, securing rooms. "Phoenix One."

"Go, Stony One."

"Your location?"

"Through the front door."

"I've got the back."

"Well, then, we better have a care in here," McCarter said lightly, "or we're going to be shooting at each other."

The sound of gunfire filled the house. Bolan moved into the doorway of a living room, identifying a number of Yakuza members taking cover inside.

One of the men yelled out a warning, pointing at Bolan.

The Executioner faded from the doorway, pausing long enough to rip a fragmentation grenade free of his combat harness and arm it. He counted down, then lobbed it inside while bullets chewed the door frame. He was already moving down the hallway when it exploded. There was no pursuit.

CARL LYONS LANDED off balance in the darkness. He kept the .45 in his hand, filling the other with the .357 Colt Python. Though he couldn't see in the darkness, he guessed there were two men ahead of him, judging from the position of the muzzle-flashes.

A handful of rounds smashed into his body armor, knocking the breath from his lungs. He shoved both pistols ahead of him, yelling as soon as he could draw a breath to intimidate them, getting his own adrenaline pumping. He fired both weapons dry, aiming at both positions he'd marked.

Groans came out of the darkness ahead of him, but no return fire.

Hurting from the blunt trauma the bulletproof armor couldn't prevent, Lyons found the wall by touch and braced himself against it while he rammed a fresh magazine into the .45, then used a speed loader on the Colt Python.

Footsteps rang on the ladder.

Lyons tapped the headset, breathing harshly. "Pol, Gadgets."

Both men answered.

"Are you guys anywhere near the office?"

"Outside the door, Ironman," Schwarz called back. "We've got some resistance here."

"Good enough. Stay back, and I'll see if I can cut down some of it for you." Lyons stepped under the shaft, both of his pistols pointed upward. As soon as he saw the man climbing down the ladder, he opened fire.

The corpse dropped from the shaft, spilling onto the ground at Lyons's feet. He took a grenade from his coverall, pulled the pin and tossed the bomb into the room above, bouncing the deadly sphere off the side of the shaft near the top.

"Fire in the hole!" Lyons called over the headset.

An instant later, the grenade went off with a loud

boom that turned into hollow noise when it entered the telephone trunk line.

"We're clear," Blancanales called out. "Coming down."

Lyons went forward, checking the two dead men. No one else appeared to be in the trunk line. A quick search revealed a flash in one of the men's pockets. He turned it on, playing the beam over the nearby wall.

He found a duffel ten feet farther on and was just opening it when Blancanales and Schwarz joined him, flashlights in hand. The three beams played over the contents of the duffel, revealing a notebook computer and other electronic equipment.

"Got it," Schwarz said. He knelt and rummaged in the duffel, then played the beam over the fiber-optic cables lashed in bundles on either side of the working area. A jumper cable snaked through the bundles, the leads gleaming in the flashlight beam. "Quick connect, they'd have been on-line in seconds."

"Yeah, well, not now," Lyons growled. He tagged the headset, having trouble making the connection to Stony Man Farm with all the interference around him.

"Go, Able One," Price called.

"Confirm mission completion," Lyons said. "We're standing down here. How are things there?"

"We're waiting."

Lyons nodded. "Let us know. I'll buzz the NYPD, let them know that we're the good guys. They should be rolling on this by now." He broke the connection and took out his cellular phone.

"LEAVE HIM," Kesar Grishin told Dobrynin. Scattered reports from his security personnel had alerted him about the black-clad warriors who'd invaded his home, but those reports were coming much more slowly now. The strike team was very efficient at its task.

"He was at the computers," Dobrynin said, pulling back from the doorway long enough to reload his pistol. "He could be accessing the files."

"Gerahd," Grishin said patiently, "if those people found us here, then they already know as much as those files are going to tell them. Smart business is to accept our losses and run, start over. Hell, we've put this operation together once. We can do it again."

"Turrin betrayed you."

Grishin listened to the sound of gunshots getting closer. He still couldn't believe how Turrin had played a part in the whole affair. Turrin was a Mafia man, yet the men attacking the estate definitely smacked of American special forces, from the clothing, the way they operated and the weapons. "Yes," he replied tightly, "and you can bet he'll never get that chance again."

Dobrynin spun around the doorway and fired relentlessly. A short burst from Turrin's Uzi clipped the doorway.

Grishin leaned his back against the wall, looking at the dead man at his feet. Angrily he kicked the corpse. If the man had simply done his job, there wouldn't have been this to worry about. He could have destroyed the computer files over the phone and launched the virus that would have consumed the Wall Street Exchange's computer systems. On Monday, perhaps another Black Monday, the world would have found out how badly the President of the United States had screwed up by letting this military action take place. Instead, the computer hadn't answered the call he'd placed over the cellular phone. There'd been no reassuring beep of the modem picking up his call, waiting for the special code that would have slagged the entire hard drive files and started a fire to consume the room.

Turrin had obviously swapped phone connections, and that meant that someone outside was in the process of trying to break through his encrypted files.

Grishin looked at Dobrynin, who was staring at him. "Gerahd, it's time to go."

"Yes, sir."

Grishin led the way out of the pantry and into the kitchen. He peered out through the double French doors that led onto a small sunroom. The jet was still on the runway, and there was plenty of fuel to get them off the island to Puerto Rico. They could put the jet on autopilot and jump somewhere off the coastline of Puerto Rico. Even if someone was able to track the jet by radar, he wouldn't be able to pick up the parachutes. And Grishin kept an inflatable Zodiac boat aboard, complete with outboard engine. They could vanish in Puerto Rico.

But the small airport was too far away.

The cellular phone in Grishin's pocket rang. He answered it automatically.

"Where are you?" Salome asked.

"In the kitchen."

"Gerahd?"

"He's with me."

"Would you care for a ride?"

Before Grishin had time to respond, he watched a bronze Mercedes 450SL crash through the wall of the sunroom, then slow to a stop less than a yard in front of him. Salome was behind the steering wheel, blood leaking down one side of her face from a cut.

Dobrynin pushed him into motion, shoving him at the car.

Grishin took the back seat, sliding over so Dobrynin could get in. "I didn't even know you could drive."

Salome swiveled her head, peering through the back glass. "I'm picking it up as I go along." She slipped the transmission in Reverse, then floored the accelerator.

Grishin buckled in. Suddenly the jet didn't seem so far away at all.

BOLAN RACED into the kitchen in time to see the Mercedes back out of the sunroom. He pulled the M-16 to his shoulder and fired a sustained burst, but the vehicle pulled away too quickly, disappearing around a corner of the house.

"Stony One, this is Phoenix Three," Gary Manning called over the headset.

"Go, Three." As Bolan rushed through the broken remnants of the sunroom, figures moved into his peripheral vision. He brought up the assault rifle as he ducked behind one of the room's surviving support pillars.

Two gunners spread out, trying to find cover as they fired at him.

"I found Sticker," Manning said. "He's in one piece."

"Good enough, Three." The Executioner squeezed the trigger, loosing blazing figure eights of 5.56 mm tumblers that cut the gunmen down.

"G-Force."

"Go, Stony One. You've got G-Force."

"Do you see the bronze Mercedes?"

"Yeah."

"Grishin's aboard. Can you assist?"

"Can't," Grimaldi replied. "We're dry. We used up everything we had except small arms in hitting the estate security."

"Can you slow them down?"

"I can try."

Bolan sprinted for the garage. Resistance at the estate house was practically nil. The people who could get away had scattered. And with Grishin's departure, none of the staff seemed intent on trying to hold the house.

Overhead, the LongRanger hurtled by, gaining rapidly on the Mercedes.

Bolan reached the big garage and found it locked. He stepped back and fired at the lock, the bullets chewing the mechanism to pieces. He rattled the door again, shaking the remnants of the lock free, then entered.

Gunfire slammed into the opening door.

The soldier crouched, spotting the trio of shooters near a white Chevy Blazer. The assault rifle chattered dry in Bolan's hands, knocking down two of the gunmen.

The third man took cover behind the Blazer and fired steadily.

Bolan dropped the M-16 and drew the Desert Eagle from its hip holster. He targeted the man through the rear glass of the Blazer, then squeezed the trigger. The big .44-caliber boattail slug shattered the glass and caught the man in the head, tossing his lifeless body backward.

A man appeared in the garage doorway Bolan had come through, an H&K MP-5 spitting death in his hands.

The Executioner abandoned his position, falling

back behind a rolling red toolbox that was almost twice his size. As he turned to target the guy, Bolan saw the man's head come apart, then David McCarter stepped in over the corpse.

"Come on, Mack," the lanky Briton said, "we're wasting time here."

"The Blazer," Bolan said. Of all the vehicles, it was the one that looked the most serviceable for going cross-country.

McCarter nodded and raced for the vehicle. "You don't mind if I take the wheel?"

"No," Bolan said, taking the passenger seat.

McCarter slid in behind the wheel. A screwdriver winked in his hands as he thrust it into the ignition. He twisted hard, and metal gave way with brittle pops. He tossed the ignition in the rear seat, then thrust the screwdriver into the opening in the steering column. Sparks flared and the engine began to turn over. "Come on, you ugly brute," the Briton coaxed.

When the engine caught, he slipped the gearshift into Reverse, then rammed through the garage door behind them.

A pair of gunners who'd been heading for the garage opened fire. Bullets cored through the windshield.

Bolan caught both gunners in the open sights of the big Desert Eagle and put them down.

McCarter whipped the steering wheel around and jammed the gearshift into First. All four wheels tore into the lawn as he steered around the garage, bringing them into view of the fleeing Mercedes and the small airstrip where the jet waited.

Grimaldi jockeyed the LongRanger expertly, setting the helicopter's pontoons on top of the Mercedes twice.

Both times, the additional weight caused the 450SL to slew out of control momentarily.

"That Mercedes is a good car," McCarter observed coolly as he shifted rapidly through the gears, "but she's a thoroughbred. Not made for rough country like this."

Bolan silently agreed.

Grimaldi made contact with the Mercedes again, leaving a dent in the top of the vehicle. However, this time Dobrynin leaned out the window with a submachine gun in his hands. Bolan heard the rattle of autofire and saw the hits run a ragged line along the helicopter from nose to stern, taking a number of them through the belly before Grimaldi could get away.

"Back off, G-Force," Bolan said. "He knows you're not armed. He won't hesitate to open up on you again."

"Acknowledged," Grimaldi called. The chopper settled back at a higher altitude.

"Going to be close," McCarter said. "We've gained some, and they're going to have to get into the jet."

The Mercedes rocked to a hard stop as the driver applied the brakes. A cloud of dust brushed over it, cloaking the individuals who got out of the car and ran for the jet. Bolan couldn't tell if there were two or three. A man standing on the fold-out steps helped them on board. The jet began taxiing immediately.

The Blazer was still eighty yards behind the jet, gaining ground more slowly as the aircraft raced along the airstrip.

Bolan tapped the Transmit button on the headset. "Jack, can you slow them down?"

"I'm on it, Sarge."

McCarter lost control of the Blazer momentarily as

it raced up the hillside leading to the airstrip and left the ground. They came down hard, fishtailing across the tarmac as the four-wheel-drive tried to sort out the suspension and redistribute the heavy weight of the Blazer.

"We can catch them, Mack," McCarter gritted, putting his foot down hard on the accelerator again. "They've got to get up to airspeed."

"Stay with it," Bolan said. He clambered out the door, then reached on top of the Blazer and found purchase on the luggage rack. The wind pulled at him, and he squinted to clear his vision. McCarter was hitting seventy, drawing closer to the Lear.

The man at the fold-out door had trouble trying to close it, and Bolan knew the pilot was having to compensate for the additional drag. It was questionable if the pilot would even be able to get the craft off the ground.

Grimaldi descended from the sky like a striking hawk, the pontoons smashing against the jet. The Lear wobbled from the blow, coasting up on one wheel as the air dynamic changed. The helicopter rocked from the impact, as well, spinning a quarter turn.

The man struggling with the door saw the Blazer come roaring up, reducing the distance to something less than twenty feet. He went for his gun.

The Executioner drew the Desert Eagle and fired a trio of shots that plucked the man from the doorway and sent him crashing to the tarmac. The soldier tapped the headset's Transmit button. "Bring me closer, David."

McCarter complied, maintaining the acceleration and closing on the bouncing door. The jet was starting to reach lift, rising in tentative hops from the airstrip.

"Stay back, G-Force," Bolan said. He leaned out over the side of the Blazer and managed to grab the open door. No one was in the doorway. He pushed himself off the Blazer just as the jet screamed into the air. The air rushing by him became a hammering force that warred with him.

The Executioner hung on through strength and determination. If Grishin was allowed to escape, there was no telling where the man would turn up again, or what trouble he would bring with him.

Bolan pulled himself into the Lear's cabin, standing on trembling legs as the wind threatened to suck him back out the door. The jet climbed steeply, throwing him from his feet to go crashing against the sofa built into the rear wall. The view through the door turned to the blue and white of clear sky.

The Executioner pushed himself to his feet again as Gerahd Dobrynin came from the pilot's cabin.

Dobrynin showed no surprise at finding Bolan there. He brought up his pistol, but the jet hit an air pocket and threw him from his feet. It also saved him from the pair of shots the Executioner fired that cut the space where his head had been only a moment ago.

Off balance himself, Bolan tried to swing around and stay erect. Instead, he ended up in a tangle of arms and legs as Dobrynin came crashing down on top of him.

The jet banked sharply, showing the green blue of the Caribbean below through the side windows.

Dobrynin lashed out, knocking the Desert Eagle from Bolan's grip. A knife gleamed in his free hand. Wordlessly he plunged it at Bolan's face.

The soldier caught the man's knife wrist, then brought up his other hand, thumb and forefinger splayed in a wide Y. He slammed his hand against the man's neck, breaking the trachea and initiating the damage that would fill Dobrynin's lungs with his own blood and drown him.

Even dying, the Russian didn't give up the fight, trying in vain to plunge the knife blade into Bolan's eye. The Executioner felt the life go out of the man as his strength left him.

Bolan recovered the Desert Eagle, watching as the door to the rear compartment of the Lear opened up. He pushed Dobrynin's corpse from him.

Kesar Grishin appeared with an Ingram MAC-10. He had to brace himself in the doorway to stand up because the jet was still flirting with disaster, then he opened fire.

The bullets tracked across the steeply tilted floor and chopped through the thin wall separating them from the pilot's cabin.

The Executioner dropped the Desert Eagle into target acquisition. He squeezed the trigger, blasting two rounds through Grishin's chest.

"Stony One," Grimaldi called over the headset, barely audible over the dull roar flooding in through the open door, "you're losing altitude. Do you copy?"

"Stony One copies." Struggling, Bolan pushed himself up from the floor and made his way to the pilot's cabin. When he opened the door, a thick cloud of smoke roiled out to greet him, sucked away by the slipstream created by the wind whipping through the holed Plexiglas windscreens and out the door.

Beyond the pall of smoke, Bolan spotted the pilot's corpse sagged over the controls. The electrical storm of sparks buzzing over the console told the soldier that any effort made to save the jet would only end in disaster.

He tapped the Transmit button. "It's done," he said. "I'm going to have to bail."

"You're out over the sea," Grimaldi called. "We'll make the pickup, then get the hell out of here."

Bolan searched the overhead luggage compartments and found a parachute. He made his way to the door with difficulty. Looking down at the ocean spread out before him, he guessed that they were only at three or four thousand feet. It would be a difficult jump, but he'd done worse.

The LongRanger came up alongside, struggling to stay up with the jet.

Without warning, a bullet slammed into the door frame beside Bolan. The Executioner whirled at once, dropping toward the Desert Eagle. He saw the small blond haired woman in the doorway leading to the rear compartment and realized there had been three people in the Mercedes.

She fired again, catching him in the chest this time, the bullet passing through the parachute he'd been about to put on before hitting his body armor. The impact knocked him off balance, throwing him through the doorway and out into open sky.

Bolan went with it. There was nothing to be gained by staying with the jet. If the woman somehow survived, they'd pick her up.

The airstream was stronger than he thought, though, and it caught him, twisting him violently. He kept tight hold on the parachute, throwing his arms out to try to gain control over the long fall. He ended up in the path of the rear-mounted jet nacelle. He flipped out of the way, narrowly avoiding the jet engine, feeling the heat and the suction as it ripped past him.

The parachute didn't make it.

Bolan reacted quick enough when the parachute was suctioned into the engine to release the straps and save his fingers, his arm and maybe his life. The parachute came out the other end of the jet engine as burning confetti.

He fell, twisting in the air, automatically assuming a starfish pattern to gain control over and slow his fall. He turned his head so he could speak over the headset. "T.J."

"Forget your umbrella?" Hawkins called back with a light tone. "I'm on my way."

Bolan watched as Hawkins threw himself from the LongRanger, an extra parachute hugged tightly to his chest to reduce wind resistance. The young Phoenix Force member sliced through the wild blue like an airborne porpoise.

Looking down, Bolan saw there was plenty of time for Hawkins to reach him before he hit the water. Farther ahead, though, he watched the jet plummet into the sea, cracking up on impact and sinking almost immediately.

"Phoenix One," he called over the headset.

"Here, mate."

"How long before you're ready to leave?"

"We're packed now. Waiting on you blokes. Stony Base has finished its operation with the computer systems. You should be seeing our finishing touches about now."

In the distance, atop the rolling hills above the Caribbean Sea, the main house at the estate went up in a blaze of destruction.

"I was thinking," McCarter said a moment later, "that it would perhaps be a shame to return to the Farm so soon. A man needs his recreation, too."

And Bolan couldn't agree more. There'd be other battles. There always were. But for now, the teams were standing down. As long as the cannibals existed, they'd be involved in the War Everlasting, but occasionally it was good for a soldier to put aside the tools of war and stand down and examine what made the fight worth fighting.

Take
4 explosive books
plus a
mystery bonus
FREE

**A violent struggle for survival
in a post-holocaust world**

JAMES AXLER

DEATH LANDS®

Nightmare Passage

Ryan Cawdor and his companions fear they have crossed time lines
when they encounter an aspiring god-king whose ambitions are
straight out of ancient Egypt. In the sands of California's Guadalupe
Desert, Ryan must make the right moves to save them from another
kind of hell—abject slavery.

**Don't miss out on the action in these titles
featuring THE EXECUTIONER®, STONY MAN™
and SUPERBOLAN®!**

The American Trilogy

#64222	PATRIOT GAMBIT	$3.75 U.S. ☐
		$4.25 CAN. ☐
#64223	HOUR OF CONFLICT	$3.75 U.S. ☐
		$4.25 CAN. ☐
#64224	CALL TO ARMS	$3.75 U.S. ☐
		$4.25 CAN. ☐

Stony Man™

#61910	FLASHBACK	$5.50 U.S. ☐
		$6.50 CAN. ☐
#61911	ASIAN STORM	$5.50 U.S. ☐
		$6.50 CAN. ☐
#61912	BLOOD STAR	$5.50 U.S. ☐
		$6.50 CAN. ☐

SuperBolan®

#61452	DAY OF THE VULTURE	$5.50 U.S. ☐
		$6.50 CAN. ☐
#61453	FLAMES OF WRATH	$5.50 U.S. ☐
		$6.50 CAN. ☐
#61454	HIGH AGGRESSION	$5.50 U.S. ☐
		$6.50 CAN. ☐

(limited quantities available on certain titles)

TOTAL AMOUNT	$
POSTAGE & HANDLING	$
($1.00 for one book, 50¢ for each additional)	
APPLICABLE TAXES*	$ _____
TOTAL PAYABLE	$ _____
(check or money order—please do not send cash)	

To order, complete this form and send it, along with a check or money order for the total above, payable to Gold Eagle Books, to: **In the U.S.:** 3010 Walden Avenue, P.O. Box 9077, Buffalo, NY 14269-9077; **In Canada:** P.O. Box 636, Fort Erie, Ontario, L2A 5X3.

Name: _____

Address: _____ City: _____

State/Prov.: _____ Zip/Postal Code: _____

*New York residents remit applicable sales taxes.
 Canadian residents remit applicable GST and provincial taxes.

GEBACK19

James Axler

OUTLANDERS™

OMEGA PATH

A dark and unfathomable power governs
post-nuclear America. As a former warrior of
the secretive regime, Kane races to expose the
blueprint of a power that's immeasurably evil,
with the aid of fellow outcasts Brigid Baptiste
and Grant. In a pre-apocalyptic New York City,
hope lies in their ability to reach one young
man who can perhaps alter the future....

Nothing is as it seems. Not even the
invincible past....

Available February 1998,
wherever Gold Eagle books are sold.